This book is dedicated to the victims of human trafficking and their loved ones searching for them.

ONE

Had I known what awaited me up ahead, I might have sought an alternative route. But knowing what I do now, if I had, they might all be dead – or worse.

Those who believe in such things might call it fate. I'm not sure what I believe, but I do know this: a lot of things had to align for me to be there at that exact moment. Right time, wrong time. Right place, wrong place. Whatever. I was there.

The drive home happened at a subconscious level. The road passed before me unnoticed; my mind on autopilot, reviewing the memories of the evening's most satisfying events spent with my girlfriend, Natalie. This night had made me think about my future and the life we might have together. Given my recent string of conflicts and dire situations, I should've been happy just to have a future, let alone someone to share it with. We'd been spending a lot of time together of late, and it had been amazing.

The idea that perhaps we were ready for just one place was on my mind a lot. A big step to be sure, but so far I'd been too chicken to bring up the idea. Things had been going so well, I was afraid to do anything that might change that. However, with

Natalie heading into work on the third shift, I decided to spend the night at home and catch up on the chores I'd been neglecting.

So, cruising down the highway on a warm, but comfortable evening in early May, I headed north on US-23 toward my house in Sylvania, a suburb of Toledo, thinking life was good. The stars were all out in the clear sky to bear witness to the glorious night.

I'd been so lost in thought, the police car barely registered; when I did notice, the officer had pulled over another car on the side of the freeway. What caught my eye was the officer with his hand resting on the butt of his weapon, standing back from the driver's door, trying to peer inside. Whatever he saw must have caused concern. The Toledo Police cruiser piqued my interest. I knew many of the Toledo police officers, because, at one time, I was a cop. I had become sort of famous, or maybe infamous, in their circles because of my involvement in taking down a few local crime rings. I wondered if I knew the officer.

The subject vehicle was a newer model, dark-colored and full size, like maybe a Cadillac. Most people checked out the person pulled over to see if they knew them. I checked out the cops. I'd liked being a policeman and thought I'd be one for the rest of my working life, but ... well, that's a different story. Now I'm a teacher in an elementary school. From one combat zone to another. They may have attitude and pop off once in a while, but they're a lot smaller than I am, and at least they're not shooting at me. Yet!

I watched the cop bend closer toward the driver's side window, keeping his body turned sideways to the car. His hand moved on his weapon as if he were drawing it. He snapped erect, pulling his gun, as a flash detonated from inside the car. In an instant, I knew the cause and slowed my car. The policeman's body stiffened. The force of the impact spun him away from the car, leaving him unprotected. His hand worked to aim his gun. A second flash lifted him off his feet. His body bounced on the highway and came to a stop lying partially across the first lane.

Tires spun, throwing up loose stones, and the dark car lurched onto the expressway. Although much closer now, with its lights off it was too dark to read the license plate.

The car raced away and I sped up, driving along the shoulder until I was a few feet from the flashing lights. I parked behind the cruiser and jumped out of the car, grabbing my cell phone. I wanted to see the officer's condition before I called 911. The wounded man was on his side, lying about three feet into the first lane. Even though I knew I shouldn't move him, I couldn't leave him in the middle of the road, especially in such an unlit area. I grabbed his legs and pulled him onto the verge, his body rolling onto his back. There was a lot of blood. I pulled him into the squad car's headlights to determine how serious his wounds were.

Keying his Motorola shoulder mic, believing it would be faster than calling 911, about to summon help, I glanced at his face.

"Oh God, no! Richie!"

His hat had fallen off when he hit the ground. He had a bump on his forehead and several large scrapes ran across the bridge of his nose, but nothing severe enough to prevent recognition.

My friend and former teammate, Richie Molten. "Richie, can you hear me?"

Memories flooded my head, my heart rate increased, and panic crowded me, losing precious seconds in getting help. I yelled into the radio, "Dispatch! Officer down. I repeat, officer down." What was that damn call sign? "10-13! 10-13! Officer down."

"Sir, this is a secured police channel. If you are not a police officer it is unlawful to cut into it," an operator said. "You must—"

"Did you hear me?" I yelled back. "You have an officer down on 23—"

"Who is this?" said a new voice. I assumed it was a shift supervisor. "Identify yourself, please."

"My name is Danny Roth. I'm former TPD. Officer Richie Molten," I choked back a sob, "has taken at least one, possibly two bullets. He needs medical assistance ... *now*."

"Stay with me, Roth. If you're who I think you are, you were a trained professional. Officer Molten needs your help. Stay calm. Now tell me exactly where you are." The voice was calm, professional and comforting.

"We're on the shoulder of the northbound lane of US-23, just south of the I-475 junction."

"Are you or Officer Molten in any danger at the moment?"

The sound of tires peeling out on a cement surface like a dragster, distracted me. "No, I ..." I looked up, drawn to the sound as it increased in volume.

"Roth," the voice yelled, "you still there? What's happening?"

Reversing toward us was the shooters' car, coming back to eliminate the witness.

Two

I grabbed Richie's legs and pulled him down the side of the drainage ditch that ran along the expressway, into the high weeds, until we were hidden from the road. If the gunmen wanted us, they'd have to get out of the car and come looking. With luck, that might buy us some time.

Pulling on Richie's Sig Sauer .40 with my left hand, I whispered into the mic, "They're coming back! Send backup. Hurry!"

Freeing the gun, I buried myself as deep into the high grass and soft ground as I could. The car skidded to a stop a few feet above us. A creaking sound signaled a door opening. Feet scraped across the loose dirt and gravel. A white male in a dark golf shirt stood in the headlights of the squad car, searching. A smile crossed his face, and he raised the gun he'd been holding at his side.

Before he could aim, I rose to my knees and fired twice. Off balance, the first shot missed him. The second bullet found its mark. The man spun around to his left, staggered a couple of steps, but stayed on his feet. He stumbled back to the car. Before I could fire again, someone shot at me from the open back door. Ducking, I waited to see if anyone else came out. I risked raising my head. The wounded man tumbled into the back seat of the car. I snapped another shot at the car as someone hauled the injured man further inside and pulled the door closed.

I stood and fired again, striking the door. A gun pointed out the front window and I dropped to the ground, rolling downhill, dodging a barrage of bullets. At the bottom of the small slope, I bolted upright and ran parallel to the car, moving up the incline until the car came into view. I loosed four shots into the car. Switching targets, I pumped two more rounds into the back seat. The window shattered with the first shot, spraying shards of glass throughout the back seat.

The driver floored the pedal. The powerful engine catapulted forward. A Lincoln Town car, older model, sped away before I reached the top of the ditch, but not before I'd read part of the license plate. I fired at the rear window, shattering it. Then the gun ran dry.

An automatic weapon filled the space around me. I did my best Pete Rose imitation and dove headfirst all the way to the bottom of the ditch. Righting myself, I crawled back up to watch the black car disappear into the darkness.

Returning to Richie, I searched his utility belt until I found where he kept his extra magazines and quickly exchanged them, ready for the shooters if they came back again. Peering over the rise, they continued north on 23 past the split.

Feeling safer now, I stuck the gun in my belt and dropped to my knees to see what I could do for Richie. From somewhere out of the night came the first faint sounds of sirens. I bent over his body, moistened my finger in my mouth and placed it under his nose. His breath had very little force.

"Come on, please let the rounds have hit the vest," I prayed, unbuttoning his shirt. Richie was bleeding, but I couldn't determine the location or extent of the damage. I ran back to my car, the engine still running, angled it to face Richie, and flicked on the headlights.

Two squad cars anchored up, tires squealing on the gravel as I checked Richie. A TPD cruiser and a state highway patrol squad car. Other sirens sounded close, too.

The doors flew open and three officers took up positions, weapons drawn, aiming directly at me. A bolt of fear ran up my spine.

In unison, they screamed at me. As far as they knew, I was the one who'd shot Richie. Any wrong move would be excuse enough for them to put me down. No one questioned shooting a cop killer.

"On the ground, now," one screamed.

"Show me those hands. Let me see those hands," said a second.

The third stayed back behind the car door covering me while the other two descended upon me. "GUN! He's got a gun," he yelled.

"NO!" I screamed back. A wave of panic hit me. My stomach heaved. I'd been in a similar situation years ago after my partner was gunned down. My colleagues knew what I had done in seeking my revenge on those guilty of his death, willing to turn their collective heads and look past the carnage. In their minds justice had been done.

My hands already over my head, I lowered – threw – myself to the ground. "It's in my belt. Don't shoot! I'm the one – uh!"

They both pounced, crushing me to the ground and forcing the air out of my lungs, rather like a burst balloon. One kept a knee pressed into my back and a hand on my head, pushing my face into the grass, while the second roughly frisked me. He found and extracted the gun and cuffed me, overly aggressive. It wasn't just *my* emotions that were running high and adrenaline pumping overtime.

They hauled me to my feet, jerking my arms, sending sharp pain through my shoulders. Two more patrol cars and an ambulance arrived. From the sounds in the night air more were on the way.

Gripping me tightly, reminding me there was no way I'd get loose, they dragged me up the side of the ditch. On level ground, they guided me toward one of the waiting cars. An officer from one of the two arriving cars sprinted in our direction, an I'm-going-to-kill-you expression on his face. A sinking feeling enveloped me. He appeared to gain speed. "Is that him? Is he the one who shot Richie?" I didn't understand why I was the only one who apparently heard him or, for that matter, saw him.

As he went airborne in front of my car's headlights, on a collision course that my two guards chose not to see, he looked like a phantom coming out of the lights.

Letting out a squeak and attempting to duck, my escorts must have thought I was trying to escape and latched on tighter. The flying tackle seemed to surprise them, and they both let go, lost their footing and we all toppled back down the slope. Winded and on my back, the irate out-of-control cop straddled me, unleashing devastating punches onto my face.

The other two cops took their time regaining their feet and pulling the man off me. At least, it seemed like a long time as I tried to slip some of the punches. Not easy with cuffed hands and 185 pounds on my chest.

Several other cops joined us, one of whom delivered an "accidental" kick to my side. Between the four of them, they managed to corral my assailant and hoist me to my feet. He screamed, "I'm gonna kill you, asshole," as he struggled against the two restraining officers. They let him get close enough to me that he jumped into the air and kicked out, catching me across the chest, driving the air from my lungs again, and sending me crashing to the ground. All while still being held by the two cops.

They yanked me back to my feet once more. One of them pointed at the man and said, "Enough! If you continue, you'll end up on report, facing a suspension."

Resisting the urge to yell, "What do you mean if he continues? How about what he's already done?" I didn't think I was in the best position to complain. They pulled me backward this time, up the small hill, while the other two dragged the screaming cop away. They slid me into the back seat of the car not bothering to guide my head safely below the frame. As my head struck, one of them said, "Watch your head." Funny guy.

The door shut behind me, and I lay across the seat trying to decide which hurt the most – face, ribs, kidneys … They obviously weren't concerned about my blood on their fine upholstery.

Closing my eyes, shutting out the pain, I focused on the information I had if somebody had sense enough to ask me questions: details of the getaway car and of the shooters. If I decided to cooperate, that is. Someone other than Richie being shot, I'd probably refuse to help them at all. As the ambulance pulled away, I hoped they weren't too late to save him. A wave of guilt swept over me: was there anything else I could have done for him?

Many images of Richie swamped me; the times we played ball together, our time at the academy, our first year on the force, attending his and Katy's wedding. Oh God! Katy. I wondered if she knew yet. A tear rolled down my cheek. I needed to tell her that I was there. I thought of their son and daughter, trying hard to remember their names. My mind refused to connect all of my thoughts. We used to double-date back when I was still married. We'd drifted apart after that and then Richie and Katy had kids. I missed those days.

I'd always felt bad about losing contact, never sure if the break was because they blamed me for the divorce or because I was single. I just no longer fitted their get-together criteria. Richie stopped going out for drinks with the guys. Maybe Katy thought I was a bad influence on him since I was back on the market again.

A sudden slap against the rear window accompanied more threats and curses thrown my way. I lay there breathing deeply, forcing a calm I did not feel. I had to help Richie. However, I also made a promise that when this was all over, that officer and I would meet again.

THREE

My thoughts returned to Richie, and I offered up a prayer for him. The driver's door opened and one of my arresting officers sat down. He fired up his MCT, mobile computer terminal, and looked at me through the rearview mirror.

"You need to sit up now, sir," he said in a tone that was anything but friendly. "I need to get some basic information from you then a detective will take your statement." He watched me for a couple of seconds. I wasn't moving fast enough to suit him. "Sir, I said sit up. Do it now!"

At that moment, I made up my mind that I would not cooperate. Not until I could speak to a detective I knew.

"So I'm guilty, right?"

"Excuse me, sir. Is that a confession?"

"By your tone of voice and the treatment I have received, you've already judged me guilty. So I guess I must be, huh? You lost all sense of objectivity because a cop was shot."

He turned to look at me through the cage. I met his cold stare with an unfaltering one of my own. He made up his mind about me right then and read my rights to me. I shook my head and waited for him to finish.

"Now, do you wish to make a statement for the

record?"

"Yeah, you're as big an asshole as the cop you let attack me." He started to say something but I cut him off. "I'll say this and only this for now. My name is Daniel Roth and since you've already let the shooters escape without getting any sort of description, I will not speak to anyone concerning this incident until you call Detective Michael Morrisey. He is the only one I will talk to. Call him." I recited his cell phone number and lay my head back down.

"This is not a negotiation. If you refuse to cooperate and answer questions now, you'll be transported downtown to answer them all night long. You'll be processed and placed in a holding cell. The entire process is extremely long and unpleasant. Is that what you want?"

"It's already been long and unpleasant. And while you're in here accusing me, you're letting the real shooters get away. Man, are you gonna look stupid when you find out the truth. Call him!" I repeated his number. It was all I was going to say.

He tried several more times to get me to respond, but gave up and got out of the car. Voices outside discussed me. A voice I wanted to remember yelled out.

"What do you mean he won't cooperate? Let me in there. I'll get a response from him."

It was my buddy, the cop that I intended to see again someday.

"Relax," a new, calmer voice replied. In a more authoritative tone, he added, "You need to move away from this area. You're already in enough trouble. In fact, you need to go home. Don't give me that look. Leave now or I'll write you up for insubordination."

There were some other grumblings, but a minute later, the passenger door opened and a short man with reddish hair wearing a sport coat, sat down sideways so he could see me.

"What's the connection to Morrisey?" he demanded.

"Call him and ask him."

"He is not involved in this case. I am. Whatever you hope to accomplish by calling him, he can't save you if you're guilty."

"Your officers have already decided that I'm guilty … doesn't make much sense to me to talk to anyone on site. I will only talk to someone impartial, that's Morrisey. The longer you wait, the harder it'll be to find the real shooters. It's probably too late now."

"Famous last words. It's always someone else. At this point, you're the only one I'm considering as a suspect."

"Good for you. You must be a great detective. Call Morrisey or you get nothing."

"I think instead of calling him I'm running you in and holding you on attempted murder, discharging a firearm in the city limits, assaulting a police officer and whatever else I can think of."

"Attempted murder?" I exclaimed, but not for the reason the detective thought.

"That's right, smart mouth. Attempted murder. That's what they call it when you shoot someone. Especially a cop."

"Does that mean you know for a fact Richie's still alive?" I sat up and looked at him.

He looked me over with a new sense of curiosity. His eyes were large, hard and observant, and in constant motion as he examined my face. He took in everything, which made me nervous, but I waited him out.

"Are you telling me that you know the officer you shot?" his voice softer, as if trying a new approach.

"I'm telling you to call Detective Morrisey and maybe you should try the dispatch supervisor to ask about the 911 call. In other words, Detective, do your job. Detect."

His jaw clenched, but to his credit, he wouldn't take the bait. He looked at me for a few seconds as if trying to make up his mind, before exiting the car. I hadn't realized his bulk, his solid build, until he stood up. The car springs groaned in relief. He shut the door and walked away. I watched for a moment then lay back down. Whatever he did would happen whether I watched or not. Besides, my head had started pounding from the beating.

Five minutes later, the door reopened and the car tilted. I decided to play nice for the moment and sat up to make it easier for him to see me. If he'd made the call, there was no sense in antagonizing him further. If he hadn't, well, there was always time to be uncooperative.

He had a phone to his ear and appeared to be listening to someone on the other end. That or he had a great iTunes downloaded. He grunted once and said, "Yeah, hold a sec." He got out of the car and opened the back door. He reached in, the phone in his hand about a foot from my head. I wondered how I was supposed to talk, then realized that it must be set on speaker.

"Morrisey?" I said.

"Danny, is that you?" came the familiar voice. I couldn't remember how many times I'd been in situations, just like this, where I'd been so glad to hear his voice. We sometimes disagreed on things, but I really owed him for all the lifelines he kept throwing me.

"Yeah, it's me. Sorry to be a bother. Again."

"Well, at least it's been a while. What the hell did you get yourself into this time?"

"Well, you know, things were going along a little too smoothly. I needed to get some excitement into my life."

"What, life with that beautiful girlfriend of yours wasn't exciting enough?"

"There's always room for more excitement."

"Detective Carbone there, who happens to be a friend of mine and a very good detective, says you may be a suspect in the shooting of a police officer."

"Yeah, right! Like I would shoot Richie," I said with all the sarcasm his statement deserved. A sudden thought struck me. "Oh God, Morrisey, someone needs to call Katy, Richie's wife."

"Don't worry about that. I'm sure that's being taken care of. What you need to do right now is give a statement to Detective Carbone. That's the best way to help Richie right now."

"I would have been glad to help them out, but things were a little hostile here. I haven't been the most popular guy around. Some of the men in blue would like nothing better than to take me into the woods here and see that I never come back out. I'm not the most cooperative person when someone's trying to beat my brains out."

"Is that true, Mario?"

Carbone looked me over and replied, "I can't say for sure because I wasn't here, but from the look of his face, it could have happened." He added for my benefit, "'Course, he could've been resisting arrest, too. He does have something of an aggressive attitude about him."

"Look, Danny, I know you're pissed, but for Richie's sake, put that aside for now. I promise we'll deal with that later. Right now, Detective Carbone needs your help. Can you do that?"

I felt like a little child being corrected by his father. I felt guilty. He was right, of course, I had to think about helping catch Richie's shooters. Because I didn't respond right away, he said. "I vouched for you. Now give your statement so we can get moving on this thing."

"Yeah, I'm on it. And thanks for the assist. Again."

"Okay. Carbone?"

The detective went off the speaker and pressed it to his ear. He listened, said "Yeah," twice, followed by a "No problem" and an "I'll let you know."

He motioned me forward and I slid out of the car. As I stood, he spun me around and unfastened the cuffs. I looked over my body as I rubbed my wrists, more a psychological response than any real pain. My face and body ached. Dried blood crusted on my face, hands, and clothes. Carbone watched me. I think at first he thought I was going to bolt.

He was a little taller than I first thought, but definitely as wide. It was a weight that at one time might have been solid, but had turned soft and hung over his belt. White crept up the back and sides of his short red hair. His crooked nose suggested he'd had his share of fights and maybe even lost a time or two.

He stepped forward and offered his hand.

"I guess I owe you—"

An angry voice yelled, "Hey, what are you doing?" The cop who had attacked me was running toward me. This time, I was ready and eager to give a little payback, but before he could get close enough to tattoo, some of the other cops stepped in and grabbed him. From their expressions, though, they didn't seem sure they wanted to stop him.

Carbone stepped in front of the crazed cop and said firmly, "Back off, Majewski. He's the wrong guy. You're about to throw your career away."

"No." I surprised myself by saying, "Let him go. See if he's man enough to attack me when my hands aren't cuffed. What do you think, tough guy? You man enough?"

"Hey!" shouted Carbone, pointing a finger at me. "That's enough. This isn't helping us catch the shooters. Don't make me haul your ass downtown."

"That's fine. I'm calm. But when this is over, I will see you again," I promised.

"You others, have the sense he doesn't and get his ass away from here. I'm telling you he's not the shooter."

With that statement, the other cops shot me curious glances and Majewski calmed down. His pained expression showed anger and frustration, but not remorse. He shook off the restraining hands, took one last look at me and walked off. He climbed back into his squad car and drove away.

Two other detectives surrounded me, one with a pad

and pen in hand. Several of the police officers also came in closer to hear what was said. Carbone introduced me to the others and explained that the victim was a friend of mine, changing the mood of the group, no longer vengeful and angry.

"Does anyone know how Richie is? Or where they took him?"

One of the other detectives answered. "He took one in the vest for sure, but the second one got through somehow. It looked like maybe under the arm. It was tough to tell how serious the wound was. I'm not sure where they took him."

I nodded once at him. "Thanks." I recounted the events from the first sighting on the side of the road until the car sped off after the shootout with as much detail as I could, albeit it limited. The first two letters of the license plate, AF, an Ohio plate, four men in the car, at least three of them armed and at least one in need of immediate medical attention. Two of the four, I was sure, were white and thirty to forty years old. At least one weapon was an automatic. I described the damage the car had taken from my shots.

One detective said, "Is that it?"

"That's what I can remember. It's difficult to focus on details with bullets flying around your head and moving Richie to safety."

He grunted and made a final note.

One of the Toledo cops and one of the troopers got on their radios, calling in a description and possible direction of the vehicle, alerting all units for any possible sightings. They advised Sylvania and Sylvania Township Police Departments, the only other cities north of where we were and sent word to the Michigan State Police. Heading north, there were only two possible routes. Either they exited on the last Ohio ramp, or they continued on into Michigan.

One of the other officers said, "No offense, detective," speaking to Carbone, "but how do we know this guy hasn't made up the entire thing?"

Carbone faced the man but spoke loud enough for the whole group to hear. "Several reasons. Mr. Roth was a member of the Toledo Police Department, since retired. He's been vouched for by members of the force, including other detectives he's worked with and by Captain Jenkins. Dispatch verifies that a man identifying himself as Roth was the one who called in the initial assault. Right now, he is a witness, not a suspect. Hopefully, that is understood by everyone. Make sure you spread the word on that. It's easy to lose perspective when one of your own is gunned down. By now, they have at least a thirty- to forty-five-minute head start. Mount up and find 'em."

Several officers had their mouths open. One averted his eyes as I swept my gaze over the group. They left with hunched shoulders rather than puffed-up chests. It was small vindication.

Carbone turned to me. "Roth, I know it's a bit late and will never be enough, but I want to apologize for the way you were treated. I'm embarrassed by their behavior and for their unprofessionalism. They reacted to seeing one of their comrades shot down. But they had no right to judge you or manhandle you. I know that's no excuse. I'll file a report on the incident. The truth is that your quick reactions may have saved Molten's life. Again, I'm sorry." He put out his hand as before. This time, no one interrupted and I took it. The treatment from certain individuals would have to wait for another time.

"If it's all right with you, I'd like to find out how Richie is and pay a visit to his wife."

"Yeah, that's fine." He handed me a card. "Call me if you think of anything else."

FOUR

Media vans had been showing up one after the other. Reporters were everywhere trying to find anyone who would give them a statement for the record. The police kept them back for the most part, but trying to control them on the side of the expressway was difficult at best. One local TV station van had parked behind me and right up to my bumper. I was tempted to ask Carbone to run interference for me so I could avoid the onslaught, or being caught on film. All I needed was to have Natalie see me on television at a crime scene before I had a chance to explain it to her.

Not seeing anyone in the immediate vicinity, I chanced escape. I moved straight to my car, keeping my head down to avoid making eye contact with anyone. Pushing the button on my key fob, I thought I had made it safely. The door on the news van slid open and two shapely legs slid out. I tried hard not to look, but the back of her skirt caught on the seat and the front rode up, exposing her panties. Without missing a beat, she smoothed the skirt down in midstride and thrust a microphone in my face as I tried to open my car door.

She used her slender hip to block it. "Excuse me,

sir, what can you tell me about the shooting?"

She had an alluring voice, like a siren pulling me to a seductive death. I risked a glance and said, "I need to leave, miss, please ..." I looked into her eyes and froze. They were the most beautiful crystalline blue I had ever seen. She must have captured a lot of interviewees just by snaring them with those eyes. Heck, I'll bet she could get just about anyone to do anything if she turned her gaze upon them, like a modern day Medusa, except instead of stone, you turned to mush.

She repeated her question. "Can you help me out here?" she pleaded, her voice hypnotic. I knew I was being played, but somehow didn't care. "I saw you talking to the detectives. It looked like you were giving them some sort of statement. Our viewers would like to know the details of what happened. What can you tell us?" She smiled. It was a smile that said, "You are mine now." Behind those hypnotic eyes, I envisioned a small cyborg woman chanting in a robotic voice, "Resistance is futile."

Noise at the back of my car broke the spell, if only for a moment. The heavyset man with the bushy hair focusing a camera on me, snapped me out of the trance, my mind my own again.

"Yes, I can help you, but that man over there," I pointed directly at Carbone, "is the man who captured the suspect. He's the real hero. You should talk to him."

She glanced in his direction and just like that, she turned off the charm switch. The alteration in her face was dramatic, like two totally different people in one body. She scared me in a very different way now. The seductress homed in on Carbone like a heat-seeking missile and beelined straight for him, dismissing me as no longer important. Smiling at what I'd unleashed upon Carbone, I jumped into the safety of my car and started it up. The van was so

Thank God.

Entering the single-story brick building, the first thing to catch your attention was the magnificent aroma escaping the kitchen. It seemed to hover by the door, waiting for someone. You couldn't help but salivate: it was Italian heaven. Tiptoeing into the kitchen, I inhaled and snuck up behind my rather vertically challenged mother to give her a kiss on the cheek. She reached back over her head and patted my cheek. She stood over a pot of sauce, gently and lovingly stirring it.

"Ah, my Daniel. How are you today? How was school?"

Everybody knew I was a school teacher, but for some reason when my mother said things like that, I felt like a student. I always expected her to ask if I had homework.

"It was good, Ma. How was lunch?"

"It was a little slow today. People are out enjoying the nice weather. They don't want to sit down and have a nice hot lunch. But we did okay."

"I'm going to check the receipts. Is there anything special you want me to order for this week?"

"Yes, dear. Check around for a better quality sea bass. That last batch, the flesh was too soft. It should be firmer."

"Okay, I'll take care of it." I started out of the kitchen, but she called me back.

"Oh, Daniel, will you please come by for dinner on Saturday? I need to talk to you about something."

"What is it, Ma? Something important? Is everything all right?"

"Yes, yes. Stop worrying about me. Is it wrong for a mother to want to spend time with her son? Just come, okay?"

"Sure, Ma." But she had me worried. It was unusual for her to ask me like that. Usually, she told me I was coming to dinner. I decided to test it out.

"Is it okay if I bring Natalie?"

She hesitated for just a fraction of a second before replying, "Yes, of course. Bring your lovely lady friend." Now I knew there was a specific reason she wanted me to go over and she would prefer I went alone.

"Look, Daniel, it is nothing bad. I would just like to talk to you about something. Now just be there, all right?"

"Okay, Ma. But please don't cook for an army. I'm trying to stay fit."

"Ah, fit. You too skinny already. You no eat enough as it is. I teach that girlfriend of yours how to cook and feed you proper."

It was time to leave. My mother was slipping into her Italian-English. Pretty soon her hands would fly as if she was swatting insects. But, that also told me whatever she had to say made her nervous, which in turn made me nervous.

I grabbed a fork and speared a meatball from a rack where they were cooling. I took a bite as I left the kitchen and the warm juices dripped down my chin. Heaven! Her homemade meatballs would have buckled the knees of lesser men.

I took it into the back office with me and plopped down into my chair. While booting up the computer, I finished munching, wiped my wet chin and started making phone calls to place the week's orders.

That finished, I ordered food for the week based on the menu prepared by my mother, then paid the bills. A smile spread across my face as I saw the remaining balance after everything was paid. Business was booming, a fact still unbelievable to me. I was realistic enough to know it was because of my mother's talents in the kitchen, but I liked to think she couldn't have done it without me. Done, I went in search of more meatballs.

As I left the office, I looked at the dining room with

pride. The tables were filling up, a good night for a Monday. Sitting at the end of the bar in his customary place was Detective Morrisey. He was a good guy. Even though we'd had our differences over the past few months, he'd saved my butt numerous times. And he really cared about my mother.

He sat in his shirt sleeves, his tie hanging loosely around his thick neck, his standard sport coat, a solid brown one this time, draped over the back of the bar stool. Busy reading the paper, he was digging into a bowl of rigatoni covered in my mother's homemade marinara sauce and topped with meatballs and Italian sausages. He wore a napkin tucked into his shirt at the neck to prevent the stains that were a part of Italian cuisine.

I patted him on the back as I walked past. "What's new? Anything more from Richie?"

"Oh, hey, hi," he replied between chews. He lifted the end of the napkin to his face but missed a small dot of sauce on his cheek. "Yeah, actually there is some news."

I waited for him to finish swallowing and wash it down with his Chianti. "Richie's doing fine. Everything looks good from that aspect. He's awake, in pain and asking for you, by the way."

I smiled, happy he was doing well. "So, what aspect is not going well?" Picking up on the way he delivered the news.

"Well, the question had been why he chased a car down the ramp to the expressway. Dispatch said he called in on a car that looked suspicious, but before he could get a read on the plate, they saw him and bolted. He was blocked by traffic when he turned on the noisemaker and the lights, so delayed getting behind them. But the thing he remembered, the reason his attention was drawn to the car in the first place, was because he thought he saw the head of a girl, or young woman, lift up above the rear seat, only to be pushed down again. He said the look on her face had been one of pure fear. He tried to catch another glimpse but never saw her again.

"The man raised his arm and brought it down forcefully several times in the direction of where he saw the girl. By the time traffic moved, they were already at the bottom of the ramp. He called it in when he caught up and pulled them over, but got no hits from the plates. He says he approached carefully, ready for trouble, but when he got next to the car, there was no woman. The men were sitting back relaxed and casual, almost too casual, which made him more suspicious. Richie swears he saw a purse on the back seat wedged between the two men. Everything was a blur after that."

"So, what happened to the girl? Is he sure he saw someone?"

"Well, here's the bad part. After hearing his story, several officers were dispatched to the ramp to search the grassy area and found her. Hilary Merritt, a young college student. Evidently, they pitched her from the car as they turned down the ramp. She had a bullet in her back, so they must have shot her as they pushed her out."

"Bastards! Why would they do that?"

"Maybe they were afraid if they were caught with her in the car she could testify against them. Maybe they killed her because she could identify them. We may never know what actually happened. Richie swears he didn't hear a shot. Maybe she was kidnapped for some sexual reason, or was being taken somewhere to be sold. Human trafficking is on the increase. Toledo has the third highest incidence in the country. Of course, there could be some other motive ... like she was involved in drugs, but at this point, it's all speculation."

"That's incredible! No wonder Richie was after them."

"Yeah, he says every time he closes his eyes he sees that poor girl's terrified face. I think he feels like he's responsible for her death."

We dropped into silence for a few moments, lost in our own thoughts. In a quieter voice,

"I also heard what happened to you at the scene." He pointed to my face. "I see some of the evidence."

Without thinking, I touched the bruises.

"The officer involved has been suspended pending a review. I thought you might want to know. I'm sorry it happened. He has a pretty good record, although he can be high strung at times. Still, there's no excuse for his behavior."

I decided not to comment. Instead, I brought the subject back to the crime. "Has the car been found?"

"Not that I'm aware of, but I'm not the lead investigator."

"What about the hospitals? Did anyone show up with a bullet wound?"

"As far as I know, the hospitals and doctors' offices have all been notified, but nothing's been reported. Again, it's still early. They're looking."

"I know. I know. I'm not pushing. It's just that ... well, if they were daring enough to kidnap someone and not afraid to shoot a policeman, these people are extremely dangerous. If they're still in the area, we're going to hear from them again. It'd be interesting to know the reason they took the girl. Could it have been a drug thing?"

"Could be. I know there is a team looking into her life, too."

Our conversation dried up, so I went in search of dinner. After making my belly happy, I said my good nights to Morrisey and my mother, and left for home. It was just a little past eight. The information Morrisey had given me still played through my mind.

Natalie had the late shift, so I decided to spend a night at my place. However, I wasn't ready to go home yet and called Tony. I figured it was about a fifty-fifty chance he'd be home and another fifty-fifty on top of that that he'd be alone.

NINE

Yo!" he answered.

"Yo? Who says 'yo' anymore? It's a new century, T. Step into it."

"How about kiss my ass, bro? Is that better?"

"Ah, see? That one's timeless. It's a classic. Classics are appropriate in any century."

"Okay, kiss my ass it is. Now, was there a purpose for this call, or you got nothing better to do than harass me?"

"Wow! Touchy, aren't we? What's the matter, your fine lady friend finally given your worthless ass the boot?"

"Nah, she's been working the late shifts again. I've been feeling very neglected lately. This one-woman thing is really a drag sometimes."

"Yeah, but if you decide to wander, she'll shoot your ass. That's what happens when you date a cop." He'd been seeing Marissa for more than six months now; a personal record for Tony. A weekend was a long time for any of his previous conquests.

"And that's why you're finding me at home … alone … and in a grumpy mood."

"Well, T, it's your lucky night. I'm about to come over and save you from the boredom of facing another long, lonely evening crying in your beer."

"Sorry, bro, but I don't swing that way. It may have been a while since I uncorralled the stallion, but I'm not willing to venture into that type of stable. You're on your own, pardner."

"Funny. I'll be there in five. Have a cold beverage waiting."

Tony was my closest friend and had been since high school. We'd been through a lot together and I owed him my life on more than one occasion. I could always count on Tony to be there if I needed him, no matter what the situation. His father was a reputed Mafia kingpin in the Detroit area, which I knew to be true, but was mainly legit now. It made life interesting for Tony now he dated a cop. We saved Marissa's life twice a few months back. In return, she saved my life and started to go out with Tony, which probably saved his life. I have never seen him as happy.

Five minutes later, I entered his home. I had a key, an access code for the alarm, my own room and extra clothes in the closet. It was my second home whenever I needed a place to crash or hide out, as had been the case several times in the past year. Tony had reciprocal privileges at my house. Lately, with both of us busy with our ladies, we hadn't seen much of each other.

Tony lived in an exclusive subdivision where all the houses were large and unique. His house was thirty-five hundred square feet with four bedrooms, two and a half bathrooms, a study, family, dining, and living rooms, a full basement, and an enclosed three-season room.

Recently, he'd added a hot tub. Funny, the changes he'd made since having a full-time girlfriend. I refused to venture into the water unless I saw it drained and cleaned. Who knew what sordid activities went on in there? Strike that. I knew. This was Tony.

Tony lounged in the family room with one leg hung over the arm of a recliner. A sofa and two small end tables separated another matching recliner. On the table by my recliner, a cold can of beer waited on a coaster. My friend! Ah!

He flipped channels between two baseball games.

"Looks like your old team is off to a good start this year," he said, talking about the Cleveland Indians, the team I once played for.

"Yeah, they've been playing well. Maybe I'll call out there and see if I can score us four tickets. Wha'dya think?"

"Sounds like a plan. Go for it. I can arrange my leisure time any way I need to. Marissa can adjust her schedule if she has enough notice."

"All right, I'll call tomorrow." I laughed. He didn't really have a regular job, so every day was leisure time for him. Tony had some businesses, but most of them you couldn't talk about. However, if you ever needed anything done, he always "knew a guy." It didn't matter what it was. The problem was that many of these multi-talented individuals didn't like to show their faces during the daytime, preferring the shadowy darkness of alleys or abandoned buildings. I knew better than to ask questions. Besides, he wouldn't have given a straight answer anyway. However, I had benefited from these shadow people on more than one occasion.

"You think they're going to remember an old broken-down pitcher like you after all these years?"

"How could they forget the best middle relief pitcher they've had in the past ten years? I may not have lasted long, but I made my mark while I was there." I took a sip of my beer. "And if they don't remember me, well, I happen to know a few things about the general manager and one of the front office girls. We'll get tickets."

"Wow! Look at you. Resorting to blackmail to get what you want. I'm proud of you. I'm starting to rub off on you in a positive way."

"Right! The day you become a role model will be the day I start robbing banks."

"Well now, there's something I haven't tried ... yet."

"Don't even think it. And no, I'm not driving the getaway car."

"Got that right, I've seen you drive. A police force of grandmothers could catch you."

"God, why do I put up with this abuse?"

"Because nobody else loves you enough to tell you the truth. You should be grateful. I make you a better person."

"Oh, dear Lord! Saint Tony." I stood up. "You need another beer?"

"Yeah. So what is it you wanted to tell me?"

I opened the refrigerator and grabbed two more cans. "Huh? What are you talking about? Can't a guy just stop over to say hi and hang out?" I gave him his beer and he looked at me in disbelief.

"Who you kidding? Come on, bro, spill it. What's happening?"

"Okay! Well, there is this one thing." I told him about the weekend. I figured he didn't know because he usually never watched the news. I broke the shooting down for him, throwing in the parts about the flasher and kidnapper around the schools.

"Man, it's like the world's become a freak show. And once again, here you are in the middle of it all. Like the ringmaster of freaks. What's the theory about the guys in the car? Just passing through and looking for some action, or was she a player, too?"

I knew what he meant. Was it random, or was it perhaps a drug or sex-related thing where she might have owed them money? "They're still running it down. I don't think they know for sure yet. But yeah, those are the two predominant theories."

"So what are you going to do about it?"

"Are you kidding? I've done enough. I'm out of it. I wouldn't even know where to begin. But, no way! Forget it! Natalie would kill me if I got involved with this thing."

"What about the perverts?"

"Well, that's a little different. I plan on keeping my eyes open and maybe take periodic runs through the neighborhood. I may go out and patrol with the crossing guards each day for a while, too. No pervert is gonna get a hold of any of those kids if I can help it. Want in?"

"Maybe. I've got nothing else scheduled and I haven't beaten anybody up for quite some time. You won't get squeamish if I catch one of these buttheads with his little worm dangling and try and put a hook through it, will you?"

"Hey, where the kids' protection is concerned, you do you want. Just make sure none of the kids are watching. Actually, make sure no one is watching. You don't need any witnesses."

"No problem. I'll be there in the morning. Just let me know where you want me."

"Oh, and I should tell you, there's an increased police presence in the area, too."

"They'll never see me."

"Hope not, for your sake. I can hear it now. 'Danny, come and bail me out. They arrested me as a pervert because I was loitering near the school. That would be hilarious."

"Anyone ever tell you you have a warped sense of humor?"

"That's what has rubbed off on me from hanging out with you."

We watched the rest of the two games and talked idly about our own upcoming season. Practice started tomorrow. We looked forward to the workout.

Just being on the field again gave us a thrill, like stepping onto our own personal Field of Dreams.

The feeling that came over me on a baseball field was difficult to explain. An inner peace descended – my own form of meditation. It was a place where I could lose the outside world for just a while and return to the simplicity of my youth. Baseball took me back to a time when life was good, simple and stress-free. The game was my ultimate escape.

But when we took to the field, it wasn't just to be recreational. We were good. One of the best teams in the state and we took pride in that fact. If the game was our religion, we worshiped wholeheartedly. The camaraderie we shared, whether teammate or opponent, was born of the same desires and dreams. The only thing separating us from the pros was the money. The pros may be the best and draw millions of fans each year to their parks, but amateur ballplayers kept the spirit of the game alive and in the imaginations and dreams of the youth.

The televised games over, I headed home, glad to have seen Tony and looking forward to working another mission together. Lord help the man who tried to dangle his wienie in front of those kids. Tony would redesign him as a eunuch.

Ten

Tuesday morning, I woke early and left for school with a couple of buttered, toasted bagels and a thermos of hot coffee. I also put my Smith and Wesson .40 in the hidden holster underneath the dashboard that one of Tony's "friends" had installed for me. I hadn't touched the gun since our assault on a drug dealer a few months before. I wanted to be prepared in case the kidnapper showed up and was armed.

Before I arrived at the school, I drove the surrounding neighborhood to make the rounds. None of the school crossing guards were at their posts yet. The guards comprised fifth through eighth-grade boys and girls. The streets were all residential. No high-traffic main street passed by the school. The guards covered four crossing points away from the building, two east, two west of the building. Two of those were out of sight. Those were the two I concentrated on.

I made note of as many vehicles parked on the street as I could. I wanted to become familiar with them so I could pick out strange cars passing through. No vans were near any of the crosswalks.

Finished with my rounds, I parked across the

street from the farthest guard post from the school. Tony called. He was on the way. I stationed him on the west side of the school to watch the farthest guard post there. The guards would start appearing in about ten minutes. I cracked my thermos, poured a cup and munched on the cold bagels.

As I ate, I took in the area. The intersection housed a large apartment complex covering all four corners. The two-story, red-brick buildings each held twenty-four apartments. About twenty percent of our enrollment came from the apartments. The entire complex included thirty buildings taking up a six-block radius.

The guards supervised students crossing on the northeast and southeast side of the road. The post closer to me was less populated, requiring one guard. The southeast side had two.

Many large trees covered the grounds. On the corner diagonally across from me, beyond the sidewalk, was a landscaped area of flowers and shrubs, including a large chiseled piece of granite displaying the name of the apartment complex. A groundskeeper was hoeing that plot. I noticed a lot of activity in the other flower beds that ran along the buildings. That was good. The more people around, the less chance someone would try anything with the children.

The three guards strolled along a few minutes later, oblivious to everything going on around them. They joked and laughed until they got on site. They crossed to the east side of the street right in front of the man working in the flower bed. Once there, they began a sword fight with the guard poles. I made a mental note to let Patrick know and give them a talking to about their behavior. With no students needing to cross yet, they all stayed on the southeast corner.

I finished my coffee and placed the thermos on the

floor. As I straightened up, I thought I saw the man with the hoe move closer to the kids. I wasn't sure if it was my imagination or not, but he seemed to be paying a lot of attention to them. He constantly sneaked peeks at them, sweeping his gaze from side to side over his slumped shoulders, as if checking to see if anyone was watching. I studied him more closely.

Then I noticed his attire. He wore a brightly colored, flowered shirt that hung loosely over his pants. He also wore a ball cap pulled down low concealing his face in shadow. He moved again, still working the hoe, now only about six feet away from the unsuspecting kids. The shirt didn't seem the type for sweaty yard work. It looked too new and too nice.

The hairs on the back of my neck stood up. I did a quick search of the area, looking for anyone sitting in a vehicle. If a car moved, the man could grab one of the kids, toss them into it and be gone before anyone had a chance to react.

There didn't appear to be anyone hiding in a car, but they could be out of sight someplace, motor running, waiting for a signal. I decided it would be better to be closer to the kids rather than sit and wait for something to happen. If anything, I wanted to let the kids know I was there and tell them to be more aware of what went on around them.

I stepped out and closed the door, standing for a second, taking another look around. My eyes were drawn to another man doing yard work. He had also moved closer to the direction of the kids, although he was as far away from them as I was. Still, I decided to watch him as well.

I crossed toward the corner but remembered my cell phone was still on the passenger seat. I reopened the door, grabbed the phone and walked forward, but now the second man had moved to an entirely different flower bed much closer to the corner. I looked back to the first man. He was within four feet of the kids. He'd been scoring the same piece of ground for quite a while. In fact, it didn't appear the hoe was even touching the ground. He kept looking back under his arm at the kids.

A hard knot formed in the pit of my stomach. I looked at the kids, who were still unaware, and picked up the pace of my approach. As I moved closer, I called Tony.

"What's up?"

"Maybe something. You got any activity on your end?"

"Nada."

"I've got a couple of suspicious characters here, eyeballing the kids. Take Crestwood East. Turn left at the first street. Come up slowly so you don't spook them and take a gander at the cars on the street. Look for a wheel man. I'm moving in now."

"I'm on my way."

I kept the phone to my ear as if still talking to someone. To get to the southeast corner faster where the kids were playing, I crossed diagonally through the intersection. The guards had yet to notice my approach. I was halfway across when a guard, Desiree Martinez, a sixth grader, spotted me and pointed. "Hey look, guys."

The two boys turned to look but didn't say anything. They probably thought I was there to yell at them for sword fighting with the poles. I glanced to my left and saw the second man was moving as well, on an intercept course with me. I now noticed movement from my right. Another man holding a rake was almost to the corner on the west side of the street.

The first man carried on as though he was working the hoe through the ground. He had his back to me as I neared the kids. A slight gust of wind or the movement of his body reaching and pulling billowed his shirt, giving me a view of a holster stuck in the back of his pants.

"Oh my God," I whispered to myself. I pushed send to reach Tony again. As he answered, I said, "Armed," and took the last few steps at a run to get between the man and the kids.

"Hey, Mr. Roth, what are you doing here?" said Bobby Smith.

"Hi, guys," I stretched my arms out wide to sort of shepherd them in close to me. I stood sideways to see the kids and the first man. I glanced back and saw the third man was halfway across the street, between them and the school, blocking any retreat for the kids. I would have to take him out first.

I leaned forward and motioned them closer to me. In a low voice, I said, "This is a drill, guys. Listen closely. As soon as I say go, you run as fast as you can back to school. You got it? I mean run all-out, but it's important that you all stay together. Go to the office and tell whoever is in there that they should call the police. That part's important. You understand?"

They all looked at me nervously, smart enough to know something wasn't right.

"But Mr. Roth," said Desiree, "if it's just a drill, why do we need to call the police?"

She was so smart and perceptive. I smiled, drawing her close for a hug.

"Now is not the time to ask questions, Desiree. Please just trust me, okay?"

She nodded, but the look in her eyes showed she was afraid. I smiled to reassure her. Glancing up from our huddle, I saw all three men converging on us. Something wasn't right, but I couldn't take chances when the kids' safety was at stake. I corralled them under my arms, straightened up and ushered them toward the man in the street blocking their path to the school. Within three feet of the man and the others following us, I disengaged my arms from the kids, stepped aside and leaned toward them. The man drew closer, his arm reaching behind him.

"Remember what I told you? On three." I put my hand in the middle of our huddle, and they all placed theirs on top of mine. "One. Two. RUN!"

The three of them bolted toward the man in the street. Distracted, he turned his head. Before he realized his mistake, I stepped forward and launched a straight right fist into his face. With a sickening crunch and a scream of pain, he stumbled back and then down.

I spun quickly to face the other two. We were in the center of the street. Behind me, to the right, a car approached. I hoped it was Tony. The first man dove straight at me, trying for a tackle. I managed to sidestep so that he didn't hit me square, though he still managed to wrap his arms around me. I spun to the side, hoping his momentum would dislodge him, and drove my left elbow down on the back of his head, driving him to the ground, but he held on around my knees, making them buckle. My arm went numb from the contact.

The third combatant jumped on my back, toppling me over his fallen comrade. I hit out and rolled, ending up on top. We flailed arms, him trying to tie mine up. Just when I cleared my right hand to throw a punch, the guy who tried to tackle me got to his knees and hit me on the side of the head, knocking me sideways. The man below me shifted his weight and shoved, dislodging me from the controlling berth.

I rolled to my feet and stood to face them as they both tackled me. I went down, my head snapping back from the impact, hitting the cement. A bright light flashed behind my eyes, stunning me. They pinned my arms and tried to roll me onto my stomach. I splayed my legs wide and head-butted one in the face. More pain lanced through me. Managing to turn on my side, I saw one of them reach behind him for what I guessed was a gun. Kicking my legs in the air violently to keep them occupied, I attempted to get an arm free. As I rocked hard, my left hand slipped free. I shot a short punch, landing it on the left side of one man's jaw. He swore and they both began pounding on me.

A blurred shadow crossed over me. In a flash, the weight on my chest had gone and my arms were free. The top man disappeared from view. Tony had arrived. The man on my left rained down ineffective but annoying punches to my head, the cumulative effect wearing me down. We grabbed each other, rolled and grappled for superior position, but neither of us could gain an advantage. Breaking free, we jumped to our feet, facing each other.

A red mist of rage clouding my eyes, I stepped forward to put the man away, when, from behind, a voice yelled, "Police! Freeze!"

Eleven

I hadn't heard them approach but was relieved the police had arrived. I backed up, thinking they would sweep in and cuff the three men. I tried to speak, gasping for breath, pointing at my opponent and attempting to signal but, to my surprise, the voice screamed again, "On the ground you two. Now!"

What? I looked up, puzzled and saw the voice came from the man whose nose I'd splattered. He was holding it with one hand and his gun in the other, aimed at my chest. My jaw dropped in shock.

"You guys are cops?" I said.

"That's right, asshole. Go ahead give me one tiny little excuse to shoot you." The blood flowed freely through his fingers. I must have hit him squarely. He's lucky the blow didn't drive the cartilage into his brain. Not taking a chance on his self-control, I dropped to the ground and laced my fingers behind my head.

One of the other two drove a knee into my back and snapped cuffs on me. As he got up from securing me, he banged my face into the cement, splitting my lip. I grunted but tried not to react.

In the distance, sirens ripped through the morning air. A mass of people lined the sidewalks, watching. Dragging me to my feet, the cop with the bloody nose grabbed me by my shirt and pulled me close. "You're lucky people are here, or I'd bust up your face. I promise you, when I get the chance, I'm going to find you and even the score." He pushed me away.

"Hey," a familiar voice hailed, "what are you doing? He's one of my teachers," Patrick said. "He sent the kids in to call the police. What's going on here?"

The bloodied cop held up his badge and said, "Police. Now step back and let us take care of this." He held up his hand to cut off any further attempt at discussion.

"You need to release these men. They are not the bad guys. They were here to help the kids."

"Sir, I don't care why they were here. They assaulted police officers. Now step back or I'll arrest you as well."

Cop cars streamed in from all over. Some of the cops recognized me, even though I wasn't sure who they were. Then the most beautiful voice in all the world barked out of the crowd.

"Roth, dammit! What have you done now?"

Morrisey, hopefully to the rescue. "I can't turn my back for a minute without you getting into trouble." He turned to the officer still holding his nose and looking a little pale. The blood loss must have been having an effect. Good! Served him right. If they were cops, he should have … and suddenly, I knew we were going to be all right.

"Sarge, what have you got here?" Morrisey asked.

"This man," he pointed at me, "moved on a group of students. He'd been observing them from the car over there. We had him under surveillance since he pulled up. He watched for a while before making a move. We saw him put his arms around the young girl. We moved in. He attacked us and we took him down. He had a friend lurking somewhere, probably to drive them off once he'd secured the kids."

I thought that was ironic, since I had the same thought about them. I decided to play my trump card. I looked for Tony, but like the shadow he was, he was nowhere in sight.

"Morrisey, excuse me ... Detective Morrisey," no sense pissing him off, "ask the sergeant why they didn't identify themselves as police officers. This could have been avoided, especially his nose. I think he needs a doctor. Really."

"Don't you be worrying about my nose, you asshole. You're under arrest for assaulting a police officer."

"Who wouldn't have been attacked if he'd just identified himself. In fact, why didn't you let the school know you were out here? I wouldn't have bothered coming if I'd known the kids were protected. Hell, I thought they were trying to kidnap our students. That's why I was out here in the first place, to watch over the guards, because of the reports of sexual predators in the area."

Morrisey put his hand on the sergeant's arm before he could reply.

"Is what he says true? You didn't identify yourselves?"

The man didn't respond and couldn't meet his gaze. "Oh God, Bill. What a clusterfuck! On top of that, I know this guy. He used to be a cop. He's the one who stopped that carload of shooters over the weekend from killing a cop."

The man looked up at Morrisey, his anger dissipating into astonishment. He put his hand to his head. His pain must have increased.

"You're way too experienced to have allowed this to happen. What went on here?"

"Things just happened fast. We feared for the safety of the kids, especially the girl, when he wrapped his arms around her. It looked way too inappropriate." The anger returned. "Then the bastard sucker-punched me."

Morrisey held up his hand. "Oh no, you don't. Don't even go there. I know him. He's a stand-up guy. Hell, he saved my life once, too. He teaches those kids. My guess is he was holding them close to keep you guys from getting them. Can you imagine the paperwork on this? There'll be hell to pay when it comes out that you didn't identify yourselves and took down one of their teachers in front of the parents of the very kids he was trying to protect. I think we need some damage limitation here, don't you?"

"What, you're just going to let him go? He threw punches at all three of us."

"Bill, I'm not going to tell you what to do. I'm not ordering you to do anything at all. This is just a suggestion, but the beating you took here will be a lot less painful than the one you'll get from the review board, or his attorney if he decides to sue the department. It's your call."

"Hell, he could sue anyways, even if we let him go. Besides, he attacked us before we had a chance to identify ourselves." He was trying to justify things, but I knew it was over.

"I think I can talk him out of anything legal. I don't think he wants the publicity any more than you do. The problem is that there was no ID given. He thought he was protecting the kids from you. This is really a no-win situation. But it's up to you. It's your bust, do what you think best. But I will say this – whatever you decide, do it fast, because you don't look so hot. You need to get to the hospital." He walked away and went to speak to the other officers involved.

The sergeant came up and stared at me. I read his face as he tried to decide whether to let me go or take his chances on a conviction on assault charges. His nose was clotting and he had to breathe through his mouth.

"Are you all right, Sarge?" I asked in a low voice. "I know it's no consolation, but I am sorry about your nose." That only seemed to infuriate him again.

"Don't worry about me. You need to shut up. Don't talk to me at all." He spun me around and opened the cuffs. As I turned, his weight pressed against me. At first, I thought he was pushing me until I felt him slide down my body. I moved fast enough to catch him before he fell.

"Morrisey!" I yelled, lowering him to the ground, his weight too much to control and afraid I would drop him. "Get an ambulance here. Hurry!"

The other cops ran to lend a hand and lay him on the ground. "Prop his head up," one of them said. Someone bunched up a jacket and slid it under his head.

"Check his airways. Make sure he's breathing."

One of them bent over him to determine if he could find a problem. As they worked on him, I backed away from the circle, in shock myself. I prayed he would be all right.

"He's breathing, but it seems rather shallow."

Patrick came and stood next to me. We watched for a while, before he turned to me. "What the hell happened here?"

"Mistaken identity. I thought they were after the students, to kidnap them and they thought I was the pervert. Lack of communication. Neither of us knew the other was out here. Everyone just reacted."

"Yeah, I see that. Once again, you seem to be in the middle of something violent. Maybe high school would be more to your liking."

I looked at him. He said it lightly, but his eyes were sending a message which made me angry.

"Now, how is this my fault? Because I care enough to spend my own time watching out for the safety of the kids? Tell me how I could have avoided this."

"I don't know how you could have dealt with it better. Maybe by telling me what you were doing. Or maybe just letting the police handle it. I don't know. But the kids don't need to see their physical education teacher brawling with the police any more than they need some guy flashing them." With that, he turned and quickstepped back to the school.

TWELVE

Fuming, if I hadn't already hit enough people, I would've added another one then. But through the anger, I understood he was right. I'd put myself in the middle of another violent situation, even though I was only trying to help. Didn't that count for something?

Tony slid up beside me and said, "Bro, you always throw such nice parties, but I think it's time for me to go. This one has turned a little too blue for my liking, if you know what I mean. Thanks for the invite. It's always a joy when I can exchange punches with some of Toledo's finest. Catch you at practice. Later."

I didn't even watch him go. Morrisey was next to bend my ear. Just about that time, the ambulance arrived and administered to the downed cop.

"Just for the record, why don't you lay out the details for me?"

As EMTs packaged up the sergeant and slid him into the ambulance, I explained what had occurred. He rubbed his short hair with his hand while I spoke.

"I'm not sure how this will go down. There may be some fallout. In truth, you were all at fault for different reasons. Walz is a good man. I don't want this to reflect badly on him. And I suppose you'd like to stay out of jail as well. This may need to be spun some. You okay with that? As long as it doesn't affect your freedom?"

"Yeah, whatever. Just let me know what you want me to do."

"I'll talk to the men and see how they feel. It will probably go down as Bill tripped and fell. Something like that. I'm not sure. It'll have to wait a couple of days to make sure no one steps forward with a statement. I'll let you know. In the meantime, let the cops do their job."

"Sure thing. And thanks again."

"Yeah, well, you just better hope I never break up with your mother. With all of the trouble you get into, you could have some serious problems. How did you survive before I came along anyways?" He patted my shoulder and walked back to the other cops. I took that as my cue to disappear and went to my car.

A couple of minutes later at the school, I went to the lounge and grabbed an ice pack for my swollen lip. It looked as if I'd had Botox injections. Crossing the hall to the gym, I found someone already teaching my first class. I turned as Patrick came out of the office and asked me to come in.

"But I have a class right now."

"I've got it covered for now. We need to talk."

My shoulders sagged in resignation. I wasn't looking forward to this, but I wouldn't let him push me around, either. I steeled myself for yet another battle and closed the office door behind me. I didn't want to sit, but decided I really needed to. The punch to the side of my head was having a delayed effect.

He got right to it. "I don't know how much more this school can take from you. You apparently like to surround yourself with controversy and violence. These kids don't need to witness that, nor do they deserve to be put in a situation where they could get hurt. Look at yourself. Look at what you've become. How many times have you been in fights over the last year? For that matter, how many times have you been shot?

"It's bad enough that it happened at all, but when it comes into the school and the neighborhood, well, it has gone too far. I seriously think you should take some time off to think about what you want to do with your life. You are obviously in some sort of inner conflict. Decide if you want to be a policeman or a teacher. You can't be both. It's not fair to the kids and it's really not fair to you."

He stopped but kept his gaze on me. He hadn't raised his voice as I'd anticipated, but kept it controlled, matter-of-fact, and concerned, although I believed the concern was more for the kids than me.

I struggled to keep my emotions in check. It wouldn't do to lose my cool now. That would only serve to emphasize his point. Besides, my head ached. He thought like Natalie did, that I thrived on danger; a violent person who went in search of it.

My bigger problem was, somewhere deep inside, I thought they both might be right. If that was the case, how did I get like this? Had I just kept my bloodlust repressed all these years? No! I couldn't accept that. I wouldn't accept it!

"Look," he continued, "I understand your motives. If it weren't for all of the other things that have happened, I could even applaud them. My question to you is, do you understand your own motivation for the danger you put yourself in? You need to give that some thought and I really think you should take some time to look inside yourself. Find out what's going on in there. Maybe seek some professional help. I don't want to see you or any of the students hurt."

I was angry again. What did he expect, that I would burn up all of my sick leave until the end of the school year, just so he could feel safer? And safer from whom? Me? Did he think me some monster, here to destroy the school?

Enraged, I lifted up from the chair, startling him enough that he recoiled from me. He must have thought I was going to hit him. "I'll tell you what, Mr. Harald, I'll stick it out for the rest of the year. I think you can survive three more weeks with a psycho as your Phys. Ed. Teacher. I'll put in for a transfer to another school for next year. Will that suit you? Well, even if it doesn't, that's what I'm going to do. Don't expect any help from me in any other way, either. You just threw what little remained of our friendship out the window." I turned to leave.

"Did you ever think that it might be out of friendship that I'm telling you this? Danny, I'm concerned for you. You've changed. I honestly think that you need help."

"Yeah, thanks for understanding, friend." I slammed the door on the way out. I blew into the gym like a tornado and gruffly told the young man who was subbing that he was no longer needed. I'm sure he wondered what he had done to be spoken to in that manner. I was too angry to feel guilty about it.

The kids finished the game the sub started while I lost myself in thought. Which one of us really didn't understand? Was I really the problem, as Patrick suggested, or was he missing the point? Maybe I was missing the point. I just didn't know anymore. He might be right. Maybe I did need some time off. But if I did that, wasn't I just admitting that I was the problem? This wasn't getting me anywhere. I was making myself crazy ... crazier. Whatever!

The class ended and students filed out. I went

across the hall to the teachers' lounge and poured a cup of coffee. Several teachers were there doing work. My mood and appearance must have unnerved them. They avoided eye contact.

One of my favorite people in the school, Mattie King, a sixth-grade teacher, followed me into the gym. "Hey, what's going on with you?"

"Oh, you mean you're not afraid to talk to me? Haven't you heard? I'm dangerous."

"Hey, I'm not afraid of you, and I don't need to be spoken to like that."

I bit back a retort. She didn't deserve to bear the brunt of my anger. I took a deep breath. "I'm sorry for snapping at you, Mattie. I just don't understand people. Am I suddenly such a monster? Am I really that different?"

"Danny, we've been friends ever since you've been here. So trust me when I tell you that people are confused, and yes, a little intimidated by you. Yes, you have changed. You are harder now. You don't joke like you used to. You're not as loose or warm with them as you once were. They just aren't sure how to approach you or what to say to you."

My shoulders slumped. An ache stabbed at my heart. Confirmation was hard to hear.

"Think back to when you broke up with your girlfriend. You never spoke to anyone. You hurt so much you shut us out. No one knew what to say to make you feel better. You got shot, not once, but twice. You got hit by a car, you became a hero. Then, back with your girlfriend, you reverted to the old Danny everyone loves. For the past few months, you've been fabulous to be around. Now, rumors of whatever happened today are spreading through the building and they aren't sure which Danny you are. Don't blame them. They still care. They're just at a loss how to act around you."

I dropped my head, ashamed. I'd never allowed

myself to see what I'd been like when Natalie left me. Only now did I realize how I had treated my colleagues and understood that Patrick was right. I needed some time away from here. I wasn't sure if I could last the final three weeks, but there was one thing I could do right now.

Mattie stepped forward and reached up to place her hands on my shoulders. "Hey, hero, it will be all right. They just need to know which one of your alter egos is present." A big playful smile spread across her freckled face. Her glasses reflected the bright gym lights up at me. She stretched her petite, slender frame and kissed my cheek.

Just then, a roar came from the gym door. We turned to see my next class standing there.

"Ah, Mrs. King, I'm telling your husband."

"Mrs. King's got the hots for Mr. Roth."

"Did you see that? They were making out right here in the gym."

Many other comments were lost as they jumbled together. I blushed, but she said, "Awesome!" She saw my confused look. "Are you kidding me? Look what you just did for my reputation. They'll all be jealous 'cause I got to kiss the hot gym teacher." She laughed and walked past the kids, slapping a few high-fives as she went.

I told the kids to come in and do some laps to settle themselves down and I went back across the hall to the lounge and said, "Hey, everyone, I just wanted to say that I'm back and that I'm sorry. I'm still me no matter what happens." I walked back to class, leaving them looking more confused than the first time I walked in.

Midway through the class, Morrisey came in. "How's the mouth?"

"Hurts. My teeth will be loose for days. I'll have to watch what I eat."

"Well, it's better than what happened to poor Walz.

He's undergoing surgery right now to clear and rebuild the damage you did to his nose." He watched the kids play for a while. "Hey, we need to go see the Mud Hens play soon."

"Sounds good to me." I waited a few more minutes, then said, "So, why are you really here?"

"I guess I was just making sure you're all right. That's all." He said it way too fast and actually appeared nervous. Something was going on.

"What, are they coming to arrest me and they told you to keep me occupied until the squads got here?"

"Huh? No, nothing like that. I was just, you know, out there and thought ... I'd check on you. Excuse me for caring," he snapped. He turned to leave, but I stopped him.

"Anything new on that other matter?"

"Nothing that I've heard. Don't worry, if they find the car, they'll call you to ID it, I'm sure."

"It's not that. I'm sure I hit that guy ... and it was a solid body shot. I may have hit him twice. Unless they have a doctor in their pocket, he should've turned up somewhere."

"What can I tell you? They're still working on it." He paused. "I hear you're coming to dinner Saturday. That's good. Looking forward to it. See ya later." He waved over his shoulder, leaving me wondering what the heck was going on. First my mother, then him. Something was up.

I called up the restaurant before lunch and had them deliver five large assorted pizzas to the teachers' lounge. We sat and joked and stuffed ourselves. Well, they did. I was still afraid to chew anything, but the laughter lightened my mood. Mrs. King and I were the butts of most of the jokes and we played along. She especially. She told everyone that now the secret was out, she could admit we'd been lovers for five years. She even came over and sat on my lap.

One of the teachers asked what her husband thought and she replied, "Oh, he doesn't mind. He's getting old now. He's more than happy to let Danny carry the load for a while. He usually falls asleep when it's Danny's turn."

The teachers shook their heads at her, their jaws falling open. I was embarrassed, but what could I do? The fun seemed to relax them enough to talk to me. One problem solved.

Thirteen

I was in my office at the restaurant, having some soup for dinner, when Morrisey knocked on the door. I found myself wondering if he was going to check to see if I was still coming for dinner on Saturday.

"I just received a call from Detective Carbone. They think they may have found the car. It's been torched and there's a body inside. He asked if you'd mind taking a look."

"Well, actually, I've got baseball practice in about twenty minutes. Can it wait?"

"You know, that's one of the dumbest things I've ever heard you say. It's a murder investigation ... and an attempted murder investigation ... the victim was a cop, remember? He also happens to be a friend of yours. Did Detective Carbone look like he'd be willing to wait until you finish practice so he could get on with his investigation?"

"Well, since you put it that way, no problem. I'd be happy to be of assistance. Where is it?"

"It's out on a side road past where you live, near Berkey. I'll follow you to your house and drive you from there."

"What's the matter? They afraid I won't show because of the beating I took, or are you coming along to protect me from getting another one?"

He smiled. "Don't be a butthead. I'll meet you at your place. God! It's a wonder you have any of your own teeth left. Everyone must want to knock them out."

We arrived on scene nearly an hour later. Berkey was a small rural community that had a large amount of new high-priced homes going up. The drive took less than fifteen minutes from my house in a usually peaceful neighborhood in Sylvania. Usually quiet, that is, until I moved in. Now there had been beatings, break-ins, kidnappings, shootings and a lot more minor stuff that really doesn't bear mentioning.

The Sylvania Police knew and welcomed me because I brought some excitement into their otherwise boring routines. They'd ask if I'd pissed anyone off lately. They didn't care if I got shot, they just wanted the chance to return fire.

The car had been found on Gibbs, a side road north of the Sylvania-Metamora Road, past a small and very old cement bridge that crossed a creek. Whoever left the car chose the spot well. Only one farmhouse down the road and it was about a mile from the site, across the Michigan state line. Little, if any, traffic passed by. The car had been driven off the road and hidden along the small creek. A line of tall trees blocked any view from the main road. Since the car was probably left late at night, there was little chance anyone saw the smoke or the flames.

That stretch of Sylvania-Metamora was rural, several miles from the actual town of Berkey. A vet called to the farm to examine a sick horse had discovered the still-smoldering vehicle on his return trip. He'd thought the burnt vehicle odd enough that he got out to take a look and notified the police when he saw the charred remains of a body inside.

We walked to the blackened shell of an unidentifiable full-size automobile. How they expected me to identify it was beyond me.

"Well," said Carbone. "What do you think? Is it our mystery car?"

"I'd like to say yes, but in truth, how do I make a connection between what I saw in the dark and what I see now? Do you have any idea what it once was?"

"Yeah, I'm told it was a Lincoln Town Car, some shade of brown. The medical examiner says the body may have been shot twice. He found melted metal inside the skeleton, which he thinks was probably a bullet."

"All I can say is, it could be. It's about the right size … and I'm pretty sure I hit the guy twice. I just don't know for sure. But it makes sense, doesn't it?"

"Yeah, it does. Well, thanks for your time." He was disappointed I couldn't lock it down for him. So was I, for that matter. But in the shape it was in, there was no way of being positive.

We hung around for a while to see if anything could be salvaged, then decided we couldn't be of any help. Morrisey dropped me off at my house without much more being said. It was almost eight. Practice would be just breaking up and I was disappointed to have missed it.

Back home, I called Natalie to say hi. We talked for a short time, but she was on her way to work. We often had difficulty seeing each other when she was on the late shift. Sometimes, if time allowed, we'd grab a quick bite to eat; sometimes, if we had been away from each other a few days, it was just a quick bite.

Normally, we were fine with the situation. But lately, I found myself missing her more and more. I wasn't sure where things were going. Maybe I was afraid of where things were going, afraid of upsetting the delicate balance we seemed to have struck. But something inside me wanted more. Was I maturing, or just getting old? We seldom spoke of our future, though. For the most part, we were happy in the here and now.

After hanging up, I channel-surfed, trying to find a

ball game. I was antsy about missing practice and needed to do something to burn off a lot of nervous energy. I thought about going for a run. The phone rang as I settled on an Atlanta Braves game.

"I was just checking to see if anybody else tried to shoot you. You weren't at practice, so I figured you were probably in some sort of trouble," Tony said.

"Oh, how sweet. You were worried about me. What a nice guy you are. I'm surprised someone hasn't latched on to you. You'd make a wonderful wife."

"Now I'm sorry I called. Next time you're getting your butt kicked by some little old man, why don't you call one of your teacher friends. Not that we missed you or anything. Practice went a lot faster not having to wait for you to hit. With all those swings and misses you do, we'da been there all night."

"Yeah, good come back. Oh, by the way, where's the money you still owe me? You know, for the bet we made last season about who would finish with the higher batting average. That'll be twenty bucks, lightweight."

"You beat me by two lousy percentage points. That's hardly worth bragging about. I'll tell you what, hotshot. Double or nothing."

"Yeah, right. And next year when I beat you again it'll be double or nothing again."

"So?"

"Great comment ... from a loser."

"So tell me, hotshot, what was so important it kept you from gracing us with your supreme presence?"

I filled him in on what had transpired. "Hey," I said, "I know what I can do instead of sitting around here. Let's go see Richie."

"What? Now? It's almost closing time for visitors, isn't it?"

"Haven't you heard? I'm a hero. They always make exceptions for heroes."

"Damn! You think you can get that big head through the door?"

FOURTEEN

We met at the elevators. I called Katy in advance to make sure it was all right to come up. She was excited and said Richie was hoping I would show up. As we rode the car up, Tony said, "I don't suppose it dawned on you that your lady friend will be here too, huh?"

"What are you saying? That I have ulterior motives for being here? As if seeing a friend in the hospital wouldn't be enough to bring me here?"

"Whoa, bro! Who do you think you're trying to snow here? Don't worry, I'm sure both of them will be happy to see you."

"Asshole!"

"Don't call me names because you're using a friend's severe injuries as an excuse to see some girl."

Luckily, the doors opened before I could reply.

We entered the waiting room but didn't see any familiar faces. Tony put the charm on a passing nurse and she directed us personally to Richie's private room. Katy and her mother were there. She stood and gave me a huge hug. "There's my hero. I'm so glad you came."

I turned my head to Tony and whispered, "See,

told you."

He rolled his eyes.

"Hi, Tony. Good to see you, too." She gave him a hug. "Thank you for coming. How have you been?"

I left the two of them to catch up and went over to where Richie lay propped up and looking much better than the last time I'd seen him. He extended his hand and pulled me forward as I took it. He wrapped his good arm around me and said, "Thank you, Danny. God bless you, my friend."

The emotional embrace made me feel uncomfortable. "How you doing, Richie? What's the scoop on your length of stay?"

He let me go, embarrassed that his eyes had watered. I turned away, pretending not to notice while I took a seat. I nodded hello to Katy's mom. "How's our boy doing? Not giving the nurses a hard time, I hope."

She laughed and replied, "No, he's been an angel, but I think he's anxious to get out. They just started letting him get up and move around a little."

We chatted for a while until Katy said, "Let's go for a stroll, Mother, and let the boys talk."

"So did you hear," he said when they'd gone, "they think they found the car?"

"Yeah, I was out there, to identify it, but it was so badly burned I couldn't be sure. At least, not a hundred percent. Tell me what you saw in that car, Richie. What drew your attention?"

He thought for a moment and his eyes drifted away, back to that zone and that time. "The woman's face, her look of horror – she was terrified. It was only a few seconds, but the look is etched into my memory, as if she was trying to reach out to me with her eyes. I was so mesmerized by the look of utter despair that I didn't react in time. They made a sharp turn for the highway ramp, taking me by surprise. I waited for traffic to clear, then pursued.

That delayed me from calling it in right away. I just blanked. The woman's face haunted me. I knew if I let them get away, she would be dead." He hung his head. "In the end, I wasn't quick enough to save her."

"Hey, man, stop that," Tony said. "There was nothing you could've done. No way they'd leave a witness, no matter what. At least on seeing you, her last thoughts were ones of hope. If you hadn't seen them, no one would've ever known what happened to her. Don't worry, they left a trail. Somebody will find it and track them down. Without you, they wouldn't even have a place to start."

"Tony's right, Richie. You gave the boys a fighting chance of catching them before they can try again. And I seriously think they will."

"Thanks, guys. I just wish that poor girl could have been saved. I won't forget her. One thing I do remember vividly, was the passenger behind the driver. His eyebrows were really big. They were black and ran almost the entire width of his face."

Tony and I laughed. "You mean he had a unibrow?" Tony said.

"Yeah, I guess that's what it was. Like a long, furry caterpillar had crawled on his face and decided to stop. I didn't think too much of it at the time. I was focused on the woman. The man had dark features. Not black ... you know, kind of Middle Eastern."

"Hey, what is this, guys' night out, or what?" Natalie said from the doorway. I wanted to ask Richie more about unibrow man, but not in front of Natalie. I didn't want her thinking I was involved in the case. She gave a big smile, walked in, and gave me a kiss.

"Now, wait a minute," whined Tony. "You can't kiss one and not the rest. That's like not bringing enough bubble gum for the whole class."

"Oh, you poor, neglected man," she said and planted a kiss on his forehead.

"Well, it wasn't earth shattering, but I guess it will have to do," he said.

She turned to Richie. "So how you doing tonight? Any problems?"

"Sore, but a little anxious to get home to my own bed."

"I hear you were up and moving a little today. Any problems with that?" She checked his temperature and blood pressure, then checked his bandages and the drip. "How's the pain? Tolerable, or do you want me to give you something so you can sleep?"

"No, I'm good, really. Any word on when I might be able to go home?"

"The doctor is expected in the morning. He'll check you out and make a decision. I'll stop back later. See you guys."

The ladies came back from their walk. As they entered, I motioned with my head for Katy to join me. We walked away from the room, stopping near the elevators.

"Danny, I just can't tell you enough how grateful I am that you saved Richie."

"I'm just glad I came along when I did. He looks like he'll be fine. His spirits are good right now. The reason I asked you out here, though, was to see how you were holding up."

She shrugged and turned her head quickly to hide a brief emotional crack. There was no sign of distress when she turned back. She was a very strong woman.

"You know how it is. As a policeman's wife, you try to stay strong for everyone's benefit. I'll be all right, now that I know he'll recover." The mask faltered and tears welled. I reached out and took her into my arms. She buried her head, let out one sob and fought for control over her emotions.

"It's all right, Katy. He's safe now. You don't have to hold it in."

She gripped my shirt and let the tears roll.

One of the elevators dinged. The door slid open and a small, tanned man with wild, uncombed black hair, stepped out. Seeing us embracing, he stopped short, gave a strange look, backed up and walked in the opposite direction, as though embarrassed to have interrupted us. His head swung from side to side as if searching for a room. He wore scrubs, so I thought he might be looking for a patient. Katy dried her eyes as we watched him disappear around a corner. We looked at each other and shrugged.

"Strange," she said.

I released her and we walked back to the room.

"You know, if there's anything you guys need, all you have to do is call me, right?"

"I know, Danny. Thank you. Everyone has been very supportive. I think we'll be fine. Especially surrounded by so many wonderful friends."

Nearing the door to Richie's room, I felt compelled to glance back over my shoulder. The strange man was peering around the corner, watching us. There was something unnerving about the way he stared. Was he checking out Katy? She was a beautiful woman and could turn heads, but this man stared at her, ogling her in a disturbing fashion.

I excused myself, walking in the man's direction. His eyes widened with surprise, the reaction of a man caught doing something he shouldn't. He ducked around the corner. By the time I reached the corner, there was no sign of him. I continued around the full loop of the corridor until I was back at Richie's room, but didn't see him again.

We stayed longer than we were supposed to and for the most part, kept the conversation light and positive. We discussed baseball and our various opinions of different teams' chances. Periodically, I got up as if stretching my legs and took a look down the halls, but the strange man did not reappear.

Natalie came back to announce we really should leave. We said our goodbyes and I stole a very sweet kiss that had wet dream potential.

FIFTEEN

It was nearly eleven when I arrived home. I wondered if Richie had mentioned the man in the car to Detective Carbone. He'd given me his card at some point, but I couldn't remember where I placed it. With no way of contacting him, I called Morrisey.

"Why aren't you in bed? Don't you have to work in the morning?" He sounded like he was in bed already. In the background, I heard a woman's voice that sounded awfully familiar. He covered the phone but some murmuring came through the receiver.

I tried not to think of my mother being in his bed. Not that I had a problem with their relationship, but there are things a son doesn't want to think about.

"So, what's, ah, on your mind?" he asked.

"I need to get hold of Carbone. Ask him if Richie mentioned that one of the passengers in the car might be Middle Eastern with a big bushy unibrow."

"He told you this?"

"Yeah, I saw him tonight, after you dropped me off."

"I'll ask him tomorrow. Let you know what he says. Anything else?"

"No, not that I can think of. Oh wait, yeah there is. Tell my mother good night."

"Sure, Danny says ..." Pause. "You just tricked me, didn't you?"

"You really are a good detective, aren't you?"

I think I heard "shithead" as I was hanging up the phone. I knew they'd been sleeping together for quite some time. I just didn't allow myself to dwell on it. She was my mother after all, and everyone knew their mothers didn't do that stuff. Our births were more Virgin Mary-ish in conception. Had to be. I remembered how strange the two of them had been acting lately, especially about this dinner Saturday night. Theories rolled around my mind.

They were either thinking of shacking up together or ... maybe even the big knot-tying thing. Wow! They were old, hence old-fashioned. Maybe they just wanted to make their sleeping together legal in the eyes of their friends. Unfortunately, those thoughts and not Natalie's long, lingering kiss stayed with me in my dreams.

The warm air on the pleasant morning drive to school made me feel lazy before the day had even begun. I decided, no matter what the situation was with the police or Mr. Harald, I would make a pass through the neighborhood anyway. I wouldn't stop, but you never know what one extra set of eyes might see.

The quick drive-by produced nothing out of the ordinary, but I did discover the new police set up. They had moved two blocks further north and were now sewer workers in a city truck. I didn't see Sergeant Walz among them, but he might not be joining them for a while. I felt kind of guilty about that. Just for fun, I honked and waved as I drove by.

At school, an unsettling sight appeared before me. A local media van sat out front of the building. The call letters on the side belonged to the same station as my reporter friend from several days ago. She was on the front lawn of the school near the steps to the main door, speaking to the camera.

Panic rising, I feared something had happened to one of the students, but I had no desire to have the reporter discover where I worked.

I parked my car as far from the door as possible and slid out on the passenger side. I waited until she turned enough not to see my approach. The forty-yard walk to the side door shouldn't have taken seconds to cover. However, as I got to the bus area, a commotion near the front of one of the buses drew my attention.

Several of the paraprofessionals who helped the multi-handicapped students get off the buses were arguing with a tall, white male, presumably one of our parents. The confrontation escalating fast. The irate man took several threatening steps toward one of the older ladies. His hands flailed erratically and the words spewing from his mouth would have made the exorcist think twice about what he was dealing with.

As I slowed my pace, my body almost unconsciously detoured in their direction. The man got louder. His language strictly street. "If the motherfucker can't drive that bitch, he oughta get a new job."

"Sir," said grandmotherly Mrs. Zink. Though slight of build, the sixty-something woman wouldn't take crap from anyone. She stood toe to toe with the young parent. He towered over her, dressed in what looked like a designer sweatsuit with a hat cocked sideways on his head. "This is the drop-off point for students with disabilities. We have children on that bus in wheelchairs. We can't get them off the bus if your car is parked …"

But the hyper man wouldn't let her finish. "Only thing with a disability is that motherfucker pretending to be a bus driver." He rocked from side to side, his finger jabbing the air over Mrs. Zink's head toward the driver. The bus driver, a large, older black man, clearly didn't know what to do. He picked up his cell phone and climbed down the steps.

"That's right motherfucker, call someone who can drive this bitch."

"Sir," continued an exasperated Mrs. Zink. "You are at a school. That language is inappropriate around children."

"What the fuck's wrong with my language? Get your scraggly old self out of my face, bitch."

"You may think it's all right to speak like that in front of your children, but it is unacceptable here. Now, you need to move your car so the bus can unload."

A sudden flash made everything quiet for a second before all hell broke loose. The bus driver had not opened his phone to make a call, he'd used it to take a picture of the irate parent. He leaned further out the door and refocused to snap one of the man's car in front of the clearly marked sign that said, "No Parking – Bus Drop Off." The driver mumbled, "Call me names, I'll have his car towed."

The man went ballistic. He tried to move past Mrs. Zink. "Hey, you motherfucking asshole, you can't do that. I got rights. You can't take my picture unless I give you fucking permission."

I moved faster, now on an intercept course, but wouldn't get there before the man reached the bus driver. Parents dropping off their children had either turned to watch or hastened their little ones away, covering their little ears as they went. Several teachers stopped to see what all the fuss was about, but more importantly, the reporter heard the screaming, too, and walked toward the small crowd with a microphone in hand, sensing a breaking news story.

I knew I should just change direction and go into the school, especially in light of the previous day's confrontations, but I couldn't leave Mrs. Zink to fend for herself. Although in my book, it would be even money between her and the butthead.

The reporter gathered speed. She hadn't noticed me yet and, at this distance, might not recognize me. That would change if I continued on my present course, but my decision was made and never truly in doubt. I would not leave Mrs. Zink to face that fool alone.

Mrs. Zink moved to block the man's advance. He put his hands on her shoulders and pushed her to the side, sending her cartwheeling to the ground. A collective gasp went up from the crowd. All other thoughts or hesitations evaporated once I saw him put his hands on her. I zeroed in on my target like a linebacker lining up a quarterback and pushed the adrenaline button to increase my closing speed. Mrs. Zink hadn't been able to stop him, but she'd slowed his advance just enough.

The bus driver stepped off the bus and lined up another shot as the tall angry man reached him.

"You motherfucker, give me that phone." He raised his hand over his head as if to strike the petrified bus driver, who lifted his own arms in a defensive gesture. I hurdled Mrs. Zink, who was just coming to a stop on the ground, launched myself at the towering man and drilled him in the back just as his arm fell, grazing the driver's head. The driver fell backward, tripping over his own feet, but to everyone watching, it looked as though the punk had tried to pile-drive him into the ground.

We went down and I landed on him. We slid on the grass a short distance, my right arm wrapped around his body, the left acting as a brake on the ground to make sure I didn't roll and end up on the bottom. As we came to a stop, I straddled his chest.

His hands flailed to keep me from hitting him, while his body bucked trying to dislodge me. He was strong and wild, scoring one glancing blow to my jaw.

I found myself wishing I still had my police ID so I could tell this asshole he was under arrest. Instead, I did the next best thing: I popped him in the jaw, only my punch had the benefit of the upper position with a lot more power behind it. Immediately, the big baby began to cry and scream. He put both hands over his face and bawled like a child.

I refrained from wrapping my hands around his neck and banging his head on the ground a few times. I sat on his chest and wondered if anyone had called the police. For the first time, I looked around and noticed a large crowd had formed.

Students pointed at us. Parents watched with mixed looks of shock and contempt, although I wasn't sure for which of us. Teachers were outraged, but again I wasn't sure for whom. Mrs. Zink sat on the ground with several teachers around her. She smiled and gave me a thumbs-up.

In a low voice, she said, "Hit the bastard once for me."

With all these people watching, it seemed reasonable one of them would've stepped forward to assist me, but they'd rather watch, point and make faces. Someone shouted, "Yeah!" and started clapping. Others joined in.

As I scanned the loose circle for signs of any aid, my eyes locked on those of the reporter. Instant recognition morphed into a smug look of satisfaction. She nodded to herself as if saying "I've got you now." She whispered to her cameraman, who'd filmed the entire incident.

Movement caught my eye, and Mr. Harald stepped from the center of the crowd. He hesitated for a split second and we both muttered, "Great!"

He walked toward me, but before he reached me, two undercover cops wearing sewer repair overalls came bursting through the circle. I thought they were going to tackle me, but as I stood and stepped over the cry baby, they swooped down on him.

As they did, I leaned in close and whispered, "Careful, cameras are rolling." The one I whispered to looked around, saw what I meant, and nodded back, "Thanks for the heads up."

They cuffed him. He was still crying when they lifted him to his feet. As they were leading him away, Mrs. Zink stepped close and whispered, "Who's the bitch now, motherfucker?" and kicked him in the shins. I wrapped my arms around her from behind and lifted her still-kicking form away from the man before she did real damage.

"Easy, Helen. Easy. There's a news crew here filming. You don't want them to see you."

"I don't give a shit," she said. "He's lucky he's tall, or I would've kicked him where I was aiming."

After handing her off to several other staff members, I went to the squad car and gave a brief statement. As they drove off, I examined my clothes and tried to brush the grass stains from my pants, a wasted effort. I sighed and walked toward the school when Patrick intercepted me. He looked stern. His first words were, "I think I'm going to have to file a safe school ordinance."

"Yeah, he's a real nut case."

"I meant on you." He spun and walked swiftly back to the building, leaving me in stunned disbelief. At that moment, the reporter stepped forward, stuck her microphone in my face and asked, "So Mr. Roth, can you tell us why you assaulted that parent?"

I brushed past her, refusing to be baited, my anger at full boil. Behind me, she said, "Careful, Jeremy, we don't want him to attack us, too."

She hurled questions after me as they followed my

flight.

"Mr. Roth, are the police here to arrest you on assault charges? Have you been suspended from your teaching duties? Do you have a history of assaulting parents?"

No, I thought, as I hastened my retreat. But I might develop a history of attacking reporters.

Sixteen

In the end, school security had to be called to contain the media frenzy that followed the initial biased report of a teacher attacking a parent. The local Fox affiliate that Miss Carolyn Monroe – I kid you not – worked for, aired the same film clip over and over as 'breaking news.' The video featured yours truly in his movie debut, hurdling Mrs. Zink and pouncing on the poor victim. Somehow, they managed to edit out the bus driver. She made it sound and look like I had instigated the fight.

The other three local channels coming into the story late, took their time, collected the facts and reported the true story. They aired a live interview with Mrs. Zink and a brief statement from Mr. Harald confirming her story. A police statement followed, showing a picture of the parent in cuffs. One reporter announced the man had a previous arrest for drug trafficking. As a result, miraculously, extra footage was added to the Fox early evening report, showing Mrs. Zink tumbling and the attempted strike on the bus driver, just before I took him down. No apology was issued.

The school day had been an ongoing circus event. Mr. Harald and many of the teachers felt I should leave school for the day so they could return to their normal routines. I refused to be pushed out. Guess they forgot about my pizza offering the day before. It was a very long and slow day.

Later, when I got to the restaurant, I retreated to my office and hid. I just sat and tried to think about what another fine mess I'd gotten myself into. It's pretty bad when you have to convince yourself you did the right thing, trying to protect the students and staff members. Anger swept over me, first at the reporter and then at Patrick. I couldn't understand his perspective of the events of the last few days.

It took some time before I was able to push the day's events to the back of my mind and start on the paperwork. Halfway through I jumped from my seat and exclaimed, "Oh shit! Natalie."

She'd beat me senseless. She had to be aware of the noon news stories by now. I had to call her to begin damage control. If I could tell her before she heard, it could go a long way in the brownie points department.

I fumbled my phone from my pocket and called. The phone rang five times, anxiety building while I waited for her to answer. A bead of sweat slid down the side of my head.

"Congratulations! You beat the allotted time for disclaiming feats of heroism."

"Ah … you heard already, didn't you?"

"Yep! It was all over the news. Both of my darling sisters called, wanting me to see what my wonderful boyfriend was up to now, although both preferred the earlier report on Fox about you being the attacker instead of the savior. You just can't get enough of the limelight, can you?"

"Let me explain, Nat …"

"Maybe I should make you a superhero costume with a cape. I could rent your services out to little old ladies trying to cross busy streets and poor little girls whose cats are stuck in trees."

"Nat!"

"Or maybe I can run an escort service. That's it! Superhero escorts. We guarantee you'll get safely to your destination."

"NATALIE!"

"Hey, Mr. Hero, don't yell at me. I'll call that reporter from Channel 36 and tell her just how abusive your alter ego really is."

"Natalie, I'm sorry." Silence. "Talk to me. Natalie?" But she'd gone. Fabulous. Next time, Mrs. Zink would just have to fend for herself.

L eaving the office, my head hanging low, I almost walked right past Morrisey.

"Why the long face? You should be beaming. You rescued another damsel in distress."

"Oh, yeah, hi. Guess the superhero business isn't all it's cracked up to be."

"What's the matter, champ?"

I looked past Morrisey at the owner of the second voice. I hadn't even seen Carbone sitting there. "Oh, hey, detective. How you doing?"

"Real good. Surprisingly, the food in this joint ain't half bad."

"The food in this joint would make the Pope think he was already in heaven," I bristled.

"Easy there, champ. I was only kidding. Don't hit me with one of those flying tackles. I admit it. The food is excellent. As an Italian, this is one of the few places I would ever bring my sainted momma. Here, she can get a meal almost as good as she could make herself."

I smiled at his accent and the way he spoke with his hands moving. I realized I was a little sensitive at the moment.

"So what is the problem, Danny?" Morrisey asked.

"Oh, it's Natalie. She thinks I'm out danger hunting again. Tell me. How was I supposed to turn my back on that little old lady when she was being harassed by that clown? Hell, if I had known he was such a baby, I would've let her kick his butt."

"I don't know what to tell you, but you should be proud of yourself for be willing to get involved helping others. There aren't many who do anymore. That's why so many crooks get away. No one will step up. I hope things work out for you and your girlfriend, but eventually, she'll accept that getting involved is part of who you are and one of the things that's special about you or ... not."

I understood what Morrisey was saying, but I didn't want Natalie to leave me again. I'd just have to wait her out.

"Hey, let's move to a table where we can talk a little more privately," Carbone said.

Curious, I went with them to the back of the dining room where we spread out on a four top table. Sheila, one of our waitresses, came over and took a drink order. Carbone placed his elbows on the table and leaned forward. He spoke in a low voice.

"Mike told me what you learned from Richie. I paid a visit to him today to re-interview him. See if he could remember anything else that might help us ID this guy. You were the only other one to see the dead man, so I thought I'd talk to you again and see if you'd come up with anything new."

He knew I hadn't seen the driver. It was logical to ask if I'd thought of anything new, but something made me think he was holding back.

"Tell me what's happened."

"What makes you think something's happened?"

"Because you're being a cop and answering a question with a question."

He smiled and glanced at Morrisey. The smile disappeared when he looked back at me. "And as the cop, the professional cop, not the amateur one, I get to ask the questions. Now give."

Now it was my turn to shoot a look at Morrisey.

Morrisey threw up his hands and said, "What do I look like, the referee? I'm not scoring this bout. You two leave me out of your tug-o-war. You're on your own. Play nice."

I laughed.

"Well, as you know, there was a little problem with bullets flying over my head, so I really didn't get a good look at anything. Even the guy who got out wasn't clear as far as detail went." I leaned back as Sheila placed our drinks in front of us. I closed my eyes, bringing the moment back.

The scene advanced frame by frame. I saw the car reversing. I heard rather than saw the man step out of the car. I jumped up and fired into him. My eyes flicked open. There was something on the fringes of my vision. A light someplace in the background. The background ... that was it. It came to me piece by piece, like the frame of a puzzle. I needed to build the border first, then fill in the middle. A light came from ... where? Oncoming headlights? No, closer. From the car itself. That was it. The interior light was on because the door was open as the man staggered back to the car. I'd ducked shots from inside the vehicle.

I stopped, rewound the picture and started again. My heart rate increased as my excitement escalated. I started again from the time I hit the gunman and he spun back toward the car. I had a fraction of a second view of the inside of the car. A quick head movement. It had to be the driver. That was it. The driver had looked back over the headrest as the man re-entered the car. For that one brief moment, he wore a halo from the overhead dome light, so quick I'd missed it before.

The dark features, jet black hair, slightly hooked

nose, a thin line of black surrounding his face in a trimmed beard … without a mustache.

In that one frozen moment, I saw him, and his eyes locked on me. Black, bottomless, soulless, deadly. The memory made me shiver, but I had it. I leaned forward, slapping the table. The drinks bounced.

"Yes!" I exclaimed in triumph. "I do recall something. Now, what do you have?"

SEVENTEEN

The excitement left Carbone's eyes as quickly as it had arrived, replaced by a stern, angry, threatening look. Morrisey broke into a laugh, snatched his beer and stood. "Oh, this is good, but I'm not gonna be here when the fireworks go off. Call me when you two are done."

Carbone and I glared across the table in a battle of wills. "You're playing a dangerous and foolhardy game, withholding evidence in a criminal investigation. I could have you arrested."

"You could, but I'd only clam up."

"I'd have a judge hold you in contempt and put you in jail."

"That's all right. The staff at my school is trying to get me to take time off anyway."

"Damn, you're a stubborn son of a bitch."

"Watch it, sir. My mother is in the kitchen. And she most certainly is not a bitch. Although after a full day of working on her feet and slaving in a hot kitchen, she could probably kick both our asses ... at the same time."

"Why is it so important to you?"

"Why is it so important that you keep it from me?"

He made a low growling sound and I could see he

was at the end of his patience. I held up my hand before he bellowed at me. "Look, I'm part of this. My friend was almost killed. I'm a witness and I more than likely killed one of them. It's not like I'm not trained, even if I'm no longer official. Let's just say I'd like to know what's going on. That's it. I'll tell you what I remembered. I'm just asking for a little common courtesy. Deal?"

He let out a long controlled breath and nodded. "All right. Deal. But no going off on your own, trying to find these guys ... I will lock you up, understood?"

I crossed my fingers and agreed. I was relatively sure that the crossed fingers thing wouldn't hold up in court, but it made me feel better. I told him of my brief glimpse of the driver. At first, he just sat there, thinking. For several agonizing seconds, I thought he would play the "Huh, gotcha" game. But he reached inside his jacket and pulled a packet from his pocket. He slid out an assortment of photos and spread them out on the table. I understood what he wanted. One or more were suspected of being in that car. The others were decoys. They had a suspect.

"Is he here?"

I thought I recognized him, but to be sure, I studied each picture, closed my eyes and brought the face back into view; I opened them and looked down at the photo. I put my finger on the photo.

"I'm as positive as I can be. This is the man driving the car. You know who he is, don't you?"

"I know I don't have to tell you how important this is. Be real sure here."

"From the glance I had, if this isn't him, it's damn close."

He nodded, swept up the pictures and stashed them back inside his jacket. He drank deeply from his imported beer and seemed to be deciding whether he should tell me more, or how much to divulge.

Then he leaned forward again. "His name is Hasheem Turfe. He's a Syrian National suspected of kidnapping American women for shipment and sale in foreign countries for sexual purposes."

"Human trafficking?"

He nodded. "Turfe travels with another man, but we have no information on him. That might have been the man Molten saw. The information comes from the FBI and isn't much. He apparently selects an area, collects four to six women aged sixteen to thirty-five, then moves on. We suspect some are to fill orders while the rest are collected on speculation. We are the fourth area to be hit by him and his group. That's where the information was gathered from. And there is precious little evidence. So far, they have picked smaller market communities, like ours and Fort Wayne, maybe thinking they're easier pickings."

A bad feeling soured my stomach. "But he's been seen here and one of his crew has been eliminated. Surely he'll move on."

Pause. Drink. Morrisey returned, having heard my last statement.

"Tell him, Mario. Tell him all of it."

"Yeah, all right. We thought so, too, until last night. Another girl was kidnapped, walking home from the library in Sylvania. Chloe Lerner, a senior at Northview High. From the pictures I've seen, she's very pretty. It'll be hitting the news by now. We initially wanted to keep it quiet, hoping strangely enough, it might be a kidnapping for ransom, but we can't take the chance. Their MO is to come into an area, round up some girls and disappear, usually in less than a week. She has to be still in the area. As far as we know, she's the first one. They haven't left. They're just getting started."

He let that last statement hang over our heads like a room full of cigarette smoke hanging in a foul cloud.

"Damn!" was all I could manage.

"So far, none of the girls from his previous jobs have ever turned up. Evidently, the Feds have every organization in Europe searching, but wherever they're being sold, they're never seen again. The popular theory is they are sold as sex slaves to wealthy men who dispose of them when they're finished with them. The news release will hopefully put everyone on full alert. Maybe we'll get lucky and someone will see him. Your identification will go a long way in helping find him. Thanks for that."

He finished his beer and made a move to rise. I placed a hand over his to hold him for a moment. "If there's anything I can do to help, just ask. Whatever I can do, I will."

He nodded. "I'll let you know. I'd better go and try to get this picture on the news. Who knows, maybe it'll help."

He thanked me and left. We sat in silence until I saw Morrisey running his hand through his short hair, his nervous thing.

Light bulbs lit up in my head.

"There's more isn't there?"

"Yep."

"Well ...?"

"The missing girl is the Sylvania Mayor's daughter."

I let out a low whistle.

EIGHTEEN

I was going to call off the next day, but with the story of the kidnapping dominating the media, I was old news. Most of the staff greeted me in a very welcoming and friendly manner when I walked in. Mrs. Zink had organized a surprise breakfast to thank me and, I assumed, to show support for me. She whispered in my ear, "I wanted you to know that most of the staff is very appreciative of all you do for them and wanted to thank you publicly. As far as the rest of them are concerned, well, they can just bid out next year or they can kiss my wrinkly old ass." She was precious. It was nice to have her in my corner.

Nice also to know I had support within the building. That went a long way in boosting my morale and in combating Patrick's efforts to push me out.

I scarfed down another donut, grabbed a cup of coffee and went to set up the gym for my classes. The day went smoothly for the most part. The only somewhat distracting part was the student comments. Many of them witnessed the previous day's altercation and seemed in awe of me. Their responses were positive, however. I had re-earned their respect. Maybe some of the troublemakers would be better behaved now.

But the most surprising response came from the community at large. Many parents had phoned in that, although they didn't condone violence or fighting, they were happy to see that a teacher was not afraid to get involved for the benefit of the students.

Most of those who had witnessed the display felt that parent should be banned from picking up his children. Many wanted his children transferred to another school. No one wanted their children to have to see such behavior or hear that type of language. Several parents stopped me in the hall to say thanks. A parent of one of the wheelchair-bound bus passengers came in specifically to give me an apple pie she'd baked for me. There were a few detractors as well, but the overall response seemed to be one of support and gratitude. All in all, it felt nice to be appreciated, even if the principal and a few colleagues disagreed.

I missed my morning drive-by, trying to keep a low profile, but after the warm, positive reception, I decided to start up again the next day.

The only bad thing was I still hadn't heard back from Natalie. I wanted to call her but felt it would be better to let her make the move. However, by the time I got to the restaurant that afternoon, I couldn't control the urge any longer.

The phone rang and I was shocked to hear a man's voice answer her cell phone. I hesitated, but when he repeated, "Hello," I said I'd dialed the wrong number.

Watching the numbers, I tried again. This time, when he answered, I knew it was Natalie's phone. I was numb. She couldn't have been that angry. It sounded like the same guy she'd been seeing when we split up.

"Is Natalie there?"

"She's in the shower. Can I take a message?"

"No! Tell her I get the message." I hung up.

My anger went from zero to mushroom cloud in the blink of an eye. It was all I could do to keep from throwing the phone. I couldn't believe she would jump ship so quickly. Especially over something so … trivial. What happened to that speech she gave me at the hospital about accepting the way I was? What about the rewards she heaped upon me? Oh, those rewards. I couldn't believe this was happening … again.

Thank God for baseball practice tonight. I needed to expend this pent-up anger. I flew through the paperwork. As I worked, my phone beeped. Natalie. I refused to answer. Nothing good could come of my answering, angry as I was. A few seconds after it stopped, a beep signaled she left a message. It would keep. I continued working, grabbed a couple of beers and headed toward Tony's house.

I started the car as another beep announced a text message from Natalie. **Call me**, it read.

"Not likely," I said aloud. I wasn't about to give her the chance to break up with me. She would just have to do it when I chose to listen. Ignoring the message, I drove off doing twenty miles an hour over the speed limit. I was fortunate no cops were around. In my mood, I probably would've ended up in jail. I could just see those headlines: "Hero who saved cop jailed for assaulting one."

Tony was outside watering his lawn. I got out, grabbed my duffel bag, handed him a beer and walked inside his home. I dropped the bag on the floor and flopped into one of the lounge chairs. By the time Tony came in, my beer was gone. I got up, snagged another one from his refrigerator, and flopped again.

"Well, nice to see you, too. Let me guess, woman

problems, right?"

"You are good, you know that?"

"Well, of course, that's why I can charge those outrageous fees. Wait till you get your bill. You'll have to mortgage your house." He sat. "So do we talk now, or do you have to calm down first?"

"Definite calm down period needed."

"That bad, huh? Well, you know where the beer is." He left to shower and get ready for practice. Tony was the only person I knew who showered before he went to work out. He was so vain sometimes. His hair had to be perfect. If I wanted to get to him, I'd say things like, "Man, you're really getting gray hair," or, "Hey, is that a zit?" It made him crazy.

I went up to my room and changed into sweats, then walked downstairs to the basement, where he had a gym set up. A speed bag and heavy punch bag hung from the floor joists. In a matter of minutes, I had a full sweat going. Alternating between kicks and punches of various sorts, I wasn't aware of how much time had passed until Tony yelled down, "Hey, are you going or what?"

I toweled off and let him drive to the field, feeling somewhat more relaxed, but the desire to hit something was still foremost in my mind. Tony tried to lighten the mood.

"You know, bro, if you could hit a baseball as well as you hit that bag, you might end up being a good hitter. It's just too bad you're a slap hitter instead of a power hitter."

"What the hell are you talking about? I outhit you and scored more runs than you did."

"I hit more dingers and drove in more runs than you did."

"Oh, right, one home run makes you more powerful!"

"No, one home run makes me have more than you. And I drove in eleven more runs than you did. Plus, I stole more bases. Huh!"

"I hit more doubles."

"I hit more triples."

"You also hit into more double plays and struck out more."

"Oh, man, that was low. And power hitters always strike out a little more than do the punch hitters who can only get on by slapping at the ball."

"Justify any way you want, but I am the better hitter."

"Only in your dreams."

"Face reality. Just look at the league's batting standings. Whose name is listed first? That's all I'm asking. Who? End of discussion."

"Yeah, but who was more valuable to the team? Me."

"This is an unwinnable argument."

"For you, yeah."

"You're pushing. I think it's time to raise the stakes. To decide once and for all. I just hope your delicate ego can withstand the truth."

"Don't you worry about my delicate ego. By the time I'm finished whupping your sorry ass, breaking up with your girlfriend will be least of your troubles—"

Silence.

"Shit!"

"Yeah! Real nice."

"Bro, I'm sorry."

"Thanks, friend."

"I didn't mean to go there, honest."

"Try to get into a good argument to take a guy's mind off of his problems and you go full circle and come right back to his problems. Nice."

"I'm sorry. What can I say?"

"Oh, I think you've said quite enough, thank you. Man, some people will say anything when they know they're losing an argument. Pathetic."

We pulled up to the field and I opened my door. He turned sideways and apologized again, but I held up my hand and cut him off. I grabbed my stuff and walked to the field without waiting for him. He ran to catch up.

"Come on, bro. What can I do to make up for it?"

"Dinner and drinks tomorrow night, place of my choice."

"Done."

It was what I'd been holding out for.

NINETEEN

Practice went quickly. I enjoyed being out on the field, even if it was just shagging balls or taking a few grounders, but the absolute best part was stepping into the batter's box.

I stepped in, took a deep breath and started hacking. The first few cuts weren't very impressive, but once I got into the groove, the ball jumped off my bat. The solid drives felt good. Really getting into a pitch and knowing it down deep in your bones is like a hitter's wet dream. I cracked about fifteen balls, then stepped out for the next hitter, feeling much better. Much of the tension and anger gone.

An hour and a half later, we were finished. It had been a good workout. I jogged the outfield from the left field line to the right field line about ten times. The final few I ran hard. Having successfully burned off my hostilities, I was ready to call it a night.

Tony invited me inside for a beer, but I declined.

"Still pissed at me?" he asked.

"Always, but I'll get over it, eventually. Dinner will help. I'm going to have one hell of an appetite. I'm thinking surf and turf, baby. Oh, yeah!"

"Whatever. Later."

On the drive home, I checked my phone. There

were two more missed calls from Natalie and seven new text messages. Plus, one voicemail from my mother. I checked the texts first.

Call me.

Call me.

Don't be stupid.

Call me back, you buckethead.

God, you piss me off.

Call me, NOW!

Fine, you butthead. Don't call. Don't ever have to call me again.

Uh-oh! Sounded serious. I wasn't sure, but it sounded like I'd better call. I checked the voicemail first to see what my mother wanted.

"Natalie said you're being a butthead. Call that nice girl, or I'll be pissed at you, too." I wasn't sure what surprised me more. That Natalie had called my mother to put pressure on me, or that she said "pissed." She'd been hanging around Morrisey too much. I decided I'd better call Natalie right away. No sense pushing my luck any further.

I pushed her number as I reached the intersection of Monroe and Main Streets in downtown Sylvania. Before the call connected, a black Hummer H3 blitzed through the intersection from the right lane and swung in front of me. The only thing preventing him from sideswiping me was my last-second, speed-of-light reflexes. All superheroes come equipped with them.

I stomped on the brakes and pulled the wheel to the left, straight into the path of an oncoming car. I swerved back into my lane, barely avoiding a head-on collision. My heart pounding at the near miss, I swore at the Hummer's driver as he sped away. Natalie's voice yelled at me. Placing the forgotten phone to my ear, I said, "Sorry, Nat. Some asshole just cut me off and ..." And I froze.

An image flashed in my mind's eye; a familiar

memory of another flash. "My God," I said into the phone.

"What! What the hell is going on there?"

It all came together with brilliant clarity. "Son of a bitch!"

"What? Did you just call me a bitch?"

Unfortunately for me, that question didn't register in my mind at the time. I was still thinking about my "accidental" discovery. The man who almost ran me off the road was the same man who'd been driving the car when Richie got shot. I was almost positive. Shoving the gas pedal down, I shot forward in pursuit. The Hummer disappeared around a curve farther up the road.

"You had better talk to me, or I swear I will hurt you."

I hadn't really heard that either, although later, subconsciously, I replayed it and realized I'd made yet another big mistake, my mind elsewhere. I had to find the Hummer and call someone. The caged squirrel that powered my brain worked double-time. I tried to focus on who to call. But first, I had to make sure it was the right guy. "Nat, I'm sorry, I gotta go. I'll call you later."

"Don't you dare hang—"

But of course, I did. I picked up speed and screeched around the curve in the road. I swerved, almost uncontrolled, with more than half of my BMW riding in the eastbound lane. As luck would have it, a car was coming. The driver hit the brakes, honked and veered to his right, avoiding my second possible head-on collision in the last sixty seconds. I was also the recipient of a one-finger salute.

I righted the car and continued at NASCAR speeds, searching the side streets as I whizzed past for signs of the black H3. At the junction of Monroe and Erie, I stopped at the traffic light and looked both ways, hoping for a glimpse of the fleeing vehicle.

The road to the left had a few small rises and dips in the distance. Just reaching the farthest of the rises, nearly a mile away, was the Hummer, heading into the beginnings of a magnificent sunset.

As the light changed to green, I sped around the turn to the left, leaving a good bit of rubber behind. The other vehicle had a good head start on me, but I had a powerful engine in my car, too. I just had to keep him in sight long enough to mark where he was going.

I needed to call someone, but who? Carbone? The Sylvania Police, whose jurisdiction it was? Maybe I should call Morrisey and let him handle it. Yep, sounded like a plan.

It took three attempts to find Morrisey's number, afraid to take my eyes off the receding taillights. I couldn't afford to lose him. There might not be another opportunity. Eventually, I had to glance down to get it right. A sharp pang of panic struck me when I looked back up. I'd lost contact. Panic seized me. My heart thudded as though I was running instead of driving. I spotted him again as I rounded another bend.

"Yeah. What kind of trouble can I bail you out of this time?"

"Yeah, thanks! Real nice! How 'bout I make your night for you, though. How's that? Will that work?"

"Okay, sorry. What gives?"

"Listen. I can't be positive 'cause it happened so fast, but I think I just saw the driver of that car that shot up Richie."

"What! Where!"

"Oh, now it's all right if I call, huh?"

"Oh, for Christ's sake. Stop being so sensitive and buy a new sense of humor. Now, tell me what's happening."

I hated being scolded, but he was right. This time.

"I'm heading west on Erie. The one in Sylvania."

There were actually three or four Erie Roads around the Toledo area. "I just passed Centennial, but he's a distance beyond."

"Define distance. You still have eyes on him, right?"

"Yeah, but he's hauling pretty good. He's driving a black H3 Hummer. I couldn't see if anyone else was in the car with him. I only got a quick look, but I think it's him. At any rate, even if it's not, it's too important not to check out."

"Yeah, you got that right. Hang on the line. I'm calling Sylvania. I'll try to get some help."

I put him on speaker so I could hear without having to hold it to my ear. Erie became the Sylvania-Metamora Road, moving past expensive suburban neighborhoods and heading for the more rural areas. I increased my speed to try to cut down his lead on me. The distance seemed to remain the same, though, despite my best efforts. My speed topped eighty-five. I blew past the spot where the original car's burnt-out shell had been found. Within seconds he'd be into the Village of Berkey. I pushed the engine harder, but in the fading sunlight and lack of street lights, it was more difficult to retain control.

Morrisey's voice startled me, interrupting my concentration.

"Okay. Still there?"

"Yep."

"Still eyes on?"

"Yep"

"What's your position?"

"Hitting Berkey now. He's already through it."

"You're in your car, aren't you?"

"Yeah. Why?"

"'Cause I told them you were a Toledo officer in pursuit in your own personal vehicle. I told them what it was. You don't want to get stopped before we can catch them."

"Are they contacting the departments down the line?"

"Yeah, the sheriff's department and Highway Patrol, too. You should have plenty of company soon. Hey, I'm putting you on hold again to call Carbone. Stay on the line and don't lose him."

As long as I don't get stopped by a local cop who is not in the loop or been contacted yet, I should ... I had to think it, didn't I? I should've known that would make it happen. Like the character in *Ghostbusters* who couldn't help but think of the marshmallow man. Out of nowhere, flashing lights bore down on me from behind.

I held the cell phone close to my mouth and yelled, "Hey, Morrisey, pick up. MORRISEY!" He either wasn't near the phone, or he really did put me on hold. Knowing him, he probably had to take a bathroom break. The cruiser was closing on me. No matter what, though, I couldn't let them stop me. So I did the only thing I could think of to prevent being pulled over. I sped up, jumping over ninety and surging forward slightly. Soon, he was right back on my tail, though, trying to pull up next to me.

Every time he attempted to go around me I blocked him. I was trying to keep an eye out for the Hummer and an eye on the police car at the same time. Turfe had to have seen the flashing lights in his mirror. He extinguished his headlights. It was getting harder to see him in the distance, but it did appear, spurred by the cop's hot pursuit, that I was closing the gap ever so slightly.

With darkness closing in, the only way I knew where he was, was if he tapped his brakes. I went all-out now. My speedometer touched one hundred.

With a quick fake to the right, the very experienced professional behind me swung out and moved up on my left. He pointed at me angrily to pull over. I tried to get him to understand I was chasing someone, but he either didn't understand my pointing in the direction of the H3 or didn't care.

Without warning, he angled in at my precious BMW. Not wanting to get hit, I reacted as he knew I would and moved toward the side of the road. There was not much of a shoulder and what was there was very rough. I bounced out of control and had to slow my speed to keep from hitting a mailbox or telephone pole.

He didn't let up but kept angling in on me. His moves were textbook and effective. He seemed unconcerned I might crash. Apparently, he was going to stop me any way he could.

Morrisey came back on. "Still there?"

"Not for long. Evidently the word hasn't reached all the way out to the sticks yet."

"Oh no! Can you out run him? We'll square it with him later."

"I tried. He's better than me. And I'm going to need you to square it with him now because I'm heading directly toward a cement bridge. I think I'm done. Plus, I can no longer see our suspect. I can't believe I'm saying this, but I wish now I'd kept that damn badge."

TWENTY

I hit the brakes hard, hoping to get him to go past, and swing back around him. But he pinned me so tight the only move I could make was to reverse. As I did, he backed across the road and was out the door with his gun pointing over the roof at me, before I had a chance to shift into drive. If he was as good a shot as he was a driver, I wasn't about to move.

"I'm a cop," I tried to yell out my window, but he wasn't having any of it. "I'm in hot pursuit," I tried to explain. A shouting match ensued with me losing rapidly. I knew I had lost when his last words were, "You will put your hands out the door and step out of the vehicle, or I will put a bullet into you. Last chance. MOVE!"

On the ground, cuffed, frisked, and on my way to the back seat of yet another squad car, before I could get a word out. Despite his anger, he shoved me into the back seat in a very professional manner – without banging my head on the frame of the car "accidentally" as the Toledo cops had done. He searched my car. Finished, he moved my BMW so it was off the road.

Back in the squad car, I tried again.

"Sir, I'm a cop ..."

"I don't care who you are. You don't go barreling through my territory like some crazed NASCAR reject.

Keep your comments to yourself. They're not going to benefit you one bit."

He swung the car around to face the way we had come. In the distance, enough flashing lights approached to have been a downtown Christmas display.

"I suppose these boys are coming for you, too. With how many of them there are, you must have done something pretty bad."

"Actually, you're right. They're here, not for me, but with me. You heard about the Sylvania Mayor's daughter getting kidnapped? Well, I was in pursuit of one of the men we think did it. You should pull over. I'll bet the Mayor will want to give you a medal."

For the first time, doubt crossed his face. The situation wasn't his fault, but adrenaline had me jittery with electric energy.

"Look, Officer. I know you did what you thought best. But just in case I'm telling the truth do us both a favor and flag these boys down. I need to tell them where I last saw the suspect car. There may still be an outside chance of finding it."

They were less than a mile from us now. The officer picked up his microphone, called his station and asked them to check with Sylvania about their pursuit. The crackle from the other end was not clear, but I heard enough.

"I was just getting ready to call you," the dispatcher said. "Evidently, there has been a sighting of the possible kidnappers of that girl from Sylvania. They have someone on site in, get this, a BMW." The officer cringed and the back of his neck tensed up. "Ain't that a stitch? These big city departments must have money to burn, huh? A Beamer cop car."

"When did you get this notice?"

"I got a call about ten minutes ago."

"Why didn't you call me immediately?"

"Well, I had to pee, Jimmy. Why? What's the big deal?"

I heard him mumble "Christ" and replace the handset

rather firmly back in its holder. He looked up again at the oncoming convoy of cars almost upon us. He flashed his brights several times and waved his arm out the window. A few cars blew past, but the following few slowed and stopped. The others screeched to a stop about a quarter mile farther down as they came to my BMW.

"You looking for a feller in a BMW?"

"Yeah, you seen him?"

"I'm afraid I have. I got him right behind me."

"Oh, no!" The cop got out and leaned his head in the front window. "Son, what's your name?"

"Roth. Danny Roth. TPD. You're looking for a black Hummer H3. Last I saw it was a little more than a mile west. Still traveling on this road. Sorry."

He turned and gave a few orders and the rest of the cars dispersed west. I counted seven cars in all. My arresting officer got out, conferred privately with his counterpart, then walked dejectedly to release me. He was visibly upset when I turned back to him after he released me from the cuffs. His teeth kept biting the top of his lower lip.

"I apologize for being difficult, Officer," I said. "This not your fault."

"Thanks. Unfortunately, maybe I was too efficient. But how was I to know? It's not every day someone blasts through my territory, doing near a hundred miles an hour, then has the nerve to try to escape me. I wish I'd known sooner."

"So do I. I wish you'd seen the suspects' car first. The way you handle that car, the driver would've had no chance. I sure didn't. You were professional in everything you did." I smiled to reassure him.

At that moment, two more cruisers pulled up. One slowed down, then continued on. The second one stopped and the Mayor leaped out, almost running to the group of cops standing around the lead officer's car. He had a map spread out on the hood, pointed out streets, and directed the troops from the radio.

"What happened?" screamed the Mayor. "Where is this bumbling fool who let the kidnappers escape?"

No one spoke up, but no one stood up, either. Everyone avoided eye contact with the irate father, which by elimination, left the Berkey cop and me as the only two outsiders. Since I wasn't wearing a uniform, he went directly for the one who was.

"What kind of law enforcement officer are you?" He was so angry spittle flew everywhere. "How can you wear that uniform or carry a badge when you're that incompetent? I'm going to speak to your boss about having you removed from your post. You may have cost my daughter—" He gasped for air.

With a break in the tirade, I took the opportunity to step in and make a whole new set of enemies.

"Excuse me, but you need to back off." The officer at my side put his hand on my arm to restrain me, but I continued. "Maybe you should get your facts straight before getting in his face."

"Who the hell are you?" The Mayor puffed his chest in my direction. Some of his officers moved to protect him.

"I'm the man who risked his life pursuing the alleged kidnappers in a high-speed chase. If this man had received word sooner from your people, he would've corralled them single-handedly. Maybe you should look at your own house before you try tearing someone else's down."

Two of the Sylvania cops inserted themselves between us. We continued to yell.

"Tell me, how important was this?"

"What? What are you talking about?"

"Just that. How important was it?"

"It's my daughter, for Christ's sake."

"Then maybe a lot more people should've been working the phones to spread the word. How many were calling? Go ahead. Ask."

Two more cops pulled me back and suggested I close my mouth.

"Check with them. Don't blame someone else for your department's mistake. Everyone knows you're upset; what father wouldn't be? But don't take it out on the people who will eventually help stop these kidnappers."

"I'm warning you. Shut it or I'm arresting you." The voice belonged to a captain.

But my temper had been ignited, which meant trouble, for me anyway. "For what? Telling the truth? And all you other so-called policemen. How can you stand by and let an officer that any department would be proud to have on its force take the heat for this? From a politician, no less."

"That's it, you're under arrest."

He grabbed me by the arm. Not good. I yanked my hand up, snapped it down, wrapping it around his arm and bending it behind him before I shoved him into the Mayor.

"You want to take me in, you come forward and pay the price. If you're man enough."

Well, he might not have been, but all of his officers certainly were. Tasers, nightsticks, cuffs and pepper sprays were suddenly in everyone's hands. They spread out and advanced on me. Once again my famous big mouth was going to get the rest of my body beat up. I squared off to meet them. If I went down, I intended to get some licks in.

My new friend stepped in front of me to try to bring order to the escalating insanity. Unfortunately, he did so just as someone fired his Taser. The prongs leaped forward and hit the man in the thigh. He jolted and fell to the ground in spastic spasms. We all stopped to watch, like gawkers at a traffic accident. I felt bad: he'd tried to defend me.

Of course, had that been a TV show, it would've been funny.

TWENTY-ONE

Just as they refocused their attention on me, two more cars drove up with lights flashing. The lead one hit its noisemaker and everyone froze. As soon as the car stopped, the doors popped open. A Toledo cop and Morrisey emerged. Once more, it was Morrisey to the rescue. I hoped.

"Whoa! Whoa! Hold on here. He's one of ours. Back down." He turned. "Captain, have your men stand down."

"Your man is way out of line, Detective. You get him under control, or we will." He motioned his men to fall back. Morrisey stepped forward.

I reached down to check on my friend. He wasn't ready to stand yet, but at least he was no longer convulsing.

"You can't get along with anyone, can you? Is there anyone left you haven't pissed off?"

"Yeah, but I got him Tasered, so maybe not."

"What happened?"

"Turfe got away. Let's leave it at that for now."

Carbone exited the second car with two other detectives. He spoke to the captain, then came to us.

"So close."

"Yeah. I was hoping he'd lead me to where they're

holding her."

"It's no longer her."

"Huh? Nothing happened to her did it? You didn't find her—"

"No, no, nothing like that."

Morrisey continued for him. "What he means is that it's no longer just her. Another one was reported about two hours ago. They're collecting. They hit their quota, they'll be gone. We have to find them fast. There's a lot of pressure on everyone right now."

"Man!" I wondered if she could've been in the Hummer. I had a new thought. "Hey, think about this. We found the burned car out here, and now a possible sighting. Maybe they're holed up out here. It's still a big area to search, but it's smaller than the entire county."

"We're already working on that theory," Carbone said.

Behind me, someone cleared his throat. The Mayor joined our little circle. Mayor Lerner was a short, pudgy man with a comb-over. I'd never met him, but since I lived in Sylvania, I knew who he was. I hadn't voted for him.

"I was wondering, gentlemen, if I could have a word with your officer." Carbone and Morrisey looked around for a Toledo policeman before realizing he was talking about me. They're only smart when it comes to the hard stuff. They walked away. I looked to see if any of his protectors were lurking about.

"I just wanted to apologize. I was out of line. I appreciate everything you tried to do. I've been so upset ... no, that's not even near. I've been scared out of my mind for my little girl. It's no excuse, I know. First, there was hope, then it was gone. I'm not handling the pressure and ... and I overreacted. I'm sorry." He stuck out his hand. I expected a politician's handshake, but his was firm and he held on long enough for me to understand it was sincere.

"I'm sorry, too, sir. Sorry that we weren't successful. We'll get her back. Have faith. I'm sure it's hard. I don't have kids, but when a group of car thieves kidnapped my mother, I was in a panic, too."

"Yes, I guess you would understand. It's like the whole world has been altered. You can't function, or think of anything else." His eyes welled up. I put a reassuring hand on his shoulder.

"Sir, may I ask one favor?" He cocked his head in unspoken query. "Would you help me get this officer to his feet?"

"Of course." We bent over and lifted the poor man to his feet. He was still a little unsteady, but could hold his weight.

"Officer, please forgive me. There's no excuse for my words or behavior. I'm sorry."

To the officer's credit, he held out a wavering hand to the Mayor. He tried to say something, but the words came out a jumble of sounds and drool. I helped him sit down on the front seat of his car and told him I'd be right back.

Morrisey stood with the Sylvania captain looking over the street map, listening to reports coming in, but they weren't promising. No further sighting of the black Hummer. The mood was grim, yet determined. Nearly two hours later, I said good night to Morrisey and the revived Berkey officer, Delbert Longley, and good luck to the Mayor.

On my way home, I retrieved my cell phone from the seat and noticed I had another six missed calls, but no voicemails. I wasn't sure if that was a good thing or not. With a huge sigh, I called Natalie's number, but I knew she'd be at work. Feeling guilty about the entire incident, I remembered why I was upset in the first place. My mood darkened.

She was angry at me about my involvement in the altercation at school and had run back to her other boyfriend. That thought rattled around inside my head for a few minutes and gathered enough speed to become resentful. I decided I didn't need to explain anything. So, instead, I just said, "Sorry, something came up. Good night."

Twenty-Two

Friday, the end of the third week in May, left just one more full week of school. The next weekend we were off for Memorial Day and the following week, school was only in session three days and one of those was without students, which many teachers believe is still the best way to run a school. At this point, I don't happen to be one of them, but I'm still new. Give me time.

After school, I went to the restaurant and sat in my office, a host of thoughts running through my mind.

The news all day focused on the second kidnapping victim and the warnings issued by the police. Every TV station had a specialist of some sort giving advice on how the women of Toledo could stay safe. Never go anywhere alone. Never be outside alone at night. Always let someone know where you're going and what time to expect you back. Try not to park next to a van in a parking lot. Be careful of anyone trying to help you with your groceries or asking you for money or a ride. Call in anything suspicious. The list went on and on. By trying to reassure the community, the media brought them closer to panic.

But many people used so little common sense thinking those things would never happen to them ...

until they were the next victim being discussed on the news. No matter how many warnings, some would never listen. With the amount of attention and publicity the story created, I wondered if the kidnappers were still in the area.

If not for Richie's discovery, a lot more women might be missing. I thought about Mayor Lerner. My heart ached for him. Sadness and guilt swept over me. If only I could've stayed with the Hummer, his daughter might be home safe right now.

The only hope for those two women was if the human traffickers stayed in the area and tried again. Perhaps we'd catch a break and take them down. There had to be something I could do to help.

Huh! I said 'we' as though I was part of the investigation. I had to push those thoughts from my mind. I'd paid dearly for past involvements. Got beat. Got shot. Lost a girlfriend; twice.

I sighed. Not for the pain and suffering, but because I knew I'd never change. If I was in a position to help someone, it wasn't in my nature to turn my back. I thought about Natalie, calling up an image of her. My heart broke anew. "Sorry, Nat."

And as quick as that, I redirected my thoughts to the case. Danny Roth, self-proclaimed superhero, was on the job. I went over what I knew so far.

If the kidnappers were still here, the fear would be that if things got too hot, they'd cut and run, leaving two more bodies behind. To eliminate the witnesses and move on might be the smartest thing they could do. But we couldn't take the chance they had moved on. The search had to continue, if not for the sake of the two women, for the safety of future victims.

Many people smarter than I am were trying to figure it all out. My thoughts kept coming back to the question of how they chose the women. Were these random abductions or had they been scouted? I also wondered if they had a shopping list. Maybe their buyers had put in requests for certain types of women, similar to how car thieves operated. I noted all three of the women, Chloe Lerner, now Darlene Northrup and the murdered Hilary Merritt, were blondes. But that connection had to have been noticed already.

A horrid thought came to mind. What if they were just the three we knew of? We knew about the first one because of Richie's interference. What if she was actually the third or fourth one, the others just not reported yet? If they lived alone, perhaps no one was aware they were missing.

It made sense the kidnappers would've scouted things out first and perhaps had an idea of who they wanted before they started abducting their targets. Otherwise, they'd be in the area for too long. That meant there must be an advance team. The entire kidnapping operation couldn't take more than a few days, tops. The risk of discovery would increase drastically with each abduction. The woman they took last night would have given them at least three victims.

I made a mental note to ask Carbone about cases from other cities to get a handle on the time frame. How did they pick their victims? If we knew that, we could wait for them to show up.

There I went again, thinking I was part of the machine, when in fact, I was on the outside looking in, like a dog outside a restaurant door begging for scraps of food. At any time, they could chase me away with a swift kick to the rump.

Finishing the little bit of work I could focus on, I went into the kitchen and made a meatball sub. On the way back to my office, I walked behind the bar. At the end of the bar, near the office door, stood three men dressed as if they had just come off a construction site somewhere. Apparently, they had been there for a while because they were loud. As I walked by, I nodded.

"Hey," one said, pointing his finger at me, "aren't you that guy on TV?"

I smiled and replied, "No, sorry. Wasn't me."

"Wait a minute, yes, it was you. Don't lie to me. I saw you. You tackled that poor guy. Yeah, I remember now. You blindsided some guy dropping his kids off at school. I'm sure of it now. It was you."

Evidently, he hadn't seen the updated version. I sensed trouble. I continued to the office door as the others murmured they remembered the story, too, even though they were too inebriated to remember their own names, let alone a news story that aired days ago. Thinking any of them even watched the news was funny.

As I reached for the doorknob, a hand shot out and grabbed my arm. I turned to look into the red eyes of the man who'd spoken. What I saw there was trouble, like a young gunslinger wanting to take on the veteran to make a name for himself.

"So tell me, why did you attack that guy?"

"Wasn't like that, bud. Now if you'll excuse me, I have work to do."

"Oh, so sorry. Am I offending you? Maybe you're just afraid to look a man in the eyes when he's talking to you." He turned his back on me. "There, is this better?" His two friends laughed, waiting to see what would happen next. I was already tired of the man's act.

"Is this how it was when you jumped that guy? You waited 'til he had his back turned. You don't have the balls to face a man down. Well, I'm waiting. Or are you too gutless?"

I shook my head in disbelief. Is this what things had come to? Instead of being baited by the intoxicated man, I turned to Beth and said, "I think these gentlemen are finished here. It's time for them to move along and find somewhere else to drink." Swinging my head back to the drunk, "You have a nice night. Just have it someplace else."

"What? You're cutting us off? That's bullshit!" His face turned red and his voice got louder. "You truly are a coward, aren't you? This how you deal with things? Get some bitch to protect you? You're gutless." And with that, he put his hand on my chest and shoved.

Prepared for it, I barely moved with his efforts.

"Beth, please call the police for these gentlemen." Over the man's shoulder, I said, "Do your buddy a favor and take him out of here."

I turned, fully aware of what might happen. I wasn't disappointed. As soon as he saw my head move, he threw a punch. Watching for the movement, I stepped back as the fist arced past me, slamming into the door frame. I stepped in toward him, fast and hard. I caught his throat in my right hand, drove the meatball sub into his face and bounced his head on the bar, just once, to get his attention. Now when he looked into my eyes, he saw trouble.

"Now who's attacking from behind? Well, you wanted to challenge me. You got your wish." I squeezed tighter and saw fear register in his eyes. He gripped my hand as he tried to choke something out of his mouth. One of his friends made a move to come to his rescue, but I planted the tip of my toe up under his sack. He grabbed his balls and fell like a rock to the floor, emitting a girlish shriek.

The third man wasn't sure what to do. My withering glare froze him in place.

"You will take your two friends and escort them out of here. You had better be gone by the time the police get here. If you're stupid enough to still be here, I will press charges against you."

He nodded and tried to help his fallen friend to his feet.

"Wait a minute!" I said. A look of panic struck him immobile. "Beth, do these gentlemen owe anything?"

"Yeah, they have a tab running."

"Pay your bill first. Oh, and add a meatball sub." He started patting his pockets searching for money. The man in my grasp tried to kick me, but with being bent over the bar, he couldn't get much leverage. To dissuade him from doing anything else stupid, I banged his head on the bar once more. The other man found his money in an instant and started throwing bills on the bar.

"And leave a tip." He obliged by throwing another ten on the pile.

He helped the moaning man off the floor and I escorted them to the door, still keeping a grip on the bully's throat. At the door, I met Morrisey.

"Need any help?"

"Yeah, get the door for these gentlemen, would you please, Detective Morrisey?" I emphasized his name.

"Sure."

In the parking lot, the man who started the trouble rubbed his bruised neck and gasped out a raspy threat. I started down the steps toward him.

Morrisey stood behind me and flashed his badge. "This is a protected establishment, boys. If I ever see you here again, you won't see daylight for years. You just threatened him, which is like threatening the entire police force. Now get!"

"Maybe you'd like to carry out your threat right now? After all, I'm just a gutless coward."

They backed away to an abused pick-up truck. As they drove off in a cloud of exhaust, Morrisey commented, "You just amaze me. You could get into a fight with an altar boy during a church service. Unbelievable!"

"Check my back, would you? Is there a sign that says 'looking for a fight' or something?"

He put his arm around my shoulder and escorted me back in.

Twenty-Three

"Y ou're rather early today, aren't you?" I queried.

"Yeah, I'm meeting Carbone here in a bit. He seems to have developed a liking for your mother's pasta. I think he's also developing one for your barmaid, too. But let's keep that between us for now, shall we."

"Actually, I'm glad you're here. I wanted to talk to you for a minute in private." I swear he looked nervous when I said that.

I led him to a vacant table in the back of the room. Fortunately, there were very few customers present to witness the little altercation. The men and one woman at the bar applauded as I escorted the drunks from the premises.

Sheila brought beers, informing us they were on the bar patrons. We raised our bottles in thanks. The lone woman blew a kiss and winked.

"Man, I sure hope that was directed at you," I said.

"Oh, sure. Get me killed. If your mother saw that, I'd be in little pieces, ready to become Italian sausage. She thinks that woman flirts too much with me. And she thinks I like it."

I gave him a who-are-you-kidding look.

"Oh, all right, it's fun, but I'm not interested. I told

your mother it was because I'm a cop. Women always flirt with cops wherever we go. Big mistake. Now she questions me about every place I go. I think she's doing it for fun. You know, to tease me. And to make me nervous. But how can you tell for sure?"

I laughed. "What do you think it is?"

"I think it's damn effective, because it sure as shit makes me nervous."

I laughed harder.

"So what did you want to speak to me about? The kidnapping?"

"Actually, it's more about what's been happening around the school lately. I thought that if I still had my badge, none of that misunderstanding with Walz would've happened. Flashing that blowhard with it a couple of days ago at the school bus would've ended that debacle before it became physical. What do you think the captain's reaction would be? I know he's not going to just hand me a badge without some sort of commitment on my part, but if I used it to help enforce the safe school ordinance, maybe he'd consider the request. Especially in light of my previous service and record."

"I don't know, Danny," he said, thinking it over. "I'm not so sure they'd think it was a good idea. After all, you're a citizen again. You made it very clear you wanted out the last time. Now, you're changing your mind again. Some people will question your motives. Others might wonder about your stability."

"I wouldn't have to be on any roster or get any compensation or anything like that. The badge would just be useful, considering I always seem to get caught up in some sort of trouble. Would you at least propose it and see where it goes?"

"Yeah … I'll ask. But what if it comes with attachments like before?"

"I just don't want them to take advantage of me. Hell, I felt like I was still on the force last time. There are times I can help out. If I can, I will."

"Okay. I'll ask. Anything else?"

"Nope. That was it."

"Good, 'cause Carbone just walked in. Let's join him."

We sat at the bar and had another drink. After a short time, encouraged by the ravenous Carbone, we ordered dinner. Tony had called earlier and begged off the dinner he owed me for being a butthead. Apparently, Marissa had the night off, and they hadn't seen each other in a while. They'd need a new bed by the morning.

Instead, I spent a leisurely evening of drinking, dining and listening to the two detectives try to top each other's stories. They went back and forth, arguing about details. They made for an interesting night.

As time wore on, I broached the topic of the kidnapped girls. "Detective, are you sure there haven't been prior kidnappings? You know, that haven't yet been discovered or reported?"

Carbone searched the bottom of his glass as if hoping it would magically refill itself.

"No, we're not sure of anything, yet. There's been a new abduction reported, though. Apparently, a young woman, Bethany Wright, was supposed to meet some friends for dinner last night, but never showed up. Phone calls went unanswered and today, one of the girls went to her apartment to see if she was all right. No one was at home, but she has a newspaper delivered and there were four of them piled up, waiting for her. Judging from her mailbox, it doesn't look as though anyone has picked up the mail in a few days, either.

"The friend got more worried when she checked where Wright worked. They'd fired Bethany because she hadn't been to work or called in the last three days. So the friend called 911 and because of the alerts, they passed it to us. A team is investigating now."

"That means if Hilary Merritt had not been killed, they'd have at least four women," I said.

"At this point, it's speculation as to whether there's a tie-in."

"Tell me, does this possible new girl have blonde hair?"

"Figured that one out, did you? Yeah, she's a blonde. Apparently, that's what they're looking for. The various agencies now being coordinated by the FBI, searched all night and into the afternoon today, but weren't able to find the Hummer you saw. You're positive about that, right?"

"I'm as sure as I can be under the circumstances. If it wasn't him, it was someone guilty of something. He drove like someone fleeing."

"It's probably a moot point anyway. If it was really the kidnappers, I'm positive they would've changed vehicles again by now. They may even have moved the victims if they were keeping them all together in that area."

"They'd need to have a lot of people to keep them in different locations," I said.

"Doesn't sound right," Morrisey said. "That would increase the chance of discovery. The more sites they have, the greater the chance that someone notices something, or they make a mistake. No, they've got them all together."

"At this point," Carbone disclosed, "we're pretty sure they have three girls. They've been picking them up at a rate of one a night. They've been watching the intended victims and getting to know their routines for a while. They know exactly who they're going to snatch."

"Hmmm. I wonder if they have a replacement for Hilary Merritt, or if they'll just go one short. That might extend their stay an extra day."

Morrisey finished for me, "Or, they may double up and grab two in one night."

We sat thinking and drinking, lost in our own thoughts.

"In the other cities, what were the age ranges?" I said to Carbone.

"As far as we can tell from the ones we're sure were kidnapped, they were anywhere from sixteen to thirty-eight."

"And were they all blondes?"

"Again, as far as we know." Carbone finished his beer and got up to use the bathroom.

I turned to Morrisey and surprised both of us by saying, "I really want in on this. See what you can do for me about that badge. Please!"

"Can't get it out of your system, can you? What's the matter, you and Natalie break up again?"

"Just when I thought we were bonding, you had to go and say that, didn't you?"

He laughed. "So, it is because of that, huh? God, you're hopeless."

"Shut up and drink your beer."

Twenty-Four

By the time I got out of there, I was feeling slightly liquefied. It was a good thing I ate dinner, or I might not have been able to walk. The glare from oncoming car headlights made me squint. I drove very slowly and almost made it home when the worst type of lights possible hit my eyes. The red and blue flashing kind. In this case, a Sylvania cop car. My first thought was the Mayor had changed his mind and was pissed at me after all. I figured I was a goner. I was pretty sure I hadn't been speeding. Unless of course I blacked out and just didn't remember. I might've swayed a little bit, but how would I know? Everything was swaying a little bit.

I guess the reason didn't matter. I pulled over. The patrolman walked up to the side of my car and shone his light over the interior. He just looked. Instead of talking on his Motorola shoulder mic, he slipped his cell phone out of his shirt pocket and punched in a number.

"I've got that vehicle you were looking for. Yeah, hold on ... your name Roth? Danny Roth?"

"Ah, yeah. That's me." Something was wrong here. Why were they looking for my ve-hic!-icle? And why didn't he just check my ID? Why ask my name?

"Yeah, it's him. By the look and smell of him, he's already been drinking. I'm surprised he got this far. You still want him? ... Yeah, I can do that. No problem. We'll be there in about ten."

He laughed when he looked back at me, either because of the confusion on my face, or because my jaw hung slack, as though I'd just been to the dentist. "Roth, I need you to drive home right now. I will follow you. You are to park the car and then get into mine. I'm driving you to a special meeting. It will all be explained to you there. Do you understand? Are you capable of driving?"

"Yesh."

He was enjoying this cloak-and-dagger shit. I thought about telling him to kiss off, but figured I'd already pissed off enough policemen in the area. I pulled back on the road and made it safely home. As I climbed into the back of the police cruiser, where I'd spent way too much time of late, the experience sobered me greatly. I still had no idea what this was all about, but for some strange reason, I wasn't as freaked out as the last time I sat in a police car. A few minutes later, deposited at the door of a local pub, the patrolman instructed me to go in.

The door had barely closed behind me when attack came from all sides. My arms pinned, strong arms lifted and carried me to a table in a separate room of the bar. I was dropped onto a wooden chair and cuffed to it as I heard the laughter. As I struggled to free my hands, I glanced around the table. Six smiling, laughing faces stared back, some of which looked familiar, especially the one directly across from me. Doug Waddell, old friend and ex-teammate, sat with a huge, stupid grin on his goofy face.

"What the hell, Doug?"

They all laughed. Doug was a monstrous human being. He had a body builder's physique and a little boy's mentality. What made those things scarier was that he was also a Sylvania City policeman. Looking around the circle, I realized all of them were cops. That's why they looked familiar.

"Doug, what the hell are you doing?"

"Hey, Danny. Long time, no see. I hear you been throwing parties and haven't invited me."

"What? What parties?"

"He doesn't know what I mean, boys. Well, let's see now. Look at all the shootouts you've left me out of. Then you chase some bad guy cop shooters right through our fair city and don't call me ... nor do you call any of my friends to join in. We're feeling neglected, so we decided it's time to have a little talk."

"Doug, let me out of these cuffs, man. Stop playing."

"Well, here's the thing. We feel that you owe us a round—"

"Two," one of the others piped in. I recognized him as one of the Mayor's bodyguards from the previous night.

"Right. Two," Doug continued, "and we want to know all the details of the kidnapping."

"You kidnapped me and chained me to this chair for that?"

"No, that part was just for the fun," another I recognized from last night said. "To compensate for showing up our captain in front of his men."

"Hell, we should be buying him drinks," another one said. More laughter.

"Shush! Quiet. You'll mess up our free drinks." They were laughing hard now.

"And if I refuse?"

Doug had a huge grin on his face now. "Let's just say the owner is a close personal friend of ours. It's a good possibility you could still be attached to that chair in the morning."

I gave up. It wasn't beyond Doug to do just that. "All right. Order them up and a Harp for me. But you know, Doug, I'm surprised you want more action. The last time you got involved with me, you got shot." I looked at the others. "It was a little scratch on his arm, and he almost fainted."

They cheered for the drinks and jeered for the slam on their brother.

"Oh, no! You did not just slam me with your hands cuffed to that chair," Doug threatened. More laughter. It was apparent they'd been there for a while. "You need to speak the truth now, or I will do horrible, fun things to you. Well, fun for me. I'll start by cutting off your clothes and practicing my dart throwing at your body. They're only plastic tips, but I'll bet I can make them hurt. Especially where I'll be aiming." He leaned closer and gave me a smile that sent a chill up my spine. He was serious, but I couldn't give in to him.

"Is this how you get all your dates, Doug? You tie them down and sweet talk them? Sorry, buddy, but Homey don't swing that way."

He turned beet red as his colleagues picked up the slams and started to verbally hammer his manhood. He turned to me and I knew I was in trouble.

"Oh, you little weasel ..." He picked me up, chair and all, and started for the door. His friends just stepped aside. It was obvious I wasn't getting any help from them.

A lone figure stepped into the doorway, blocking Doug's path.

"Doug, put that chair down right this minute," the voice boomed. She was tall and as muscular as Doug. She was attractive, but in a scary way. She looked hard. Hands on her hips, legs slightly spread, she looked formidable. Her tone suggested she was used to giving orders and having them followed. It was the first time I'd ever seen Doug back down from anyone. He slowly lowered the chair to the floor.

"Now, be a good boy and slide the nice man back to the table." He did.

"Do I have to uncuff him?" he asked in a little boy voice.

"Not just yet. You can play with him a little longer. Just play nice."

The room had gone quiet when she entered. Now it burst into laughter once more. My savior stepped in to join us. She sat down on my lap and wrapped her arms around my neck. "Didn't someone say something about drinks?" She rubbed my head like a good luck charm. I was more afraid of her than I was of Doug.

Someone went to get the drinks and the big woman got up. I stared at my legs, hoping they would still function. A beer manifested in front of me and everyone sat back and watched, waiting. Instead of complaining about being cuffed, I moved as close to the table as I could, bent forward, wrapped my mouth around the neck of the bottle, lifted and drank. I took several gulps and almost made it without spilling any, but tilted it, dribbling some out of the sides of my mouth. The large female finally had mercy on me and took the bottle from my mouth, setting it on the table.

"What do you think, guys? Should we trust him to talk?"

"I think we'd better, or he might drown himself," quipped Doug.

My new girlfriend, Sergeant Julie McIntosh, uncuffed me.

"Oh, I haven't paid for the drinks yet." I headed for the bar while reaching for my wallet, veered and walked out the front door. I looked at them through the front window. They sat frozen in place, surprise caught perfectly on their faces. I waved goodbye and disappeared around the corner. I waited a minute, walked back inside, paid for the drinks and sat down. They burst out laughing again.

For the second time that night, I sat back and drank with cops and talked shop. I explained about a third possible kidnapping. They already knew many of the details, but I filled them in on whatever they didn't know. I decided to float a theory for discussion. I might have actually insinuated it was my theory, but they were getting me drunk, so no apologies.

"The two occasions they've been seen have been in this direction. What are the chances they're hiding somewhere to the west?"

One cop said, "It's pretty much all residential neighborhoods out this way. Someone would notice something strange."

"Yeah," said another, "if they're out here, they're past Sylvania. Probably even past Berkey. Somewhere with few people."

We debated back and forth for an hour before the silence of inebriation settled upon us.

Then Doug said, "We should form a search group in our own time and drive each and every street. We could chart what we do and eliminate possibilities as we go."

Swiftly, a new excitement took over.

"We'll work in shifts and upgrade the map after each tour," Julie said.

One of the men went out and brought in a map from his car. He spread it out on top of a table. The map showed a street-by-street blow up of the entire area, including Sylvania, Sylvania Township, Metamora, Berkey and several others along and just over the Michigan line.

"Let's start at the outer corners and work our way to the middle," Doug said. He pointed to the four starting points. "Check every house, door to door if you have to. Tomorrow we can get individual street maps. Do a drive-by of every residence on the street. If you can, verify who lives there and check it off. For those we can't, we'll go back and knock on doors."

"Something I should tell you," I chipped in, "these guys have done this before and apparently are very organized. They scout out their intended victims, which I assume they have already done, and snatch targets from their list until they have as many as they need. Usually, they're out of town in less than a week. If Bethany Wright was one of theirs, then they have three of the six they usually try for counting the one they killed. They won't be around much longer. I'm surprised they still are, since we're on to them now."

Doug said, "So, if we're going to do this, we have to work it hard. We're working someone else's jurisdiction, so we can't very well do it officially. I'm not sure how many more guys will help us."

"I think that Berkey cop would be happy to help," I said. "I'll join in as well. We need to make up a schedule so someone is out searching at all times."

"I'll take this corner," one of the men said, pointing at the southwestern corner. "I'm off tomorrow, so I'll start early and spend the day."

"I'm off, too. I'll take the southeast corner," another said.

The rest of them filled in the chart. I volunteered to search the next two days until early evening. "I'll contact Officer Longley and see if he wants to help."

We agreed to meet at the bar for shift changes and updates. The map and charts would be left in the pub and updated as each person finished working an area.

As we were about to break up, I got their attention one last time. "I think there's something that needs to be said here. These guys thought nothing of killing that girl to eliminate a witness, or of shooting Richie Molten, the Toledo cop who pulled them over. We have to be very careful that, if we do discover where they are, we don't trigger a mass elimination. We can't go in there guns blazing, or we'll lose the women. I just thought we should keep that in mind."

"Good call, Roth," McIntosh patted me on the shoulder. "But we still have to find them and if it's a choice between them getting away with the women or stopping them, I'm going to try to stop them, however I have to. Remember, this is technically unofficial, but I'll support you in any way I can. Just keep me posted as to your progress."

Everyone nodded their agreement.

Doug gave me a ride home. The topic and subsequent planning had sobered us.

"Hey, no hard feelings about tonight?"

"No, it's cool. I was glad to meet the guys and even happier to be accepted by them. That's a good group of dedicated professionals there."

"They are that and much more. I'm proud to serve with them. Let's nail these guys, Danny."

"Sounds like a plan."

He dropped me off and shook my hand. "Thanks for being a good sport."

I smiled and went inside. An interesting night, to say the least. But oh, man, would I have a headache in the morning. I popped a couple of pain pills and lowered my head gently to the pillow.

TWENTY-FIVE

It was nearly 10:00 a.m. by the time I managed to drag my butt out of bed. My head throbbed, but not as bad as anticipated. I dressed in sweats and forced myself to go for a run, but after a little more than a mile, my body had had enough. After showering, I headed to last night's bar, praying they had coffee.

Brady's Pub was a fair sized bar, located in the center of a strip mall. The shopping center was located a quarter mile from my house. Somewhat smaller than my restaurant, the space was divided into two separate rooms. A small kitchen served typical bar food; burgers, wings and the like. The back room had a sliding accordion-style partition for use during private parties, but otherwise stayed open. The room was closed now.

I ordered coffee from a bartender and went through the door in the wall to the private room. The map lay spread across one of the tables. The street chart had been updated once already. Someone had been up early. I looked the chart over to see how they were marking it. I studied the streets while I drank my coffee. Someone had entered the names of the current residents of each property. That would be helpful.

Armed with a list of streets to check, I went to the bar to pay my bill before getting started. A large, barrel-chested man in his fifties came over and waved off the money. "I think it's a great thing, what you guys are trying to do. That room is yours for as long as you need it. Also, your money's no good here." He stuck a large callused hand out for me to take. "Name's Brady. Retired SPD."

"Danny. Nice to meet you. And thanks for the coffee."

He reached behind the bar and came out with a large to-go cup. Filling it, he handed it to me. "Here's one for the road."

I thanked him again and as he turned away, I put a tip down on the bar. "When I turn around I better not be insulted by seeing a tip there, either," he said, using the eyes in the back of his head. He would've made a good teacher.

I pocketed the money and left.

The area I chose to patrol was the northeast corner of the search pattern. Butting up to the Michigan line to the north, it was about five miles away, located between the villages of Morenci and Berkey. I drove west on the Sylvania-Metamora Road, the main east-west road in this area. The north-south boundaries stretching from the Michigan border to Brint Road had been established as the search grid. That covered quite a bit of land, though there wouldn't be a lot of houses. I skipped Morenci and Berkey. The kidnappers wouldn't take the chance of some nosy neighbor turning them in. Strangers were noticed in small towns.

I had an idea in mind of what to look for, but couldn't risk passing up any possibility. All houses and commercial buildings needed checking and verifying. The search group had agreed to pose as donation collectors for the Special Olympics. I took a milk jug with me and seeded it with several dollar bills and some change to make it more realistic. I studied the list of homes and the owners' names. According to county records, most of the properties had been owned by their current residents for several years with few turnovers.

On my way toward Berkey, I called information and asked for the number of the Berkey Police Department. Once connected, I asked for Officer Longley. He wasn't on duty, so I left my number and asked that he call me.

I arrived at Lucas-Fulton County Road and traveled north first. I drove to the Michigan line, turned around, and went back and forth across the road, stopping at each house. Working steadily, I made my way south until I hit Brint. Turning east to the next north-south cross street, Lathrup, I moved north. So far, the search had taken nearly two hours. Even though there hadn't been many houses to check, I'd only eliminated one entire block of my search area.

Only one house could not be verified, but even though I marked it as such, I felt its proximity to the road and to another house made it an unlikely hideout. The most positive thing to come from my efforts so far was that I'd collected twenty-three dollars for the Special Olympics.

Lathrup, south of the Sylvania-Metamora Road, was barren. Two massive pieces of farmland covered the entire area, with just two houses across the street from each other. Both occupants made donations.

I pulled over when I reached the main drag and finished my coffee, mentally replaying the houses and owners encountered so far. I crossed to the north side of Lathrup. Several homes lined the road and were more realistic possibilities. The houses were spread out and a fair distance from the road.

One had a row of small pine trees that ran about a hundred yards back from the road. Another had trees around the house, blocking it and the outbuildings from a drive-by view.

Opting to continue on down the road rather than stop, I wanted to observe for a few minutes and get a feel for the properties. Neither one had shown any signs of life on the first pass. I drove down to Yankee Road, which was just across the Michigan border.

On the corner of Lathrup and Yankee was an old gray, shingle-sided, two-story house. About forty yards past the house sat an old weathered barn that had seen better days, but looked in good enough condition to be useful. What drew my attention was the newer single-story, vinyl-sided building that stood between the two.

At first I thought it might be a garage, but there were no doors big enough to allow a car to pass through. There seemed to be only one door facing the street, with two small windows on either side. My second thought: was it built as an apartment? It appeared vacant, although not deserted. The grass had been trimmed and the buildings did not have an abandoned look. No one might be living there currently, but someone was taking care of the property.

Even though it was in Michigan, I stopped and knocked on the door. No one answered, so I looked around. I went to the smaller building and peered through the window, but could not penetrate the darkness beyond. The door was locked. I walked the perimeter, but found no other doors or windows. At the car, I made a note to recheck it at a later time.

Moving back toward the Ohio border, I came to the house with the trees screening it. Newer and larger than the last house, a large, old-fashioned red barn sat at the rear of the property with a separate smaller building between the two. The row of small pine trees ran the length of the property and then some on the Michigan side of the house. The trees probably served to block the wind blowing across the open fields to the left. I didn't like the house as a potential hideout because it was too close to the street.

The other house sat across the street about half a mile down. Horses walked a fenced pasture. Obvious signs of life, as well as tell-tale evidence of multiple children were everywhere. Toys, bikes, and a swing set filled the side yard. I crossed it off the list and returned my attention to the tree-lined property. I watched the house for a moment, but nothing moved. It didn't look empty, nor did it appear anyone was home. "Only one way to find out," I said aloud.

I drove up the long driveway that led past the smaller building to the barn. I stopped next to the house, got out and looked around. Still no one in sight. I walked up the steps to the door and knocked, listening for any movement within. No one responded and I knocked again. There didn't appear to be a door bell. Moving along the wraparound porch, I peered into windows.

The inside looked neat and clean. If someone lived here, they probably didn't have any kids. Steps led down the back from the porch. I took them and moved to the second building. It was a good size and could have been a garage, a storage shed, or an apartment. There was a window on each side, but it was dark inside and difficult to make anything out.

Next, I strolled to the barn. The large weathered double doors were locked. Although the barn was old, other than the need for paint, it was in good repair with no sign of gaps or busted, eaten, or eroded boards.

As I stood, hands on hips, spinning in slow circles, I heard a vehicle pull up out front. I moved cautiously for a better view. A postal carrier had pulled up to the mailbox and made a deposit. I stayed hidden until it pulled away, then made a move to the box with a glance down the street in both directions to check for witnesses, lowered the door and slid out the assorted mail.

The bills and other items all bore the name of the people listed on my sheet as the owners. I put the mail back, closed the door and went back to my car. I noted that no one was home and it should be checked again. It was probably nothing, but the location and the house fitted the image in my mind of what the kidnappers would need. It wasn't necessarily a good idea to have preconceived notions of what that might be, because I could miss the real hideout. But some of the houses could be eliminated. Like the next house on the right.

On the same side of the street as the house I'd just checked, stood several buildings fronting acres of farmland. I veered off the road in the gravel pull-off in front of the structures, looking around to make sure no one was there. I didn't know much about farming, but the space appeared to be a storage station for whichever farmer worked the land. A green and white striped aluminum building stood about twenty feet deep and forty feet wide, with large sliding doors on both ends. It probably housed equipment. In front of that structure, nearer the street, sat two large grain silos. They weren't very high as silos went, but had great width to them.

Just past them was an old-style Quonset hut, overgrown with shrubs and brush. It wasn't very big, but at one time might have been used to house field hands. It didn't have any obvious breaches in the roof or sides, but didn't look habitable, or disturbed for a long time. Behind that, farther from the road, was a long mobile home sitting almost flat on the ground. It looked as though it might have been moved from another location and dumped there. The front section was crushed, as if a large tree branch had fallen on it. No electrical lines ran to it. The back section sat higher off the ground than the squashed front end. It, too, was overgrown and forgotten. Two doors were on the side facing me, but there wasn't enough room there to hide three women.

I watched the house across the street with the horses and kids' toys. A few minutes later, the side door burst open and three children ranging in ages from about six to ten, ran out into the yard screaming and laughing. I crossed it off the list and moved on.

As I was checking off the last houses on my list, Officer Longley returned my call. I explained what we were doing and he agreed to help. He knew his area better than we did and would know immediately if anyone new had moved in. He'd report after he finished his shift and gave me his cell number.

It didn't take much longer to finish the chart. The next road over was the beginning of a subdivision with maybe forty newer houses, located just inside the Berkey Village limits. The houses I passed along the Sylvania-Metamora Road all looked as though someone lived in them. They were too close to the road and to each other to be realistic choices. Most had people moving around the outside doing chores. I checked those off, then headed to Brady's to make my report.

Back at Brady's, the place was coming alive. Brady was in the kitchen filling lunch orders. Replacing him behind the bar was a very tall woman with extremely high hair and a lovely, friendly smile. She greeted me and I ordered a pop. I explained why I was there. "Some of the boys are in the back room," she said. I thanked and tipped her.

Everyone stopped to look at me as I entered. I recognized two of the guys from last night. Two new members of the team were introduced as fellow officers, one from Sylvania and one from Sylvania Township.

I placed my collection jug and chart down and explained where I'd been. My route was checked off the map and the rechecks placed on a list. A lot of ground had been covered already, but we still had so much territory to cover. One of the guys, Marty something, assigned areas to the new guys and they took off.

"You know," I said, "these guys are not likely to be moving around during the day, especially now that a composite of the two men we've seen has been all over the TV. Somehow, we have to be able to cover these same locations again, only at night. Anything that looks suspicious needs to be double-checked again in the dark."

"Yeah, good point," replied Marty. "That's an awful lot of territory. There might be too much to cover all over again. Especially at night. There's no street lights out there to make it easy to see anything. If we go flashing spotlights, we may spook them. If we find them at all. Let's see what comes in today as far as possibles go ... we can go back tonight and check those. It'll be easier just having to check a few houses. What do you have?"

"There are three I want to recheck. One fits the bill, but it looks too lived-in and too close to the road. Still, it should be checked to be sure."

"Well, look what's up and moving," boomed Doug. "You're such a lightweight I figured we'd be lucky to see you by six, if at all today." He clapped me solidly on the back, sending me forward a step.

"Sorry to disappoint you, but I've already been out and finished a shift while you were trying to catch up on your beauty sleep. Which, by the way, you're a couple of decades behind on."

He put me in a crushing headlock. "I just love a smart ass in the morning."

"Well then, you should enjoy looking in the mirror each morning."

He squeezed tighter to emphasize his power over me. He had tremendous strength. "I don't think you fully understand the seriousness of your predicament. Keep spouting off and I'll pop your head like a zit."

"And you should be an expert at popping zits. Oh, and I don't think you fully understand the importance of using deodorant."

The others laughed at the bantering, but none were dumb enough to step in to try to help me. I couldn't blame them. There weren't too many people stupid enough to mess with Doug when he was joking. I couldn't imagine how dumb a criminal would have to be to tangle with him. I had no doubt that he could pop my head like a zit. The man truly did not know his own strength.

"Okay, smart mouth. You're really looking for a beating."

"Let go before I have to embarrass you in front of your friends." I was trying to keep it light, but the pressure was giving me a headache.

Fortunately, the barmaid chose that moment to walk in carrying a tray full of sandwiches and baskets of fries. "Doug, you big gorilla, leave that poor man alone, or I'll have to hurt you."

"Well, in that case ..." He let go and I dropped to my knees, letting out an involuntary gasp. "I wouldn't want to piss you off, honey. Although it might be fun to wrestle a round or two with you. Besides, I had to let him go so I could eat."

"Yeah, in your wet dreams, big boy," she replied.

Marty came over and offered a hand to help me up. "Hey, Doug, I thought you told me this guy was tough." More laughter.

"Yeah, let's see how tough you are with your nose stuffed in his armpit," I said.

"Good point," he conceded.

"The sandwiches and fries are on Brady. The beers are on you guys," the barmaid said.

"No problem. Thanks, sweetie."

"Yeah, and Doug's got your tip," I added.

"She don't want the tip. She wants the whole thing."

"Yeah," she countered, "but I'd want a man's whole thing, not that little boy toy you got."

She left the room, getting in the last dig. The rest of us gave Doug the oohs and aahs that he deserved. As we ate, we talked cop shop, telling funny stories. Others came in from patrol while some just stopped in for lunch. It became a party that I had to excuse myself from, afraid that if I stayed, I'd go home and pass out. If I missed my mother's dinner, I wouldn't be able to show myself in the Greater Toledo Area again.

TWENTY-SIX

Saying my goodbyes, I promised to return later to go out again. The sun was bright and the day quite warm. I actually looked forward to mowing the lawn, knowing I'd be able to sweat out some of the beer intake of the past few days.

After unlocking the door, I went upstairs to change. While sitting on the bed tying up an old beat-up pair of sneakers, I noticed two messages on the house phone. I depressed the button and heard a voice that made me cringe.

"You didn't think you could stay hidden from me for long, did you?" Carolyn Monroe, my favorite reporter. "You may have dodged me so far, but I know you are a story and I am going to tell it. I'm just trying to decide which angle to tell it from. The ex-cop-turned-teacher who has violent tendencies. Do you want this man teaching your children? Or, the man who supposedly saved the life of a cop, but no one else saw the shooter. Who really shot a cop? Let's see ... what else have I got here? Oh yes, coming to the defense of some children who might have been targeted by a flasher. Then gets into a fight with the police, gets himself arrested and puts one of the cops in the hospital. Who were the children more in danger from, the flasher or the teacher? Aw! How about this? The teacher might be the flasher."

The recorder ran out of space at that point and cut her off. However, the second one was a continuation of the first. "Oops! Now, where was I? Oh yes. You are definitely the story. I can smell it. Call me if you want to have some input into how the story is written. I'd better hear from you soon. I won't stop digging until I come up with something. Trust me, it will be better for you to cooperate with me. Much better. You might even find it fun. CALL ME!"

Great! Just what I needed. Just then the phone rang. I stared at it wondering if she was calling back. My anger grew in increments with each ring, like the degrees on a thermometer. Snatching it up, I shouted, "What?"

"Well, is that any way to speak to your mother?"

"Oh, God, Ma, I'm sorry. I've been getting some harassing calls and thought you might be them calling back. I'm sorry."

"Well, you should be. Let that be a lesson to you. Always make sure you know who you are yelling at before you start yelling at them."

Huh?

"I just wanted to remind you about dinner tonight. I ... I mean we ... look forward to seeing you."

What? "Yeah, I didn't forget. I'll be there. See you then. 'Bye, Ma."

"'Bye."

I had a lot to think about while I mowed the lawn. And suddenly a lot of energy to do it. I went over each item of concern, starting with the kidnapping. There were so many problems it was difficult to focus on one for long. My mother and whatever was going on with her. The perverts around the school and Mr. Harald. The pestering reporter and, oh yeah, Natalie. I'd been burying her under all of the other problems, trying not to think about her.

I thought about calling but wasn't in the mood to fight with her. My mother was expecting Natalie for dinner, but I didn't think she would care if she wasn't there. I remembered the way she hesitated when I asked if I could bring her. I thought my mother would be happier with whatever she had planned if I was there alone.

It took a little more than an hour to finish up. I did a lot of perspiring and even more thinking. My conclusions were inconclusive. I'd continue to work the case and get through the rest of the school year, hopefully keeping a low profile. I would avoid Ms. Monroe until I stopped being newsworthy. And Natalie ... well, I didn't know what to do about Natalie. We both needed to deal with whatever this was, if for no other reason than to have some closure. That situation deserved more thought, but in the end, we needed to talk.

After a shower, I went to see Tony. I should've called. He wasn't home. I still had some time to kill before dinner, so I drove to the restaurant to see how things were going. Near the door, a voice called to me from the back of the parking lot.

"Mr. Roth. Excuse me, Mr. Roth. Can I have a word?" It was Carolyn Monroe. This time, she was not being followed by a cameraman. I didn't trust that she was alone though and scanned around her for a hidden video set up someplace.

I turned back to the door as she caught up to me. The gentleman that I am, I stepped aside and allowed her to enter ahead of me. My first instinct, however, was to use my key to lock the door, delaying her pursuit, and hightail it to the hills. Except we don't have any hills in Toledo, and I know that would only make her all the more determined.

As we entered, I walked past her to the bar and spoke with the bar manager for a few moments before poking my head into the kitchen. One of the cooks said, "If you're looking for your mother, she left about an hour ago."

I was surprised she had come in at all. "Thanks. I was just checking on things." I snagged a slice of capicola and munched it down. Turning around to go to the office, I found Ms. Monroe blocking the kitchen doorway.

"Did you get my messages?"

"Yeah. Why don't you go bother someone else? I've got nothing for you."

"Somehow, I don't believe you. And even if it were true, you intrigue me. I would really like to know more about you."

If another girl had said that to me I'd be excited, but when she said it, all I could think of was a circling shark with a mouth full of sharp teeth. She scared the hell out of me.

"I'm sorry. I've got work to do. Please don't come here again." I tried to move past her, but she stretched her arms out and grabbed the door frame on both sides. The sly smile on her face told me she was daring me to try to move her. The waitress, Sheila, had been watching the entire scene and chose that moment to intercede on my behalf.

"Excuse me, honey. I need to get into the kitchen."

The reporter glanced over her shoulder and the smile fled her face, replaced by an even scarier look. For a second I thought she might actually challenge Sheila and refuse to move. That might have proved very interesting. Sheila had been waiting tables for years. If she didn't take shit from the customers, she wouldn't take any from the likes of Carolyn Monroe. She might think she's hard-nosed, but she was out of her league with Sheila.

Grudgingly, one arm came down allowing admittance. Sheila came in, rinsed out a bar towel and moved into her path, forcing her to drop the other arm. Basically, setting a pick for me just like in a basketball game. Her move enabled me to slip past and walk behind the bar. From there, I made my way to the office without looking back. Safely inside, I closed and locked the door behind me.

Sheila's voice came through the door. "Sorry, honey. Is there something I can get for you? Something you can actually sink your teeth into?"

There was a knock at the door and someone jiggled the knob. "Come on, Roth. Just a few minutes of your time. I'll try to make it as painless as possible." Silence. She tried the doorknob again, slowly. "You might even enjoy it. Are you afraid of me?"

Yes, I thought. Very afraid. She was the worst possible combination: beautiful and lethal.

"You are, aren't you?"

Her voice changed to that of a charmer. Soft, seductive, alluring, trying to reel me in like a fish. The hook baited and dangling, trying to get me to take a nipple, uh, nibble.

"Just five minutes of your time. Tell me about yourself. If you do, I'll leave you alone."

I couldn't take any more. I just wanted her to go. I stood up, turned the lock and yanked the door open. It put me literally face to face with her. She must have had her head pressed against the door, trying to hear what I was doing. We were inches apart and I had to admit that my first reaction wasn't one of surprise, fear, or revulsion. My first thought was to kiss her.

She must have sensed it because a victorious smile played across her face. She was in control and knew it. Instead of pulling back, she actually moved slightly forward. A test, I knew, but I flunked before I started. I pulled back faster than she leaned forward.

"You are afraid of me! How sweet! Or are you really just a shy man after all?" Her face kept inching closer until she was leaning halfway through the door. She smiled and bit her lip, suddenly and uncharacteristically unsure. "You really have beautiful eyes, you know that?" Her eyes explored my face. "What was your first thought just now?"

"My first—? Wh-what do you mean?"

"You know what I mean." She was inside the office now. "You wanted to kiss me. Don't deny it. I could feel it. Your body heat was overwhelming."

"You're crazy. I'd never want to kiss you. I'd be afraid my lips would turn black and fall off."

She laughed, but there was little humor in it. "You really don't think that. Why don't you take me out to dinner someplace nice and get to know me? Who knows, maybe you'll like what you see." She put her hand gently on my chest and traced a soft line downward.

I felt like a slab of meat in a butcher shop and she had just traced where to start slicing off prime cuts.

I dropped into my chair, and she leaned forward. Her tongue flicked across her lips and had the desired effect on me, traitor that it was. Her eyes were a hypnotizing deep blue. Her smile was different somehow. The open door to the dining room was the only connection we had to the real world. The office had somehow been transported to a different place. She reached down and stroked the side of my face, which brought just the slightest quiver to her lip. Her touch brought a massive tremor to my entire body.

"I can't." The words seemed to stick in my very dry throat. She was very attractive. "I have to go home and have dinner wi-with my momma." It sounded just as bad to me as I'm sure it did to her.

From behind her, a voice that seemed to come from far away called to me. "Excuse me, Danny, your mother called and wanted to make sure you weren't late for dinner." Sheila to the rescue once more.

"Huh? Ma?" I was still lost in the trance.

"Yo, earth to Danny. Your mother!"

"Oh, yeah. See?" I said. "I'm having dinner with my mother."

Carolyn turned around and sneered at Sheila. I think I heard a hiss. She straightened up and looked down at me. "Perhaps another time. I'd really like to get to know you better."

I wasn't sure where she pulled a business card from. As far as I could tell, she hadn't been carrying a purse, but magically it was in her hand. "Please. Call me." She gave me one more sweet smile, pushed past Sheila and was gone.

Light seemed to pour back into the room. Now I had enough air to breathe. I wiped my hand across my forehead. It came away wet.

I exhaled a breath, which apparently I had been holding for a while. Sheila looked at me and just shook her head.

"What!"

"Pathetic!" was all she'd say. But she said it several times.

TWENTY-SEVEN

I stayed in the office, recovering. A strange, overwhelming, inexplicable desire for a cigarette came over me. I felt guilty, but as I thought about Natalie, I realized if she was already with someone else, there was no reason why I should feel bad about being attracted to Carolyn, er, Ms. Monroe. But the guilt refused to let go.

My legs less rubbery, I made my way out. As I passed Sheila, I stopped and said a quick but sincere "thank you." On my way to my mother's, I recalled the details of the erotic episode, as if replaying a steamy love scene from a movie. In the absence of a cold shower, I lowered the window and stuck my head out.

Arriving at my mother's apartment building, I was about fifteen minutes early. I leaned against the car and wondered with much regret, if I should have at least called Natalie to see if she still wanted to come to dinner. She and my mother had become close over the past few months. Close enough that my mother had actually given her one of her secret family recipes and taught her how to prepare it properly. Now, in light of our separation, I wondered if Natalie had signed a non-disclosure and non-competition agreement.

I climbed to the second floor of the three-story building, after being buzzed in. Morrisey met me about a third of the way down the brightly-lit hallway and handed me a beer, surprising me. "Nice to see you," he said. In a softer voice, he added, "You're going to need that."

The confusion on my face remained as I entered the apartment and found Natalie and her new boyfriend sitting at the dining room table. The people in the apartment below probably dialed the super to complain about the noise of my jaw hitting the floor. Snapping my mouth shut, I spun to leave as anger welled up. Morrisey stood, blocking my retreat.

"Unh-uh!"

"Move or be moved. I'm not playing."

My mother stepped out of the kitchen folding her apron. "Ah, there you are, Daniel." She wrapped her arms around me in a hug, then grabbed my arm and forcefully spun me around. I looked back at Morrisey and said, "I'll remember that."

"Oh, you do that," he said with a smile that made me see red. I wanted nothing more than to pound it off him. I missed what my mother said. The sound of the tide crashing against a rocky shoreline filled my ears.

"Daniel, pay attention, please. I want you to meet someone. Of course, you know your lovely girlfriend—"

"Mother, I need to—"

"Hush, now. I want you to meet her—"

I pulled my arm away from her and said, "No, I—

"—brother ..."

"I can't stay—"

"... Robert."

Silence.

Brother? Everyone watched my reaction. Now I was not only angry, but I was also embarrassed. I looked from one laughing face to another. They had set me up and played me. I tried to calm down, but couldn't. It was too much for my fragile male ego. Too much confusion swam through me. A battle brewed between relief at learning Natalie didn't have a boyfriend and my ... my what, embarrassment? That was lame. I was actually in sensory overload. I needed some air and some space to regroup.

"Sorry. Nice to meet you." I fought for control, but knew I was losing. As soon as Morrisey moved from my path, I turned and walked right out the door. The slamming door silenced their words. The stairs flew underneath me, two at a time.

Natalie bounded through the doors as I shifted into drive. I caught a glimpse but couldn't bring myself to look. The car lurched forward. I couldn't even trust myself to look in the mirror. I knew I should go back and face the situation, but it was too late. I needed some time to myself to gather my composure. I ignored the phone calls. Instead, I called Tony as if he were my shrink, though at this point, I really needed a professional one.

"Yo, what's happening?"

"Hey, T, you wouldn't believe what just happened."

"When it comes to you, bro, I'd believe about anything. Shoot."

And I did. I laid it all out and like the true friend he was, he understood completely.

He laughed his head off. "Man, I wish I could've been there to see the expression on your face. That would have been great. Got to hand it to your ma, man, she's the best. Her brother, that's great! That's why you been moping the whole week? What a chump!"

Not what I expected. "Yeah, thanks for your support, friend. What am I supposed to do now?"

"Do? You go back, you putz. You go get some flowers and crawl back with your tail between your legs, like the whipped dog you are. That's what you do. You know damn well you're relieved and you want nothing more than to be with her. So stop being the oversensitive, whiny bitch you've been and go back and say, 'I'm sorry for being a jerk.'"

"Great! Thanks for those words of wisdom. I thought you were so good with women. That's the best you can do?"

"That's right, bro, I am good with women. So good, in fact, that I would never get into the situations you find yourself in on a regular basis. Good luck with that crawling stuff. Hey, maybe you should get some knee pads, too. I have a feeling you're gonna be on your knees a lot. Hey, Marissa, wait 'til you hear what ol' Danny boy did this time." He hung up.

Fifteen minutes later, I was back at my mother's door with an armful of flowers, boxes of chocolates, a nice red Italian table wine and a case of beer. Morrisey let me in without saying a word, went back to the table and continued to eat. Of course, they would have started dinner without me. I couldn't blame them.

I made my apologies to everyone as a group; when they continued to ignore me, I made them individually. I dispersed the gifts and my mother told me to find something to put the flowers in. As I returned, Morrisey was busy collecting five-dollar bills from everyone. They all froze for a second, then started to laugh.

Morrisey looked at me as he pocketed the money.

"We had a pool. I won. Fifteen minutes."

"Shit." I sat down next to my mother. Everyone laughed again, including red-faced me. My mother reached out and did her world-famous *thwack*, smacking me on the top back of my head. "And watch your language at the dinner table." That brought another round of laughter. Plates were passed to me. I took one from Natalie, but she wouldn't release it until I looked at her.

"You deserved that for being a butthead," she said and stuck her tongue out at me.

"I'm sorry. I've been a jerk. Not intentionally, though. You have to admit, it wasn't all my fault."

"We'll talk about it later when you have a better chance to make it up to me. Now meet my brother properly."

I shook hands with Robert and apologized again. He was gracious in letting me off the hook with, "It's all right. I might have misunderstood and freaked a little, too. And for the record, I didn't know anything about this setup. It was all my sister."

I looked at her, and she stuck her tongue out again. A sudden pain in my head announced the second *thwack*.

"And that's for being a butthead to Natalie. You be nice to her, or I thwack you again," my mother threatened.

"You two have gotten entirely too close," I said.

The rest of the meal passed pleasantly with idle upbeat chatter. I felt like a huge weight had been lifted from my shoulders. We cleared the dishes and sat down for dessert. Morrisey raised his glass and asked to make a toast.

"Here's to a delicious dinner and a hugely entertaining ... and profitable night." They chuckled. "And to the best chef in Toledo, a wonderful and beautiful woman, who has done me the honor of accepting my proposal of marriage."

"Oh, that's great!" exclaimed Natalie.

"Wow!" contributed Robert.

Then, everyone looked at me for a response, like they thought I'd get all emotional or upset and go storming off or something. I smiled and nodded my head, "Yeah, awesome. It's about time. Congratulations!"

We took turns giving my mother congratulatory

hugs. Morrisey shook my hand. More drinks were poured and more toasts made.

Then my mother made one more announcement.

"This means, however, that it's also time for me to retire from the restaurant."

"What?!" I jumped to my feet. Okay, now I felt like stomping out of there. "Why?"

"Daniel, please sit down. I need you to listen to me for a moment." I sat but felt panicky. "I'm not getting any younger. I don't want to work away my life. I've been granted many second chances, most of them when I moved down here with you. A second chance to get to know you, a second chance to rekindle my love for cooking, a second chance to feel alive and now … a second chance at love. I don't need the money. Please, Daniel, don't be upset with me."

She was right, and I knew it. I couldn't very well argue or be mad at her. She deserved this opportunity. "It's okay, Ma. I understand. I want you to be happy. Frankly, I could use a break myself. Maybe, since it's doing so well, it's time to find a buyer."

"That would be fine. You sure you won't miss it?"

"Oh, I'll miss it, but not more than the free time I'll get by not being there. Yeah! Let's do it."

"In that case, I'll continue to work until we find someone to take it over."

"That's great, because if you left first, the value would drop. Without you, that place is worth very little."

"Oh, Daniel, thank you. That's sweet."

"Well, I was just thinking of the loss of money," Pause. "What! Stop looking at me like that. I'm kidding."

Thwack!

TWENTY-EIGHT

Robert, Morrisey and I were talking sport while my mother and Natalie were in the kitchen doing dishes. I know it sounds sexist, but they wanted it that way. My mother wanted to talk to Natalie and we were chased out. Anyway, we were talking, when out of the clear blue, *thwack!* I swear, this time, I saw stars. I grabbed my head and turned, "What the heck!"

It was Natalie. "Your mother told me to try it out. She says it's the best way to keep you in line. She swears by it."

"Well, she didn't try to knock my head off. Not a great lesson, if the first time you do it, you knock the person unconscious."

"Well, I'll just have to practice."

"Not on me, you won't."

"Oh, stop being such a sissy."

"Oh yeah?" I poked one finger into her side, which made her jump and squeal. She was very ticklish in certain spots. I waved one finger threateningly in front of her. "Okay. Thwack me, but every time you do, I'm going to tickle you until you can't stand it anymore." I jabbed her once more to emphasize the point. She blocked my hand and jumped backward.

"Okay! Okay! You win. For now."

It was good to see her smile again. My heart seemed to float. The warmth I felt when near her returned. She explained about her brother. "He works aboard a freighter whose route comes through Toledo three, sometimes four times a year. He usually stays with me when he's in town."

I explained what happened the day I cut her off. "I was chasing the man thought to be the mastermind behind the kidnappings. Speeds were such, I had little opportunity to continue our conversation. Unfortunately, he escaped. Afterward, it was very late and I was exhausted."

She squeezed my hand in understanding. "We still have much to talk about, Danny, but it'll wait for another time and place. But, soon."

My throat seemed to constrict, my eyes dampened. "Okay. I promise."

She wiped a wet spot and placed a gentle kiss on my cheek. I was so happy to be with her again. I recovered and said, "Yeah, well, it was still a pretty rotten way to get flowers."

"Hey, I'm a woman. Get used to it. The best thing you can do is to bring me presents all on your own and save me from having to guilt you into it."

"You're not a woman, you're a ballplayer."

"Oh, really? Not according to the last time you were at my house."

"Sorry, I'm male. I can't remember anything that took place that long ago."

"You just proved you're a typical male with a comment like that. But even if I were, 'just a ballplayer,' as you say, what was your batting average last year?"

".431," I stated proudly.

"Yeah, and mine was over .500. So I guess that means I have the bigger bat. And in those terms, that makes you the woman."

"You know, I think I liked you better when I thought you were shy and quiet."

"Get used to it, baby. And get used to never winning another argument as long as you live."

"Wow! Is that a promise or a threat?"

"It's a promise to be a threat." She walked back to the kitchen.

Morrisey, enjoying the interplay, said, "Eh, she looks better wearing the pants anyway."

I'm just surrounded by supportive friends.

The night ended and I held Natalie in my arms, leaning against her car. Her brother was already in the passenger seat waiting.

"So, call me tomorrow and we'll talk, all right?"

"Yeah, I promise." We kissed long and soft. Letting go, I said, "Oh yeah! For sure."

They left and once more the world seemed balanced. Driving home, I remembered I was supposed to check the four houses past Berkey once more. It was late, but …

It took eight minutes to get from my house to the edge of my search zone. I didn't waste time stopping at Brady's first. If anyone was still there, I'd check in with them afterward. If I went there first I'd get too buzzed to go out looking.

I turned right on Fulton-Lucas County Road, crossing into Michigan. The first property I came to was the older house and barn and newer outbuilding that sat on the corner. Lights were on in the house and a white van advertising a traveling automotive repair business, in the driveway.

Slowing, I tried to see any movement in the windows. The shades were drawn. I stopped the car down the road, grabbed my gun and flashlight, and walked back. The property had open ground with no fences or bushes bordering it. I pressed against the brick foundation and slid to the large picture window. The shade hung crookedly, leaving a small gap, allowing a clear view of the interior. Sitting in a lounge chair with the foot rest extended and her feet up, was a woman in a robe and a head full of large pink curlers. A man entered from another room and handed her a glass of water, then he parked on a couch. The changes of light coming from the corner indicated they were watching TV. I felt like a Peeping Tom, which in fact, I was.

I lowered my head below the height of the window and walked behind the house to check out the small vinyl-sided building. It had a single door and no windows. Walking its exterior, I found a small garage door on the far side hidden from both streets. Too small for a car, it had to be for a riding mower or tractor. I moved to the barn. The weeds around the barn needed trimming and didn't look like it was used often. On the far side, away from the house, I switched on the flashlight and aimed it through a gap in the door. Scurrying sounds came from inside. I saw some very old and rusted farm equipment. I walked back to the car and crossed it off the list.

Reversing to the intersection, I retraced the route taken earlier in the day to Lathrup Road. Slowing as I came to the dark, tree-lined house. It didn't look disturbed since I left it. No vehicles in the driveway, no outside lights, no automatic night lights. I drove up next to the mailbox. The mail was still there. Vacation? Possibly. I drove up the driveway. Stopping next to the house, I got out, climbed the steps, flashed the light inside and peered through the windows. Darkness. This one would stay on the list.

Backing the car out of the driveway, I drove toward the third house. Something to my left drew my attention. I stopped in the middle of the street. Whatever I'd seen was near the last house I checked.

I searched the rear view mirror, then looked back over my shoulder. Nothing but blackness out there. The only light for miles in that direction came from the shaded window of the house on the corner. But as I focused on one spot at a time, I made out a shape slightly darker than the area around it.

A car had stopped on the side of the road in the knee high grass. It hadn't been there when I passed minutes before. Perhaps shutting off the headlights was what had caught my eye.

Inching forward, I watched for movement. The shape stayed put. A hundred yards ahead on the right was the house where the kids had been playing. Immediately on my left were the two silos and the aluminum building. I pulled off the road and drove the fifty yards to the Quonset hut.

Shutting off the headlights, I grabbed the Maglite, and jumped out of the car. I ran to the edge of the building and peered around the corner. Several very long minutes later, the shape appeared. The headlights were still off. From this distance, I couldn't make out any details about the driver or if more than one person was inside. The vehicle stopped short of where I turned.

I wanted to know who was following me. But what if they were waiting for me to leave the area so they could do whatever they were going to do? Another minute passed, and I decided to find out who was in the car.

Keeping low, I ran for the silos. Once there I checked the car's position. A shadow moved inside. I went around the silo, coming out at an angle behind the car and sprinted forward.

As I neared the car, I aimed the flashlight and turned it on. A head dropped below the window but moved too slowly. I recognized the blonde head. Carolyn Monroe. Disappointment then anger swept over me. I'd hoped to strike gold and find Turfe.

Instead, I'd struck fool's gold. Really annoyed, I slapped the window, swore, and ran back to my car. She called after me but I didn't hear what she said.

I reached the car and sped directly toward her. The headlights caught the look of fear on her face. I turned a hard left, spraying up stone and dirt, and drove off, determined to lose her before I got to the bar. I raced to the first intersection and squealed around the corner. My last glance as I turned showed me she was still sitting in the street. Good, I thought, maybe her car wouldn't start.

Increasing my speed, I hit the next intersection, swung right and doused the lights. Slowing in the dark, I spun around the next corner without touching the brakes, thus staying dark. Certain she hadn't followed, the lights on now, I drove straight to Brady's.

Seven men and one woman gathered around the map table. They hadn't noticed me enter.

"That covers our entire target area. We just need to check the houses we couldn't verify."

"Here," I said, handing over my chart. "I've eliminated two of my four possibles. A third one is occupied, but no one is there. They could be on vacation or something."

The group parted and let me into their midst. I laid down the paper, and the map was updated.

"How many properties need to be rechecked?" one man asked.

"Looks like thirteen."

"Is anyone free to check them out in the morning?"

Several officers said they could. I volunteered to check my remaining properties once more. So far, locating the traffickers' hideout did not look encouraging. On the positive side, no word on any new kidnappings or attempts had been reported. The Toledo Police were treating Bethany Wright as a kidnapping now, too. That meant three women out there somewhere.

I didn't hang around long. If I was going back out in the morning, I wanted to get some sleep. I said good night and drove back to my house. Upstairs and ready for bed, I noticed I had two new messages on my home phone. The first was from Natalie saying how nice it was to see me again and maybe we could find time for make-up sex. I smiled and hoped the same.

The second message was from Carolyn Monroe. "So, Roth, what was it you were looking for out here? I don't see a thing. What's the big mystery? I don't get it. Obviously, it's something you think is important. You hiding something out here? Or are you hiding someone inside the mobile home? Maybe you've got a secret girlfriend out here. Lucky her. Anyways, you left a light on in there. Don't worry, I'll track you down eventually and get answers from you. Have a good night. Wish I was sharing it with you."

That gave me pause, remembering our brief encounter in my office. I shook my head to clear the image. I did not want to go to sleep with her the last thing on my mind. She was a royal pain in the ass. I would have to be more aware from now on. I didn't want her following me. It was like having a stalker.

Sleep took its time in pulling me under. The only thing that helped make the final connection was thinking of baseball. I was back on the mound again in my youth, firing fastballs past all comers. If a smile wasn't on my face as I slid deeper into slumber, there surely was one in my heart.

TWENTY-NINE

The constant ringing of the phone woke me from a deep and restful sleep. Checking the clock before picking up, it was already after nine. If not for the phone I could've slept until noon.

"What?" I said, in my best you-just-woke-my-ass-up grumpy voice.

"Mr. Roth?"

"Yeah. Who is this?"

"I'm sorry to disturb you, sir. My name is Martin Brocklin. I'm the news director for the Fox TV news department. I was wondering if you could help me with something."

Shocked awake, I sat up on the edge of my bed. "What is it you think I can help you with Mr., uh, Brocklin, was it?"

"Well, quite frankly, I'm not sure. We seem to have lost one of our reporters and as strange as it might seem for me to be asking this, I wonder if you might know where she is."

"Excuse me? What are you talking about?" Fully alert now, I sensed trouble on the horizon, like the beginnings of a headache nibbling around the edges of my brain.

"Please don't be insulted ... but you know, young

people sometimes get attracted to each other and they, uh, sometimes spend the night with each other."

"Whoa, Mr. Brocklin. Let's back up a step or three or ten. Start from the beginning. Who's missing, who's shacked up with whom, and more importantly, what does it have to do with me?"

"Ah, maybe I shouldn't have called. Apparently, you don't know what I'm talking about. I'm sorry to have disturbed you. Good day, sir."

"Whoa! Whoa! Hold on a minute! You've already disturbed me and I have a feeling I'm about to be even more disturbed, so why don't you fill me in on what the hell it is you're talking about?"

"Well, if you truly don't know, perhaps it's best not to go into it. I shouldn't—"

"Does this have anything to do with Carolyn Monroe?" The headache was growing in direct proportion to the amount of patience I was losing.

Pause. Silence.

Bingo.

"Have you seen her?"

"Yes. Now tell me what's happened."

"Well, she missed her morning deadline. She was scheduled to go out on assignment. No one has heard from her since last night when she said she was still working on a story about you. Frankly, I didn't see much of a story there, no offense, but she was on her own time, so I let it go. She seems to be obsessed with you, so naturally, when she didn't show up, I assumed, obviously incorrectly, that you two might have – how do the kids put it? – hooked up. Now, she's on my time, though, and I'm concerned. I'm sorry if I presumed too much, but young people do strange and ill-thought-out things sometimes. I was almost hoping that she had got entangled with you romantically. That would at least explain her absence. Where did you see her?"

"She was following me last night. You've tried to call her, of course."

"Yes, all three of her numbers. Following you, where?"

"Out past Berkey. Has anyone checked where she lives?"

"Yes. Her roommate, who also works here, said she never came home last night or called in to say she wasn't coming home. What was happening in Berkey, Mr. Roth?"

"I was doing a search. Is that normal for her to check in?"

"Yes, any time she isn't going to be home. Searching for what?"

"Hiding places. Has she ever done anything like this before?"

"No, never. Hiding places for what, Mr. Roth?"

"OK, is it me or is this getting weird?"

"How so? Have you done something with her, Mr. Roth?"

"Must just be me then. No. But I'm going out to look for her."

"I'm notifying the police."

"Good idea. Oh, shit! She's a blonde."

"What have you done, Roth?"

"Me? You got it wrong, bud. Contact Detective Carbone and tell him what you just told me. And tell him she's a blonde."

I hung up. No! It couldn't be.

I ran to the bathroom. A quick cold shower, a couple of aspirin and I was dressed and backing out of my driveway. My speed was well above what it should've been for the subdivision I lived in. Several early morning walkers gave me nasty looks.

The cell phone became plastered to my ear as I made one call after another, the first to Morrisey.

"It's Sunday morning. How could anyone get into trouble this early on a Sunday? You didn't get into a fight with a priest, did you?"

Funny man. I felt like rescinding my marital blessing. I explained the reason for the call and asked him to check in with Carbone. Next came Tony.

"Bro, do you know what time it is? Do you know what happy couples spend Saturday night doing? All night? It's why we sleep in on Sunday. You should seriously try it sometime."

God, it was like a freaky version of the *Blue Collar Comedy Tour*. I told him I might need some help in my search. "Yeah, all right. Tony to the rescue, again."

I told him where I was heading and moved on to the next number. Doug.

"Hey, I'm glad you called," he said. Finally, someone who wasn't trying to be funny. I knew I could count on Doug to be sensible. I started to explain, but he cut me off. "Unfortunately, I'm not here right now, so leave a message and I'll get back to you."

"Bastard!" I said in frustration. "Call me. It's urgent." I hung up before realizing I hadn't told him who to call. Hopefully, he had my number in his contacts and my name displayed. If not, screw it! I'd try him again later.

I screeched into the parking lot at Brady's, but found they didn't open until noon on Sundays, so flew out again toward Lathrup Road. I hit the wheel with the palm of my hand, realizing I'd taken my gun and flashlight into the house last night. I called Tony again and got Marissa.

"Hey, Danny. Tony's in the shower. What's up?"

"Tell him I left the house empty-handed. He'll know what I mean."

"You need him to bring you a gun?"

Pause.

"Oh, please. I'm stupid, right?"

178 | Ray Wenck

"Uh, sorry."

"If you get my boyfriend shot, I'm gonna come gunning for you. Just thought I'd warn you."

"Yeah, I'll try not to. I promise."

"OK, I'll tell him. Good luck.

My speed climbed to well over eighty. I slowed down when I hit the Berkey Village limits. No sense getting pulled over again, which gave me another idea. I called Delbert Longley and left a message on his voicemail.

As I neared Lathrup, I slowed and took the turn easy. Cruising to a stop in the middle of the road, I surveyed the length of the street. No cars in sight anywhere. I passed the first house with the kids and gave it a cursory glance. Nothing moved at the moment. No cars visible. They were either in the garage or they weren't home. It was Sunday. Maybe they were at church.

Increasing my speed slightly, I moved past the silos and focused on the house where no occupants had been about. Pulling onto the side of the road, I looked over the property for any recent signs of activity. My vantage point did not allow me to see the entire area. Sliding out to check on foot, closing the door as quietly as I could, I walked toward the white decorative border fence, keeping one of the trees between me and the house.

The fence only stood three feet high, so I jumped it and peered around one of the pines. Watching the front windows, the place still appeared empty. I moved to the corner of the porch and climbed over the rail rather than going up the steps. Pressing myself against the wall, I leaned forward to see inside. No lights and no one moved. If anyone was here, they weren't on the main floor. I was sure of that.

I climbed back over the railing and looked at the side of the house. The windows had curtains covering them. I looked for basement windows: none on the side and none at the back of the house. The house didn't sit up high enough to have a full basement. There were some vents, however, which might indicate a crawl space, or maybe even a partial basement.

Climbing the wooden rail of the back porch, I looked in the kitchen. The room looked clean and unused recently. No dirty dishes in the sink or used pans on the oven. Feeling bold, I tried the door knob. Locked.

Next, I did a close-up inspection of the small outbuilding. That was locked as well. A window on the far side showed me a complete view of the interior. With the sun coming over the barn and shining into the window, the inside was well lit. The structure contained yard tools, including a riding mower, with all of the usual attachable accessories. There was a small plow, a spreader, a cart and just about everything you could ever need to go along with the mower. Chainsaws, lawn trimmers, augers, a full-size workbench loaded with hand and power tools, and much more. But no space for annoying reporters.

The large barn was next and also locked. Windows on both ends gave a partial view of the interior. Nothing seemed out of place. It was just a big open space with large farm vehicles parked in the middle. The ground showed no recent tracks or footprints in the dirt.

Dead end. What have you gotten into, you pain in the ass? With all the trouble she'd caused me, I couldn't believe I was actually looking for her. But the thought of even her in the hands of human traffickers was more than I could stand. I let out a long breath and a chill ran up my spine.

THIRTY

I walked down the driveway, no longer caring if anyone saw me. Making my way back down the street to where I left my car, I stood staring at the spot where Carolyn had parked. I closed my eyes and tried to remember exactly what I'd seen. Could there have been someone else in the car with her? I didn't think so, but anything was possible.

Then I tried to recall her message. Where had I been when she saw me? I turned as the memory came back to me. Behind the silos hiding from her, before I ran at the car and saw who it was. Damn! I should've confronted her right then.

What else had she said on the message? She was curious about what I was looking for. Some gibberish about keeping a hidden girlfriend out here. Yeah, right. And where would I keep her? I looked around. The silos? Not likely. The Quonset hut? Sure, but you'd need a machete to get through the weeds. The smashed mobile home? If you were a midget, maybe.

What else? Something about leaving a light on. Where did she see a light anywhere? She must have seen the reflection of headlights in one of the windows. There were no lights out here. Or were there? She might be a pain in the ass, but she wasn't stupid. It was dark. If there was a light, she would've seen it. But that didn't make any sense. If she had seen a light, why didn't I?

Answer: I wasn't looking.

I wouldn't have noticed because I pulled in here to see who was following me. I never took the time to investigate the area. Oh God, it couldn't be. Twice I'd been here and never really looked the buildings over. I was sure no lights shone the first time when I did the drive-by. But it was daylight when I checked. A quick glance showed lights on the outside of the silos. A power line ran to the Quonset hut, but nothing to the crushed mobile home.

Checking the silo, all access was locked. The ground around the hut showed no footprints and the weeds were untrampled. No one had been there in a long time.

Turning, I faced the mobile home. It was truly just a wreck of a structure, although all of the damage appeared to be at the front, leaving about sixty feet in reasonably livable shape.

As if drawn by some mysterious power, I moved toward the mobile home. It was about eighty feet long and maybe twelve feet wide. Originally, the color was two-tone; white skirting the bottom half and dark brown around the top. Since then, many other colors had intruded.

Two doors were on the side I approached; one, maybe a third of the way down, the other about ten feet from the far end. Windows lined the side. I formed a mental picture of the interior based on other mobile homes I'd been in. The living room was up front where it was now an unlivable room. The middle portion would be the kitchen and in the back section there would be two or three bedrooms and a bathroom.

Working my way through the overgrown weeds, some of which looked suspiciously like poison ivy, I reached the end of the metal heap and squatted. I scanned the area around the mobile home. There was no way to tell if anyone was inside.

Staying in a crouch, I crept along the crushed front section. Nothing moved. It was impossible to see through what was once the front window. The roof was flattened almost to the floor and the entire front lay flat on the ground, the rear end elevated, still on the wheels.

I slid around the front and pressed myself against the side wall. The structure angled downward, giving me clear sight through the busted side windows. I was right about the floor plan.

Continuing with caution, I came to the first door. No steps. I stretched for the doorknob. Locked, but the knob was loose. Not wanting to move it too much, for fear of announcing my presence, I didn't force it open.

I kept thinking this was crazy. Who would be out here? There was nothing to indicate that anyone had been here in years.

The angle of the mobile home made the windows a little too high for me to see in, so I made my way toward the back door. A mound of garbage and debris leaned next to a small tree between me and the door. I scanned the waste to see if I could step on anything to get up to window height. Broken furniture stood to one side. I dragged what was once a recliner from under the trailer and positioned it near a window. Placing a tentative foot on the cushioned seat, I pressed down. The chair held, so I put more pressure on it and the seat cracked and shifted, icing my veins.

No one responded to the noise. Either they didn't hear, or there wasn't anyone here. I felt silly taking my actions this seriously.

I grabbed onto the tree, which stood about ten feet high, pulled myself up and grabbed the edge of the roof. Though awkward, the position offered a view inside. To the right was the kitchen as surmised. To the left, a hallway had two closed doors in the wall in front of me. The place was as it looked, deserted.

I climbed down and wiped my hands together. This was a waste of time. I was about to give up when I noticed the cinder blocks by the back door, stacked high enough to grant access. By themselves, they weren't that suspicious, but they kept the possibility of this being something more alive in my mind.

The mobile home was at its highest point here; maybe three feet off of the ground. I crawled under the trailer, waited, listened, and moved again. No sound came from above.

Sidestepping next to the blocks, I squatted and examined the ground. There, in the dirt, were clear shapes of recent footprints. My pulse went into overdrive. Pressing my ear to the bottom of the door I listened. There! What was that? A light thump. Something moved. Son of a bitch! I wished I had my gun.

Fighting down the adrenaline rush, I stepped onto the first block. I didn't want to get too excited in case the sound was nothing more than a rat. The door knob turned. It wasn't locked. What sounded like footsteps sent a vibration through the door from the knob to my hand. I jumped from the blocks, ducking underneath the building and smacking the top of my head on the metal frame. I wanted very badly to curse but had to settle for rubbing my head instead.

The footsteps stopped almost above me. I envisioned someone peering out the window. It couldn't be any of the girls. If they could get up and move around, then they could find a way out.

Another thought dawned on me. The inhabitant could be a vagrant or homeless person. That made more sense than anything else. I crawled to the opposite side of the trailer and looked for a way to see inside. To my surprise, all of the bedroom windows were covered. Not just by curtains. Dark paper had been taped to the glass covering them completely. No one could see in and no light could shine out.

Crawling underneath again, I waited to see what would happen next. A minute later, the door opened. A foot stepped down the cinder blocks and legs walked in a hurry toward the aluminum building out back. As he moved farther away from the trailer, a short, slender dark-haired man, dressed in jeans and a pullover shirt came into view. This was not a homeless person.

He carried a black garbage bag that appeared to be half full. I watched him disappear around the back of the building. As soon as he was out of sight, I crawled to the steps and climbed up slowly. I paused at the doorway and listened. He'd left it slightly ajar. Hearing nothing, I ventured forward. If anyone else was inside, maybe they'd think the other man was returning.

The door opened into a narrow hallway running left and right. Dark brown paneling lined the walls on both sides. To the right was the living room, or what was left of it. Three doors in the wall opposite faced me, with another one at the end of the hall to my left. So, three bedrooms and a bathroom.

Stepping in, making as little sound as possible, I pulled the door closed, but not shut. Placing my feet close to the wall, my best bet at preventing floor squeaks, I moved across the three-foot wide hall to the first door. I turned the knob slowly and pushed it open. A small eight-by-eight-foot room revealed itself. A mattress lay the floor. Nothing else was in the room. No people.

Another light thump sounded. I suspended breathing. Thinking the man was returning, I swung around looking for someplace to hide. A scraping noise came from behind the next room. Someone else was here, as well. Taking a quick peek out the door to make sure the garbage man wasn't coming back, I slid along the wall to the next door. Taking a deep breath and placing my head against the door, I listened. Someone or something moved inside. Placing my hand on the knob, I twisted slowly. Pushing it open, it creaked. I stopped. Not much of a sound, but in my heightened state of awareness, it was a cannon shot, or at least loud enough to be heard inside.

I waited, my thumping heart the only sound I heard. I was just about to resume the push when a voice almost made me jump in the air.

"Farouk, is that you?"

Afraid to breathe, if breathing were even possible, my muscles locked.

"I'm almost done cleaning up. I think I got it all." The voice had a Middle Eastern accent. "What'd the boss say about the girl?"

THIRTY-ONE

The girl? What had they done? Sickening thoughts assailed my mind. I flashed back to the garbage bag the other man carried. Could it have held body parts?

My shock morphed into anger. Even though afraid of what I might see, I had to look in that room. I chanced a peek through the small crack. It was a bathroom with a sink to the right, but I couldn't see anything more past that. What sounded like a spray bottle squirted followed by more light scraping. Not scraping. Scrubbing. The cracked mirror above the sink allowed me more of a view into the room. A man on his knees, his back to me, leaned over the bathtub.

He lifted up and called, "Hey, Farouk. You out there?" I pulled back before he could turn his head.

At that moment, the door I came through opened, and the first man stepped in. His eyes widened as he saw me. For an instant we hesitated, then sprang into action simultaneously. He reached for something behind his back and yelled, "Hey!" as I landed a straight punch to his mouth, knocking him backward, out the door to land squarely on his back.

The second man emerged from the bathroom

holding a gun. I pivoted and fired my right fist into his chest. He staggered back, arms flailing, discharging the gun into the ceiling. I grabbed the gun arm with my left hand and drove my right knee into his groin. He crumpled and loosened his grip on the gun. Wrapping a hand around the barrel, I twisted it violently toward him until his trigger finger snapped. He screamed, releasing the gun and pulled the injured hand to his chest. He collapsed to the ground, clutching his arm. He kicked his feet to keep me away.

Outside, a series of shots penetrated the thin outer wall. The bullets hit high in the paneling to my left. I ducked into the bathroom, stomping on the injured man's head as I went. He stopped moving. Wedged between the toilet and the sink for protection, I fired two shots blindly back.

I wasn't as concerned about hitting anything as letting him know I was armed, too. Sure enough, the shooting stopped. Suspecting a trap, I waited. I slid the magazine out and checked my load. It was a Glock nine millimeter with five rounds left, plus one in the chamber. After a minute with nothing happening, I worried about him sneaking up on the other side of the trailer and shooting me from behind. The walls wouldn't be much good at stopping bullets.

The sound of a car engine drew my attention. I jumped out of the bathroom and stepped to the outer door just as Carolyn Monroe's car sped past. I ducked back as the driver fired several more shots.

As he cleared my position, I stepped to the edge of the door and lined up a shot. Just before I pressed the trigger, I stopped. What if she was in the trunk? I couldn't risk hitting her.

I jumped from the steps and raced after the car as it turned out of the driveway. Drawing level with my car, the driver stopped, lowered the window, leaned out and fired a round into my back tire, then the front. I lined up a shot again, but knew I couldn't let it loose for fear an errant or ricocheted shot might hit my favorite reporter. I ran after Carolyn's car, even though I knew it was in vain.

The car sped away heading north. I screamed in frustration.

From behind me, a car horn blared. I didn't recognize the vehicle speeding down the road toward me. I raised the gun and steadied my aim. I was on the verge of firing when arms flailed out of the passenger window. A head leaned out, "DON'T SHOOT!"

Recognizing Marissa, I lowered the gun and ran the last few steps to the car and was in the back seat before it came to a stop. Tony was in the driver's seat. "What's up?" he said.

"I think one of the kidnappers just fled in Carolyn's car. There's another one in the trailer." I turned to Marissa, "You got your cuffs with you?"

"Ah, well, actually, they're still attached to the bedposts. Sorry."

Saving Carolyn was more important than making sure the other guy was secure. "Drive," I said. "If we don't catch that car, we're going to wish we had the other guy under our control."

The car leaped forward. We were silent for a minute. I said, "Bedpost?"

Marissa was totally unfazed, but Tony cast a sideways glance and blushed.

"Not a word," he said. "Not one single word."

"Right."

"I mean it."

"Uh-huh."

"I'm serious."

"Apparently."

He caught my eyes in the mirror. "What?"

"Cuffs. Pretty serious stuff."

"Oh, shut up."

"Drive, bondage boy." The other vehicle disappeared around a corner. "Don't lose them. Would it be too much to hope that you brought a gun? Or did you leave that under the covers?"

"I'm warning you, bro."

Marissa chipped in, "Don't need a gun to get him into bed. He's usually pretty willing. Keeping him there is why I need the cuffs."

"You're not helping," Tony said.

"Besides, he brings his own gun. I don't need mine. It's fully loaded. Well, it was."

"Stop!"

"Sometimes he fires a quick burst."

"Marissa!"

"But he's pretty much always on target. The only problem, at his advanced age, is that reloading can sometimes be a slow process."

"OK, I think I've heard enough," I said.

"Yeah, put a gag in it," Tony begged.

"Gag's still on the nightstand," she said.

Thirty-Two

As we chased down the fleeing car, only managing to gain on it slightly, I used my cell to call in reinforcements. I gave a description of the car, but after giving the location, the operator informed me I was in Michigan.

"So?"

"So, we can't do anything to help you. I need to call the Michigan State Police."

"Uh! Then do it. Please. We're desperate for some assistance here."

I hung up and called Doug's number. This time, he answered.

"Got your message. Where you at?"

"Evidently, we crossed into Michigan. We're chasing someone who might be connected to the kidnappings. Can you help us?"

"You bet. I'm not passing up another opportunity to shoot someone."

"I left a man unconscious in a mobile home on Lathrup, just south of the border. Can you send someone there to take him into custody?"

"Yeah, I'll call it in."

We coordinated our routes to hem in our escapee. I warned, "Doug, we need him alive and able to talk, so—"

"Yeah, your point?

"Ah, so, go easy with the whole 'shoot first' philosophy."

Silence stretched from the other end of the phone. "Doug?"

"Can I wound him? Just a little?"

"Doug, those women's lives are at stake."

"Oh, all right, but before this is over, I'm shooting someone." He disconnected.

"Uh-oh," said Marissa.

"What? What do you mean, 'uh-oh'?" I looked down the road we were speeding on. "Where's the car?"

"Hence the 'uh-oh.'"

"Tony, we can't let him get away. Lives depend on it."

He didn't respond. I knew he understood the circumstances and felt enough pressure without me reminding him of the importance. The car lurched forward as he floored the accelerator. We sped past farmland and huge farms, blindly flying through intersections. We saw nothing.

"How is this possible?" I yelled.

"I don't know!" he yelled back.

Marissa spoke more calmly, "Turn around. We missed something."

Tony braked hard and spun the wheel. As the tires screamed for purchase, the car slid off the road and tilted in a small ditch running the length of the road. Without letting the car come to rest, he started the car moving forward. At first, I thought we were stuck in the soft dirt. Inch-by-agonizing-inch, we gained traction until we blasted from the ditch as if we'd been launched.

This time, we slowed to look down each intersection. We passed a small wooded lot with a hidden driveway.

"STOP!" I yelled. He slammed on the brakes. "Back up."

"What is it?" Marissa asked. "See something?"

"There's a hidden driveway there. Everything else is too open, too long and too straight. There shouldn't have been any way for him to slip away. Not at the speed we were going."

We backed up until we were at the dirt driveway. The pathway wound through the trees with no clear line of sight into the woods. We couldn't tell how far back the road went or if there was a house back there.

"If we go back there and he's not there, we lose him for sure," Tony said.

"What do you suggest?"

"I'm just saying, that's all."

"Let's try it," said Marissa. "We got nothing else."

Tony turned the car onto the eight-foot-wide dirt drive. The path wound to the right about ten yards, then curved back to the left another ten. After that, it straightened out.

"Look!" exclaimed Marissa, pointing ahead.

Tony braked. Fifty yards in front of us, in the middle of the road, sat the car, the trunk lid up. A man bent over the trunk trying to lift something. Whatever it was did not want to come out. His hand went up and shot down, striking whatever it was once, then again. He pulled a woman out, throwing her over his shoulder and turned toward the trees.

My hand was on the handle ready to spring.

"He's got a gun!" Marissa said and pulled hers out.

"Shit! T, he's eliminating the witness like they did before. GO!"

Tony floored the accelerator. The man heard our approach and snapped a shot in our direction, throwing the woman on the ground.

"T!" I said, panic rising in my voice. We had thirty yards to go.

The car closed in a hurry. I had the window down and leaned out. The man extended his gun arm toward the woman. A vice pressed my chest, making it difficult to breathe. I tried to steady my hand, but couldn't afford to wait. I pulled the trigger and loosed two rounds, drawing his attention away from the woman. He flinched, ducked and turned our way.

He fired three times. Two of the rounds struck the car. We closed to within twenty yards, the car bouncing, making aiming difficult. He turned toward Carolyn again, who, even with her hands and feet bound, was trying to crab walk away from him. The horror on her face was in drastic variance with the beauty she was known for.

Steadying my arm as best as possible, I fired two shots, knowing hitting him was unlikely without a lot of luck, but I had to keep him occupied or she was dead. He ducked again, but stood up and aimed at her.

Ten yards.

I screamed, frustration and angst threatening to pummel my heart through my chest, and fired the remaining rounds. One bullet crossed close to his face. He brought his hands up as if swatting away insects and took a step back.

Tony braked, throwing me out the window. I bounced on the ground, knocking the air out of me, as shots were exchanged. Marissa was out of the car, standing behind her door, gun bucking in her hands, before I rolled to my knees.

Ignoring the pain in my back, I pushed off the ground like a track sprinter. I ran for cover hoping to come up next to Carolyn, trusting Marissa could keep the gunman pinned down long enough.

Reaching the trees, I grabbed the trunk of one and used it as a pivot to swing me like a slingshot in the direction of the shooter. Another barrage of shots erupted. Seconds later, I exited the woods to find Marissa and Tony holding sights on a fallen man. Marissa advanced and kicked the gun away while Tony covered her. She knelt next to him and felt for a pulse at the same time I reached Carolyn. Dropping to the ground, I tore the duct tape from her bruised and bloodied mouth.

"Oh, Danny!" she cried, shaking violently. "Oh my God! Oh, Danny!" I pulled her face to my chest with one hand and let her sob while I undid the tape that bound her hands and feet with the other. Finished, I held her tight, letting her emotions run their course.

Tony searched the car while Marissa bent down next to me. I gave a questioning look and motioned with my head toward the shooter. She shook her head.

"You better call it in," I said to her.

She nodded and moved away just as my cell phone sounded. I reached into my pocket to retrieve it.

"I heard shots!" Doug yelled. "Where are you? Don't you dare tell me it's all over. Danny, talk to me. Don't you tell me I missed the shooting again."

"Sorry, Doug. The bastard wouldn't wait for you."

"Oh, man. I can't believe this. Next time, I'm sticking to you like glue. Wherever you go, people get shot. I'm sick of being left out."

Great. Just what I wanted to hear.

"I'm propping his ass up and shooting him anyway."

I explained where we were, not really knowing for sure, and asked him to call the Michigan office of whoever's jurisdiction we were in. "Did you send anyone to the trailer I described?"

"Yeah, but nobody was there. Whoever it was took off."

"Start a search, Doug. He might be on foot and hurt. He's not going far."

"Yeah, sure! Give me the grunt work while you get to shoot people. I'll get right on that."

"Thanks! And if it's any consolation, I didn't shoot anyone."

Thirty-Three

Within the next thirty minutes, swarms of police from every organization within thirty miles descended upon us. Some were calm, some questioned us, some queried our involvement. Others yelled and threatened, while still others congratulated us.

Carolyn used the few minutes she was granted alone to call the station and have them send a remote truck and crew for a live broadcast. She couldn't help herself. It was her scoop and she was going to run with it. She made me wonder if her kidnapping had been staged to get a story.

Carolyn thanked me, her words giving way to hugs and kisses, ending with a promise to find a better way to reward me. She seemed almost like a real person for a few minutes before her on-air personality crept out and a totally different person emerged. She winked and took the microphone from the cameraman.

Carbone and Morrisey huddled with the local detectives and sheriff and state police. Doug sulked around the scene grumbling to himself. After a short while, Mayor Lerner made an appearance, hoping for news of his daughter, but another lead had slipped away. The hope and disappointment taking its toll, evidenced in his sallow skin and dark circles defining his eyes.

A Toledo cruiser drove up and Richie Molten stepped out to see if he could identify the dead man. He frowned and shook his head. "I'm not sure. The attack happened so fast, but this could be the man in the rear seat."

I described the other man in the trailer, but the description didn't ring any bells for him.

Carolyn came over, wanting to do an on-air interview with her rescuer, but I firmly declined. I pointed her in Doug's direction, explaining he had been responsible for organizing the search. He gave me a withering look, but flushed and melted when the seductress cast her spell.

Later, Carolyn came over to me, I thought to say goodbye, but she flung her arms around my neck and attached her lips to mine, giving me a way too long and uncomfortable thank you kiss. I tried to dislodge her from my face, but it was like trying to remove a tick.

Releasing me from the death grip, she smiled and said, "I will never forget what you did. Thank you. I love you." She laid her head on my chest for a moment, then pushed away, trailing her fingers down my chest, and walked away. As my gaze followed her, the cameraman lowered the camera away from his shoulder.

With acid climbing into my throat, I realized she'd played me. That little staged scene would be all over TV. The film would make undercover work impossible and would give Mr. Harald more fuel against me. My face would be everywhere. Reporters would hound me for days. But most importantly, Natalie would kill me. Just when we'd started talking again.

I wanted to vomit. The only thing that stopped me

was the fear the camera guy would record me. Next time that viper was in trouble, I'd wait for Doug before making the rescue.

I closed my eyes, trying to remember the scene. Was there anything I had to worry about? I mean, other than the way too long kiss, which probably looked like me wrapping my arms around her. There was her proclamation of love, and of course, the guilty look I'm sure that had consumed my face. Yep! I was a dead man.

My only hope was to get to Carolyn and try to convince her not to use that recording. I found her in the TV van, sitting in the passenger seat, talking on her cell phone to her news director. The van was about to pull away when I caught up. I latched on to the handle and tried to open the door. She turned and smiled at me. "Hi, my hero."

"Please, Carolyn, don't use that last bit of film. I'm begging you."

"Oh, silly man, of course I'm going to use it. It's too precious not to."

"But you swore you would do anything to thank me."

"I meant sex, you goof. This is news, honey. I could never hold back a good story. See! I told you there was a story someplace about you. I have to go now. My deadline is drawing near. I'll call you about the sex. 'Bye now." She blew me a kiss.

They drove off leaving me wishing I still had bullets in the gun. I just wasn't sure if I'd use them on her or me.

"Another tough day at the office, dear?" said Tony from behind me.

"You know, for a school teacher, you sure do see a lot of action," contributed Marissa.

"Sounds like he's going to get all the action he can handle from Little Miss News at Eleven. I'd be careful about sex with her. It might be on the air someplace."

"Thanks for being understanding, you guys."

"Hey, what are friends for?"

"There's a question." We walked back to the talking heads to see if we could leave yet. "Natalie is going to kill me when she sees that clip."

"We could always catch up to them, shoot out their tires and burn the camera," offered Tony.

I raced for the car.

"Wait, bro. I was only kidding. Seriously! It was just a joke. Man, get out of the car."

THIRTY-FOUR

My car was towed to a local repair shop where one of the Sylvania cops knew the owner. The cop explained the situation and the owner offered to come in and fix the flats, even though it was a Sunday.

Tony drove the three of us to Brady's where we joined close to thirty other law enforcement personnel. Drinks were on them as long as we were willing to recount the story.

It was a bittersweet celebration, though. We saved one woman, but three more were still out there.

"Damn, T!" I shouted in frustration. "I was right there. Twice!"

"Can't beat yourself up over it, bro. Even though you stumbled on to them, there's no proof the other women were ever there."

"They must have been. The guy was on his hands and knees scrubbing the place down. He was trying to obliterate any evidence that might link the place and whoever was there to them. They wouldn't have done that otherwise. They were that close ... and I missed them. It never occurred to me to check the place. I was too narrow-minded in what I was looking for. It just never dawned on me ..."

"You saved one of them, Danny," soothed Marissa. "Without you, we might not have found your friend, Ms. Monroe. We might still find a clue that will help locate the others."

"Or they might decide to cut their losses and run. And don't call her my friend." We drank in silence for a while. "We're too close to them. That's three times we almost nabbed them. If they were smart, they'd run."

"All law enforcement agencies from here to the Canadian border are on the alert. The FBI entered the picture a few days ago and issued statements for cops all over the area to check anything suspicious. All we can do is wait and hope for the best." said Marty Kreutz, an older officer with more than twenty-five years on the force. "We did well these past few days. A lot of concerned men and women joined together to find those girls. It was a good thing to see and it worked. Maybe not like we wanted, but it did smoke them out."

A waitress brought another tray of drinks bought by one of the cops. They passed them around and I grabbed one. I was depressed about the near miss. It would have been easy to spend the day getting drunk.

"Hey, bro, go easy," Tony said. "You can't drink the problem away. Besides, practice is in a few hours and Lord knows you need it. You're bad enough sober."

I offered a smile and took another drink.

"Hey! Hey! Quiet!" someone shouted.

The TV announced a special news bulletin on the local Fox affiliate. The story of the kidnapping and daring rescue of Carolyn Monroe was breaking. A stern-faced older man restated the earlier story, adding more detail. He cut live to Carolyn at the station.

The camera started full figure and zoomed in close

on her pretty, but scratched and bruised face. In dramatic, emotional fashion, Carolyn went through her ordeal in detail, mixing in shots and interviews from the scene, including one with Doug. She mentioned my name as her savior and added Marissa's for her assistance, fine shooting, and overall compassion.

I wondered how long she practiced her expressions in the mirror. She performed with Oscar-nomination brilliance. I marveled at her skills.

I breathed easier, thinking she'd had a change of heart and decided to leave out the film of her thanking me. The panic subsided. Relieved, I took a drink of beer. There it was. The shot of her throwing herself into my arms, expressing her "everlasting love and gratitude." The kissing part followed and seemed to last forever. I swear she doctored the film to make it longer than it was. I choked, spraying beer everywhere.

The others hooted and hollered about the possibilities of future involvement with the luscious and beautiful news reporter. I thought of the possibilities of being beaten to death by my girlfriend. The story ended. The damage done. Sweat beaded my forehead.

I wiped up the mess I made, and to the laughter and comments from the peanut gallery, raced outside to do some damage control. Praying she hadn't seen the news, I called Natalie.

"Hi, Nat," I said in my sweetest voice. "How you doing?"

"I'm fine, hon. I'm glad you called. I was just finishing up your superhero cape, wondering what name I should put on it. I was thinking maybe Kissing Man, or how about Hot Lips Crusader? Oh wait, I've got it, Dead Meat Man. Yeah! That might work."

"You saw, huh? Let me explain before you kill me.

Please! It really wasn't what it looked like. She set me up and doctored the recording to make it look like that."

"Well, that bitch!" But her tone wasn't one of anger. It was sarcastic, which put me on immediate defense. I swallowed hard. "She really is good. Imagine, doctoring a live broadcast while she had her tongue down your throat."

Damn! I'd forgotten the original broadcast was live from the scene.

"You seemed pretty involved. You enjoyed it. Admit it. Otherwise, why did it last so long?"

"Uh, trick photography?" It sounded as weak to me as I knew it did to her. This was a fight I couldn't win. "Look, Natalie. She was grateful and played it up big time, putting on a show for the camera. She's a total player and would do anything for a story. I swear it was nothing more than that. Think about it. Why would she have the camera running if all she really wanted to do was thank me? It was a key element to her story. "

"Anything, huh? What else did she do?"

"Nothing! Nothing! I swear it!"

From the other end of the phone came the sound of laughing. Starting as a giggle, the laugh grew, ending up as a full blown, roaring laugh that included two loud snorts. Confused, at first I thought she was sobbing. As the volume increased, I realized Carolyn Monroe wasn't the only one playing me.

"God, that was fun."

"I'm glad you were enjoying yourself. At my expense. Again."

"That's what made it so much fun." She laughed some more, but I was relieved she wasn't mad. "So when do I get to hear the latest adventures of Lip Lock Man?" She laughed again, with another snort. I had to admit, that one was funny.

"It all depends on your schedule. But I have to check to make sure I'm not needed anywhere. You know, in case of a crisis. Lip Lock Man is on call. Have lips, will kiss."

"Yeah, kiss this!" she said, leaving me to imagine where. "How about 'have tongue, will lick'?"

"Uh, yeah. I love it when you talk dirty."

"Well, if your lips are free, why don't you bring them over here tonight? I don't have to be in until five tomorrow afternoon. You can practice before saving the world with your mouth."

"I'll be there. After practice, I'll go home and shower ..."

"No, I can't wait that long. Shower here," she blurted. "I mean, it would be easier to shower here."

I smiled. "Easier for who? You're just horny, aren't you? Can't wait to get into bed with a superhero!"

"Don't need a superhero, need a super stud. If you see one on your way, bring him along."

"Oh, wow! That was cruel. I think I'll just take a pass and go home tonight."

"Not if you know what's good for you, buddy. Not if you know what's good for me! Besides, we both know who holds the real superpower."

I laughed. "I'll see you later. And leave B.O.B. in the closet."

THIRTY-FIVE

We left twenty minutes later, but not before I was coerced into buying a round of drinks. Tony dropped me off to pick up my car. The place was locked up and the owner had gone back home.

At home, I gathered my duffel bag containing my baseball gear and some bottled water and was out the door, looking forward to unwinding a bit at practice, followed by some extreme relaxing at Natalie's later. I turned the radio on to the Cleveland Indians' game to get into the mood.

The phone rang. A restricted number. I hesitated but chose to answer.

"Hi, honey. Did you like the story?" It was Carolyn. She seemed excited.

"Uh, no, not really. You could have left the kissing part out."

"You've got to be kidding. That was the best part. In fact, that's why I'm calling—"

"And speaking of calling, how'd you get this number? I don't remember giving it to you."

"Oh, that was easy. During one of the many hugs I bestowed on you for saving my life, I slipped your phone out of your pocket and called my cell number with it. Now you're in my phone book, forever."

"Great!"

"I knew you would think so." She missed the sarcasm. Or chose to ignore it. "Anyway, the reason for my call is that, well, I really like you. That kiss just keeps replaying in my mind. I would like to do it again. Maybe over dinner tonight? Besides, I owe you now. I would love to make it up to you in some really spectacular way. If you know what I mean."

I knew exactly what she meant and I was sure Natalie wouldn't approve of Carolyn rewarding me the way she did. Even if I were a superhero.

"I'm sorry," I said, trying to be polite, "but I already have plans for the night. Thanks, anyway."

"What could be so important that you would rather do it than me?"

Wow! That was putting it right out there. This girl was real trouble. I needed to put a stop to her advances, now. "Look, I appreciate the offer, I really do, but I have a girlfriend. And why would you be interested in me, anyway? I'm just a story to you."

"Well, honey, it's your loss, but girlfriends can be replaced, you know. And yes, you are a story, but you've kind of grown on me. I'd like to get to know you better and spend some time with you. I'm sure I can make it worth the effort. Just give me a chance." Her voice almost sounded pleading, which was uncharacteristic. But I couldn't show any sign of weakness with her or I'd regret it. Besides, she could be acting again.

"I'm sorry, Miss Monroe. Your interest is very flattering, but I can't."

"Huh, I hope you don't end up regretting your decision. I won't make the same offer twice." She hung up, angry. I had a bad feeling she would make me pay for the rejection. I had no doubt, if she chose to, Miss Monroe could make my life very difficult.

I parked at the field and grabbed my equipment. My step was a lot heavier than when I got into the car. I had some serious issues to work out. A debate raged between the mini me on my left shoulder and the mini me on my right.

"You should tell Natalie."

"Don't be a chump. You'll ruin the evening."

"Tell her in case she finds out some other way. She'll be pissed if you don't tell her now."

"If you tell her now, you won't get laid."

"If you don't tell her tonight, you may never get laid by her again."

"Enough!" I yelled out loud, leaving my teammates staring at me. I was driving myself nuts. A short drive, granted, but I didn't need to increase the speed.

I decided to tell Natalie. I just wasn't sure when. I had a strong desire to hit something hard. I needed to bat.

Stepping on the field had an almost immediate reaction, relaxing mind and body, like visiting an old friend. Baseball was my therapy. By the end of the session, I was smiling and joking with the rest of the guys. Retelling the same stories that never got old, and verbally abusing each other's skills, or lack thereof. By the end of practice, I was ready to spend the night wrapped in Natalie's arms. By the time the rest of my teammates had pulled off their spikes, I had already driven off.

The trip went by much faster than usual. Eighty miles an hour might have had something to do with that. Even the car was anxious for me to get laid. I wondered if the State Troopers would accept, "because my girlfriend is horny and I dare not be late." Probably not.

Anyway, there was no shower in my immediate future. The door opened and my clothes were ripped off me like a shucked ear of corn. We barely made it to the bedroom. The first round was over fast, leaving us both panting and a little awed at the intensity. My pulse raced. I tried to get up to take a shower, but she pulled me back down and said, "Where do you think you're going, super stud? You're not done yet." And surprisingly, she was right.

Almost an hour later, extremely more spent than before, she agreed it was time for me to take a shower. She joined me, which made the cleaning process more fun. Clean and glistening, we moved to the kitchen where we made a light meal out of canned tuna, hummus, and mixed greens.

Afterward, we curled up on the couch and watched TV. I still had to get up to go to school in the morning, but Natalie tried to convince me to call in sick and spend the day with her. While I debated, holding out for some incentive, she slid to her knees and opened my robe.

She was on the verge of convincing me when my phone rang. No way I wanted to answer it, but she thought I might need to see who it was, so she reached out, without stopping, picked the phone off the table and handed it to me. Morrisey. Uh-oh. Now what?

She heard me sigh and took a break. "Well, go ahead. Answer it. I'm not doing all this work for nothing. You need to concentrate or forget it."

The call had already gone to voicemail. Punching in my code, I listened. "Just thought you should know that a female student was abducted earlier today. She attends one of the Catholic schools near your school. It'll be on the news in about five minutes." I looked over my shoulder at the clock in the kitchen and noticed it was almost eleven. He finished with, "Call me when you get this."

I ended the message and stared off. Natalie curled up next to me. "What?"

"A student was kidnapped today near my school. He wanted me to know and call him."

"Oh, God, that's terrible! Do they have anything to

go on?"

"I don't know yet. I need to call him. Do you mind?"

"Are you kidding? Not when it's something important like this. After all, you are a superhero. They need your help." She said it with a smile, got up, kissed me and walked into the kitchen for a glass of water.

"What's the story?" I said, when Morrisey picked up.

"Fifth-grade girl, walking home from doing homework at a friend's house, never made it home. Because of the previous threats and attempts in the area, police took it seriously immediately and were on site within minutes. Witnesses report a dark-colored van prowling the streets, but no one thought to take down any information. They can't even agree on make or color. I just thought you should know and be aware. There will certainly be an increased police presence out there tomorrow during school hours."

"Yeah, I appreciate the heads-up. Unfortunately, whoever it was isn't very likely to stay in the area. I'll do some drives-by. Do you think this is tied to the other kidnappings?"

"There's nothing to indicate they're connected, but who knows. Human traffickers target all ages, especially young girls. I'll be in the area tomorrow. Maybe I'll drop in to see you."

"Okay, see you then."

Natalie sat down to cuddle. I wrapped my arm around her shoulder and pulled her in where she was a perfect fit. She drank from her glass but said nothing. We watched as the nightly news led with the kidnapping story. They broke to the on-site reporter. I flinched when I saw Carolyn. Natalie felt it.

"There's your girlfriend."

I felt guilty remembering the call from earlier. "Shh! I want to hear this."

"Of course you do."

The report went on to explain what Morrisey had said and that currently, the police had no leads. She then gave some tips to help prevent the same thing from happening to other children.

"I can see why you'd want to kiss her, she's very pretty." A defensive tone in Natalie's voice.

Guilt pangs pierced me like daggers. Time to come clean. My lower head yelled, "No! Let her finish first."

"Natalie, you have nothing to worry about. I have no interest in her. She used me to make a very traumatic story more dramatic. You're more real than her and ... and much more woman."

"What's that supposed to mean? I'm fat?"

Oh, God! She wasn't going to make this easy. I shook my head. "Stop that. You know what I mean. I have my perfect fit right here."

"You sure? I mean, you could have a fine, blonde TV celebrity for a girlfriend. Not some overweight, frumpy nurse."

"Stop fishing. You're infinitely more beautiful than she could ever be. You have a soul and a heart, something I'm not sure she possesses. Besides, she couldn't hit a softball worth a darn. Who'd want her?"

She smiled and hugged me. "Well, if you're sure ..."

I hesitated but knew I had to tell her. "However, there is something I need to tell you ... and I don't want you to be mad or misunderstand."

She pulled back at the tone of my voice. "What?"

I explained the entire phone conversation to her.

She listened in silence. She stood up and went for another glass of water.

She drank half of it, came back and sat down.

"Am I going to have to hurt this girl?"

I laughed. "I don't think so. She was just looking

for someone to add to her collection. She's like a female Tony. She'll have a new flavor of the week within a day and I'll be old news."

"You'd better be old news or she'll end up in the obits. If she tries to kiss you again, I'll use her for batting practice."

"Ah, do I sense a little jealousy?"

"Don't go testing me, buddy. I keep a sharp pair of scissors in the drawer next to my bed. Beware when you sleep." Her fingers spread like scissors, she made a cutting motion and said, "Snip! Snip!"

"Maybe you need to remind me why you're number one. Where were we before the phone call?"

She gave me a withering glare, but reached down and caught me in a death grip. Still giving me a hard look, she slid down, opened her mouth, snapped her jaws shut, making me jump as I 'felt' the sharpness of her teeth dig into me.

Her laugh was light, but the look in her eyes was sinister. She'd made her point. She pulled back and said, "And don't you forget it."

Then she gave me another reason not to forget.

Afterward, we went to bed, making tentative plans to get away when school was out for the summer.

THIRTY-SIX

The alarm on my cell phone sounded and Natalie reminded me once more why she was number one on my scorecard, number one in my heart. She sent me off to school with weak legs, but a huge, content smile. Near to the building, I drove around the neighborhood but sighted nothing menacing.

The teachers were buzzing about the previous night's news story. Mr. Harald made a special announcement to the entire school, reminding them about the dangers of going anywhere with strangers, or going anyplace alone.

Midway through my morning classes, Morrisey and Sergeant Walz paid a visit. Walz still had the protective cover and bandages over his nose. I was surprised to see him and again offered my apologies for breaking his nose. I offered my hand and said I hoped there were no hard feelings. After a slight hesitation, he took my hand, but I had the sense he still held a grudge.

Morrisey handed me my badge. "The captain said he thought having you back on active duty would be a good idea, at least until we capture this nut case, but that you need to understand you don't have any real authority. Use this wisely and don't let anyone know unless necessary. This is also voluntary. You're not getting paid." I started to complain, but he held up his hand to stop me. "Seriously? With everything he could make your life miserable about, you're going to argue? Besides, lack of pay has never stopped you from sticking your nose in things before."

"True," I had to admit. "Still, the extra money would be nice."

Morrisey continued. "The captain also said, 'shit or get off the pot,' meaning, this is the last time he'll do this. You're either in or out. You'd better think long and hard about that."

I had, that's why I gave it back the last time. I didn't like being used as bait to pull out a drug smuggling killer. "Okay."

"He also cautioned about overstepping your bounds and misusing your privilege. Danny, you need to understand, this isn't sanctioned. The captain could get in deep shit for doing this. Basically, he meant, don't shoot anyone …else."

I assured him that wouldn't be a problem. Then asked about Walz.

"Don't worry about him. He'll get over it. He's a pro. You embarrassed him in front of his men. He might not easily forget that, but he's also smart enough to know the whole situation was their own fault."

After they left, Mr. Harald came over to me to ask if there was anything new on the kidnapped girl. "It was just a courtesy call to let me know they were in the neighborhood. They were checking in with me. They promised to let me know if they found out anything," I didn't tell Patrick I had my badge back. I didn't want any more trouble from him.

On my lunch break, I took another drive around the neighborhood. The weather was a comfortable seventy-three degrees, though breezy. Perfect end-of-the-school-year weather. It was hard enough to keep the students' attention with summer break drawing near, let alone when it was too hot outside. I didn't see anything out of the norm, except an increased number of squad cars on patrol. I waved to several of them as I passed, and went back to school.

Later in the day, I received a text from Morrisey to call him. After my last class of the day left, I contacted him. The news wasn't good. The kidnapped girl had been found on the east side of Toledo, walking some railroad tracks, in shock, her clothes or what was left of them, hanging from her bruised and battered body. She was rushed to the hospital.

From what they could get from her, she'd been repeatedly raped by several men. She wasn't sure how many or how many times. She could offer no description of them. In fact, any mention of them sent her into severe shakes and whimpers. She would have a long road to recovery before she would be able to talk about the assault. If ever.

As Morrisey gave the details, a horrendous picture came to my mind. Revolted, an acidic wave churned in my stomach. I vowed that if those men ever crossed my path, I would make them suffer, too. The lowlifes had ruined her childhood and possibly her entire life.

I went to Mr. Harald's office and let him know the details. Following a deep, sad silence, I left him lost in his thoughts. This could be a sick, disgusting world sometimes. Regardless of my current official standing in the law enforcement ranks, I wanted in on this one. These men had to pay.

After school, I found myself sitting at the restaurant bar with a beer in front of me, staring at the bottle. The thought that I might not own the place much longer was very strange to me. I'd grown used to the extra work and hours. The long hours made me think about how little I'd done with my life before this.

Before the restaurant and meeting Natalie, my routine consisted of going to work, doing a couple of errands, going home. The sad truth was that without baseball, I wouldn't have had a life at all. The restaurant had shown me I was capable of so much more.

I'd miss the chaos and the daily grind. I'd miss the people and the notoriety. I was proud of what my mother and I had built. But, as always, she was right. It was time to go. Financially, now was the best time to sell. We packed the place nightly. The value had skyrocketed. Yeah, I would miss the place, but I'd sure as hell get over it.

Finishing my beer, I decided to leave early and do some grocery shopping. An hour later, with enough food and supplies to last a family of four a month, I pulled into my garage. With the groceries all in their proper places, I went out to do some yard work. I was in the middle of edging the lawn when a Sylvania Police car pulled up and stopped. Doug stepped out, hitched up his belt, looked around the neighborhood as if he were searching for someone; he strutted over in his slightly bow-legged way, reminiscent of an old-time sheriff. The type of walk you see on bodybuilders when their thighs are so big, they rub together. It looked as though it would chafe. Not that I'd know.

"What's up, Officer Dougie?"

"Well, I'm guessing if you're asking me that, you haven't heard the news."

His expression was serious, he wasn't joking around as was his norm. My shoulders drooped, my stomach hollowed in anticipation. "What news?"

"I'm not sure if it's good news or bad. I guess it depends on how you look at it. But there was another kidnapping late last night."

"Oh, damn!" I let the edger fall to the ground. "Where?"

"A twenty-eight-year-old woman from Perrysburg. She's a waitress at a blues club down there. Evidently, she got off work a little early 'cause business was slow and called her boyfriend to tell him she was on the way home. She hadn't arrived an hour later, and the boyfriend called work and was told she'd left a while ago.

"Thinking her car might have broken down on the way, he hopped in his car and went looking for her, didn't see her on the way ... he found her car in the parking lot at the club, the door unlocked and her purse on the passenger seat. He called the police. She's a blonde."

"Son of a bitch! The bastards!" I shook my head as a light bulb went off inside my brain. "But wait ... that means—"

"Yeah," said Doug, "it means they might still be working the area. We still have a chance to catch these assholes. If you look at it that way, that's the good news."

I pulled my cell phone from my pocket to call Morrisey, but he beat me to it.

"I was just about to call you," I said.

"So you heard, huh?"

"Yeah, just now. What's the scoop?"

"Name's Ellen Crane. She's a waitress at—"

"Yeah, that part I know. Are there any details? What are the bigwigs thinking? What's Carbone got?"

"Whoa! Whoa! It's not my case, remember. If I find out the details, I'll let you know. Thought you'd want to hear."

"Yeah. If you hear anything else, if there's anything I can do to help, call."

"Just can't stay away, can you? It's in your blood, calling to you at times like this. I know. I've always felt it too."

"What are you talking about?"

"The pull of the adventure. The thrill of the hunt. The chance to help. The adrenaline rush of the chase. You have it bad. Don't let it control you. Don't be its slave. Learn to step back and leave it alone. There's nothing you can do, other than what you already have. Let this be, Danny. The desire and frustration will consume you."

"I'm just curious, is all. That's the extent of it. I'm not a cop. I know my limitations. Don't worry about me." I was thrown by his comments. Not that they were cruel or insulting, but that they were the truth.

"Uh-huh!" was all he said before disconnecting.

Doug looked at me strangely, having only heard my half the conversation. "So do your limitations prohibit you from filling me in?"

"He doesn't have any more than what you told me. He's not really the D in charge of the case. He said he'd keep me posted as more became known."

We chatted a while longer before he went to complete his rounds. Some time later I realized I had finished the edging, so lost in thought I didn't even remember picking the edger up. It was as if I'd taken a catnap standing up.

I tried to find arguments against what Morrisey had said. I was afraid I had become a violence junky. Well, maybe not violence, but at least a thrill junky.

After putting the lawn tools away, I traipsed through my house, grabbed a cold beer and plopped down in my favorite lounge chair, not caring I was all sweaty. Turning on the TV, I found a Tigers' game, staring at the screen without really seeing the game. I was so intent in my self-examination, I'd sipped from an empty beer can for several minutes before realizing nothing was wetting my throat.

It was ridiculous. I was not addicted to danger or a thrill seeker. Snagging another beer, I plodded upstairs to take a shower. Later, I sat propped up in bed watching the news story about the kidnapping victim, which made me angry again. What truly motivated me to get involved was an honest desire to rid the world of scum. If I got a little excitement out of doing that along the way, so what? With that thought, I went to sleep, finally at peace with myself.

Thirty-Seven

Tuesday morning, I left a little earlier to make a slow pass through the school district. I widened the area to include the Catholic school that shared the neighborhood with ours. I spent time searching the parking lots of the apartment buildings to the east of the school, focusing on vans, minivans, and SUVs. The only thing the kidnapped girl remembered was being lifted up into the vehicle. She didn't recall seeing any windows.

The fact the attack took place in the evening made me wonder if it was the same kidnappers. All previous attempts had been during the day. The thought there could be more than one group of perverts trying to kidnap children turned my stomach anew. The only good news had been that the flasher seemed to have disappeared, at least temporarily. If a flasher showed himself once, he usually did it again. It's a sickness they can't control. They're most often harmless exhibitionists with deep-rooted problems, but you still don't want them near kids.

Seeing nothing suspicious, I drove to school. Part of me wanted the kidnappers to try again so I could get a shot at them. But the smarter part of me would be happy never to see them. I'd be devastated if one of our children was assaulted.

The staff room talk was all about the two kidnappings. A feeling of sadness and empathy hung over the building. I couldn't blame them, it was scary with the victim an area student.

I decided I needed to carry my own gun again in the special bracket installed under the dash. Since I was such a thrill seeker, it was a wonder I didn't keep a gun there all the time, but I still didn't want to accept Morrisey's assessment of me. I was just a guy. A schoolteacher. A teacher of little children. I was just a normal guy, for Christ's sake. Just a guy ... who had killed several people in the last year, but still just a guy.

I made the rounds again at lunchtime and once more before I went to the restaurant, where I found my mother sitting in one of the booths with a tall silver-haired man in a suit and tie. He looked like a salesman. She motioned me over to the table and introduced us, and I knew he was a salesman by the way he shook my hand. You know, that quick, energetic pump and release, as though they are afraid you can read their thoughts through osmosis, just by touching their skin.

His name was Ralph Pallotta and he worked for a local commercial real estate company. He had bright white teeth set off by a dark midsummer tan. I sat next to my mother and listened to him ramble on about his experience, how he would market the property and how he would establish a value based on assets and sales.

"I'm not real thrilled with the location," he said. "I'm afraid you will lose some value because of where it is. If the building were on the other side of town, I'm sure I could get top dollar for it. Seems like a nice place, though. Maybe a little rundown, but I can make some suggestions to help spruce it up and make it presentable."

To me, he was saying he wanted to low ball the price for a quick sale, or had a client who might be interested. "And what is your commission rate, Mr.

Pallotta?"

"Well, let me tell you, David."

"It's Daniel," corrected my mother. I'd have just let it go.

"Right! Sorry. Daniel, my rates are pretty well established and will be justified by the price I am able to bring in for you. I'm sure you can appreciate all the hard work that goes on behind the scenes. That's what I will be doing. Working behind the scenes to get your business sold. That's what all of us want, isn't it?"

"Uh-huh, and that fee is …?"

"Well, let me put it to you this way, if I can get you your bottom line for the business, does the commission matter? If you can walk away from here with the amount of money you were looking for, or maybe even more, the commission shouldn't make a difference. That's what I'm going to do for you. Get the best possible price for your business. Sounds good, doesn't it?" He slid a piece of paper in front of my mother. "Now, Mrs. Roth, if you will just sign here authorizing me to begin marketing your business, I can get started immediately."

"Well, first off, Roger—" I said.

"Er, that's Ralph."

"Right! Sorry. First of all, my mother doesn't own any part of this business. I do. Secondly, it does matter what the commission rate is, because it's my money. And lastly, you came in here, having never been here before and simply assumed that because we're in an area you deem inferior to others that we're not doing the numbers that would command a top price. That tells me you haven't done your homework and hoped to low ball the price to make a quick commission check. And with as little behind-the-scenes work as possible. Have you ever even dined here? I thought not."

I didn't give him a chance to respond. "But that's okay. You go do your little appraisal of our business and let us know what your numbers tell you. Then, when you work up a price, you come back and see us. Okay? In the meantime, we have appointments with three other top performers in commercial real estate here in Toledo. I'm sure yours will be the best one, though, because you have all that experience."

I slid the paper back to him and said, "Thanks for coming in. Call when you're ready to talk numbers." I slid out of the booth to signify his dismissal. He looked in dismay at my mother, who bless her, smiled the most innocent smile and said, "What can I do? He's the boss."

The befuddled man collected his things and promised to get back to us soon. He shook my hand as he left, looking stunned. Obviously, he wasn't used to leaving without getting the listing. I pumped his hand once and released it on the downward motion so the force made him bend over slightly. He drew himself up and walked, ramrod straight, out the door. I couldn't help but wonder how many sticks he shoved up his ass to achieve his posture.

My mother muttered, "Snakeskin salesman!"

I laughed and corrected, "I think it's snake oil salesman, Ma."

She looked confused. "You can get oil from snakes? Can you cook with it?"

I just hugged her.

"If you're serious about doing this, I'll call around and make some appointments. Okay?"

"Yes. I think I really do want to do this. But I will miss it. I met a lot of nice people here. It's been fun." She paused, reminiscing. "Yes, I am sure. Now it is time."

THIRTY-EIGHT

An hour later, Tony called to see if I wanted to do dinner before practice. He named a place and time and I set about getting my work done. We used to meet for drinks and/or dinner before every practice, but now that Tony had a full-time girlfriend, we didn't see each other as much. It seemed so weird, Tony having a girlfriend. I still couldn't picture him as a one-woman man, but he seemed happy. And I was glad for him.

I packed up, told my mother goodbye and left, bumping into Morrisey on the way out. I asked about the little girl. He said she was going home today. "What about the other case?"

He shrugged. "We have the whole city on alert and hopefully on the lookout. The kidnappers are lying low. The department is under fire for not being able to find these guys. There's a lot of political pressure on the Chief. The politicians are involved and if ever there was a self-proclaimed group of experts on everything, it's them. They're calling for the Chief's head if he can't solve this. Everything else has been put on the back burner."

"If they hold true to form, you should probably know by tonight. Right?"

"Yeah, if they do. Otherwise, they've packed up and left town. Makes you almost hope they try again tonight, just to have a chance to catch them. Every available car will be patrolling tonight. Hopefully, we'll catch a break."

"I have to go. Let me know what happens."

He chuckled and patted me on the back.

"What?"

"Nothing. Nothing at all."

Tony was late, as usual. I'd already polished off one draft beer and was working on the second when he made an appearance. We were at a small family diner specializing in homemade meals, at higher than normal prices, because the food was served by lovely, long-legged, young, well-built women in very short skirts. We called it Legs and Eggs. They called it Happy's Diner. There certainly were a lot of Happy customers. Pun fully intended.

We flirted with the waitress and watched her walk away, as we were supposed to. We jumped into our favorite topic – our other favorite topic – baseball. With the season starting soon we discussed this year's team.

As we ate, I filled him in on the events of the past couple of days. He offered to patrol the neighborhood again some days, but after school. He was not a morning person. The benefits of being self-employed, especially since some of his more profitable business deals took place late at night and in total darkness and were not always entirely legal.

We split the check, even though he still owed me a dinner. I wanted something that would add a sting to his charge card. We paid, then moved to the practice field. With the first games coming up this weekend in a Memorial Day tournament, we went through a quick round of batting practice, then separated into teams. We scrimmaged until it got too dark to see the ball.

Afterward, we decided to have a preseason team drink and stopped at a small neighborhood bar. The early crowd of regulars had most of the bar stools, so we pushed three tables together and bunched around them.

Several hours later the party broke up. Without a doubt, I'd be a little hungover at school the next day. There's nothing like having a bunch of wild kindergartners running around, screaming at the top of their lungs to enhance a hangover. I popped a couple of aspirin, something I seemed to be doing a lot lately, and slid into bed.

The throbbing was just fading when the phone rang, something else that was happening far too often lately.

"Time to earn your keep." Morrisey. "Detective Carbone just called and said they found a body along the edge of a creek out there someplace by you."

My heart leaped to my throat. "One of the girls?" I asked and cringed, waiting for the reply.

"No, a guy. He wants to see if you recognize him."

I said, relieved, "What makes him think I would know this guy?"

"Because evidently, someone broke his wrist."

"Shit!"

"What's the matter, afraid of losing out on your beauty rest?"

"No, afraid of being hungover in the morning."

"Ah! One of those nights. Oh, well. Go quick, make the ID and get back in time to catch a few hours. You're young, you'll survive. I'll call Carbone and tell him to call you with directions."

I dragged myself out of bed, redressed and got back in the car. The call from Carbone came a minute later. The body was in the creek off the same road where the burned-out car was found. One of the dogs from the farmhouse up the road found it and drew the attention of its owner, who called the cops.

Portable lights had been set up at the site. A forensic team was busy working the scene. Squad cars from Toledo, Sylvania, Sylvania Township, Berkey, the Sheriff's Department and the State Highway Patrol lined the road. The county morgue guys waited near the body. Officers gathered together talking.

As I walked near, they looked up. Carbone stepped forward offered his hand and said, "Hey, I appreciate you coming out at this late hour. It shouldn't take much time. We just need to know if you recognize him."

I nodded. "No problem." I nodded to Delbert Longley and several Sylvania cops I recognized.

Carbone led me down the bank of the creek where crime scene techs worked on the corpse. The trees lining the creek served as a barrier that could have prevented the discovery of the body for a very long time. The farmer up the road was probably annoyed about his land being used as a dumping ground.

I leaned down to get a closer look. A crime scene tech shone his light on the face. I had no doubt it was the guy from the trailer. The only difference was now he sported a third eye.

"Yeah, that's him. I think he still has my footprint on his head."

The tech pointed the light and leaned in for a closer look.

"No, I was kidding. I stepped on his head when we fought."

The guy looked at me as if I were a nut case.

I left Carbone there and walked back to the herd of law enforcement.

"So, is it your man?" asked a Sylvania cop.

"Yeah, it's him."

Delbert Longley said, "What's your thinking?"

I shrugged. "Just a guess, but maybe his boss was mad the guy got caught. He either wanted him punished for failure, or eliminated because his broken wrist made him a liability. Whatever, the head man is ruthless."

The others nodded in agreement.

The Toledo cop said, "How's he gonna move the victims? If Richie saw four men in the car and three are now dead ..."

"Good question." I hadn't thought about that.

"Maybe this guy helped snatch the woman from Perrysburg before he got shot," the Trooper said.

"Or maybe this organization is a lot bigger than we know," said the Township cop.

"I'm surprised they're still here," I said.

Carbone walked over. "Four kidnap victims and four dead bodies. This case just keeps getting worse."

I said, "You need me for anything else?"

"No, you're good. Thanks again for coming so quickly."

Twenty minutes later I was back in bed, my headache gone.

THIRTY-NINE

On my way to school, Morrisey phoned. He told me the traffickers were still in the area because there had been another kidnapping last night. That made five. He didn't have much information at the moment, but the FBI and the local task force were meeting in minutes. He hoped to know more after that.

Once more I made my rounds through the neighborhood, pulling over in the same spot I stopped several days ago and watched the guards at the intersection in front of the apartment complex. I needed to think. I didn't see undercover cops anywhere, but it didn't matter because I had no intention of getting out of the car.

The guards went about their job crossing the students. The two boys on the west corner chatted to each other. The two girls on the east side just walked around, not paying attention to anything in particular, unless a student needed to cross.

A small male who looked like a high school student approached from the far side of the girls' location. He had long, thin, black hair, but it was the unnatural black created by hair dye. Dressed in all black, Goth style, and wearing a long black overcoat, his hands in his pockets holding it closed.

I might not have paid him too much attention except for the coat. It was eighty-some degrees outside. He had to be hot in that outfit, unless he didn't have anything else on. I chuckled, then stopped. I looked closer and noticed something seemed odd about the pants showing beneath his coat. He might be nothing but a strange kid, but I decided not to take any chances. I stepped out of the car, aiming to be inconspicuous.

I walked around the back of the car and bent down. Judging the distance and the time I would need to get to the corner, I waited and watched the man approach. The two girls hadn't noticed him yet. He was still ten yards away and walking at a pretty brisk pace. I decided to shorten the distance. I was about thirty yards from the guards. I moved up two cars, staying to the curbside and using them for cover until I was out of vehicles. He closed the gap on the girls and I sprinted to the tree in front of me.

Peeking around the trunk, I watched as he glanced at the girls and looked around, as if making sure no one was watching. That was all I needed. I ran toward them.

The girls had now seen him. They stopped moving, their attention focused on the man. As I closed on the corner, I did my own sweep of the streets to make sure it wasn't a grab and go, but didn't see any moving vehicles.

Just then, the man made his move. He jumped to a flat-footed, open-legged stance and whipped open the trench coat. He laughed and said something. I was still ten yards away. The girls screamed in unison, but did the unexpected. The taller one, Deidre, kicked out and caught him square in the jewels. Obviously, he hadn't expected that, because he made no attempt to dodge the blow. Letting out a knee-buckling howl, he dropped to the ground. His knees crunched on the sidewalk.

The second girl, Rose, lifted her orange guard pole and brought it down repeatedly across the top of the man's head. The man reached up and caught the pole in a downward swipe and wrenched it from Rose's hand, hurling curses as he attempted to stand.

Before he made it to his feet, I tackled him and knocked him flat, sending his face scraping across the sidewalk, leaving skin deposits as he slid. I straddled him from behind. He lifted his head and screamed in protest, but I had him pinned. He continued to yell.

The girls cheered me on. I grabbed the man by his greasy hair, looked at the girls and pointed behind them. "What's that?" I said in an astonished tone. Both girls turned to look, and I bounced the screaming man's face on the cement. He wailed. As the girls turned back, I leaned forward and whispered in his ear. "Shut up, or I'll do it again." The screaming stopped, morphing into a steady and annoying whimpering.

I took out my cell phone and called 911. After giving them the details, I called the school and asked for Mr. Harald to come down to the corner. Done, I told the girls to stand across the street with the two boys who had been too afraid to move.

Within minutes, two cruisers and an unmarked car screeched to a stop. This time, they recognized me and grabbed the right man. They cuffed him and slid him into the back of a car. Mr. Harald arrived in a frenzy just as I finished my statement.

"What happened this time?" he said, scornfully.

I shook my head and said, "Not me this time. The girls took care of the problem all by themselves. I just came along to hold him until the cops got here."

"Apparently," Sergeant Walz explained, "our flasher there," he nodded to the man in the back of the squad car, "showed his goods to the girls and they took offense. One of them kicked him in the groin. The other clubbed him over the head with her pole. Mr. Roth here was nearby and saw the whole thing."

"Yep! You would have been proud of how the girls handled themselves," I said, beaming a smile at him. "Of course, now that they've protected themselves and been violent, you'll probably want them to transfer to another school."

He scowled at me.

"Hey! Maybe they can go to the same school I transfer to. We could form a club."

He walked away to have a word with the girls.

Walz said, "Trouble in paradise?"

"Yeah, I guess my efforts to protect the students of this fine school are unappreciated. I've been asked to take my violent ass someplace else."

"Imagine that. My face agrees with him." He walked away. I guess he wasn't a friend, either. I was tempted to ask how his nose was.

I was about to leave when Mr. Harald came back to me. It seemed strange to call him that now. I used to call him Patrick, but with the tensions between us, I hadn't felt it appropriate. "Well, I hope you're proud of yourself now!"

"Huh? What's that supposed to mean? I didn't do anything."

"Do you know why those two girls attacked that man? Because, as they put it, they saw you beat up that man at school and wanted to be like you."

"And what's so wrong with that?"

"Those girls could have gotten themselves seriously hurt trying to emulate you. You've become some sort of hero to them."

"And again, what's so wrong with that? I'm proud of what they did."

"You would be."

"Would you rather they just stand there and be abused? Would you prefer they be so docile that if someone told them to get in a car, they would? Personally, I'd prefer to believe they have a fighting chance against an assailant, rather than be a victim. They did good. Can't you see that?"

"They did fine ... this time. I think the whole school has gone crazy and is way too drawn to the violence surrounding them."

"Meaning me!"

"Meaning you're a major part of it. If they witness violence constantly, they will start to believe it is acceptable behavior. Is that what you want to teach them?"

"Not that it's acceptable behavior, but that it's an unfortunate necessity in today's world. In order to survive, you'd better be able to defend yourself. Maybe what I need to do is teach an after-school self-defense class."

"I would never approve it. Maybe what you need to do is bid out, as I requested."

"Don't worry. I'll request a transfer when school is out for the summer."

We glared at each other and he spun and walked away. I watched his retreat, not sure how this ended up my fault. I hadn't even thrown a punch. Well, not technically.

I went back to my car and drove to school. Excitement coursed through the building. Several teachers wanted details of what happened. I told them to ask Mr. Harald.

One bad guy down. Maybe he was the same pervert who kidnapped that poor girl from the Catholic school. It would be nice if the threat were over.

After setting up the gym up for the first class, I walked to the office and asked Mrs. Luckett, the school secretary, for a transfer form.

"What? Transfer? Why would you want to leave us? Don't you like us anymore?"

"It's not that. I've been asked to leave. Apparently, not everyone here wants me to stay."

"What bonehead told you that?" she said, visibly shocked.

"That would be me, Mrs. Luckett," Mr. Harald said from inside his office, "I suggested it might be better for everyone if he moved to a different school. The events of this past year have been very distracting for the students. They could use a break from all the excitement."

"They could, or you could?" she replied.

After a brief pause, he responded, "Both."

"Yeah, well," she said, half under her breath, "I like having one member of the staff you can count on in an emergency."

I smiled, thanked her for the form and told her I'd complete it by the end of the day. Nothing would happen until the next school year anyway, but if I got the form in early, I'd get first crack at any openings. The thought of leaving the only building I'd ever taught at was a sad one. But I wasn't going to butt heads with Mr. Harald every day. That was as tiring as battling perverts and irate parents. Maybe, just like the restaurant, it was time to move on.

At lunchtime, I filled out the form and dropped it off with Mrs. Luckett. She was angry and tried very hard to change my mind. I told her it was probably for the best and she said, "Bullshit!" which dropped my jaw. I'd never heard her swear or raise her voice before.

"This is ridiculous. You two have been friends for years. Sit down and talk to him!"

"I guess friendships change. I've tried to put myself in his place and I can't say for sure I wouldn't feel the same if the roles were reversed."

Again, she said, "Bullshit!" Her phone rang and

interrupted us. "I'm not giving up on this," she said, pointing a finger at me.

I spent the rest of the afternoon dodging questions about my possible transfer from every teacher I saw. Mrs. Luckett apparently leaked the information to the staff. My answers were noncommittal and I left most conversations with, "We'll see."

It made me happy that I'd be missed by most of the staff. A few felt that I'd become too much of a distraction, but overall, the teachers supported me.

Just before school let out, Mrs. King found me. Before I could say a word, she reached up, grabbed the front of my shirt and pulled me down to her height. Face to face she snarled. "Why are you leaving?"

"Because Mr. Harald wants me to leave," I squeaked.

"Yeah, well, who scares you more, him or me?"

"You, by a long shot."

"So I'm telling you now, if you leave, you will make me an enemy. I will find you and beat you senseless." With that, she threw me backward, as much as her petite frame could. Without another word, she stormed away.

What a great lady. I smiled all the way to my car.

Forty

That afternoon when I walked into the restaurant, Morrisey and Walz were just sitting down at the bar. I told the bartender their drinks were on me.

To Walz, I said, "I know there's nothing I can say to offset the pain I've caused you, but I just wanted to say once more, I'm sorry for our little misunderstanding."

He took a long drink, then said, "Well, if by 'misunderstanding' you mean breaking my fucking nose, you're right, there's nothing you can say. But the free beer helps. Keep 'em coming."

I wasn't sure how to take that, but I told the barmaid to put whatever he wanted on my tab.

In the kitchen, my mother was adapting a recipe for more portions. I put my arm around her shoulders and asked if I could help.

"No ... no... I think I got it now. I just want to increase the recipe so it makes forty servings instead of twenty-five. You see? Not quite double, so I have to adjust it."

"I don't know why you bother," I laughed at her. "You'll end up eyeballing it and adjusting it to taste anyway."

"So? It works, doesn't it?"

"Yeah, very well. So why tax your brain? Just do it the way you always do."

"Okay, smarty. How was your day?"

"Good. Real good." I decided not to tell her about the pervert. She would only worry. I grabbed a piece of garlic bread, fresh from the oven and went back to the dining room and sat next to Walz.

"So, what's up there, Detective?"

"I hear you had another busy day," Morrisey replied.

"Busy and productive. I'm just glad my favorite news reporter didn't show up to pester me."

He laughed. "Giving you a hard time, is she? I'd have thought you'd like all that attention from such a beautiful woman."

"Not that kind of attention. That woman scares me." The bartender slid a beer in front of me and I thanked her. "Besides, I don't need that kind of attention. I'm having enough trouble trying to keep my job. The principal wants me to transfer to another school. Apparently, I'm too much of a distraction."

"They should interview those two girls. You didn't do anything but sit on the guy," stated Walz. "They did all the work."

I knew he was trying to insult me. "I agree. Let them take the bow. They deserve it. God, you should have seen them! They were awesome!"

Just then, the door flew open, as if some magical force was at work. Carolyn Monroe made a grand entrance, walking with singular purpose directly at me. My stomach lurched, then fell. I almost spit my beer all over her. I choked it down, but some dribbled down my chin.

"Oh, no!" I said, wiping at the beer with the back of my hand.

"Good afternoon, Mr. Roth. I was wondering if I might have a word with you outside, please."

"Ms. Monroe, unless this has to do with a restaurant review, I don't have anything to say."

"Well, you either speak with me off camera, or I will bring my cameraman in here to film you. Which do you prefer? One way or another, I'm going to interview you."

I turned and looked at Walz and Morrisey for support. Both pretended not to know me, their beers lifted to their faces.

"You should talk to the two girls who were involved. They're the real story."

"I tried, but the parents refused to allow them to speak to me. There should be a law preventing them from doing that." She actually sounded serious.

"I'm sorry about that, but I only came in at the end. You need to ask someone who was there the whole time."

"But that was just the girls, wasn't it?"

"As far as I know. Yeah."

"Oh, go on, hero," said Walz from behind his beer. "You know you saw the whole thing. Talk to the pretty lady. Don't be shy. You were just saying how much you liked her."

Her face lit up like someone turned a flashlight on under her chin. "Really?" she exclaimed.

I sat forward and gave him a withering stare.

"Come on, Danny, just a few words. Don't make me have to bring the crew in here and disrupt your dinner service."

I could've told her no, banned her from the premises and threatened to call the cops, but that would've caused a scene and only motivated her further. I slid off my stool and said, "All right. But just a few words and I'm done. Right?"

She pursed her lips, as if trying to blow me a kiss. She crossed a long, sensuous line across her left breast, hesitating enough to make it more alluring. "Cross my heart, Danny."

I resisted the temptation to say, "Don't you have to have one first?"

She turned to the door and I followed. Before I'd taken two steps I stopped, leaned back and told the bartender. "He buys his own beers from now on," pointing to Walz. I went out the door like a man going to his own firing squad.

Outside, Carolyn moved to the end of the building where the same cameraman as before waited for me to join them. She gave him some direction on how she wanted it filmed and where to stand. I approached reluctantly.

"Okay, let's get this over with."

"Oh, relax, honey. It won't hurt too much. Besides, it gives us some time to spend together. Hey! You know what would really be great? If after we're done here, you take me out to dinner someplace nice."

I wasn't sure which part made me angrier. The part about taking her to dinner or the slam that my place wasn't nice. "That's not going to happen, Carolyn. Can we just get through this? I'm not comfortable being in the spotlight. Especially when I didn't have anything to do with the takedown."

"Why can't you take me out? Am I that repulsive?"

I bit my tongue. "Look, I've tried to explain it to you. I have a girlfriend. Plus, I can't just leave here. I have a lot of work to do."

"Well, drop your girlfriend and I'll meet you at your place after you get done with work. I still have to thank you for saving my life," she said, coyly.

Before I could respond, she leaned forward and put her arms around my neck. "Here, let me adjust your collar. Can't have you looking disheveled for the camera."

Just about the time I realized I wasn't wearing a shirt with a collar, she pressed her breasts against me and kissed my mouth hard. I tried not to return the kiss. No, really! But her snake-like tongue forced itself between my lips and through my teeth. I know, it seems unlikely. That's what I thought, too. But it happened. And that's my story.

I reached up and pried her interlocked fingers from my neck, then gently guided her backward. As we separated, she pulled my hands down so that the backs of them brushed across her breasts. I had to keep my distance from this woman, or she'd cause me a lot of trouble and probably some severe pain.

A devilish smile lit her face, a mischievous twinkle sparkled in her eyes and the small, but strong, tongue licked the corner of her lip. How could a mere mortal resist such charms? Fortunately, I reminded myself, I was a superhero and with superhero strength, I stepped back.

"I have to go back to work now." I backed away from her, trying to widen the gap. She stood there smiling at me. She knew she was getting to me. "Please," I begged, "don't follow me inside." I almost added, "have mercy on me." I turned and ran back up the steps and disappeared beyond, to what I hoped was the safety of the door.

Inside, I fell into my seat and hoisted my beer, drinking deeply. Replacing the bottle on the bar, I looked sideways. They were both laughing.

"Back from your date already?" quipped Walz. "Can't have been very satisfying for her."

"Funny man. You're a very funny man."

The door opened again and in she pranced. This time, however, my mother intercepted her.

"Can I help you, miss?" she said, in a stern voice. She must have seen the earlier exchange from the kitchen.

The sight of my mother holding a large, wooden spoon halted Carolyn's progress. She turned and in a very sweet girlish voice, replied, "Oh, uh, I'm just here to speak with Danny."

"He's busy working now. You call and make an

appointment next time. You should go now."

"Okay. Danny, I'll call you later." She turned on spiked heels and left in a flash.

"What are you two gawking at?" she said, catching Walz and Morrisey watch Carolyn's withdrawal. "You'd think you'd seen a pretty girl come into this place before." She shook the spoon at Morrisey. He seemed to shrink in his seat. She winked at me and went back to her domain.

"What are you smiling about, sissy boy?" Walz said. "Had to have your mother come to your rescue."

"Damn straight," I laughed, "and proud of it." Then we all laughed.

"Great ass, though!" Walz said

"Don't you get me in trouble, now," answered Morrisey.

I added, "Oh, yeah!"

We clinked bottles and smiled cautiously, not wanting my mother to catch us.

Forty-One

I called Natalie on my way home. She was just walking into the hospital to start her shift, so we didn't have much time. We arranged to meet for dinner the next evening as it was her day off.

I created a list of things to get done. One being to call some realtors as I'd promised my mother. I still had mixed emotions about selling the restaurant. I would miss it, and though I'd enjoy the free time, I had a feeling before too long I'd be very bored. Of course, there was that new superhero business.

With a load of laundry in the washer, I sat down to watch the end of the Indians' game. I did a roster count and only came up with three players still with the organization from when I'd played. Several others were still in the league or with the team in other capacities. Another sign of my getting older. A month ago I'd turned thirty-three. It didn't seem like that should be old, but suddenly, it just did.

I shifted the load to the dryer, then went outside for a run. I made it a slow-paced, almost leisurely jog. Just enough to work up a light sweat. Returning, I folded the laundry, showered and was in bed when the phone, once again, became my enemy.

"Hello," I checked the small alarm clock next to my

bed. Eleven thirty-six.

"Big trouble!" Morrisey.

"Wh-what's going on?" I stammered, sitting up on the edge of the bed.

"The kidnappers hit again. This time a lot closer to home." He paused. "They got Katy Molten, Danny. Richie's wife."

"WHAT!" I shouted, standing up.

"Look, I'll explain as we go. Just get to Flower Hospital right now. Call me on the phone when you're in the car. Go. Now!"

He left me trying to get answers from a disconnected line. I swore and ran to the bathroom. I wasn't sure if I needed to throw up or splash cold water on my face. Maybe both. Oh God! Not Katy! How could this happen? Not bothering to wipe my face from the cold water splash, I threw on some clothes, grabbed my backup Sig Sauer 9mm and an extra magazine. The Smith and Wesson .40 was already stashed in the car. Taking the stairs two at a time, I was in the car and on the street seconds later.

The hospital was minutes from my house. As I drove, I called Morrisey.

"So," I said, when he answered, "why am I going to the hospital? Is Richie back in? I thought he was home already."

"He was. Just listen. Katy drove Richie to the hospital for a checkup. Back home, she realized she could not find her wallet. She knew it was in her purse, so thinking she'd dropped it at the hospital, and not wanting to wake Richie, she left a note and went back alone looking for it. She retraced her steps. She talked to several nurses, asking if anything had been turned in. She also talked to Natalie. We know she got that far. After waking and not knowing what time she left, Richie started calling when she hadn't returned after more than an hour.

He tried her cell, but it kept ringing. He tried to get someone at the hospital to look for her. He couldn't get any cooperation, so he drove there himself.

"He found her car, still in the parking garage. After searching inside, he identified himself as a police officer and asked for security. He explained the situation and a search was organized. They found nothing. Next, they went to the security office and started checking the monitors. They're looking through those now. Carbone wanted you there in case you recognized anyone."

"Okay. I'm almost there now. Anything else?"

"Yeah. I know it won't be easy, but try to calm Richie."

"Right! If it happened to you, could you be calmed? Never mind. I already know the answer. I'll do my best. I'm parking now. Call them and let them know I'm here. Clear me through. Talk to you later."

"Right."

I parked on the top level of the garage and took the stairs down to the walkway that led into the main building. My pace was quick and my mind occupied. Down at the far end of the hall, a figure in light green scrubs walked away from me. Something about the way he moved struck a chord. I pushed it aside as being unimportant.

I neared the information desk and turned toward the security office. The man ahead glanced over his shoulder, saw me, and paused. I couldn't be sure, but he reacted as though he recognized me. A look of panic crossed his face and his last steps before disappearing around the corner were running.

Curious behavior, but I didn't have time to pursue it. At that moment, someone called to me.

"Are you Mr. Roth?" A uniformed guard approached, waving me over. I gave a last look down the empty hallway and followed. He ushered me into a large three-room suite where banks of security monitors lined the tables and walls. There had to be twenty of them showing various aspects of the hospital. Two hospital security guards sat at work tables scanning the various displays. The head of security was in the adjacent room with Richie, Carbone, and another detective I didn't know. Several Sylvania policemen were spread out around the room watching the screens and waiting for instructions.

We didn't waste time with introductions. The older man at the controls of a playback recorder motioned me over and said, "Look at this. Tell me what you see."

Katy came into view walking down a hall. They all looked so alike it was difficult at first to determine where she was. The cameras had blind spots and she disappeared for maybe two seconds then reappeared. She went through a set of glass doors. Now I knew where she was, recognizing the doors to the walkway that led to the parking garage. I'd just come in that way. The camera followed her to the doors but not past.

"Is that it?" I asked, a little anxious. I reached out and squeezed Richie's shoulder. He grabbed my hand and held it tight as if it were a lifeline.

"Hold on. These just came in from the garage," the security chief said. He pushed a button and the screen next to the first one showed a set of legs. They could be Katy's, but it was difficult to be positive. A car broke the picture as it drove by. It cleared and a more distant picture showed more of the person, though still hard to tell, with the picture so grainy. But we could see more of her now. She was the same height and general build as Katy. Her hair on the black and white picture could have been blonde, but it was certainly the right length and style.

I turned to Richie. He nodded. "It's her."

The chief said, "Part of the problem is the lack of

light in the garage at night time."

As we watched, another vehicle blocked the camera. Katy was on the opposite side. The vehicle stopped for seconds, and when it cleared, the woman was no longer in view.

"Whoa!" the Sylvania detective said, "Run that back."

"Doing it now," the chief said, working the various buttons and knobs.

Richie, Carbone and I all leaned forward for a closer look. We watched again as a white panel van with no side windows, pulled up. I turned to Carbone, but he was already on his radio calling dispatch to put out an alert. The other suit in the room did the same for Sylvania.

The chief called one of his men and gave commands. The two of them coordinated the monitors to show slow motion and more close-up photos.

"Yeah!" exclaimed the chief. "Here. Look here. You can see the van dip slightly here," he pointed at the screen, "and here. As if someone was getting in or out of the van. It's very quick. Mack, back it up and pull back. Let's see what we get through the windshield."

They worked while I asked, "What's the time on these tapes?"

"20-38."

"Eight-thirty," I said to myself."

He nodded. "We have her arriving at just before twenty." He continued to move knobs. The front of the van appeared, but no matter how hard they tried, they could not get a better shot of the driver, although there appeared to be only one person in the front seat. I left them and went out into the main room where the monitors were still on real time. I heard Carbone ask, "Do you have complete coverage? Can we get a different angle and catch a glimpse of the license number?"

I put my hands behind my head and looked toward the ceiling, offering up a silent prayer for Katy. Richie came out and stood next to me, fear etched deeply into his ashen face. We looked at each other, too numb to speak. Finally, his face crumpled and he cracked. I grabbed him as he fell forward sobbing.

"Oh God, Danny, what am I going to do? Please tell me she'll be all right. Please tell me this isn't about getting revenge on me. Oh God! My poor Katy."

He slumped almost to the floor and I half dragged, half carried him to one of the chairs by the wall next to the outside door. I knelt in front of him.

"It's not over, Richie. We'll find these bastards. Don't you dare give up. Your family needs you. So does Katy. You need to be as strong for her as she was for you. You hear me?"

He put his face in his hands and rocked back and forth. I worried he would have a meltdown.

I stood and paced across the room, trying to think of something I could do, but kept coming up blank. I turned at the far end of the room when something moving on the screen caught my attention. I moved closer and leaned over the tech's shoulder for a closer look.

"Excuse me, sir, but—"

"Shh! Who's that, there?"

"Sir?"

"That man, right there. Who is he?" I touched the screen. The memory flooded back. The night Tony and I came up to see Richie. I was in the hall with Katy and that strange little man was checking out her ass. That was the man right there. On the screen. He might be nothing more than a pervert, but what more did I have?

"I'm not sure, sir."

"What do you mean, you're not sure? Don't you

know everyone who works here?" I yelled in frustration. The man on the screen moved fast, constantly looking over his shoulder, as if someone was chasing him.

"Well, no, not everyone. That's why they have to wear their identification badges."

Hearing the tension in my voice, Carbone poked his head out of the other room. Even Richie listened. I grew anxious watching the man on the monitor. He was afraid of something.

"What's the problem?" Carbone asked.

"We need to catch that guy. Where is he right now?" The security guard hesitated not knowing if he should respond to me or not. After all, I wasn't his boss.

"NOW!" I shouted. My need for speed made me tense. "Where is he?"

The chief yelled from the other room, "Tell him what he needs to know, Bert. And you, stop yelling at my men."

The security guard said, "He's heading toward the parking garage from the ground floor level where employee parking is."

"What is it?" Carbone asked again.

"Maybe nothing, just a hunch. Maybe grasping straws, but I need that man stopped. Call someone. Please!"

The Sylvania detective came out and watched me now. They all stared at me as if I were crazy. I knew they wanted an explanation, but time was running out. A fire burned inside me like a furnace. I threw my hands up. "UH!" I looked at all of them and something jumped into my head. I began to ramble to myself. Maybe a piece just fell into the puzzle. Maybe. But again, what else did I have? I felt ready to explode.

"Okay! Okay! Listen. Just please do this. Check where the other girls were before they were kidnapped. See if any of them were here any time within a week before they were abducted." I looked from detective to detective. I pointed toward the escaping man. "He could be the key."

The Sylvania detective became very animated. He turned back into the room and instructed the two cops, "Go with this man and do what he asks." They moved to the door and he added, "The Mayor's daughter was here for a blood test the morning she disappeared."

FORTY-TWO

It was all I needed. I yelled over my shoulder on the way out, "Check the others ... and stop that man."

The three of us sprinted down the hall. We were joined by a hospital security man who led us to the door to the garage. We burst through it, slamming it backward with a loud crash. My phone rang in my hand. I answered while running.

"He's in a small car, looks like maybe a Honda. Light-colored. He's making the turn into the exit lane. We have a call into hospital security to cut him off. The Sylvania Police are on the way." Carbone disconnected not wanting to delay me.

"We need to get to the exit before he gets his car out of the garage," I yelled and took off across the grass along the outside wall at the back of the garage. I was in the lead as we closed in on the end of the structure. Adrenaline flooded my veins. Desperation ignited.

I rounded the corner, my hand dragging along the wall to give me control of my turn. The car crossed in front of me. I slowed. The overhead lights along the road made it difficult to see at first. The next cone of light illuminated his face. It was him.

Changing direction, I raced straight for him. I wasn't sure what I would do since my weapons were in the car. I just ran right at him. He turned and saw me closing on him.

Surprise, recognition, then panic appeared on his face. He accelerated and pulled away. I was six feet from him as he sped up. Without any thought going through my crazed brain, out of desperation, I launched myself at the car. I seemed to stick there, attached to the side for a second, before I slowly slid down and peeled off like a flattened Coyote from a Roadrunner cartoon. I was fortunate the fleeing car didn't run over my arm. I hit the ground on my back and rolled several times. If I were stunned or in pain, my fear for Katy blocked me from feeling anything.

The two Sylvania cops had their weapons drawn but were afraid to fire. The headlights from an oncoming car momentarily blinded them. Once the car passed, their only target was the retreating taillights.

Despite my scrapes and bruises, I ran as hard as I could for my car. The two cops followed. The security guy took out his hand-held radio and reported in.

In the absence of stairs at this end of the garage, we ran up the ramp to the rear of the garage. I ripped open the door leading to the stairs and took them two at a time.

I was sucking in air hard by the time I reached the roof but did not slow down. We piled into my car and I took the ramp down doing fifty. Twice I almost sideswiped the wall. I bottomed out leaving the garage, sending sparks flying. Screeching into the turn, we passed the security guy, who pointed the direction the car had turned. I followed the winding hospital road until hitting the main street outside the hospital. There I redialed Carbone.

"Where to?"

"North on Harroun. West on Monroe. That's as far as the guard could see. We have other units converging on the area. Hold on ... yeah ... good ... okay. Danny, there are two cars blocking Main Street at Monroe as we speak. He can't get through there. That doesn't leave many options. Keep your eyes peeled."

"Keep a lookout along here, guys," I said. "They have a roadblock across Monroe and Main. If they don't stop him there, he has to be in a parking lot somewhere."

"Unless he turned up Summit, heading toward Michigan."

"Shit! That's right. One of you call and have them relay to somebody in Michigan. If he gets across the border, we'll need help." Then into my phone, "Carbone, did you hear that? We're turning onto Monroe now." I ran a red light to get on Monroe. "If he went straight, the roadblock should have him now. Or at least see him."

"We're checking, hold on ... negative, Danny. They don't see him. He couldn't have gotten through, but he might have turned off."

"I'm going to gamble on Summit." I could see some taillights. There weren't many and some could be eliminated by size. More and more brake lights flashed on as the cars backed up at the roadblock ahead. "At this point, we got nothing to lose. We have to cover all options. If he's in the traffic at the roadblock, they'll catch him, but if he turns off, he'll get away. I'm turning toward Michigan." I accelerated. "Carbone, get someone at the hospital to identify this guy."

"Already working on it."

I had a sudden thought. "What happens if we find him?"

"What?"

"You heard me. What happens if we find him? What will you do?"

"Not my jurisdiction. Hold on, I'll ask."

A minute later, I got my answer, and it was what I feared. "The usual, Danny. Questioned and depending on what we learn, arrested and processed. We'll start an investigation into his life and try to negotiate a deal for information."

"Bullshit!" I exclaimed. "Those girls don't have that much time. They could be out of the area or worse, the country, by the time a deal gets worked out."

"I know. But our hands are tied here. We have to follow the law or lose the case."

"What's more important, losing the case or the girls?" I swung a hard right onto Summit and pressed the pedal down. The powerful BMW leaped forward throwing the two officers back in their seats.

Silence. "What are you proposing? No, wait. Don't say it." More silence. "I'm having trouble hearing you. Your signal must be breaking up. Call me back. If you can't get through, keep trying."

He was gone. I thought about his words and liked him all the more for his decision. He understood the problem and basically washed his hands of the solution. I looked in the mirror at the two men's faces. They'd only heard my half of the discussion, but understood the situation. Now the problem was whether or not they'd be okay with what I might do. I couldn't stop and let them out, but I did have another idea. I punched up my phone book and scrolled down until I landed on Doug's number.

He answered on the first ring. "What's up, buddy? Is there another chance to shoot someone?"

"Doug, shut up and listen. We're chasing a suspect, probably up into Michigan. I'm going to need your assistance if we catch him."

"Where?"

"I just crossed into Michigan on Summit."

"On my way. Don't shoot him."

I laid the phone down and maneuvered through an S curve. The car slid dangerously, threatening to leave the road, or flip. The road turned right then left, forcing me to slow. On the more open two-lane road, I floored the accelerator again. The problem with farm country was the lack of lighting.

"There!" shouted the cop next to me, pointing down the road. "A car just stopped at Stearns Road. Floor it." He got on his radio to report the finding. I heard him say, "In pursuit," but missed the rest.

All we had to go on was the brake lights flashing a little less than a mile in front of us.

"You guys know what's at stake here. I need this guy to talk and now."

"Hey, man," the cop next to me said, "let's catch this bastard. We can figure out what to do after we catch him."

I nodded. We shot forward at full throttle, closing the gap. I expected the man to turn east and get on the expressway. Instead, he turned west on Stearns, heading into more rural areas. Now I wasn't sure we were chasing the right man. It didn't make any sense. Still, I continued on. I couldn't take the chance, even if only slim, that it might be him.

Then I had another thought. If it was him, I wasn't so sure we wanted to catch him too soon. It might be better if we kept our distance and followed. Maybe he'd lead us to where the women were being held.

My phone went off again. Carbone. "You were right on the money, Roth. Two of the other victims had been to the hospital within the last week. Don't let him get away."

"We're on it. I thought your phone was having problems."

"What did you say? I'm having problems with my phone." Click.

I got to Stearns and turned after him, his taillights less than a mile ahead now. I called Doug again.

"Direct me," he said.

"He's heading toward two-twenty-three. Where are you?"

"Perfect. I'm coming up two-twenty-three. With any luck, I'll intercept him."

"Yeah, about that. Don't take him until you hear

from me. Okay!"

"Uh, sure, I guess."

"Trust me. I'll get back to you."

My passengers looked at me. "What are you thinking?" the one in the back asked.

"What if this guy leads us to the rest of them? I mean, first, we have to make sure it's our guy. But if it is, what if he's joining up with the others?"

"Tough call. Especially if we lose him."

"Call your boss. I'll call mine. Best we have an answer before we close on him."

"Carbone, what if this guy is running to meet the others? Should we intercept or tail him?"

"Fuck!" I waited. "Hold on." In the background, I heard someone else say, "Fuck!" Must be detective code for something. Probably for something that was fucked.

"Do you think he's made you yet?"

"Don't know, but if he's looking, he's probably not expecting a BMW to chase him. It's dark and he can't make out who's behind him."

"Good point. Hold … where are you now?"

"He's stopping at the four-way stop at Stearns and two-twenty-three. He's signaling a turn, believe it or not, heading north. I'm less than a half mile back."

The headlights of the car we chased washed over an oversize, red pickup truck. Doug had arrived; he slammed on his brakes when he saw the car. The truck slid, fishtailing from side to side, trying to come under control. The man in the Honda changed course. He shot straight across the road instead of turning right.

"Well, we're made … I'm taking him now."

"Might be for the best," said the cop next to me. "Do it."

The man in the back added, "It's definitely a Honda."

FORTY-THREE

I shut down the phone and concentrated on catching our prey. The road had small rises and dips, making it difficult to follow, and it was hard to see what we were driving over in the dark. Also, the road was not very well maintained. The many bumps and potholes made driving at high speeds difficult. The lighter-weight Honda bounced out of control. The brake lights kept going on, allowing me to gain steadily. We closed to under a hundred yards. Doug was right on our tail. And I mean right on our tail. If he were any closer, we'd be in the same vehicle.

Within thirty yards of the Honda, I told the officer next to me to lean out of the window and put a couple of shots in the Honda's direction. I didn't expect him to hit anything at this distance and speed, bouncing around as we were, but it might spook the man enough to make him stop.

"Just don't blow him up," I said.

He leaned out and steadied his aim as best he could. Just as he was about to squeeze off his first shot, I hit a pothole. The bounce sent us airborne, almost dislodging the man from the window. I grabbed a leg and pulled. He hung out the window, his head dangling dangerously close to the road.

His partner leaned over the seat, grabbed his belt, and we managed to haul him back in. The poor man must have seen his life pass before his eyes. "Thanks for slowing down for me."

I said, "No problem," before I realized he was being sarcastic.

To his credit, he leaned out to try again. This time he got off several shots. One looked like it might have made contact. Brake lights flashed on longer now.

The ground was more open and level at this point on the road. A loud roaring noise of machinery next to my car startled me: Doug's truck passed me. Evidently, he had grown impatient with the chase. Either that, or he'd seen his fellow officer getting to shoot at someone and was afraid he'd be shut out of the fun once more.

He drove along the dirt shoulder of the road, which must have been in better condition than the road because he wasn't bouncing nearly as much as we were. He closed on the Honda, crossed in front of me and used his bumper to push the Honda sideways.

The car soared through the air, landing on the opposite side of the drainage ditch and into a plowed field, bounced twice, and came to a stop. I hit the brakes, barely missing Doug's truck. As we watched, the Honda drove across the field away from us.

Doug took off in hot pursuit. He hit the bottom of the ditch hard but had better suspension than the Honda. His large tires quickly grabbed dirt and made up the gap. I got out, grabbed my Sig Sauer and ran into the field. The others were slower but followed. One of them said, "Shit! Here we go again!"

The ground was soft, almost as bad as running on sand. Up ahead, Doug caught the Honda and cut in front, blocking it by running his oversize tires up and over the front end like a monster truck. It was incredible to see. That put a halt to any forward progress by the Honda. Doug jumped down from the cab and straightened up. Seeing Doug's size, the man exited his car and fled, screaming, without looking in front of him and ran right into my arms. I hit him with a forearm and dropped him to the ground.

"Where are they, asshole?" I shouted, dropping on top of him, pinning him to the ground.

"Please! Please! I know nothing. Why are you doing this? What have I done?"

"You know what you've done, you sleazebag. Tell me where they are or I'll beat you to death."

"No!" He covered his head as I attempted to push it into the soft dirt. "You cannot do this. I have done nothing."

"Oh, you've done something, all right. And trust me on this, you are going to tell me, or you will feel pain like you've never felt before."

The others caught up to us and stood watching. One of the Sylvania cops cleared his throat to get my attention.

"Ah, police. You must help me. This man has attacked me. Arrest him."

"We can't do this, Roth. We have to take him in."

"Yes, yes, take me in. Save me from these crazy men."

My crazed, insane look stopped the prisoner from saying any more. "No! He stays with me. He talks or dies." I chambered a round, cocked the hammer and jammed it under his chin. He shrieked and flailed his arms and legs. I wasn't sure I had enough control over myself not to pull the trigger. The adrenaline pumped double shots.

One of the cops was on his phone while the other approached with his hands up in front of him to show there was no intent to attack or harm. Doug stood over me and held a hand up to the advancing officer.

"Doug, we can't allow this. It could mean all of our careers."

"Who's going to argue about it, the Mayor?" asked Doug.

"And it could mean those girls' lives. Or worse," I said.

"What do you mean, worse?"

"Come on, man, you can't be that dense. Why do you think those girls were chosen in the first place? What do you think their lives will be like if these bastards get away? Do you understand what they will do to them? They'll be some rich guy's plaything until he gets tired of his new toy and throws her away. Get with it, man. We may be the only hope these women have."

"Is he for real here, Doug?"

"Yeah, man, he is."

"Not to mention they not only have your Mayor's daughter but now, they have a cop's wife."

Doug cocked his head in a question.

"They got Richie's wife, Doug."

His jaw dropped open then snapped shut, his face the epitome of anger. I stood and pushed my captive down with my foot. "Look, I know it's not right, but I have to get that information. If you can't handle it, I'm asking you to walk away. File charges against me later if you want to."

"No. If what you say is true, fuck that asshole. Do what you got to do. We'll be by the car."

I turned to Doug. "You all right with this?"

"More than all right." He bent down and lifted the petrified man off the ground. "In fact, so all right, I insist on doing the honors myself. Come on, little buddy, let's go have us a little talk." He tucked the man under his arm like a running back carrying a football and headed for a copse of trees twenty yards away. The man whimpered for help. I stopped them with a slap across the head.

While Doug went to play with his new friend, I searched the Honda, finding a cell phone on the front seat. Beneath it was a copy of yesterday's local newspaper. I opened the phone and checked the call history. Almost all of the calls coming in were restricted. The man made several calls earlier in the day which showed numbers. I flipped my phone open and called Carbone.

"What d'ya got?"

"I've got a phone. If I give you the numbers, can you check them?"

"Give 'em."

"Anything else?" he said when he'd written them down

"Not yet. I'll call when something breaks." A scream emerged from the woods. "Sounds like something just did." I hung up and trotted toward the trees, not entirely comfortable with leaving the information-gathering process to Doug. He literally didn't know his own strength. I had a scary vision of an old cartoon where the big strong dolt held two halves of a toy, saying, "Duh, gee, George, it broke."

It was so dark in the trees, the only way to get my bearings was to listen for the whimpering and occasional cries of pain from our, uh, informant. Doug had the man pinned by the neck against a tree, dangling three feet off the ground. The man couldn't breathe, let alone speak.

"Ah, Doug, if he isn't breathing, he can't talk."

"Huh, is that right? So you want me to let the little bastard breathe? You're too nice." He let the man drop to the ground, gasping for air. He stomped past, whispering, "Call if you need me."

Ah, good cop, bad cop. He had me worried for a moment. I walked over and squatted next to where the man sat sucking in air, holding his throat.

"Okay, here's the deal. We know all about you and your friends. We know that you spotted the girls and the others did the actual abductions. So technically, you're not in as much trouble as they are. We know all about Hasheem Turfe." I couldn't be sure in the dark, but I thought I saw him flinch at the mention of that name. "The only thing we don't know is where they are. You can help us and help yourself ..."

The man shook his head. "No, no, no."

"Unh-uh, don't start that with me. We both know that you know. If you want to get out of these woods alive, you need to talk to me now."

"You can't hurt me. You are a policeman. You won't kill me. It is the law."

"I hate to break it to you, but we're not cops. The other two were, but we sent them away. It's just you and us. No one will ever know what happens here tonight. Whether you live or die will depend solely on you. There won't be a trial. You either talk and live, or don't and die. It's that simple."

"But I know nothing of what you want."

"Okay, if that's how you want to play it." I stood up and started to walk away. "Doug," I yelled to the darkness, "he's all yours."

"No," wailed the man. He tried to rise and run, but out of the darkness, Doug came flying like some demon and tackled the man. He pinned him and began slapping his face. The cries grew in pitch, pain, and desperation.

I walked far enough away from the scene to call Carbone. Although, as loud as the poor guy screamed, I could've been home and still heard his cries.

"Anything?"

"It'll take a little time, but it's in the works. What have you got?"

"I know this is touchy, but I need the Sylvania detective to pass a message to the two cops with me." I spelled out what I wanted them to do, hung up and walked back. I was just in time to hear the man crying out, "Okay! Okay! Please, no more."

"Take a break, Doug. My man here wants to talk to me."

Again I squatted down next to him. He rolled to his side and spit out blood. At least I thought it was blood. It was kind of hard to tell. I gave him a minute to compose himself.

"So, what was it you wanted to say?"

"You're going to kill me anyway. Why should I talk?"

"Well, because you want the pain to stop? And just maybe I'll let you live. In fact, if you tell me what I need to hear, I will let you walk out of here and disappear."

"You would never do that. You are lying to me."

I was getting seriously pissed. Every second's delay could be taking the girls farther away. "Last chance, bud. I don't give a damn about you. I want the girls back and I want Turfe. I'm not a cop. I'm not gonna arrest you. Tell me where they are and when we find them, you'll be free to go." I watched the wheels spinning behind his eyes as he thought about this. "But I'll tell you this. If you lie or if you take so long to answer that I miss getting the girls back, I will rip you apart piece by bloody piece. I will leave your remains scattered in these woods for the animals to feast on. I may even strap you down alive and let them eat you while you're still able to feel their tiny teeth tearing into you. My patience is at an end. Talk, or I call my friend back."

"You don't understand. They have my wife and children," he gasped. "They will kill them."

FORTY-FOUR

Well, that kind of changed things.

I sighed, squatted next to him and softened my voice "Tell me more. Who has them and where?" Tears welled, his expression one of desperation and defeat. "Talk to me. We may be the only ones who can save your family. These people do not leave witnesses. Help me to help them."

"This man came to me and said he needed my help. If I did well, he would reward me. If I refused or caused a problem, he would take my wife and two daughters to replace the ones he lost. All he wanted me to do was find women who looked a certain way and pass along the information. They had someone watching from outside. They would follow the women home watch them and learn their routines. He wanted six blondes, then they would go."

I called Carbone. "You had better be telling me the truth right now." I reached down and grabbed his ID badge, which was still swinging from a lanyard around his neck. I slid it off and looked at the photo. It was him. Kahlil Saher.

"I swear it is the truth."

"Hold on," I said into the phone. "Where are they taking them?"

"I'm not sure. But they have two blue vans parked in my garage. I think they will use these to move them. The two men at my house were getting the vehicles ready when I left for work today. I was to report to them if there was anyone getting too close."

"Who did you call?"

"I had a number to leave a message. I reported early that there was nothing. I had a bad feeling when I saw you, so I told my supervisor I was ill and had to go home. I wanted to call on the way, but when I saw the roadblock, I got afraid and didn't get a chance."

"Did you hear any of that?" I asked Carbone.

"Yeah, most of it. Enough to get the picture, anyway."

"We need to get a SWAT team to this man's house. There could still be someone there." I thought of something else. I turned back to the man and asked, "What time do they expect you home? For that matter, where is home?"

"I get off at three and I'm usually home by three-thirty. They keep my family together in one room so they can watch them easier." He told me his address.

"We don't have much time," I said to Carbone. "We need to find out where they're heading. His name is Kahlil Saher." I gave him the address in Toledo and let him get on with organizing the raid.

I stood thinking, then called Tony.

"Oh, bro, this better be good. If you only knew what this woman was doing to me right now."

"Tony, they took Richie's wife, Katy."

"Fuck! I should have known it'd be really good. Okay, what do you need me to do? Ouch! Hey, you gotta stop now, babe."

"What are the phone exchanges for Dearborn?"

"Dearborn? Ah, let's see, it's 313 in that area. But the numbers vary. In the east end, a lot of them start with 58."

I checked the phone I'd confiscated from the Honda and ran down the numbers again: several with a 313 area code and one 58. I showed them to the man. He acknowledged they were numbers he called to report when he had a girl for them to watch.

"Shit, T, road trip. Meet me at twenty-three and Stearns ASAP. Call Big Vic for some referrals. We're going to need an army up there." I clicked off before he could reply.

Back to Carbone. "Two of those numbers are in Dearborn, Michigan," he told me. "One's a land line the other probably a disposable cell.

"I'm going up there. If they've already gone, there's a good chance that's where they're heading. It makes sense. With a large Lebanese and Syrian population throughout the city, they'd have a lot of support up there to help hide and move the victims. Can you call up there to get the ball rolling, maybe get me a contact name and an intro?"

"Yeah, but I'm going to have to wake some bigwigs to do the greasing. I'll get back to you on that, too. We've got tentative approval on SWAT, the assemble call went out just now. Keep me posted on what you're doing. And for God's sake, remember you're not in a jurisdiction where we can help you. Don't get arrested ... and try not to shoot anybody!"

Sheesh! Did everyone think I was some sort of Wild West gunslinger or something?

"Hey, guys," I yelled to the two Sylvania cops. "I need you here now."

The two cops jogged up. "What's up?"

"I need you to babysit our friend here. Keep him safe and away from his home and any phones. Keep him away from the station, too, in case word leaks out somehow. Use my car, the keys are in it. I'll call you when it's clear. And, thanks, guys. Let's go, Doug. I need a lift."

We jogged back to his truck. "Where to?" he asked.

"The Stearns Road overpass at twenty-three."

He turned the truck around and headed east. "You sure you want to do this? It's not like you have any authority anywhere. You're carrying a gun, hopefully with a permit."

"Fortunately," I said, "Michigan has reciprocal carry laws."

"You plan on chasing down bad guys like you're some bounty hunter?" Doug said. "I'm not putting you down, 'cause I've seen you in action, but maybe it's time to leave it to the real cops."

His comments stung me. Heat flashed across my face. He was right. I was nothing more than an ex-cop in the middle of the whole thing. I tried to let my anger flow out before I spoke, but too late. My mouth worked faster than my brain.

"I may not be a cop, but I'm in this whether they, or you, like it or not."

"Easy, tiger, I'm not the bad guy here. I'm just pointing out the facts."

"Well, here's a fact that keeps running through my mind. They've got Richie's wife, Doug." Something caught in my throat. I cleared it. "You played with him, too, man. He's our friend. That's what friends do, Doug. They help out in times of need. Richie and Katy need all the help they can get. If they get her out of the area, we may never see her again. Can you live with that?

"I'm in the middle of this thing, up to my eyes. I'm seeing it through, right or wrong, legal or not. They took his wife! They have to pay for that. Do you know what they'll do to her?"

"Okay! Okay! I was just saying. I'm in all the way. Let's do this." A silence loomed between us as we let the tension fade. After a long moment, he said, "And for the record, if I were ever in a jam, you'd be the first person I'd want coming to my rescue."

We neared the entrance ramps to the expressway.

I brushed my eyes with my fingers and they came away wet. I kept thinking of how I'd feel if it were Natalie. I knew if I ever caught who took her, they would die. I felt the same emotional response about Katy. She was a friend. I couldn't even conceive of not trying with everything I had to save her.

I made a call and instructed Doug to stop. We waited about five minutes when a dark SUV shot up the ramp and pulled next to us. Tony lowered his window and nodded, a serious, all-business look on his face. Marissa sat next to him.

"What's the plan?"

"I'm only speculating here, but if there's no sign of these guys in town, I think they're heading toward Dearborn. SWAT is entering a house they might have been using. Two ways to play it. Sit and wait until we hear what they find, or start now to get a head start, in case they find the place empty."

"You're running the show, what's your decision?"

I wanted his input, but he was right. I had already decided what I wanted to do. Sitting still was too hard. "We go now."

He nodded. "Good choice."

Morrisey drove up at this point. "Oh yeah," Tony said, 'forgot to tell you, I brought some help."

"Wow!" I said. Tony had come a long way from the days when he didn't trust cops. I guess sleeping with one changes your mind.

"It was my idea," offered Marissa.

I nodded. "That explains it."

"Eat shit!" he said.

Morrisey got out of his car. "What's the plan?"

"Are you the voice of reason in all of this madness? Are you here to stop me?"

"I'm always the voice of reason, but I'm off duty and on my own time. Consider me a liaison."

I gave him a quick smile and told him what I planned.

"Let's take two vehicles. Ride with me and coordinate by phone. Do we know what we're looking for?"

"Two dark-colored vans. Neither has side windows. The backs are probably tinted to prevent anyone seeing in." I climbed down from the truck. "Questions?" No one said a word. "Then let's rock. Thanks, Doug. I appreciate all your help."

I climbed in with Morrisey. He put the car in gear and was about to drive off when the back door opened and Doug scrunched his huge frame into the tight space.

"What are you doing, Doug?"

"What does it look like, pea brain? I'm coming. I'm not missing the fun this time."

"Doug, what about your career? What about those things you said to me in the truck? I don't want you getting in trouble over this."

"In the truck, I was checking your resolve. As far as the job goes, hell, if I save the Mayor's daughter, he'll probably give me a medal and her hand in marriage. Besides, I smell gunplay here. The chance to shoot someone far outweighs having a job."

"You're a scary man, Doug."

"Yep! Let's roll."

FORTY-FIVE

Kahlil Saher had said when he called home a little after eleven, the men were still there. They allowed him a few moments to speak with his wife. She told him their daughters were fine. They had been ignored all day. His wife had told him it looked like the men were getting ready to move. They spent a lot of time in the garage.

It was almost one in the morning. If the kidnappers had left immediately after Kahlil's call, they'd have nearly a two-hour head start. The drive to Dearborn would take an hour. We plotted out the possible courses they might take. The consensus was they were unaware of our pursuit and would not have taken evasive action. They'd stay on the main roads and keep their speed below the legal limit. I had Tony call some of his father's friends in the Dearborn area and start a lookout patrol for the vans. With Morrisey's light on the roof, we made good time.

From the back seat, Doug said, "I don't suppose you two stellar intellects thought about the fact this route passes Detroit Metro Airport."

I had thought about that. If they took the girls to one of the smaller private or charter lines, we could be way too late. I looked at Morrisey. He frowned.

"Anything we can do to check on that?" I asked.

"What, you mean, like see if any flights are scheduled for the Middle East marked Human Trafficking Express?"

"There must be someone you can call to have them check private charters. Airport security is much more than rent-a-cops now."

"I know. I know," he snapped. "I'm just thinking. With the head start they may have, they could be long gone by now. I'm afraid for those women."

"All the more reason to call now. We still may be able to stop them."

He punched in a number. "I'm calling the captain. This will have to be handled by someone further up the chain of command than me."

The captain had been asleep, but fortunately was not one of those who said stuff like "Do you know what time it is?" or "This had better be good." Instead, he asked Morrisey what the problem was and what he was needed to do.

After Morrisey explained the details, Captain Jenkins told him he'd see what he could arrange and get back to him. He suggested in the meantime, contacting the Michigan Highway Patrol and see if they'd start looking. A good idea, except we still weren't sure what we were looking for. Still, it was better to have them alerted and involved for when the word came about what the traffickers were driving. At least they'd be in motion.

We turned off twenty-three and drove east on I-94. Five minutes from the turnoff for the airport, Morrisey got a call from Carbone. He put it on speaker and handed it to me.

"I hear you joined the pursuit," he said. "What are you doing so far into Wolverine Country? As big a Buckeye fan as you are, I'd have thought that'd be like spraying holy water on a vampire. Your skin would be burning."

"It's joke time now, is it? Nothing better to report?" replied Morrisey.

"Relax, old timer, don't have a stroke. SWAT went in several minutes ago. Their commander reports the house is empty. They must have taken the family with them, hopefully to use as further incentive for Saher's continued cooperation. Otherwise, they may have already disposed of them.

"There were definite signs of more than just the family staying there. The family was in one bedroom. The other three bedrooms had mattresses spread out on the floors. Could have been up to six other men ... or the kidnapping victims ... or maybe a combination of the two. Anyway, it looks like our man Saher was telling the truth.

"They found a license plate. They probably switched the plates with a stolen set. The plate we found is registered to Ronald and Rose Taylor of Rossford. It belongs on a dark blue 2009 Ford Econoline van Mr. Taylor used to deliver carpet for his installation business. They reported it stolen earlier yesterday morning. It has no windows on either side and tinted ones in the back."

"Okay, that at least confirms what we're looking for. We need to put out alerts immediately."

"Already done. There's one more thing. Someone, we're guessing Saher's wife, kept track of the time on a piece of paper she hid under the bed in the master suite. She marked off the time every five minutes they were there. I think she was trying to tell her husband how long they had been gone. The last time written down was twelve-twenty-five. If that's when they loaded them into the van, we can probably add five minutes and assume they left about twelve-thirty."

"So they have just over a half hour head start. That's encouraging. Harder to board a plane and get out of Dodge in that time."

"That's what I'm thinking. With any luck, less than that."

"I hear ya. Okay, we're pulling into the airport right now. Are we cleared?"

"Wait." He talked with someone else. Morrisey pulled over while we waited for directions.

"Hey, Mike, we just got word from the chief of the Metro security department. He assures us that currently there are no planes departing that match our criteria. He will send officers to all of the smaller companies. No one flies without a flight plan, so he'll be notified if something happens. He'll make sure that all charters and private aircraft are checked before departure."

"Where does that leave us?" Doug wanted to know.

Good question. I thought on it. "Doug, call Tony." I gave him the number. "Tell him to get back on the road and look for one, maybe two, dark blue Ford vans. We'll follow in a minute."

Morrisey said to Carbone. "Any ideas? We don't have a lot to go on here."

"I know. I'm still waiting to hear back on the phone numbers. If they don't pan out ..."

He didn't bother saying the obvious. We could be screwed.

"I still think it has some connection to Dearborn," I said. "What do we have to lose?"

Forty-Six

Without a word, Morrisey swung the car around and in minutes we were back on I-94, speeding east. We were about twenty minutes from Dearborn. Tony and I had grown up there. It had three distinct sections of town. The east side was predominantly Italian. The south side was mostly Lebanese and Syrian, while the west side was basically rich. No one ever seemed to notice that we didn't have a north side. In fact, Detroit surrounded Dearborn on three sides.

We lived on the east side, which, in the years since we had been gone, had become primarily Middle Eastern. Most of the places we'd known no longer existed, or had been converted to an Arab business of some type. It made me feel like the place where I had grown up no longer existed, as if it had all been a dream.

We exited onto Shaffer Road going north. We came to the downtown area around City Hall. Michigan Avenue was once the main shopping center for Dearborn. Not wanting to drive up and down every street in the city, we pulled into a gas station and bought a street map. We sat in the car and pored over the map. I pointed out all of the residential areas as we discussed where they might be.

Doug said, "They're gonna be in a house or group of houses in a neighborhood where the residents are all Arabic-speaking."

"Maybe, but let's not stereotype. Just because they're Middle Eastern doesn't make them bad. If someone sees something that looks wrong, they'll call the police."

"That's naïve thinking. Just being good or bad doesn't define the lines. Indifference and fear controls people's lives. They may see something but will choose not to get involved."

Morrisey tended to agree with him.

In the middle of our disagreement, Morrisey's phone sounded. By the expression on his face, it was important. He listened and nodded silently to the person on the other end.

Finally, he started taking part in the conversation. He motioned for me to check the map. "Uh-huh, yeah, we got a map right here. What's the … yeah, 3297 Oakman Blvd. Okay, we'll find it and check it out. Don't worry, we won't. I'll call you." I knew exactly where it was. I found it on the map and refreshed my memory about the surrounding area and the side streets that connected. Not that I would remember every street after thirteen years, but Oakman I knew. It was the main street in that section of town and I remembered the street was commercial, not residential.

Morrisey filled us in on what he learned. "The phone is listed as belonging to a corporation, Old World Bakery, specializing in Middle Eastern breads and pastries. They sell and deliver pita breads and baklava all over the state and into northwest Ohio. It appears to be a large, profitable company. With all the delivery trucks they'd need to cover that much territory, they'd have the perfect cover to transport anything without drawing undue attention."

"Ah! Here it is." I displayed a website on my phone. Morrisey leaned closer and Doug bent over the seat to get a better look, then I called Tony.

"T, we got a possible location. Where are you?"

"Driving around the old neighborhood. It'll take forever searching this way. I got some of the boys from the area driving around looking, too. Wha'dya got?"

"Old World Bakery on Oakman Boulevard. Ever hear of it? It's between Michigan and Ford, down the street from Italian-American Hall where we had our high school sports award banquets. Maybe a block north."

"Yeah, I've heard of it. I've actually been there. They have a walk-in retail business in the front on Oakman. The commercial portion is in the back. I think you have to drive down a paved alley or something to get into the back. If I remember right, it's all fenced. They could easily see anyone approaching by car. The alley entrance is between a couple of side streets. Ruby and ... oh hell, I can't remember the other one. The building fronts a residential area. A street of houses backs up to the property. You can see the place from the backyard of one of those houses. If we're gonna check it out, we'll have to be on foot."

"Let's drive by first," said Morrisey. "I want to see this building before we do anything else."

That sounded right to us. It was a five-minute ride to the bakery. Tony would come toward us from the north. We approached from the south.

Oakman had a large landscaped median dividing the north and south lanes. Each side was two lanes wide. The building sat on the corner of Ruby and Oakman, located on the west side of the street, which put us on the far side of the boulevard. Both the street and the parking lot were well-lit. The large fenced complex held a single-story, brick building that dominated the lot.

A fence ran from the building to the fenced backyards of the houses behind the site on the next block. Another section of fence ran north along Oakman connecting to the business next to it. Trucks gained access to the yard through a large sliding gate on the Ruby Street side. The tops of the trucks were visible over the fence, but the fence itself had green slats running through the links, blocking our view from the street.

We drove past and went down the street far enough to be out of sight from the building. While we were making our turn crossing the median to the opposite side, Tony and Marissa went by in the southbound lane. We waited a few seconds, then followed. Tony continued past the bakery.

Morrisey slowed to get a better look. A parking area for walk-up customers was on the side of the building. Plenty of security lighting surrounded the building and lot.

Behind and to the north side of the bakery, the large parking lot held about a dozen delivery trucks. They were lined up along the fence away from the building. None were as small as a van and all had Old World Bakery and its logo painted on their sides.

Morrisey went a block past Ruby, turned right, then right again at the first street behind the bakery, where he pulled to the curb. We looked past the row of one-and-a-half and two-story homes that lined the street. It looked like a nice neighborhood. The homes were well-maintained and probably forty to fifty years old. Most had a garage in the backyard lined up at the end of a driveway that prevented a clear and direct line of sight to the parking lot. Morrisey edged forward from house to house until we found one without a garage in the backyard. Here we had a clear view. We studied the area for a moment.

"I'll go take a look," I said. My hand was reaching

for the door when Morrisey stopped me.

"Wait. Let's think this through. I think all three of us should take a look from different perspectives. Doug, go around the block that way." He pointed in the direction the car was facing. "Come around the front and take a good look at the building from there." To me, he said, "If you're going through the yard, I'll go along Ruby and scope out the driveway and side of the building. I'll take a look through the front window where the customers enter. Look for any activity, security cameras or anything unusual. I don't have your number, Doug."

They exchanged numbers while I called Tony and explained what we were doing. He parked in case he was needed. With that, we were out of the door.

"Watch out for any signs of a dog. And try not to look too suspicious. They may be monitoring the area around the building. Try to notice as much as you can while looking casual," Morrisey said.

The house I approached was a smaller vinyl-sided, one-and-a-half story home with a small fenced yard. No lights shone inside. Walking to the gate of the backyard, I checked for a dog house, a worn-out path through the grass, or any doggie landmines that might lie in wait for me to step in. It was difficult to see, but the way looked clear. I lifted the latch and pushed the gate open. It let out a slight squeal that sounded loud to me. I waited before entering to make sure no one responded, sliding through the gap, leaving it open in case I needed to make a fast retreat. Keeping low, I crept to the six-foot-high chain link fence bordering the rear of the property, and sidestepped toward the corner where a small bush, growing wild through the fence from the neighbor's yard, offered some cover.

The bakery's lot was about sixty feet wide and eighty feet from where I was to the fence to the nearest the main road. The driveway ran to my right behind the building, exiting on Ruby.

The building had one outside door at the rear by the driveway and another on the side, two-thirds down the wall. Two overhead doors for loading and unloading trucks were in the side wall. Two black Cadillacs were parked near the front of the building by the door.

The roof was flat with a half dozen powered vents spaced out on it. I could see a small camera mounted on each corner overlooking the lot. Other than that, nothing caught my attention as being out of the ordinary. The place seemed to be what it was, a bakery.

To my right, Morrisey came into view, walking along the sidewalk by the driveway. He stopped to examine the gate while pretending to tie his shoe. His head moved back and forth scanning the building and lot. He moved on and out of sight. Thinking this was a waste of time, and that there had to be somewhere else we could check, I wondered if Carbone had been able to get a fix on any of the other phone numbers.

My phone vibrated. Doug. "Anything?" he asked.

"Nah! I think we need to move on."

"Nothing here either. What ...oh, it's Morrisey peeking in the front door. Thought I had some movement there for a moment. Okay, I'm heading back."

"Right."

I was about to return to the car and call Carbone when the back door opened and a dark-haired man in jeans and a dark windbreaker stepped out and moved to the gate. He typed a code into a keypad mounted to a pole on the left of the driveway, near the gate. Seconds later, the motor engaged and the fence pulled back. Morrisey approached from the other direction. As he drew near, the man stepped in front of him, blocking his path.

"What you do here?" the man asked in accented broken English. "Why you look in window? You try rob us? You try break in? You talk. What you want here?"

"I'm just out for a walk. I couldn't sleep. I'm not bothering anyone. Excuse me." He tried to step around the man and stopped suddenly.

"What? What are you doing?" I heard Morrisey say.

The foreign man blocked my view. I couldn't see what Morrisey was concerned about. I was about to move for a better view when another voice spoke.

"Just stand still, bud, until my friend here has a chance to go through your pockets and see who you are."

I thought I'd been spotted until Morrisey spoke again.

"Is that a gun?" Morrisey said loudly, trying to make sure I could hear him. "What is this, a mugging? *OOF!*"

"You need to keep your voice down and be patient," the unseen man said. "If you're who you say you are, we'll let you get home."

"He's got gun," the first man announced. Then he found Morrisey's badge wallet and flipped it open. "He's cop! From Ohio."

"Ohio? Now what would a cop from Ohio be doing up here checking on a bakery? Must like good bread. Is that it, Mr. Cop? You come all this way to get some of our famous pita bread?"

"*OOF!* You need to stop poking me with that gun."

"Or what, tough guy? Let's get him off the street and find out why he's here." The first man stepped back to make room for Morrisey and the other man to come through the gate. "Just keep moving, cop. In case you're wondering, I got no problem with blowing your spine in half."

Morrisey came through the gate with a taller man

following close behind. Inside the lot, the first man punched in a code again and the gate closed. The man behind Morrisey prodded him toward the door with the gun. The second man by the gate took another look around the area, then followed. They walked through the door, closed it behind them, and just like that, Morrisey was gone.

Forty-Seven

About to climb the fence, I realized I'd left the gun in the car. Instead, I called Doug.

"What's up?" he said calmly.

"Trouble! Where you at?"

"Leaning up against the car waiting on you two. What's the trouble?"

"Two guys just took Morrisey inside the bakery at gunpoint."

"I'm on my way."

"Wait! You got your gun?"

"Of course!" He said it as though I'd just insulted him.

"Can you get into the car? I need my gun. It's under the seat."

"I can't believe this. How the hell did you ever shoot anyone when you can't even remember to carry your gun with you?"

"Doug ... hurry." I hung up and called Tony. "Morrisey's in trouble. Get over here. Pull up behind us and call me."

I watched the door. I knew I should call in legal backup, but didn't know if Morrisey had that much time. Still, I thought I should at least make a report. I called Carbone, deciding to let him handle the details concerning who to call. He answered on the first ring.

"Morrisey's been taken."

"Taken? What are you—"

"Listen. We're at Old World Bakery on Oakman Boulevard in Dearborn. Two guys took him inside at gunpoint."

"I'm already on my way north. I'll call it in. Hold tight."

"He may not have that much time. We're checking it out. Get someone here fast."

"Danny."

"What?" I answered, not going to be put off.

He hesitated. "Be careful."

"Always." I hung up and thought, well, sometimes.

Doug came up behind me, startling me into a defensive stance.

"Damn, man!"

"Easy, tiger. Here's your piece."

I took it, dropped the mag, checked it, and slid it back in, chambering a round. I looked at Doug's anxious face and said, "Well, you asked for it."

He ignored me, more nervous than I would have thought. "Give me the 411."

"Two men took him at gunpoint through that first door closest to the gate."

At that moment, the door nearest the two Cadillacs opened and two different men came out. One kept his head down and climbed into the passenger seat of the first car. The second man acted as a bodyguard, scanning the area as if looking for potential threats. We dropped down, prone, grateful we were outside the arc of the pole lights.

He walked around the car, climbed in. As they drove past, I got the briefest of glimpses into the car and felt a tug of recognition. The passenger looked like Turfe, but I wasn't positive. As the gate slid opened, I called Tony.

"There's a black Cadillac leaving the lot right now. I need you to tail it. Leave Marissa, though."

That last comment was met with silence. I quickly explained. "T, you know the area better than she does and we might need her."

He didn't respond. The line went dead. Minutes later, Marissa joined us carrying a Sig Sauer .40, her patrol piece.

Doug said, "We need to get in there."

"Agreed," I replied. I pointed toward the nearest corner of the roof. "But they have security cameras on the roofs. There's one on each corner of the building."

They looked from corner to corner.

"How about this?" Marissa said, "There is probably a blind spot in the middle of the two cameras that face the parking lot. They're angled away from the building to watch the trucks across the lot. Along the wall, between the far door and the first overhead door, the cameras can't see you. They're positioned with the idea that no one would start that close. An intruder would have to come from somewhere to get to the building. They'd be able to see them long before they got there."

"Yeah," Doug said, "and how does that help us?"

She looked at him and smiled, "Here's what I see, big boy. Scale the outside fence where it connects to the end of the building down there." She pointed to the farthest corner of the bakery. "You can come up behind that camera, walk to a midpoint between the two cameras and drop to the ground without being seen."

"Okay, I repeat, how does that help us? Someone will be trapped inside with no place to go."

"I guess I'm the one doing all the mental exercise around here, huh? One of the others climbs the fence to serve as bait, drawing them back outside. The one by the wall gets the drop on them from behind and uses them as a shield to get back into the building."

Doug looked at her with new respect. The scrunched look on his face told me he was thinking. "Okay, as I said, good idea. I'll climb up."

"I don't think so, thunder foot. They'd hear you clumping around up there. It would be better if I did it. I'm lighter and much more agile than you could ever hope to be, Mr. Muscles."

"Yeah, okay, girlie, but do you have the strength to climb up there like I would?"

They glared at each other.

"Excuse me," I said, "but I get this same behavior from my second graders. We don't have time for this. Remember Morrisey? He's probably in there getting his butt kicked, waiting for us to rescue him. Here's how it's going to go. Marissa, you climb. Doug, you're the decoy. I'll cover you both. Questions?" I didn't wait for them to reply. "Good! Get moving."

Marissa took off at a trot. Doug stayed next to me. While we waited, I adjusted the plan.

"Doug, hop that fence there into the next yard and scale the ten-footer leading into the business next door to the bakery. That way, when you climb into the bakery's lot you can use the trucks as cover if shooting starts. Remember, we want to get Morrisey out first, before we start shooting people. Right?"

"Yeah, whatever!" He took the first fence, hurdling it with one hand on the top cross bar, his legs out to the side like a gymnast. It was a smaller four-foot fence though, so I only gave him a seven for degree of difficulty. The other two were higher, so he actually had to climb them. He tried to hang over the first one and flip his feet over his head, but his hand slipped and he almost landed on his head. Not that it would have hurt that big rock, but it would have been embarrassing for him. He straightened back up and turned to see if I'd been watching. I gave him a thumbs up. He flipped me off. He crept toward the joining fence between that business and the bakery. There he stayed crouched behind a truck while he waited for Marissa to get into position.

We waited for what seemed an eternity before Marissa's head poked up above the roof. She swung a leg over the cross bar, staying tucked as close to the building as possible. She lowered her body down, not more than a foot from the camera.

Hanging by her hands, she dangled a good eight feet above the ground, high enough to break an ankle if she landed wrong. I found I was holding my breath, waiting for her to drop. She landed in a squat with all fours touching the ground. Quickly, she stood erect, back pressed to the cement block.

Hugging the wall, she slid toward the door. There, she ducked under the peephole, crossing to the hinge side of the door. She waved, indicating she was ready. Doug began his climb.

This time he climbed up straight, swinging his meaty leg over the top bar and descending foot below foot until he set down. He crept to the cover of the first truck and waited. Either the people inside hadn't seen him, or no one was watching the monitors. He looked over at me and shrugged before he stood up and walked around the cab of the truck and slid between the next two. He couldn't have been more obvious. Maybe they didn't know what to do.

All of a sudden, the back door near the gate flung open and the same two men who'd grabbed Morrisey ran out. The only problem was they came out the other door at a good angle with every opportunity to see Marissa.

Understanding her predicament, she dropped flat to the ground. Fortunately, the two men had eyes only for Doug. They separated and ran past the building, their backs to her. They raised weapons and aimed at the space between the two trucks, their movements quick, but cautious.

Doug had scooted under the second truck and behind a wheel.

Marissa crawled along the wall, keeping her eyes and her gun focused on the two men in case they turned around. She turned at the corner of the building and jogged to the back door, improvising on the original plan, which made me nervous. Grabbing the doorknob, keeping her back to the wall, she pulled it open, waited a second, then peered in. Whatever she saw, or didn't see, she must have felt it was safe to enter. With gun poised, she disappeared within; not what we had talked about.

It was time to adapt.

It was my time to move. I waited until the man closest had his back to me, then stood up. With as much stealth as possible, I scaled the fence in front of me, keeping my eye on the two armed men yelling for Doug to come out, threatening to shoot if he didn't move. With time running out, I had to sacrifice caution for speed, and swung over the crossbar, hung for a second, then let go. I landed in a squat, my reconstructed knee making an audible pop. I froze. Neither man turned toward me.

One man advanced between the two trucks. I approached at an angle, trying to stay out of their peripheral vision. The man closest to me squatted, facing the truck, his gun pointed underneath. He said something to the first man, who backed away in a hurry. Evidently, Doug had rolled from the second truck to a position under the third one.

I picked up speed and was within ten feet of the man squatting when he decided to stand and move to help his comrade. He heard me coming and turned. Without hesitation, I went airborne once more and drilled him chest high. I had been doing so many flying tackles lately, I should be accumulating frequent flier miles.

I drove him backward, landing on top of him. His head smacked the cement with a thud. He groaned. I tried to hold on to his body and his gun hand, but with the gun in one hand and momentum carrying me, I slid over and past him, rolling to get back to my feet.

His gun went flying after the impact, careening off the side of the truck. I bounced to my feet and pointed my gun at the fallen man and backed away, smacking the back of my head on a truck mirror with a solid thud. "Ow!" Stunned momentarily, and fearing the advantage to my opponent, I refocused my aim, but to my surprise, the man had not moved. In fact, he looked unconscious.

The other man came around the truck. Seeing me with a gun pointed at his partner, he swung his weapon toward me. Dazed and slow to react, I dove and rolled over my right shoulder, hoping to throw off his aim and get off a shot of my own. I kept moving until I came up onto one knee, aimed a snap shot in the general direction of where I thought him to be, but at the last second, froze. Standing where the man now lay crumpled on the ground, was Doug.

"Christ!" I exclaimed. "I almost shot you."

"See! That's how you are. You don't care who you shoot as long as you get to shoot someone. I like that. Don't be in my way if I get overly anxious to press my trigger."

"Yeah, thanks." I picked up the first man's weapon, while Doug showed me he had the other man's. We tucked them away for future use and dashed for the building. If someone inside was watching the security cameras, they already knew we were coming. We moved fast, not wanting anyone to have time to prepare a warm reception for us.

Without warning, the overhead door rose. We ran back to the trucks for cover in case someone came out shooting. A dark blue Ford van burst out of the loading bay, drove straight at us and spun a hard left, its tires squealing on the way toward the gate. A man hung out the passenger window firing wildly.

Taking cover, Doug raised his gun to return fire.

"Doug, no! The women might be inside."

"Damn!"

The van screeched to a stop at the gate. The driver punched in the exit code and the passenger got out of the car and laid down suppressing fire to keep us from following. Bullets came from the loading dock, smashing into everything around us. Metallic pings ricocheted off the trucks on both sides of us. We ducked and moved to the back of the trucks and returned fire into the open door.

The van scooted through the gate, not waiting until it was open, to the sound of loud rending of metal meeting metal. The driver swung the wheel hard, cutting the corner too close and sideswiping the gate post, leaving a four-foot-long scrape behind the door.

My heart fluttered, wondering who else was inside besides Morrisey. Or was he – dead? The thought was so frightening I went rigid.

FORTY-EIGHT

A bullet smashed into the back of the large truck mirror above my head, snapping me from my fugue, forcing me to dive for safety. More shots were fired inside the building, but not directed toward us. Marissa? A more horrifying thought entered my mind. Panic arrested me like a cryogenic freeze. What if the kidnappers were shooting the women, Saher's family, or Morrisey? I couldn't allow that to happen.

Without the benefit of intelligent thought, I raced toward the building to the right of the overhead door. Doug saw my insane move and fired a covering barrage. Fire from inside was sporadic. I envisioned the killers moving from body to body, making sure they were all dead. The thought made me more reckless.

Several rounds peppered the ground near my feet, but nothing like I had anticipated. I made the safety of the wall and tried to become one with the bricks. Pausing for just a second, I crept toward the open overhead door. More shots from within. I feared for all the captives' lives, but common sense had surfaced, and I rationalized I couldn't help them if I were dead. At the corner, I knelt and took a quick peek inside. Nothing came flying out at me, so I stood and took a longer look.

A dim light in the back of the loading dock illuminated dozens of wheeled baker's racks against the back wall. Two doors on either side of the dock had steps leading up. I didn't see or hear anyone inside, but the space in front of me was completely open, offering no cover for me to enter safely.

From somewhere deeper inside the building, another round of shots rang out. It seemed as though all the action was happening elsewhere. Marissa was making a pest of herself. A sound on the opposite side of the door grabbed my attention. Doug had joined me, a demonic look on his large face. He'd finally got his wish to get involved in gunplay, except he didn't seem to understand it wasn't play. He could get shot just as well as shoot someone. I wondered if he ever really considered that.

"Cover me," he said. He darted inside, staying low. I pivoted and brought my gun up, searching for a target, ready to shoot anything that showed itself. Doug made it to the cement steps on the left without incident. He stopped and motioned me forward. Since I was already practicing to be a human target, I made it more interesting and ran for the steps on the right.

Again, nothing happened. We looked at each other across the bay and nodded. Slowly we crept up the stairs, guns trained and sweeping. We stopped at the two doors. The doors were heavy metal with small square windows in the top half. I stayed to the side of the door and glanced through the window to a narrow hallway on the opposite side. I pulled the door open and peered through. The only movement I saw was Doug doing the same.

The hall went in both directions. To my right, it ended at another door that looked the same as the one I was at now. At the other end, to my left, stood another of the same type of door. Across the hall on the opposite wall were two more doors, but these were white, smaller and swinging. The one across from me was marked 'Out', while the one near Doug was labeled 'In'. They also had small windows near the top portion. I guessed they led to the kitchen.

Somewhere to the left, someone squeezed off another round. I ran to my right to look through the window in the metal door. The action might be in the other direction, but I didn't want to chance someone sneaking up behind us.

The room on the other side of the door contained cubicles and offices and another door. That one was all door, no window. It looked like the outer door the two men took Morrisey through. I took a chance that no one else was out there and went back toward Doug, already scoping out the door at the opposite end of the hall. I saw him duck below the window. He must have seen something.

I stopped at the 'Out' door, gave it a push, dove in and rolled to my feet. As I came up, I banged my head into a stainless steel worktable that ran the length of the room. The blow knocked me back on my rump.

Thankfully, this room was empty. I stood, rubbing my head and looked around. To the right was a dry storage area where shelves lined the walls. In between the shelves was a walk-in cooler door. On the other side of the table across from me was a series of ovens, dough mixers, prep tables, and coolers. To my left was a wall that was half partition and half glass. Another door swung in the center of that wall. I advanced. It led into the display and retail sales area.

A noise behind me made me spin, my heart in my throat. I caught sight of something on the floor below the ovens. I jumped onto the table to prevent whoever it was from shooting me in the legs, or worse. I rolled across the top, brought my gun over the edge, and aimed directly at the lifeless face of a man who had already been shot once. I was so startled that I almost left a deposit on the table. I sighed and stepped down.

My nerves were fried. I went to the glass door, keeping low and looked out into the cash and carry area. Two large glass display cases filled one wall with a walkway for the workers behind them. Several metal racks that held bread formed aisles. The walls were lined with wooden shelves that had a variety of products on them. In the far wall was another door, not all glass. Kneeling on the other side of the case was Marissa, her back to me.

Wanting to avoid getting shot, I ducked and pushed through the door keeping the glass display cases between her and me. I called out, "Marissa, it's—"

Bang! Bang! Two shots smashed the glass window in the door behind me, raining shards of glass down upon my head. "Fuck!" I said as I felt several pieces dig into me.

"Danny! Is that you?" she whispered.

"Ah, yeah!"

"Sorry."

"Is it safe to come over there?"

"Yeah, come here."

I crawled to her and sat with my back against the wall.

"You're bleeding."

"Imagine that!"

"Sorry, but you startled me. You should have warned me."

"I tried, but your trigger-happy finger must be hard of hearing."

"Okay! Okay! I said I was sorry." She bit her lip. "Don't tell Tony, okay? Please! He'd never let me live it down."

My shocked look stopped her from making any further comments. "Why don't you tell me what's happening. Oh, and by the way, Doug's out there somewhere. Try not to shoot him, either."

"Sure, rub it in. One little mistake and I'm marked for life."

"Yeah, well, I'm scarred for life. Now what's the situation?"

"Well, as far as I can tell, there's just one guy left. He's in that next room, but he has Morrisey tied to a chair. They must have been beating him. I haven't been able to see anything else. He keeps yelling that he's going to kill them all. But I haven't been able to determine who else, if anyone, he has in there with him. It's an office and he has it barricaded." She sat back and bit her lip again, then added excitedly, "Hey, did ya see I capped that guy back there? And one more over there someplace." She waved her gun to indicate where.

Jesus! "That's great! I'm proud of you." Not really knowing what to say to that. Wow! And they thought I was attracted to violence.

Suddenly, another shot ripped through the room. A voice screamed out, "I'm warning you. Come closer and I'll start killing them, one at a time. Stay back."

"That must be Doug," I said. "Cover me."

I lay down on the floor and crawled around the display case to the office door. I inched the door ajar until I could see into the room. The shooter had lined up an overturned desk, a sofa, a four-drawer file cabinet and an upended table across the room. Several wooden chairs had been stacked on top giving the shooter wall-to-wall coverage. Behind the mound, sitting up in a chair with his arms tied behind his back, sat Morrisey. I couldn't see anyone else in the room.

I slid back and pulled out my phone.

"Doug, I need a diversion so I can get into that room."

"Diversion? Hell, yeah, I can do that."

"Whatever it is, keep it going as long as you can. Give me a minute to get ready."

"Got it."

I slid back behind the counter and looked over at the anxious Marissa. "When I get through the door, stay here and cover me. If he makes a move for Morrisey or me, shoot him."

"I can do that."

With a humorless smile, I said, "I know."

As I crawled back to the door and waited for whatever Doug was going to do, I thought how funny that both she and Doug had said the same thing. I might have killed more people than they had, but they were the gun crazy ones. Maybe that was because I took no joy from shooting people in the way they seemed to. I'm not saying the people I shot didn't deserve to be put down, just saying sometimes I struggle with the fact I've taken lives.

Of course, the old adage, "it was him or me," does go a long way in the justification department. I can live with that.

From the other room there came a loud crash followed by two gunshots, then two more. Doug was doing two-shot bursts. As I peered through the door again, I could see the source of the crash. Doug had picked up a huge commercial dough mixer and heaved it through the window into the office. I crawled into the room as a metallic crash sounded right next to me. The baking tray almost had me jumping to my feet in fright.

I glanced back to see Doug throwing round metal pizza pans like Frisbees into the room. He was so accurate that the man with the gun had to keep his head down or risk losing it. I managed to reach the edge of the barricade and squeezed through a gap between the upended table and the file cabinet.

The gunman was behind the sofa, reaching his hand up without looking and pulling the trigger. A half dozen handguns and several boxes of ammunition lay on the floor next to him. No chance of him running out of bullets anytime soon. I eased forward to get a shot at the man. I raised my gun and was about to fire, when another pan flew over the makeshift wall, slamming into a mound of blankets piled on the floor along the wall on the opposite side of the shooter. The mound moved and made a noise. A noise that sounded like the squeal of a scared little girl. I backed up and rolled to my back. Now what? I couldn't shoot; they were in the line of fire. If I missed, I risked hitting whoever was underneath the blankets. Even if I hit my target at this range, the bullet could go through him.

I moved forward again until I could see Morrisey. His head drooped. His eyes seemed unfocused. Signs of a beating decorated his face. The shooter was on the other side of him, his attention, for the moment, concentrated on Doug. An idea came to me. I looked around the floor until I found a piece of glass and flicked it at Morrisey, hitting him in the cheek. His eyes cleared and he looked around until he found me. I used my hand to indicate what I wanted him to do. At first, he looked at me like I was nuts. He should've been aware of that fact already. I repeated the motion. He sighed and nodded.

He put his feet flat on the floor and in one powerful motion, pushed off, toppling over backward. He fell several feet away from the gunman. The man, taken by surprise, almost popped up high enough for either Doug or Marissa to put him down.

I knew we should try to take him alive. We needed the information he was sure to possess, but I wasn't going to risk the lives of the other people in there.

He slid to where Morrisey now lay, climbed up

over the chair and pushed his gun into Morrisey's cheek. "You want to die? I kill you now," he screamed in a frantic, high-pitched voice, evidently losing control. I couldn't wait much longer but still needed him to move about a foot farther away from the blankets.

Unable to wait and risk Morrisey's life, I decided to chance a head shot from the side. I lined up the shot. Morrisey looked at me as if to say "what are you waiting for?" At that moment, the blankets moved and a young dark-haired girl scrambled out and climbed the furniture in a frantic attempt to escape. The man heard the movement and spun, drawing a bead on the girl as she climbed.

A voice roared, "NO!" Multiple shots followed, driving the man backward with each consecutive impact until his gun fell harmlessly to the floor. He slid down the wall, leaving a red smear as he went. His eyes were still open, but we wouldn't be getting any information from him. It was only after I stood over him that I realized the scream as well as the shots had come from me.

Doug and Marissa burst into the room. Doug gathered up the little girl who tried to kick him and scratch his eyes out. I helped Morrisey get free from the chair, while Marissa went to the blanket. She pulled them back, revealing a woman and another daughter. I guessed were the Saher family. They had been duct taped together. Somehow, the little girl had gotten free.

While the family hugged each other, we tried to decide what to do next. One thing was for sure. We needed more information and we needed it fast.

"How long has it been since that van took off?" I asked.

"It hasn't been that long," replied Doug. "It just seems like it. Maybe five minutes."

He was right. At times like this, time always seems

longer than it really is.

"Any guesses where they're going?"

"That's all they would be at this point is guesses."

"God, so close!" I turned to Morrisey. "You okay?"

"Hell, no."

"If it's any consolation you don't look okay, either."

"You're an ass. Next time you get tied to a chair, I'm gonna order a pizza first before I come to the rescue."

"You want to call Carbone and see if he has any ideas?"

He mumbled something, found his phone on the floor and made the call.

Mrs. Saher came to us and said, "I can never thank you enough. You have saved our lives. We will be eternally grateful."

"I'm glad we got here in time. I just wish we could've gotten here earlier to save everyone."

"Yes, those poor women. I know what is in store for them. There are many bad people that make my people look bad. But we are good and law-abiding people. Can you not stop them before the ship sails?"

The whole room went on pause. Then, as though we had just come back from a commercial break, we all said at the same time, "Ship?"

"What ship would that be?" Morrisey asked

"The ship they have waiting in the lake to transport the slave girls. I thought you knew all of this. How did you find us if you didn't know?"

"Now, there's a question."

Forty-Nine

By the time we were ready to leave, we'd lost time, but gained valuable information. I called Carbone, who wanted us to wait for the locals. Like that was going to happen. Moments later we were running for the cars.

Morrisey and Doug hurdled the fence toward the car on the street. Marissa and I climbed into the Cadillac after finding the keys in the man's pocket. As we moved off, she yelled, "Stop!" She hopped out and ran to the man I had knocked out, now sitting up and holding his head. She jammed her gun under his chin and said something to him. He replied. She said something else and he nodded. She seemed satisfied and started back to the car. As an afterthought, she went back and cracked him over the head with her gun, sending him back to sleep.

I looked over at her as she buckled her seat belt. She returned my amazed look. "What?"

"Nothing."

"Well, how did you plan on getting out of here?"

"I was going to ram the gate. You know, like in the movies."

She sniffed at that, "Well, I guess you don't want the code number."

"Marissa?" She just looked at me. "What's the number?"

"Well, if you're sure you don't want to do the movie thing." She told me, but I was still looking at her. "Now what? Oh, the guy? He was tired and having trouble getting to sleep. I just helped him with a new sleep aid."

I started toward the gate. "Old home remedy?"

"Yeah, something like that."

We were out of the gate and on our way back to the expressway. Morrisey contacted Carbone who, though unhappy, would meet the local authorities at the bakery. We left the Saher family in the offices near the back door. The police were minutes away. If we stuck around to answer questions, we'd lose any hope of catching the kidnappers.

From what Mrs. Saher had overheard, a ship was waiting on Lake Erie about a mile off shore. A boat was waiting at a marina somewhere south of Monroe. That narrowed the possibilities somewhat but still left a lot to check. After passing the information along to Carbone, he contacted the Monroe Police Department. They put me in contact with a Detective Morales, who would coordinate things his end. Two-man crews were dispatched to the area marinas as well as public launching sites. Unfortunately, since a portion of this city was on the lake, there were quite a few places to check. Marissa called Tony when we reached the expressway.

"Where are you, honey?"

I couldn't hear his response. "Put him on speaker." She did, but we missed what he said. I said, "Can you repeat that, honey?"

"Yeah, I said, kiss my ass, dear. I'm on 75 south, nearing Monroe."

That put him about thirty minutes farther up the road than us. The van was hopefully somewhere between. I prayed they didn't stop and decide to eliminate the witnesses.

Marissa said, "Tony, we think they're meeting a boat someplace south of Monroe. Don't lose them, we're on the way."

"I'm on it."

Detective Morales called back to say his crews were on the road. He also contacted the Michigan State Police, putting them on alert for the van. I told him where they were last reported and what we were driving, hoping he could run interference for us so we wouldn't get pulled over. He said he'd pass that information along, but no one wanted us involved in any take-downs or shootouts. Otherwise, he'd keep us out of it completely. I think he saw us as a bunch of vigilantes or bounty hunters. He wasn't about to let us have free reign in his territory. I crossed my fingers and agreed to his terms.

Morrisey called and asked where we were. He was a little behind us, running with his cop top flashing, and caught up quickly. We slowed until he passed us, then drafted off him. The van couldn't be that far in front of us. We were traveling near a hundred miles per hour; the van would be hard-pressed to match that speed.

We had to slow when the expressway ended. Southfield Expressway became Southfield Road. We traveled the slower road for about a mile before catching the ramp to I-75. At the speed we flew, Monroe was less than twenty minutes away.

Tony called. "The Cadillac turned off at the Luna Pier exit and is heading toward the lake."

I tried to recall what I knew about Luna Pier. One main road ran through the center of the small town. Another went north and south following the shoreline. At this hour, everything had long ago closed up. The main attraction was a nice pier that stretched out into Lake Erie. People liked to walk out and sit on the benches, watching the water, the gulls and the ships in the distance. The pier also served as a break, which created a small cove for public boat launching. Lakefront houses and cottages lined the shore behind the break. Each had a small dock.

I didn't know the area that well, but Natalie and I had stopped one day on the way back from Detroit after watching a Tigers' game. We bought ice cream cones and walked hand in hand out on the pier. We sat for a while and enjoyed the warm summer breeze coming off the water. Eventually, though, we were overwhelmed by seagulls fighting for the remains of our cones and forced to leave.

I started thinking aloud. "Neither the Cadillac nor the van had a boat attached to it. So if they're going out on the lake, there must be one waiting for them. The public launch in the cove is for small boats and would be too open. Anyone, including the Luna Pier Police Force, would see them easily. The boat has to be somewhere more private. I can't remember where there were other docks or marinas in the area ... unless it's attached to one of the homes along the water, which are more secluded and shielded from view."

"There's not much traffic," Tony said. "I'm pulling over. I'll be able to see which way they turn." He didn't speak for long seconds. "Hold on, I'm moving. They turned left and drove past the public access. I can't just follow around the corner. I've got my headlights off, but there's no way they wouldn't see me. Right now, they're out of sight. I'm getting out of my car to take a look around this house."

There was a slight pause. Air whispered past the small microphone on the cell phone.

"Shit!"

It wasn't said into the phone, just picked up by it.

"What?" I yelled. "Shit, what?" But there was no reply, making me nervous. Marissa slid to the edge of her seat. Then, what sounded like running, and a car door slamming.

"They're gone."

"What?"

"Troubles with your ears, bro? I said they're gone. The road goes around a bend farther down, but they shouldn't have disappeared that quick. Unless they're on to me, or pulled into one of these houses."

Silence. I knew he was thinking, so I hung back from interrupting.

"If I follow and they're watching, I'm made. If they've stopped at a house and see me, I'm made. No matter what, they'll be suspicious if they see another car come down this street at this time of night. I might have to go on foot. The problem with that is if they continued beyond the bend, I'll never catch up to them or find them again." He sighed. "I'll just have to chance it. They've never seen me before, so if I'm caught, I'll just have to bullshit my way out of it. You're close, just in case, right?"

"Oh yeah, right around the corner," I lied. I was sure he knew that.

"Okay, I'm keeping the line open, but keeping the phone down. Put Marissa on."

I handed her the phone.

"Keep him on the line."

"Yeah," I heard her say. "Don't worry, honey, I've got your back. I've got your front too, but that'll have to wait for later. So don't get anything important shot off, 'K?" She was silent after that, just listening.

A sudden thought came to mind.

"Marissa, have him call you back on your phone. Morrisey might try to contact me. We don't want to lose contact later when it's important."

She nodded and relayed the request to Tony. A minute later, we were still waiting for his call.

"Shit! Call him back," I said, anxiously.

"I can't. What if he's not calling because he needs it quiet? The phone might give him away."

"Damn!" She was right. "Text him. He'll have the phone on vibrate. It'll just buzz once."

She felt that was a safe enough option and sent it. We waited impatiently for a response, but nothing happened. My phone rang. We both jumped. However, it was only Morrisey.

"I think we may have caught the van. Doug can see a dark-colored van up ahead, maybe a mile. He's using the binoculars. Even though it's dark, he seems pretty sure it's a Ford. At this speed, we should intercept them in about five minutes."

"I don't think it'll take that long. Tony was following the Cadillac. It exited at Luna Pier. We should be there in less than five minutes. He was following the Caddy, but lost it. Now we've lost contact with him. We may need to let the van get there to help us find Tony."

"Man! I'm turning the overhead off so they won't get antsy and play hide and seek." He was quiet for a moment, then said, "Here's what we do. Just in case they've spotted me because of the lights, I'm going to pull off at the next exit. You keep going and when I get to the top, I'll stop for a minute, then come right back down behind you. We want them to meet up with the others so we can take them all at once."

"Right. My thought, too. Okay."

"I think it's time to call the State boys and let them know where we are."

"I'm not sure that's a good idea," I said. "If we don't hear from Tony, I don't want their presence to make them eliminate witnesses and run for the hills. Or in this case, open water. Let's wait to see what we're dealing with first. It's not a big area, they'll see anything that's coming, unless we can get them to agree to blockade the area without going in. Just make sure no one gets out. If I remember right, there are only three ways out of there."

"I don't think that's going to happen. We're the

outsiders, remember! We place the call, they'll come in force and take control."

"Hey," shouted Doug, "did anyone think to call the Coast Guard or whatever harbor patrol they may have up here?"

"No, but that's a good idea," said Morrisey. "I'm pulling off on this ramp. Don't lose them."

"Got 'em." I hung back just enough that I had a good visual on the taillights of the vehicle in front of us. After passing under the overpass, I saw Morrisey in my mirror descending on us. He stayed about a half mile back. I slowed to a speed matching the van. In the seat beside me, a worried Marissa was trying Tony again. Still, with no luck.

"He knows what he's doing, Marissa. He's probably in a position where answering his phone might distract or give him away. Have confidence in his abilities. He'll call when he's ready."

As we watched, the van pulled to the side of the expressway. We had to make a quick decision, either to pass and try to pick them up later or take them now. I wasn't sure what Morrisey planned. He was farther back, but there was no time to call him. I decided to pass and come back on the north side of the expressway. As we passed the van, Marissa slid over to me. Instinctively, I put my arm up around her shoulders. She turned her head to me showing the back of hers and blocking me from view. The darkness might hide us but it was a good move.

By the time I called Morrisey, he'd already followed me past them. It might have been a huge mistake, but we didn't have much choice if we wanted them to lead us to wherever they were holding the ladies, and now, perhaps Tony. Despite what I told Marissa, I was concerned about him too.

A call came in. "Doug has them in the glasses. They're moving again."

I slowed our speed.

"They're going up the Luna Pier ramp," Morrisey said. "Wait until they cross over the expressway, then we'll double back."

The next exit was still a distance away. I started looking for the emergency vehicle turnaround usually sited between every two spaced-out exits, except now, when I needed one. A sign showed the next exit was a mile away. This stretch of highway was unlit and would help hide us as long as we shut down the lights and stayed off the brakes.

"Is it okay to exit?" I asked.

"Wait! They're still on the overpass. They're moving slowly. They must be watching us. Okay, there they go. They're driving fast now. Probably hoping to get as much distance between us as possible, in case we do come back. Go! Go! Now!" he yelled through the phone.

I'd almost gone past the ramp by the time he gave the command. I turned off my lights and changed lanes, turning the wheel sharply to get up the ramp without rolling the car in the ditch alongside. I was moving too fast and bounced us over the edge of the median between the ramp and the expressway.

"Ow! Fuck!" I looked over and saw Marissa holding her head.

"That's why they tell you to always wear your seat belt."

"Kiss my ass!"

You just gotta love cop lingo.

Fifty

I waited until the last possible moment to step on the brakes, not wanting the lights to give away my position. I didn't have to worry, though. The long, curving ramp had a lot of trees between us and the highway, completely blocking us from view. I cut the stop and turn too close, almost flipping the car. If it had been lighter, I might have. Marissa had her hands pressed flat on the interior roof. Even in the dark I could see she was scared. For some strange reason, that gave me a moment's pleasure.

We sped across the overpass and I whipped the car down the entrance ramp to northbound I-75, flooring it. At the bottom, a semi blared at us as we cut in front of it. I'd forgotten we were still running without lights. We pulled away from the semi and flew toward the Luna Pier exit, which came up fast. I slowed just enough to keep on the winding ramp. We had temporary cover from the hotel that sat to the right of the ramp.

I stopped at the top and waited while Marissa rose up in her seat to look down the road. It was not a long road, only about half a mile until you hit the lake. Several side roads connected. They could have chosen any, but the main one would lead to where we'd last heard from Tony. Morrisey brought his vehicle up next to the

Cadillac with the window down.

"Wha'dya think?" said Doug. His eyes had an eerie glow to them from his adrenaline rush. They could have lit up the road without benefit of headlights.

"The last we heard from Tony," I said, "the Cadillac turned to the left on the last street before the lake."

"We need to split up," Morrisey stated. "All of those streets have to connect somewhere by cross streets. There can't be that many of them. We'll turn left at the first one by that restaurant, you go on up to the one by the lake."

I nodded and drove off. "Keep watching on your side," I said to Marissa, "in case they're sitting somewhere waiting for us." Morrisey and Doug turned left on Harold Street. We continued for on two short blocks through what passed for a downtown. At the corner of a public parking lot, the pier sat straight ahead. Lake Erie beyond that. The road curved in front of the lot.

I stopped short of the cross street, creeping forward just far enough to see around the row of hedges lining the property of a summer rental home. The street was deserted. Some lights lit the parking lot, but none down the street. The Luna Pier law prohibited anyone on the beach or the pier after dark. Evidently people here obeyed the law because the pier was deserted.

The street, appropriately named Lakeside Drive, only went left, running about four very short blocks in length. Past the houses the road branched out and moved more inland. If they were truly going to launch a boat from here, it would have to be within those four blocks. There were maybe eight to ten houses on the lake side of the street. I was certain some of them had docks in the small cove behind the pier. The pier itself ran into the lake, first straight east, then curved north. From my previous visit I recalled a small jetty of about sixty yards in length on the north end of the small cove, running out from the shoreline, on the far side of the houses. Together they formed a c-clamp shape, leaving enough room between the pier and the jetty for a boat to safely navigate the shallow water, to enter or leave the inlet. And, it couldn't possibly be that big a boat. Too much draw would cause it to ground in the soft bottom.

"Well, what are we doing?" Marissa said, her voice tense.

"Be patient. If something happened to Tony, it won't do him any good for us to follow suit." I faced her. "Look, I'm concerned about him too, but let's do this right. And to do that, we have to put aside all emotion. It'll only interfere with and delay the thought and reaction processes. Think about what Tony would say to you if he were here."

She appeared to do that. "Yeah, okay. You're right. So what are we going to do?"

"I'm getting out and approaching on foot. Give me a minute to get next to that first house on the right, then drive down the street. Drive at the speed limit, and act like you belong, not like you're looking for something. If you spot Tony's car, don't stop, don't hesitate, just keep on driving. Go all the way to the end and around that bend down there. Call me when you get clear of the area. Got it?"

"Of course I got it. I'm not stupid, you know."

"Hey, Marissa, lose the attitude. You're worried, but don't take it out on me."

"Whatever!"

"Right."

I got out and slid the gun in my belt behind my back.

"Hey, Danny!" I looked in at her as she climbed into the driver's seat. "I'm sorry. Just promise me he'll be all right."

"You know I'll do whatever it takes."

"Yeah, I know."

I patted her arm, checked that the phone was still on vibrate, and trotted across the street to another row of matching hedges, higher than I could see over, along the front side of the parking lot. I moved along them until I stood at the side of the garage of the first house on the block. It was a small gray one-story, aluminum-sided home with a connected one-and-a-half car garage. The garage stood out from the house, the closest part of the structure to the street.

I looked around it and down the street, trying to pierce the darkness, but couldn't see anything moving. Crouching, I ducked behind a bush near the front door and studied the house. It was totally dark.

Looking back, I motioned Marissa forward. She turned on the lights and drove slowly around the hedgerow. I wanted the lights shining down the road to help me identify any potential ambushes. As she passed me, I ran to the corner of the next house and squatted.

There really wasn't anywhere for someone to hide on my side of the street. Most of the houses were very close to the road and had nothing in the front except a mailbox. However, there were plenty of dark areas across the street that could serve as a hiding spot for someone. I waited to see if anyone reacted to Marissa's progress.

Almost at the end of the road, she hit her brakes briefly, as if she wanted to stop and thought better of it. I checked the second house, a brick and wood constructed two-story. Like the first one, it too was dark, except for a small night light by the front entrance. I moved on to the third house, a yellow two-story home. In an upstairs room, the constant flickering light rebounding around the walls told me someone was still awake, watching TV.

Marissa's taillights disappeared around the curve at the end of the road. I moved to the side of the next house. I hadn't picked up on anyone on either side of the street who appeared to be interested in Marissa's passing. I waited a short while, in case she called. I didn't want to be moving if she did. I was just about to step out and inspect the next house when I heard a voice.

Somewhere out in front of me and possibly to my left

... maybe across the street. I halted and listened carefully. The houses faced the opposite direction and actually were on the next street over; their backyards faced Lakeside Drive. Those backyards had lots of places to hide. Sheds, above-ground pools, assorted parked vehicles. The voice could have come from anywhere.

The sound of a hand slapping bare skin echoed down the quiet road, like maybe someone swatting a mosquito. The slap came from near a large wooden shed in the backyard lined up across from the next house, the fifth one on the block. The one I'd been about to move to next. I heard the whispered voice again, but couldn't make out what was being said. I was positive someone was there, and I had them pinpointed.

Marissa called as I was trying to decide how to approach. I stepped back to prevent the light given off by the phone from catching the watcher's eye. I answered and hung up on her. I typed in a text, **No tlk. Sum1. Stay.** and sent it.

With great care, I crossed the street and came to a three-foot-high fence surrounding the yard and shed. The shed was in the center of the yard about six feet in from the fence and in front of a double gate that opened to the street and wide enough for a car to pass through. Whoever was there was either on the far side of the shed or inside it. The wooden double doors of the shed faced the street and did not appear to be locked. But they were closed.

Placing one hand on the ball on top of the corner post and checking the ground on the opposite side of the fence for anything that might announce my presence, I placed my right hand on the cross bar and hurdled the fence. My landing was perfectly silent, or so I wanted very much to believe. But the person in the shed must have heard me somehow. Maybe he had superhuman hearing, like I had superhero stealth, because the voice stopped, mid-sentence. I thought I heard a whispered,

"Quiet."

Regardless, if I stayed where I was, and someone peeked out from that shed, I was caught. Everything seemed to get quieter.

I duck-walked to the back corner of the shed. My gun had somehow attached itself to my hand, trained on the front doors of the shed. Whoever was here was playing the waiting game. Whoever made the first sound lost. It felt like ten minutes by the time I reached the corner of the shed. My thighs burned from the exertion of walking quietly in a squat. The door creaking gave me the warning I needed.

A face appeared at the edge of the shed directly in front of me. I slid behind the building as the man scanned the darkness, a phone to his ear. "Thought I heard something ... Nah, I told you it was just some girl. She drove past and never even looked at any of the houses. She knew where she was going. Probably just some local coming home. Don't worry, I got a good look at her. If she comes back, I'll handle her like I did the other one."

So they definitely did something to Tony.

"When are we leaving? These 'skeeters are eating me up ... Okay, don't yell, just call me when you're ready."

There was a slight pause as the connection must have been severed.

"Fucking bastard! He's not the one out here getting eaten by bugs."

The voice had been whispered, but clear. He was less than ten feet away from me. "Fucking bastard. Thinks he's fucking King of Arabia or some shit!"

He clearly wasn't happy with whoever he'd been talking to. With his mind preoccupied, now was the best time to take him. I took a deep breath to calm my heightened nerves and let it out slow. From my squatting position, I looked around the corner. It was dark, but not so that I couldn't see ten feet away from me. He was no longer at the end of the shed. He was either in front of it or inside.

I stepped along the side of the shed and waited, my weapon pointing the way. I sidestepped again and waited. One more step and I was inches from the front. I ventured a quick peek and pulled back. Although I didn't see him standing in the open, I knew he was close. The two doors were slightly ajar. If he was standing at the edge, he wouldn't see me move. If he were standing back, however, he might catch a glimpse through the gap near the hinges.

I took a longer look this time but still couldn't decide where he was. Smoke rose through the doors and up into the night, and a hand appeared as he flicked away the discarded butt. The hand grabbed the top of the door to pull it shut. It was now or never. I stepped to the door and put my shoulder into it, slamming it shut on the man's fingers, trapping them between the frame and the door.

He let out a howl, but as fast as I slammed the door, I whipped the left side open, stepped forward with my gun raised and smashed him in the mouth with a short jab. He fell back. Stepping in, I closed the doors and jammed the gun under his chin.

"Move and die. Simple rules. Drop the phone on the floor. Now!" Something hit the floor. It was hard to tell what it was, but by the sound it made, it could have been a phone. "Turn around. Don't give me an excuse to shoot. I don't need much."

I felt him turn, then patted him down. He had a gun of some sort attached to a holster on his right hip, a switchblade in one of his pockets. I relieved him of both and put them in my pockets, and shoved him toward the back of the shed where he collided with something. It turned out to be a riding lawnmower. With my gun pointed at his chest, I called Marissa.

Fifty-One

D anny," she squealed, "Tony's car is at the end of the row of houses, parked up on the grass by the metal dike by the beach."

"You didn't go near it, did you?"

"No, but I wanted desperately to. Danny, he could be in serious trouble."

"I understand that, but we can't help him if we get caught, too. Have you seen Morrisey?"

"Yeah, he's parked just down the road from me, waiting to hear from you."

"Wave for him to join you, but for now, stay where you are."

I turned my attention back to my prisoner. "You and I are going to have a talk. But before we do, I want you to understand I will hurt you as much as necessary. The amount of pain you feel will depend on your level of cooperation." He sat against the mower with both hands covering his bloody face. "You and your friends have two of my friends. If they've been harmed, I promise you will be, too."

"I don't have any idea what you're talking about, man. You're the one who jumped me! I was just out here having a smoke when you attacked me."

"If you want to play it that way, that's your choice.

But you should know that I already heard you talking to the man in charge. What's his name? Oh yeah, Turfe." I heard a voice coming from my phone. I lifted it back up and heard, "Danny! Danny! Can you hear me?" She was yelling.

"Quiet, girl! Listen. Is Morrisey with you?"

"Yeah, I'm here, Danny. What d'ya got?"

"I have one of them in a shed across the street from the lakeside houses. There's a big gray house on the lake side with a smaller gray house next to it. The shed is in the backyard of the house across the street. Come down Second Street from the lake. The shed's at the end of the driveway. Don't let anyone see you from the house. Leave Doug watching the road from that side. If they run, they'll head that way."

"On our way."

I closed the phone and started on the man again. From the way he was watching me, he was trying to find the right moment to make his move. I smiled. "Go ahead. Try it. I want you to."

"You're crazy. And you're in big trouble. People are coming here to pick me up soon. They know I'm waiting for them in the shed like I always do. If they don't see me come out, they'll come looking for me. Then we'll see how tough you are."

"Brave talk from the man who let himself get caught. My guess is that when your friends discover how you failed at your guard duties, they'll shoot you themselves."

He glared at me but held his spot. "Sit down, right there. I said sit! Right there, in the center of the floor." Keeping my gun trained on him, I backed out of the shed and swung the left side door open all of the way. I had to hope no one was watching from the house. I did a quick peek around the shed. Morrisey and Marissa entered the yard at a crouch, picking up their pace when they saw me. I stepped back inside just as the man attempted to stand. I lifted my foot and shot it forward, catching him on the shoulder and spinning him back to the floor.

At that point, Morrisey and Marissa joined me inside and closed the door behind them.

"Is this the guy?" said Marissa, in a very threatening tone.

"Yeah, but so far he denies all knowledge."

"Is that right?" Without warning, she launched herself at the unsuspecting man, knocking him backward into the mower. Her fists rained blows down on his head like a two-piston engine. The attack was so sudden and so ferocious that he couldn't fend off the blows.

We let it go on for about twenty seconds, then after looking at each other and shrugging, we pulled her off him. At least for now. I worried about the noise drawing unwanted attention.

"Keep that animal away from me. I don't know what you guys are talking about. I swear!"

"Well," I said, "if you're sure. I guess we'll have to leave you in here with her while we go check out that house."

Even in the darkness of the shed, there was no mistaking the panic in his eyes. Hell, I'd be afraid of her, too. I reached into my pocket and pulled out his switchblade. It opened with a smooth snick. "Here," I handed it to Marissa. "I don't want to leave you in here with this mad man, defenseless."

"No!" he almost screamed. "You can't leave me alone with her, she'll cut me to pieces."

"Yeah. Probably. The last one was in teeny, tiny, bite-size pieces. But hey, that's your choice. See you in a little bit, Marissa. Oh! I probably shouldn't have said little bit, huh?"

We were out and closing the doors when I heard a last desperate plea, "No, wait! I'll tell you. Please don't leave me here with her."

314 | Ray Wenck

Morrisey looked at me and smiled, "You're evil. You know that, don't you?"

"Me?" I said. "I'm not the one inside, foaming at the mouth and holding a knife."

We went back in and closed the doors. "Okay, bud, last chance."

"Wh-what do you want to know?" He looked at Marissa as though he was about to jump out of his skin. She stood to his side, repeatedly closing, then snapping open the blade.

Morrisey took over the questioning, "Let's start with which house."

The man hesitated, but finally seemed resigned to his situation. "Are you cops?"

"No!" I said, cutting Morrisey off so he didn't have to lie. "That means I'm not going to worry about any laws or feel guilty about any pain I may cause you. Stop stalling."

"Which house?" Morrisey restated.

Marissa stepped toward him and all resistance crumbled, "The gray one across the street," he said.

"Is that where our friend is being held?"

"Friend?"

"No time to play stupid. The guy you took out of the car a little while ago."

"Okay, yeah, him. He was checking out the houses and saw the car parked on the side. I called inside and snuck up behind him. I had a gun on him when they got out here. Hasheem hit him with a Taser and they dragged him inside. From there, I don't know what happened."

"How many inside?"

"Six, that I know of."

"What about the women?"

"They've got them in there, too. They're all drugged to make them easier to handle. Not so they're out of it completely, but just so they won't cause any problems."

"Where are they holding them?"

"I'm not really sure. I never made it into the house. They just sent me out here."

"How are they getting them out of here?"

"Boat."

"When is it due? Or is it here already?"

Just then my phone vibrated. "Yeah? Right now. Okay, move in closer to the break and keep low. Let me know when something happens." I disconnected. "Doug says a boat is coming in from the lake right now. Whatever's going to happen, it'll be real soon. We've got to move now."

"What do we do with him?" asked Marissa.

Morrisey looked around the shed and found a fifty-foot extension cord. We set about hog-tying him to the riding mower. Marissa shoved an oily rag into the man's mouth using another one to hold it in place by tying it around his head.

"That should keep him for a while," Morrisey said.

We closed the doors, climbed the short fence and made our way across the street. I stopped short when I realized Marissa was no longer with us. From behind I heard the quiet squeak of the shed door. A moment later she reemerged and joined us below the front porch of the dark two-story gray house.

"Forget something?" I whispered to her.

She held up her gun to show what it was she forgot. "Yeah, and wouldn't you know it, but when I reached for it, the darn thing fell and hit that poor man in the head. I sure hope he'll be all right. He's sleeping now, though. That should help, don't you think?"

We stayed crouched on the street side of the front steps, while Morrisey did a quick scan of the house. "I'm calling the State Police," Morrisey told us. He motioned for Marissa to move around the building to the right and for me to go left. He was going to go up the steps and look in the windows.

I crawled out from the cover of the steps, staying below the windows. No lights shone inside. At the corner of the house, I allowed myself to stand erect, my head still below the level of the windows. I did a quick glance around the corner. Three vehicles parked alongside the house in a half-sized extra lot. One looked like the Cadillac from the bakery. The other two were matching vans, similar to the one we'd been tailing. We were in the right place.

Crouching again, I made my way to the rear bumper of the first van. Checking both sides, I determined no one stood guard over them. Staying to the side, I pulled on the back door of the van and opened it. Leading with my gun, I stepped forward into the open space, moving my gun arm from side to side. It was empty. I moved between the two vans, stooping down to use them for cover and checked the second one. Halfway through, Doug called again.

"Hey!" his voice sounded desperate. "There's movement out on the dock in that little inlet. I'm not positive, but from here it looks like two guys just escorted a woman to the boat."

"How big is the boat?"

"How big? How the fuck should I know? Do I look like Popeye?"

"Guess. Does it look big enough to put eight to ten people on it?"

"Yeah, maybe. If there's room below."

"Keep me posted. But whatever happens, don't let that boat get back onto the lake."

"Got it."

FIFTY-TWO

The house had a low white picket fence lining the backyard on the sides. The dockside was open. A small gate abutted the corner of the house. I hid behind it and peered through the slats. I could see the boat docked at the end of the twenty-foot walkway. Someone moved on board. As I watched, the sliding glass door overlooking the water parted and two men led two women into the yard. One of them reached back and closed the door before they proceeded toward the dock. The women walked as if they were drunk, appearing to have little control over their bodies. The two men held them, one hand under their elbows and one on their backs, guiding them, rather than dragging them. The women gave no signs of resistance, but neither did they display any awareness of their surroundings.

I wanted to call Morrisey but was afraid we were too close to the bad guys. I reached over the gate and quietly unlatched it. It swung open with only mild protest. No one seemed to notice so I stepped in and pushed the gate so it looked closed. Patio furniture was spread out over a cement slab in front of the sliding glass door.

I moved to the large table. A vinyl tablecloth

draping it gave me extra cover. Looking back at the house into the room lit by a pair of table lamps against the far wall, I realized anyone standing there would have seen me.

The house was deceptive in size. From the street it was a two-story, but from this side, the sliding glass door was at basement level.

The night air carried voices from the dock. They'd reached the boat and were trying to get the women to step down onto the deck. The man on the boat guided their feet so they wouldn't fall.

To the right of the dock, I caught sight of a darting movement. Whatever it was, dropped down onto the grass knoll separating the house from the waterline. The yard went back about thirty feet from the house to the mound. After that, the ground, covered with large stones, dropped off steeply toward the waterline. A set of white, wooden stairs led over the knoll and down to the dock.

I looked closer and saw Marissa's head rise above the top of the mound, just enough to allow her a good angle for watching the boat. The two women were now on board and out of sight. They must have taken them down below. One of the men headed back toward me while the other stayed on board. Holding my breath, I waited for what I feared would be sure discovery. The man was in a hurry though and walked past me and through the sliding door.

I waited until I was certain he was no longer in the room and left the cover of the table. Inching the glass door, the room opened up before me. Sofas and chairs were arranged around a large flat screen TV mounted on the wall. A fireplace took up one corner and a bar dominated another. Along the rear wall were stairs leading up. There were doors to the right and left. The one on the right was closed, the left one open.

Without warning, the man emerged from the open

door on the left, his back to me while he guided another woman through the door. I dropped behind the nearest of the three sofas, my gun ready. The patio door slid back, then closed. I sat up and watched as he led her toward the boat.

Crawling on all fours toward the open door, I glanced in. The room was empty. Damn! Were all six women on board already? I had to find Tony fast. I needed to check the other room before I decided what to do.

The door on the other side opened, and two men came out.

"He will not talk," the first one said. I recognized him from my brief glimpse the night he shot Richie. It was Turfe. "We are almost ready to leave. Finish him, now." The second man saw me and tugged at his weapon. Turfe saw me and dove for cover behind a sofa. I stepped through the doorway into the empty room, just as a hail of bullets punctured the wall where I had just been standing.

Angry with myself for allowing Turfe's presence to distract me, not thinking very well, I stuck my head out, not wanting to deprive the poor guy of having a target to shoot at. A bullet struck the door frame a fraction just above my head. I fired back, ducked and moved just as bullets ripped through the wall above me.

Reaching my left hand around the corner, I fired two quick shots blindly, then dove out into the family room and scampered toward the smallest of the three couches. A bullet hit the armrest above me. Silence. I waited and listened.

Another, different, shot sounded – a whole lot closer. I spun, pointed and almost shot Morrisey, who was hiding around the corner on the stairs. He winked at me, reached around the corner and shot twice. I scurried around the length of the sofa to my right.

The sound of gunfire came from the dock area. My only thought was that at least now, Doug would be happy. A series of shots inside reminded me where I was, then the sliding glass door exploded. Someone had thrown a lamp through it. A body followed immediately after it. I tried to get a shot off at the fleeing Turfe, but his partner was still shooting, keeping our heads down. I looked over at Morrisey, who motioned at me. He wanted me to distract the shooter. Basically, he wanted me to be bait.

Heck with that. I reached my hand up and shot in the general direction of the shooter. Evidently that was enough, though. Morrisey reached around the corner, lined up his shot and double-tapped. The sound of a body hitting the wall and then the floor told me he'd made his target. He stepped down the stairs with his weapon in front in a two-handed grip.

I watched and waited. I was just about to stand when another man came down the steps firing an automatic weapon. He was almost at the bottom and swinging his gun back toward Morrisey when I stood up and emptied my remaining bullets into him. He danced backward, landing on the stairs, sliding down them until he hit the floor, leaving a red trail on the carpet.

We kicked away the weapons from our kills and I pointed at the door the men had come out. We moved to it and took up standard entry positions on either side. He ticked off three with his fingers and went in from left to right, while I went right to left, crossing behind him.

The room was empty apart from Tony strapped to a chair. From the looks of his face, he'd taken one hell of a beating. His once proud, slightly hooked Italian nose looked like it might be broken.

He smiled through a bloodied and swollen lip. "'Bout time, butthead." he lisped.

I went to cut him loose but remembered I'd given

the knife to Marissa. Morrisey handed me his key ring with a Swiss Army knife on it.

From outside, the sound of the boat starting up caught my breath short. Oh God, we might be too late. I turned to run outside to lend a hand but came face to face with two Michigan State Policemen with their guns trained directly on us.

"Hands! Let me see hands, now!" the first one screamed.

The second one yelled, "Gun! They both have guns!"

Then they began screaming at us at the same time as we screamed back trying to explain.

"Let me get my badge out," Morrisey said, trying to sound calm.

"The boat's moving!" I said. "We have to stop that boat!" An almost blinding pressure throbbed behind my eyes.

"I know. I know. Gentlemen, I'm placing my weapon down and getting my badge out. We have to stop that boat out there, or six women could be very dead."

"We don't have time for this," I shouted, putting my weapon down on the floor. I was about to explode.

"Put your weapon down and get on the floor. If you're who you say you are, you know what we have to do."

More gunfire erupted from outside, causing everyone in the room to flinch. I used the distraction to propel myself through the broken glass door, slicing my left bicep as I did.

"NO!" I heard Morrisey scream behind me. A crash and a gunshot happened but neither affected me. Whatever he had done, the shot I was expecting in the back never came. I did a shoulder roll, coming to my feet just as an automatic weapon opened fire from the direction of the boat, peppering the grass and rock mound where Marissa hid.

I stayed down until the shooting ceased, got to my feet and started running toward the mound. I saw Marissa lying on her belly on the far edge of the knoll to the right. She returned fire with the man on the dock with the automatic weapon. Doug was at the end of the fence shooting from the left.

"Doug!" I shouted to be heard. "The women are on board, man. Stop shooting at the boat." I looked at Marissa, but at this distance, it would be pointless to try to get her attention. She was shooting at an angle that would take any missed shots harmlessly out over the water.

As I looked down on the escape boat, I heard two things. The first was the state cops running outside, away from the house with Tony and Morrisey right behind. The second was the boat throttling up. If we didn't stop them here, it could be too late. An automatic weapon opened up from the cover of the boat. Shots flew over the mound and struck one of the two cops high in the chest, dropping him instantly. Morrisey dragged him back inside. The second trooper overturned the patio table and squatted behind it, returning fire when he could.

That instant, I knew what I had to do. I backed up a few steps from the mound, keeping my head down and ran for all I was worth toward the break at the north side of the inlet. The man on the dock flung the rope off its mooring and about to clamber aboard when a shot from Marissa struck him in the side and pitched him past the boat and into the water. As the boat pulled away from the dock, she got up and ran toward it.

Doug, seeing me running, followed. I reached the cement walkway and leaped from the sloping grassy mound to the jetty, almost overshooting and sliding down onto the large rocks on the far side of the wall. I caught my balance with one leg hanging over the side, righted myself and sprinted for the end. The narrow jetty, covered in seagull shit, stretched about forty yards long. As I ran, head down, arms pumping, I recalled running forty-yard dashes for time when I was a young rookie in A Ball. This needed to be my best time ever.

The pilot of the boat looked over each side at the water to keep centered in the channel, then increased speed. He couldn't safely go to full throttle until he cleared the jetty. As yet, no one had seen me approaching. All attention and gunfire was directed behind them at Marissa, Morrisey and the State Cop, who were all giving chase along the bank. I prayed they would hold the gunman's attention, my only thought was if I didn't reach those women, they might as well be dead.

I closed the gap and had but twenty feet to go, when the pilot spied my approach. He yelled to his companion with the automatic weapon. I knew at that instant, that if there truly was a God, I was now in his hands.

I lowered my head and barreled forward. Fifteen feet and the first bullets started tearing into the cement just behind me. It would only take a minor adjustment to swing his weapon on target.

Twelve feet, the driver increased his speed and I let out a wild war cry as a ward to the pain I was about to feel. Ten feet. The bullets kicked at my feet. My time had run out. Still, I raced on as if I could outrun a bullet.

Eight feet. A sharp pain lanced my calf.

Six feet. A bullet pierced my inner thigh. I almost stumbled but righted and pressed on. The boat drew close to the jetty's end. A few more feet and it would be into open water. I ran straight down the AK-47's barrel.

Another shot sang out and the shooter spun around to his right, giving me the break I needed, or the miracle. The shooter's finger stayed down, spraying the cabin with wild shots. It made the pilot duck as the windshield blew out.

Four feet and I knew I'd make it.

At two feet, with the boat just beginning to pull past me, the pilot stood back up, pushed forward on the throttle, just as I went airborne.

I soared over the huge stones at the base of the wall, over the side of the boat and crashed into the driver at such a speed, ripping him off his feet and sending both of us over the gunwale into the murky water. As I hit him, his hands pulled the wheel and turned it on a collision course with the pier on the opposite side. The boat sailed past, missing us by less than three feet. It hit the large rocks, bounced, and landed with a crash, grounded, the propeller blades still churning. The hull was breached but was far enough up the rocks that it was in no danger of sinking.

But it could still attempt to climb the rocks or explode.

We hit the water with me on top of him. I held on and used my momentum to drive him to the shallow bottom where he hit his head on the sharp rocks below. A gush of air escaped his lungs and he went limp. I left him there like the fish food he deserved to be and stroked to the surface. As I broke into the night air with a gasp, I saw that the gunman had regained his feet after the crash, and was lining up a shot at my head. I took a deep breath, about to dive, but knew my luck had run out.

The shots came. I yelped, believing I'd been hit and clutched at my body. Feeling no pain, I looked around in shock, thinking it to be a trick of my mind because I was in the water. The man took one step forward, dropped his weapon overboard and toppled headfirst into the water. I couldn't believe my eyes.

To my left, Doug stood at the end of the jetty, still

looking down the sights of his gun. Thank God! Doug had finally got to shoot somebody. He continued to watch the water while I swam to the grounded boat.

I crawled out of the water, exhausted, but determined to get to the boat. I climbed the large rocks leading up to the pier. Gripping the gunwale, I pulled hand over hand up the boat. Leaning over the side, I reached through the shattered windshield and switched off the engine. As I hauled myself over the side, a man with blood dripping from a gash in his head emerged from below decks and sighted me.

He screamed a curse at me and raised a shotgun. I let go of the railing and dropped back to the rocks as the blast blew apart the section of railing I'd been holding. I couldn't see, but a series of shots followed, then silence. I lay on the uneven, jagged rocks and for a brief, excruciating moment, thought I might have broken my back.

Then I realized if I had, I wouldn't be feeling any pain. Marissa looked down at me, her head appearing upside down from my position.

"Danny, are you all right down there?"

I tried to sit up, but found the effort difficult and oh, so painful. I shifted my weight onto my arms as Marissa climbed down and squatted next to me. Doug still stood covering the boat in case there were any more surprises.

Then Tony was next to Doug. "Bro, what'd I tell you about midnight swims with my woman?"

I started to laugh. I couldn't help it. It kept the pain at bay.

FIFTY-THREE

We climbed aboard and dragged the body out of the doorway. I went below to find the ladies. There was a door at the bottom of the stairs. I had to push hard to get it to budge. Heaving it far enough to squeeze my big head through, I found the crash had thrown the women in a sprawling heap against the door. They were so disoriented and drugged they couldn't seem to untangle themselves. Legs and arms stuck up in all directions.

Katy looked up from the middle of the pile, saw me and let out a sob. "Oh God, Danny!" She burst into tears. The others followed her lead. Evidently the crash had a very sobering effect. They cried and hugged each other. I kept trying to get their attention, but they were too emotional. "Katy!" She looked up through teary eyes. "Can you get the ladies to move back so I can open the door?"

It took several moments for them to work out the puzzle of whose limbs were where. One of the ladies had a severe laceration on the back of her head and another had what looked like a broken arm. With the drugs beginning to wear off, the pain would soon sink in. They all had bruises and scrapes of some sort, but one thing they all had in common ... they were safe.

Morrisey and the uninjured state trooper came to lend a hand and shortly after came an army of paramedics and law enforcement agents from all over. The women were treated and transported to the nearest hospital for further evaluations. Carbone had someone contact their families. The wounded trooper was airlifted, his injuries stabilized, but serious.

Another helicopter, dispatched along with Coast Guard vessels, searched the lake for whoever the kidnappers were trying to rendezvous with. A large freighter lay anchored on the lake just over the horizon.

The ladies all transported, we gathered in the family room of the gray house to debrief. Tony, Morrisey and I had been treated and stood looking very much like the walking wounded we were.

Detective Morales was there from Monroe. He was angry.

Captain Robinson was there from the local State Trooper station. He was pissed.

Sheriff Billings was there from the Luna Pier department, along with the Mayor, a middle-aged blonde woman, who just wanted it all to go away.

They were all in different stages of ballistic. Carbone stood at the back and just smiled. He was making me angry.

Eventually, the clamoring for our heads subsided for the moment and someone finally decided to ask for details. They agreed to argue over who could do what to us at a later time. We took turns explaining how everything went down and why it happened the way it did. The scariest interview was Doug's. At the part when he shot the gunman, his eyes rolled back in his head and he grinned as though he'd just had the best orgasm of his life. I decided to take the lead and accept the blame for not involving everyone else from the beginning. That started them all baying for my blood again.

They were still arguing with one another when Mayor Lerner of Sylvania entered the room. He walked straight to me and clasped my hand. He pulled me to him and gave me a hug. He held on and broke down on my shoulder. The room fell silent. Recovering, he backed off and patted my shoulder. "Thank you. I cannot possibly express what I feel, other than to say thank you. Thank you all," he said to the others.

He went to Doug and shook his huge hand and smiled, "God bless you, son. If it weren't my daughter, I would simply tell you how proud I am of you. But those words just don't seem to be enough." He turned to the other dignitaries and looked into each of their eyes. "I know you feel you have to justify this somehow to the powers that be, but don't be too critical of them. They're good people and they brought a lot of lost young ladies safely home to their loved ones. If you are parents, then you can understand what these wonderful, wonderful people have done. Just accept it as a job well done and everyone, share in the glory.

"The bottom line is that deadly criminals have been stopped from doing something unthinkable. They willingly put their lives on the line to save those girls. As far as I'm concerned, they're heroes and deserve medals."

He walked out of the room and for several minutes, no one spoke. Then Doug had to ruin it.

"He called me son. I wonder if he'd let me date his daughter now."

Everyone started talking at once again. I looked at Doug, shook my head and laughed.

In the end, a multi-jurisdictional task force was created, giving us credit, but allowing each organization their fair share as well. They seemed happy with that arrangement. They left us out of the politicking, which suited me fine. I didn't care who took credit as long as they left me out of the spotlight.

Morrisey and Carbone vouched for Marissa and me being Toledo Police. A phone call to Doug's superiors cleared him. Tony was sold as a civilian, unfortunate enough to be in the wrong place at the wrong time; easy to convince them, since he'd been a prisoner and had the bruises to show for it.

As the meeting broke up and we were allowed to head home, a report came in from the Coast Guard. They'd boarded a freighter with French registration. They had refused to respond when hailed and tried to escape into Canadian waters. An overzealous crewman fired on the Coast Guard ship and a brief battle ensued. Ten more kidnapped women were discovered in a secret hold. The episode had the makings of an international incident. Apparently, this had been a much bigger human trafficking organization than first thought.

Hasheem Turfe was fished from the water. I'd split his skull open on the sharp rock. When they told me, I didn't bat an eye. He got off easy.

Marissa and Doug argued over who shot who. Amazingly, Tony hadn't shot anyone and seemed okay with that. Personally, I think he was more hurt than he let on.

The guy from the shed was arrested and taken into custody by the state police. I think they wanted him close in case the trooper who'd been shot didn't make it. Somebody would pay.

I sat in Morrisey's car and watched the sun rising over Lake Erie, too exhausted to move. The colors, pretty and soothing, promised a beautiful day, belying the events of the evening.

Marissa and Tony and disappeared quickly. She'd been concerned about his condition and wanted him to go to the hospital, but he refused as I knew he would.

Morrisey slid into the driver's seat. Doug jumped into the back like some hyperactive five-year-old on a sugar high. We had a police escort, either out of respect or to make sure we got out of town. Maybe both.

I turned to Doug. "Thank you. You saved my life. Probably those of the women, too." I didn't know what else to say. Honestly, there just aren't words enough to make an expression of thanks seem appropriate when someone saves your life. It was humbling.

"Yeah, it was pretty awesome, wasn't it?"

So much for humble.

"I knew that if I hung around you long enough, I'd get to shoot someone. Hell, I should be thanking you." He was beaming. "Of course, I ain't letting you off the hook for the save, though. You still owe me big time. I'm just saying, I appreciate the opportunity to save your life by shooting someone. I feel complete now – like I just lost my virginity again. It's like the best wet dream a guy could ever have. You can pay me back by buying drinks at Brady's and telling everyone the story of just what a hero I am. Yeah! That'll work."

That was all I could take of that. I was glad he saved my life, but him saying that hanging around me would eventually get him to shoot someone wasn't a testimonial I wanted to hear. I closed my eyes and slid down in my seat with an overwhelming need for sleep.

"Make sure you dream of me," said Doug. And as sick as that statement was when he made it, when sleep took me, that's exactly what happened.

I walked down an endless street with all the bad people I had ever known in my life walking by. I pointed at them, telling Doug to shoot them. He did so with a huge, satisfied smile. The more he shot, the bigger the smile, until his entire face was a smile. Like some perverted arcade game.

I woke with a start when Morrisey nudged me. We were in my driveway. I was surprised to see my car there. Doug had already been dropped off. I was groggy and exhausted. Even more so when I realized I had to be at work in about two hours.

"You did a great thing tonight. I just wanted you to know that. It was the craziest thing I've ever seen — charging straight down the barrel of a gun, but it worked. I shudder to think what would've happened to those women if you hadn't gone all kamikaze. You should be very proud of saving those girls."

I was too tired to reply, I smiled and winked at him, then went in for a short nap. I knew I should call off, but I also knew I wouldn't. One more day and it would be the weekend.

Hey! I realized, with muted excitement, our first baseball game was tomorrow, I mean tonight. The thought usually would have buoyed my spirits, but now it just made me more tired.

I climbed like a zombie into my house, into my bed and into my slumber, for an hour.

FIFTY-FOUR

I went through the motions of preparing for work in a mechanical fashion. I didn't have the energy to make my own coffee, so I stopped on the way and got a large dark roast. The strong bitter brew had an immediate effect on me. I jolted awake. I hurt and ached all over. My bruised ribs flared to life whenever I took a deep breath. My back was already an artist's landscape of assorted colors.

But when I flashed back to the relieved and grateful faces of those women, of Katy sobbing on my chest, the pain eased. For some reason, swallowing became difficult and my vision blurred. I didn't care what Harald thought, I did serve a purpose, even if it was a violent one.

As I drove, I called Natalie, even though I knew I'd be waking her up. I thought it would be better telling her myself of the night's adventure, rather than hearing about it on the news. And I had no doubts it would be all over the news. Catching human traffickers would be a huge story. I thought about it while I waited for her to answer. The fact that those women would be returning to their families, instead of having to live the life they had been destined for, gave me a massive sense of pride.

"Hello?" the sleepy, gravelly voice said.

"Hi, hon. Sorry to wake you, but I needed to tell you something."

Her voice was alert in an instant. "What is it? You're not hurt again are you?"

"No," I laughed, "I'm not hurt." Why make her worry more than necessary? "But I wanted you to know what happened last night. There was another kidnapping."

"Oh, no! Not another. That poor girl! Who was it?"

"Well, that's the thing. It was Richie's wife, Katy."

"What?"

"Yeah. They tried to keep it quiet. But, well, the thing is, I kind of figured it out and we tracked them down late last night and rescued them all." I paused to let my words sink in.

"Oh, Lord! In other words, you were out playing superhero again. Tell me all of it, Danny. What happened?"

So I spent my drive to school filling her in on the events of the night. I was so engrossed in my story that I didn't even realize I'd taken the alternate route to school. The one I'd been taking to check on the students each morning. It was a longer drive; maybe I wanted enough time to finish telling my tale. Whatever the reason, I was now driving through the winding streets of the apartment complexes.

The sidewalks were full of students on their way to school. It was very close to starting time and I was later than usual. As I came around the last bend of a one-way street around the corner from the school, my eyes widened and I cursed. Dropping the phone on the floor, I swung the wheel sharply to the right to avoid a head-on collision with a van barreling down the middle of the road, traveling way too fast for a school zone. I flipped the driver off as he passed and continued on. I reached down and blindly snagged the phone while watching the road.

"What was that?" asked Natalie.

"Oh, just some stupid fool driving down the middle of the road. He almost hit me. I'm so tired, I almost didn't react in time. God, what a butthead." I shook it off and came to a stop at the sign. Natalie was saying something.

"... it's getting to the point where you have to be constantly on the lookout. You know? There are just so many crazy people out there. You just can't afford to let your guard down for an instant. Right?"

Something she said fought for my attention. I was just too tired to grasp it. I wanted to shake it off, but somehow the nagging tidbit seemed important. I turned onto the road the school was on.

"Danny, are you all right. What's the matter?"

I said more to myself, "Yeah, what is the matter?" I stopped in the middle of the turn and sat staring at the road unfocused.

"Danny, are you still there? Say something."

I snapped out of my fugue with an actual shaking of my head, "Huh? Oh yeah, sorry. I just kind of zoned out for a moment. I just couldn't shake this feeling ... I don't even know what."

"Oh Danny, you're exhausted. You should go home. You need sleep after your long night. There's just one way, that's going ..."

That was the trigger and I was suddenly wide awake and pumping adrenaline. I didn't hear anything else she said.

The van wasn't just driving down the middle of the road, it was a one-way road, going the wrong direction. I was so tired, it didn't register. They were moving fast because ... why? They knew they were going the wrong way ... or was it because they were trying to run from something?

A chill passed through me. It was a van that was spotted driving in the neighborhood when the girl from the Catholic school was abducted. Could it be the same one? And if it was, if they were in this neighborhood, they could have taken one of my students. A car horn blared and brought me back. Natalie was still trying to get me to respond from the other end of the phone. I whipped the car around and turned back the other way, following the direction the van went.

"Natalie, I have to go. It's important. I'll call you later, I promise."

At the intersection, no van was in sight. To the left the road was one-way. The direction I had just gone. To the right was two-way traffic. I moved my car into the intersection to see down the street. There was only a small area from the point the van passed me to where I was looking, that I couldn't see. The odds were the van had passed this point and I needed to turn right. As I turned, I picked up the phone again and called the school. Mrs. Luckett answered.

"Mrs. Luckett, it's Danny Roth. I need—"

"Oh, hi, Danny. How are you today?"

"Mrs. Luckett, please listen, this is important." She tried to speak but I wouldn't let her. "I need to speak to Mr. Harald immediately. Call him now!" I yelled to prevent her from asking questions. I knew she was miffed, but I needed to speak to Patrick.

It took longer than I hoped, but eventually he picked up. "What's the emergency now, Mr. Roth?"

I was put off by his tone and hesitated before I told him off. Taking a deep breath for control, I said, "I just saw a van speed by that might match the description of the one that kidnapped that girl from our area. Do you know if anyone who should be there has not reported to class yet?"

"Ah, no, I wouldn't know that. The attendance cards haven't come down yet. Are you sure?" His voice was a lot more concerned now, less hostile.

"Not positive, but I don't want to take a chance. Call me if you find out someone's missing. And, oh, by the way, you may want to have someone cover my first class. I'm going to be late."

"Right. God! I hope you're wrong."

"Me, too." But my gut told me otherwise.

Damn these superhero powers.

FIFTY-FIVE

By the time I hung up, I had passed the last apartment building. I glanced into every parking lot and scanned the streets. Nothing. Panic set in. I stopped in the middle of the road, looking to my right where the apartments continued and straight ahead, where two blocks of houses lined the street. I opted for straight ahead. The road ended at Lewis, a busier road. If it were a kidnapping, they'd want to get out of the area in a hurry.

I raced down the first block and screeched to a stop at the second, taking a moment to look down each. I accelerated toward Lewis, braking hard at the stop sign. I called Morrisey, relieved he answered right away. He, too, had opted to go to work this morning. I was just about to say something, when, from the corner of my eye, to the left, I spied the van making a right turn at the traffic light at the junction of Lewis and Laskey. They must have been stuck at the light. It was a big break.

"Danny, what the hell's going on?" Morrisey yelled into the phone.

"Hold on a minute." I forced my way out into the northbound traffic, much to the annoyance of the southbound drivers. I sat across their lane blocking their progress while I waited for an opening in the opposite lane. Blaring horns and extended fingers described the mood. One courteous driver motioned me to pull in front of him. I waved thanks and sped to the light. I was caught at a red behind two other vehicles with no alternative but to wait for green. My frustration growing, I looked down Laskey to the right and could still see the van fading into the distance. I cursed, slapped the wheel as if it was at fault for the delay, and started filling in Morrisey.

"I'm not positive, but I think I just saw the van that kidnapped that Catholic schoolgirl. It was flying away from the area around my school. I thought maybe you might want to call Walz to let him know."

"What? Tired of going it alone?"

"Hey, that's uncalled for. There's more at stake here."

"Yeah, sorry. I'll call him right now. Where are you?"

The light turned green, but the cars in front of me just weren't moving fast enough. I wanted to scream. Finally making the turn, I said, "I'm heading west down Laskey, going toward Bennett. The van is past Bennett now and speeding toward the Detroit and Telegraph Road split. Give him my number."

"Okay, don't lose that van." He disconnected.

By the time I reached the split, I hit another red light with a semi in front of me trying to turn right. A car in the northbound turn lane and the angle of the road made it impossible for the semi to complete his turn. I couldn't afford to wait, so I pulled around the semi into the oncoming lane and almost smashed headfirst into a minivan.

The driver hit his brakes and I swerved left, going up on the grass and onto the sidewalk. Slamming down the gas pedal, I shot forward along the sidewalk until there was an opening in the traffic. Running the light at the intersection, I caused two other cars to swerve to avoid colliding with me.

I hit the edge of a curb and bounced through the intersection. I'd lost sight of the van. Had they turned and I missed them? It was too late now. My decision made, I continued straight on. Once more, my BMW's powerful engine accelerated past whatever traffic had been witness to my madness. I drove north on Detroit Avenue, tension rampant within me.

With no sign of the van up ahead, panic soared again. It couldn't have evaded me in this direction ... unless it turned off somewhere. Frantically swinging my head back and forth, I scoured every business and parking lot. Nothing. My stomach churned up more acid. No wonder so many detectives lived on Tums.

I decided to go as far as Alexis Road. If I hadn't picked the van up by then I'd double back. The chances of finding it from that point were extremely slim. Alexis was still a mile away. I sped past the old race track on the left where the trotters used to run. There was nowhere they could have gone in that direction. I concentrated on the right side of the street.

My phone rang. "Danny?" Mr. Harald sounded as frantic as I felt. I hoped he would tell me everyone was accounted for and I was stressing for nothing. I could take the embarrassment as long as all of the kids were safe. "I did an all-call announcement that we needed the names of any student not currently in the building to be sent to the office immediately. I told them it was an emergency."

"And ..." I prompted.

"... and, we have eleven students we can't account for right now. Wait, here comes the Fosters, late as usual. Now that leaves eight."

"Who best fits the ... uh, profile?" I said for lack of a more frightening term.

"Yeah, one. Diana Mossing."

The silence hung there as the image of the girl's face danced in front of me. "Shit!" She was one of those girls who had developed early. If you saw here from behind you would think her much older; a small, but well-built, twelve-year-old with dark blonde hair. A sixth grader and one of the sweetest students we had. An honor roll student who had never been in the principal's office for bad behavior her entire school career. I was very afraid for her.

"Look, Patrick, call Detective Morrisey and tell him what you just told me." I gave him the number. "Call me if she shows up."

I reached Alexis and came up empty. After scanning both directions, I turned around at a corner gas station and flew, desperate now, in the opposite direction. I was so intent on the road and the horrid possibilities of what Diana might be facing, that I almost missed an old abandoned house on the left, set back from the road. Overgrown with weeds, it backed up to a large field.

There, behind the back porch of the house, partially hidden by a tree, was the van, so well-hidden I never would have seen it from the other direction.

I stomped on the brakes, but had already gone past the house. I angled the car toward the curb, hit and bounced. The front wheel drive gripped and pulled the rest of the car up and over, stopping on the grass belt alongside the race track's outer fence.

Leaping out of the car, I stopped myself. I knew what I needed to do, but worried whether I had the time. I grabbed my badge and gun, then ran across the street, trying to call Morrisey. The first attempt I fumbled and had to retry. I stopped in front of the house, waiting to be connected.

"Morrisey," I said, before he could speak, "I may have found them ... I'm on Detroit at an old abandoned house. It's across from the track. I think it's the only house on this part of the road. Send help. I'm going to check it out." I closed the connection and pocketed the phone. With my gun in one hand and badge in the other, I moved around the side of the house.

At this point, I had no idea if they were in the house, a rotted, two-story, wood constructed house with a large stone porch in front, or still in the van. Most of the windows had long since fallen victim to someone's barrage of rocks.

I peered around the corner of the porch along the side of the overgrown gravel driveway and saw the remains of what once must have been the garage. The van was still hidden from view. I jogged to the back of the house where the wooden back porch had completely collapsed. They'd need a ladder get inside the house, or have to physically climb up.

The vehicle, now in plain view, rocked a couple of times and a yelp came from the van. Without warning, as I stepped out from the cover of the back porch, the sliding door on the side of the van burst open and a man stepped out backward.

"Fucking little bitch kicked me in the face." He wiped his mouth with his hands. Blood smeared across it as he did. The man spat. "Fuck. That's it! I'm not waiting any longer. Let's rip the little bitch's clothes off and get started. I'll make her pay for that."

The sounds of a struggle inside set my blood on fire. There were two of them for sure. I edged closer. Inside I was cheering. Thatta girl, Diana! Don't give in. I heard a slap and a scream, then a dull smack followed by crying. I moved to get behind the man to look inside the van.

The man outside the van pulled something out of his pocket and fiddled with it. He stepped forward and lowered his hand. He held a small knife. "I'm going to cut those clothes off of you, you bitch. I'm going to enjoy myself."

He was younger than I first thought, but quite large. He had to be six-three and weighed at least two-forty. Another louder smack sounded. Diana kicked her feet as the big man knelt on the floor, his feet sticking out the door, his body filling the frame. Diana's legs pumped ferociously, fending him off. The other person in the van must have been holding her arms.

I edged closer, keeping his large body between me and whoever was inside. I was still thirty feet away.

"Hold her, man. That's it, baby, give us a good fight."

"NO!" I heard her scream. "Please! HELP!" Another slap and Diana cried some more.

The large man grabbed one of her legs and sat on it. She tried to roll on her side but had little wiggle room. Quickening my step, I saw the man reach up and grab Diana's uniform skirt and pull it up, exposing her pale legs. He reached under it and I feared he would cut her. Instead, he stuck the knife through the fabric and ripped a long slit all the way to the bottom. It stopped at the hem. By the time he finished cutting, I was in full sprint. He would pay severely.

I came up behind him and slammed the butt of my gun into the back of his head. He didn't go down, but was dazed. "Ugh!" I grabbed the back of his shirt and ripped him backward out of the van. As I did, I pointed the gun inside the van at a small pimply-faced teenager with stringy, unwashed brown hair. At the sight of the gun, he let out a squeal and jumped back, colliding with the sidewall while the big man landed on his back with an "*OOF*," the wind knocked out of him. He clutched his head and rolled from side to side, emitting a low moan.

"Don't you fucking move, you perverted little shit."

Tremendous anger and hatred for these vile men coursed through me. If it had been a student from another school, someone I didn't know, I would be tearing these two lowlifes apart.

I reached out my hand to Diana and tried to sound calm. "Diana, it's Mr. Roth. Take my hand, honey. Let's get you out of there. Come on, Diana. It's all right."

She looked up at me through teary eyes and cried, "Oh, Mr. Roth." Huge tears rolled down the poor girl's face. She slid forward, her sliced skirt riding up her thighs, her blouse shredded. Her face was bruised and swollen. A tiny trickle of blood formed a fine line from the corner of her lip. The sight of her condition stoked the fires of my anger even more. As soon as I got her to safety, they were mine.

The man on the ground moved. He rolled to his knees with his head down on the ground. A low growl escaped him. As Diana reached out and took my hand, I pulled her the rest of the way out of the van. She jumped into my arms unexpectedly, clinging to me like a toddler holding on to her father. Her legs wrapped around me and her arms circled my neck so tightly, I had trouble taking a breath. She buried her face in my chest and let the horror of the last half hour flood out.

The teenager in the back of the van started crying, the sight of the gun pointing at him apparently too much to handle. Such a nice sensitive boy. Suffer, you asshole. I took a step back away from the van and said, "Now crawl out of there. Do it slowly and do it now, because I'm just angry enough to shoot you for no reason whatsoever."

With my attention split between Diana and the second attacker, I was too slow to react to the downed man's move. He kicked the back of my legs and suddenly, I was falling. I held Diana with my left arm so she would land on me and tightened my grip on the gun. Diana's weight and momentum were too much for me to counter. I landed on my butt, jarring my spine, throwing my head forward to avoid banging it on the ground. My legs came off the ground about a foot before slamming down.

I pushed Diana away from the man. *"Run!"* I screamed, as she crawled on all fours, whimpering in panic.

Sitting up immediately and taking aim, my assailant, already on his knees, grabbed and brought down a branch squarely on my wrist and the gun went flying behind me. I rolled on my left side, the pain in my hand excruciating. Still on his knees, the man lifted the branch high for an all-out downward strike at my head. With time against me, leaning on my side, I kicked my right leg in a forward strike, snapping it against the side of the man's head, sending him sprawling. The branch sailed through the air.

I'd only just rolled to my knees when the younger boy jumped from inside the van and knocked me back down. He unleashed a wild flurry of punches that had little force behind them but kept me occupied while the other man staggered toward the gun.

I caught hold of both of the kid's arms and pulled him toward me and sat up to meet him, crashing my forehead into his nose. I heard and felt the crunch of cartilage. He screamed and fell back, clutching at his bloodied nose. Harder than expected, the blow momentarily stunned me. Instinct kicked in and I rolled to my left, jumped to a four-point football stance and pushed off hard at the larger man, now bending for the gun. I tackled him just as he grasped the handle.

The jolt wrenched the gun from his hand and we tumbled over and over several times before skidding to a stop a couple of feet from each other. Faster to my feet, I planted a well-aimed front kick deep into his groin that easily would have resulted in three points from fifty yards out. He actually lifted off of the ground before landing hard on his knees.

The strike had been so quick and so perfectly placed, and drove the air from his body so completely, there was none left to give any volume to his scream.

Noise from behind threatened to distract me, but I needed to finish the big man off. I stepped back one pace and delivered another front kick directly below the man's chin. Defenseless and still trying to find where his balls had disappeared, his jaw cracked shut, his head whipped back and his eyes rolled up into his head. I watched as he fell forward, unconscious.

I had just taken a deep breath when someone grabbed my hair and yanked it violently. Raising my hands to grab my assailant's, I felt the cold hard steel touch my exposed neck. With my head back, taken completely by surprise, dread tickled my soul.

I knew death had finally come for me.

The blade bit into my flesh.

Oh God! my panicked mind screamed, Not like this!

My skin parted like butter beneath the finely-honed edge. I gripped the arm, my legs buckling, hoping to drop from the deadly grip. Mind-numbing fear encompassed me. Natalie's face flashed like starburst fireworks.

I never heard the shot. My mind had shut down by then. Nothing registered. I remember falling and clutching my severed neck, the warm blood running between my fingers. I dropped to my knees, the body of an unknown man fell in slow motion to the ground beside me. My veiled eyes looked up. How many precious moments did I have left?

A slideshow of vivid images played across my vision. My mother. Natalie. Tony. I blinked and they were gone, replaced by tears.

Another man stood twenty feet away from me, arms extended, a gun pointed my way. I wanted to tell him not to waste his bullet; I was already dead.

With a last moment of clarity, I realized the figure with the gun was Walz. He and other men were running toward me. I smiled to myself. I wanted to say thanks anyway. I wanted to say, "Tell Natalie and my mother I love them," but the haze grew thicker and the words disappeared.

I tried to stand. My legs would have nothing to do with the process, though. Once more, I was falling to the ground. Walz caught me before I hit. My hands still clasped my severed throat. I wanted to speak, but couldn't make my mouth work.

"It's all right, son. I've got you. You'll be okay."

But I knew that wasn't true. They always told the dying man that on TV. I shook uncontrollably. I was scared. Natalie! I tried to say, but no sound came out. A calmness descended as the darkness closed in. My last thought, At least Diana is safe.

FIFTY-SIX

In the back of an ambulance on my way to the hospital, two EMTs leaned over me. I couldn't see what they were doing and couldn't feel them touching me. I couldn't remember why I was in an ambulance. They were speaking, but I couldn't understand a word they said. Then I understood. I was dead. My spirit was leaving my body. Any second now I'd be able to look down upon my lifeless form. The thought relaxed me and I thought I could feel the tug of a smile cross my face.

The lights slowly dimmed.

A beautiful ethereal woman in all white moved around me. She had a warm, comforting smile. She spoke in a language I did not know. I told her I was disappointed she didn't have wings. That made her smile more. Evidently she could understand me. She left with the light.

The lights came back on a little while later. A lot of people had crammed into the tiny room. I looked around and decided I must be at my wake. Suddenly everyone was talking at once. Someone noticed me. My mother and Natalie were instantly by my side, both crying. It felt like the thing to do, so I joined them. For some reason I didn't feel like myself, as though a part of me was missing.

A distant memory seeped through the haze. The overwhelming sensation was fear. I started to shake again, which seemed to upset everyone. Soon the wingless ladies in white were back and leaning over me.

Sound came back to me as my thoughts cleared. Now, everyone was smiling. My wake must be in full swing. There was so much noise, I had trouble filtering through it. Finally, someone said, "Let's give him a minute to adjust and relax." They all left, wishing me well. The party must be over. I was saddened.

I lay there staring at the ceiling, thinking how strange I was not in a coffin.

My hand went up to my neck. Bandages. Wait! They don't bandage a corpse. My memory cleared and with it, I was delivered back to reality. My neck was sore. I couldn't turn my head without pain.

A hand gently removed mine and a light soft voice told me I was fine and not to touch my neck or move too much.

"Wh ... wh ..."

"Shh! Where are you? Is that what you want to know?"

I couldn't even nod. I grunted.

"You're at St. Vincent's."

"Wh ...wh ..."

"What happened?"

Grunt. I sounded like a caveman.

"We stitched up a cut you had on your neck."

Cut? What did she mean cut? Did she see the thing? My entire head was hanging by a thread.

"Wh ...wh ..." This was ridiculous.

"Will you live?"

Huh? Now she was just making shit up.

"Of course. Your injury wasn't that bad. It took eight stitches. Just a little scratch is all it was."

"Bullshit." Oops! That actually came out of my mouth.

She laughed. "Ah, figured out how to use your voice again, I see. I'll tell you what, I'll let the doctor know you're awake and let him explain it to you. Now, do you feel up to seeing visitors?"

"Yeah ... and, uh, sorry."

"That's okay." She laughed and left. The door hadn't completely closed before my mother, Morrisey and Natalie were by my side. My mother kissed my left cheek, while Natalie moistened the right. Morrisey, knowing what was good for him, stayed right where he was.

"Michael," my mother said, talking to me through Morrisey, "you tell Daniel to stop trying to be a policeman. He's no good at it. He always end up ina hospital." She was slipping into her Italian-English.

"Thanks, Ma."

Then Morrisey started in, "I'd think you'd be sufficiently tired of seeing the inside of hospitals by now."

"*Et tu*, butthead?" It was getting easier to talk now.

"Personally," Natalie decided to pitch in, "I think he likes meeting new nurses. I think he's getting tired of me."

"Pretty bad if he has to get beat up all the time in order to meet girls." A new voice from an old friend. Tony had entered without anyone noticing. "Hey, bro, I'm not sure who taught you your pick-up moves, but it usually impresses the girls more if you occasionally win a fight."

His face looked like an abstract painting by some new age Goth artist. He sported a bandage over one eye and had a protective splint on his nose. "Looking good, T."

"Yeah, kiss my ..." He paused, pointing at me, but speaking to Morrisey, and said, "How 'bout this guy. He nicks himself shaving and he's lying in a hospital bed. I get beat by an army of guys and I'm walking around like nothing happened. And still looking better than he ever could."

Morrisey laughed. My mother put a hand to her mouth, but I knew she was smiling.

"Nurse! Can we clear the room, please? Where's that nurse when you need her?"

They beat me up verbally for a few more rounds before the door opened and the doctor walked in. He was a short, bald man with very non-reassuring coke-bottle glasses. I suddenly felt like my neck was leaking on the inside.

"Hello, Danny. Would you all move aside, please? I'd like to examine my handiwork."

He moved to my left and peeled the bandage carefully, as if not wanting to open the stitches, and peered as if through a high powered microscope. "Well, that looks perfect, if I have to say so myself. I'll have the nurse put a fresh bandage on. I'll give you a script for some pain pills and we should have you out of here in about an hour."

"Huh? Wh ...what do you mean, an hour? My neck was almost cut in half ... I was almost decapitated, for Chrissake. How can I get out of here? My head might fall off."

Everyone laughed, but I failed to see the humor. It wasn't their neck. It might not be much of a head, but it was all I had.

The doctor sat down and explained what he had done. "He's still a little doped up," he explained to the gathered masses. "First of all, you obviously weren't decapitated. Not even close. The fear of a knife to your throat probably made you envision that. I'm not sure I wouldn't have felt the same way.

You're a very brave man. Secondly, the actual cut, though fairly deep, was only a little less than an inch long. It only took eight stitches to sew you back together. Your head is now firmly attached."

"'Bout time," quipped Tony.

"Look, Danny, I'm not going to lie to you. It's not a serious injury, but it could have been. The cut stopped a mere fraction before nicking or severing the carotid artery. If that had happened, the chances of us having this conversation would be next to nil. You are lucky. As they say, you were 'saved in the nick of time.'"

He stood up and placed a reassuring hand on my arm. "You will live. I promise you. And for what it's worth, I'm honored to have met you. This city owes you a debt of gratitude for saving that girl from a horrible ordeal. Go home. Rest. Be with your loved ones. You will be just fine. There will hardly even be a scar. But that's because you had a truly gifted surgeon." He patted my arm and smiled. "Goodbye and good luck."

Fifty-Seven

For the next hour, a steady stream of well-wishers poured through the door. Representatives from the police department, the FBI, and the Mayor's office all showed up to say job well done. The media was kept at bay and forced to move off hospital grounds. It was hectic, but I needed it to be. In the few moments I had to myself, my mind returned to the knife at my throat. I couldn't shake that horrible memory. It had scared me. It had robbed me of my self-confidence. There might not be much of an outer one, but inside, the scar ran deep.

I just didn't feel the same as I did before. It was as if a portion of me did die.

Perhaps, faced with my own mortality, I had finally come to understand just how fragile life was. In a heartbeat, it could all come crashing to an end. I didn't want to be less of a man, but despite facing life-threatening situations over the past few days, I suddenly felt incomplete.

I found myself lacking and doubting my own abilities. I thanked God I had rescued the women first because had I felt that knife at my throat beforehand, those women would be long gone and I would've failed. The man with the knife had cut out an important part of me. He might not have killed me in the physical sense, but he certainly slew me mentally.

A few minutes before I was released, Sergeant Walz came in. I was standing next to the bed staring blindly out the window, still mentally numb. I turned to face him and my entire body trembled again and before I knew it, I was blubbering like a baby, uncontrollably, against his chest. He never said a word, he just held me and let me work it out.

Spent, I stepped back and dried my eyes, embarrassed at my lack of control and backbone. I'd been shot, cut, and beaten, all to a point where I could have died. And yes, I'd been afraid. Very afraid. But nothing could compare to the fear I felt as that knife penetrated my neck. I wasn't sure if I was strong enough to overcome this one.

"Thank you, sergeant. You saved my life."

"Hey, don't ever think for a second that tears make you less of a man. In truth, they make you more of one. You may be one of the bravest men I've ever known. I was wrong about you, and for that, I apologize. You can't always be strong. But you were when you needed to be. You were there when that girl needed you, just as I was there when you needed me. We can't understand what God has in mind for us, but we can be thankful when it all works out. And son, you've had a good string of things working out. Don't let that son of a bitch steal who you are. Do not let him alter your life."

"I feel so hollow. Like I died and there's just this empty shell left."

"Tell me something. Was it worth it?"

"I'm not sure I know what you mean."

"Was it worth it? Saving that girl. Knowing you might be sacrificing your life to save hers."

"I never thought about it in those terms. I just knew I had to help her."

"Of course you did. So was it worth it?"

354 | Ray Wenck

"Yeah."

"Could you have lived with yourself knowing you might have saved her, but were too afraid to do so?"

"No."

"You feel empty now, although you saved her. But how empty would you be if you had failed?"

I didn't know what to say.

"You saved that girl because of who you are. You might feel a little shaky right now, but it will pass. If you had failed, it would never pass. I'd bet my life, if another situation came up that required you to save someone else, you wouldn't hesitate. And I'd be proud to be there to help."

He reached his hand out to me and I choked up again as I took it. This time, I maintained some control, though. I didn't blubber on his chest, but my eyes still leaked.

"You'll think about that moment. Perhaps for a long time. And yes, it will shake you – for a while. But you'll get over it. Especially every time you see that girl smile. You'll remember that it was you that put that smile there. Because without you, she might never have smiled again. And when you wake up in the middle of the night, remembering how that knife felt against your throat, lie back and close your eyes with the knowledge that he's dead, not you, and she's still smiling."

Later that night, I woke in fright. My face was soaked, as was my pillow. I clutched my neck to make sure it was still holding together and I remembered, just like Walz had said. My confidence had been shaken badly. It would take a long time to recover, if at all. But as the image faded, I flipped my pillow over, laid my head back down and focused on the pretty, smiling face of Diana Mossing and knew, eventually, I would be all right.

FIFTY-EIGHT

I spent the day in bed, having no energy or motivation to get up. Natalie accepted that and waited on me constantly. She kept up a steady upbeat conversation that, for the most part, remained one-sided. Twice I caught her staring at me, concern etched into her beautiful face. I worried about what I was doing to her. She didn't deserve to have worry lines at such a young age. We would have to face and deal with this latest departure into insanity at some point. But not today.

The dream returned that night and as before, I focused on Diana and got through the worst. I was aware of Natalie checking on me, but it could have been a dream. She stayed the night, but in one of the guest rooms.

The next morning, I climbed out of bed, showered and sat down at the kitchen table. Natalie served me a light breakfast. I didn't have much appetite but managed to force down some toast and a glass of juice. She still had that apprehensive look in her eyes, but she used lighthearted chatter to distract me.

It was the Wednesday after Memorial Day. I had missed the entire weekend baseball tournament.

That didn't seem to matter. The empty feeling inside continued unabated. It would have been very easy to sit there all day and do nothing, but I decided I wasn't missing any more school. I had to return to a normal routine or risk losing myself further. There was only one week left. I can do this, I kept telling myself.

Natalie took the day off work to drive me. I wasn't sure I could make it through the day, but remembering Walz's words, felt I had a better chance doing that than staying at home with my own thoughts.

What I hadn't counted on was the media circus at the school when we pulled up. We were in Natalie's car so no one noticed us. I slid down in the seat until we were in the parking lot.

"Are you sure you want to go through with this? You could easily take another day off. No one would blame you."

"I know. But I need to do this. I need to feel normal again. I need this connection to who I am. I'm almost desperate for it."

"Hey, I'm really proud of you. You really are a hero, you know? But you never have to prove anything to me. No matter what, you'll always be my hero."

My eyes blurred. "Thanks," I wiped my eyes, "but for now, I think I'd just like to be my alter ego."

She smiled at my joke. "You ready?"

"Yeah. Let's rock."

We flung open the doors and hurried the short distance to the school. Someone saw us and sounded the alarm. A herd of reporters stampeded around the building, but we were inside before they could catch us. School security stood at each door to prevent any reporters from entering. I realized how stupid it was for me to be here. It was selfish. I was letting my needs outweigh that of the four hundred students and staff who still had work to do. I went straight to the office to find Mr. Harald.

It took some time to get there. Everyone wanted to shake my hand and hear the details of the rescue. It was a bit overwhelming and emphasized my decision to take the day off. I finally made it to Patrick's door, knocked and walked in. He was just finishing up a phone call and motioned for me to wait.

He hung up, smiled and stood. From behind his desk he came with an outstretched hand, which surprised me.

"Look, Mr. Harald, I'm sorry for all of this distraction. I'm gonna leave. If you want to call a sub in for me, I'll stay until he gets here, then get out of your hair."

"Nonsense. No need for that. Distraction? What distraction? Besides, we're getting used to it." He sat on the corner of his desk and looked down at his folded hands. His eyes had changed when he looked up, his voice soft.

"I wanted to tell you that I'm sorry. I was wrong. What you did for Diana is just incredible. I don't want you to bid out. Please stay and say that you'll forgive me. I shouldn't have been so narrow-minded or so damning in my criticism. I should have known you would never do anything to hurt these kids. Please stay."

Once more, I didn't know what to say. "Ah, yeah, sure."

He said, "I called the board about having you transferred out this year. They were going to take it up with the union. At the last minute, I changed my mind. I'm not even sure why. Maybe it was divine intervention, or just plain luck. Or maybe it was me not wanting to destroy the friendship we once had and hopefully can have again. But the end result is what is important. If I had pushed through with the transfer process, you wouldn't have been here to save Diana. It's eerie. And again … I'm sorry."

We talked a few more minutes and I went to class. Natalie had gone, promising to return to pick me up later. The kids had all heard about my exploits. It had been all over local and national TV news. The newspapers had picked up on both rescues. This time, however, I was unable to keep my name out of the press. Thanks in large part to my good friend, Carolyn Monroe. Her report was over-flattering and hinted at a romantic relationship between us.

Fortunately, I didn't have to explain it to Natalie. She called her 'that lying bitch' and swore she'd contact the news director. I decided not to respond. It would be safer not to state an opinion that could only be turned against me in one form or another at a later date.

The day progressed and many people I did not know kept coming to the gym doors and watching me through the windows. They made me nervous, as though I was some animal on display, or maybe some circus freak show. At lunch, my fellow teachers could talk about nothing else.

It would have been real easy to develop a big head over my exploits, if it weren't for the fact that I knew how shaken I still was. Having to relive the story over and over again was giving me a headache. I was on edge. Nervous about my own notoriety, I reached a point where I had to get up and leave or I would explode.

Ms. Bieniek, the first-grade teacher of one of my afternoon classes, asked if instead of taking her students in the gym, if I would take them for a long walk around the block. I wasn't sure why, but I agreed. Being outside and away from the attention would be a nice change. The reason for her request became clear when I returned from the walk. The school, the Board of Education, the Mayor and the city council had joined together for an award ceremony for me. Embarrassed, I also wasn't sure that emotionally I could handle it. The entire student body was seated on the floor of the gym. Parents lined the walls and many notables and local celebrities were up front waiting for me to arrive. I didn't want to go in and almost walked away until I heard one voice call my name.

"Mr. Roth!" I stopped, knowing who it was and knowing I couldn't walk away from her. I turned back as Diana Mossing came over and took my hand. Her touch had a warm, comforting effect on me. She smiled and again Walz's words came back to me. She led me into the gym to a thunderous round of applause. The kids all stood, clapped, screamed and howled; perhaps more to make noise than to show their praise.

Diana wrapped her arms around me in a big hug. Tears streamed down her face. I put my arms around her and held her as much for me as for her. It was at that moment I knew I would be all right. It might take time, but I knew I would do it all over again if I had to. Of all of my accomplishments in life, whether on the force or on the ball field, there were none more important than what I had achieved in the last two days. My throat grew tighter and I was actually filled with a sense of pride. I prayed I was strong enough not to get too emotional in front of the kids and on TV.

The Mayors of Toledo and Sylvania presented awards and made proclamations. Mayor Lerner's daughter was there as well. She hugged me and gave me a kiss on the cheek. The superintendent of schools, along with a host of other administrators, stepped up to shake my hand and say a few words. All four TV stations covered the event. Several local politicians had to get their faces seen as well.

The Chief of Police and assorted law enforcement head honchos all felt compelled to step forward, shake my hand and give a short speech.

The kids had to be bored shitless. I know I was after about ten minutes.

In the midst of them all stood my mother, Morrisey, Natalie, Tony, Marissa, Doug, Richie and Katy Molten. One after another, dignitaries came forward to heap praise and awards on all of us. The final act was a card with a picture in it presented to me by Diana and her parents. Her mother hugged me and broke down in my arms. It was at that point my eyes began to leak. Where the hell was that damn doctor when I needed stitching?

It was a long, emotional sixty minutes. In the end, I thanked everyone and reminded all of the students to beware of strangers. I really didn't know what else to say, in every way possible.

The students had all filed out and most of the presenters had gone back to their offices, having done their political duty with the obligatory press interview. The only people left were the ones closest to me – and Carolyn Monroe. I had consented to an interview as long as she stayed just to the story. For the most part, it went smoothly. She huddled with her cameraman when it was finished. I had a sneaking suspicion that something else was going on.

In one of the few moments I had to myself, I leaned back against the wall and thought to myself, Yeah, I'll be all right. I can and will get through it. Although I wasn't sure if I meant the words or was just trying to convince myself. I smiled for the first time, actually meaning it. I looked up and Carolyn was approaching. Uh-oh, I thought, here comes trouble. I hoped Natalie wasn't paying attention, but I knew better.

I put on a smile as Carolyn approached. I thought

she was going to ask me something personal but instead, she kept coming and threw her arms around me. I tried to step back but was too slow. Honestly!

"My hero," she said, as her lips moved in for what I was sure would be a sensual kiss for the camera. Before her lips could home in, her arms were ripped from me. Natalie stepped in and pushed the shocked and somewhat scared Carolyn away.

"This is my superhero, bitch. Go get your own." She stepped in and showed Carolyn how a real woman rewards her superhero. I was breathless when she finished. I stuck my tongue out just to make sure it was still attached. Carolyn thought I did it at her. Well, maybe, but she turned heel and stormed off. Natalie whispered in my ear what my other rewards were going to be. My smile grew bigger.

Oh, yeah! I think I'll get through this just fine.

ACKNOWLEDGEMENTS

As always there are many people to thank when taking on a work such as this. First, my daughter, April, for her constant help with promoting, searching out opportunities and keeping my website as current as my forgetfulness allows.

Next, my son, Jon, who is always first to pick up my new books and tell me about the mistakes he finds. Thanks, Jon. (I think)

And then, my son Jeremy, who, when he does read, motivates me to impress him with comments like, "Really, dad? That's all this is about?"

A special thanks to Nancy Kueckels-Averill, RN, BSN from Michigan Institute for Clinical & Health Research for always being ready to offer her knowledge and assistance with medical procedures.

Thanks to the staff at the Reynoldsburg Staples for their last minute help with some emergency printing needs and especially John Remmer for all his assistance on the many promotional materials I order with each new release.

Thanks also to Crystal Lewis and Ronnie Bloebaum from the Geek Squad at Best Buy for helping me out of a bad situation, keeping my computer purring and allowing me to make my deadline. It was touch and go for a heartbeat or two.

As always, an enormous thank you goes out to the great people at Rebel e Publishers for their support and confidence in my writing and allowing me to keep putting out new works. Thanks Bill and EJ. And to Jayne, my editor, you're awesome. You complete me. No, seriously. Stop laughing.

And lastly, and most importantly, to all those individuals involved in rescuing victims and putting an end to human trafficking. They need all of our help to end this horrific and growing industry.

To Investigator Deana Lauck, and the members of the Lima-Allen County Interdiction Task Force, thank you and bless you for the difficult job that you do on a daily basis.

And to you, the reader, thank you. Read On!

AUTHOR'S NOTES

I first became interested in this disturbing topic perhaps twenty years ago, when a young woman disappeared from her office early one morning. There were no witnesses and few clues, but many theories were offered as to what happened to her. One stuck in my mind; she was kidnapped by human traffickers. I remember being outraged that something like that could happen, but to my surprise and horror, I discovered the prevalence of this modern day form of slavery.

Years later, I was approached by representatives of a local church who were sponsoring an event entitled Taken, Stella's Voice, real life stories of young girls who survived and escaped enslavement and were sharing their personal experiences. I spent a long time learning from these representatives and knew then, that although this story touches on a different aspect of human trafficking, I would do what I could to draw attention to the problem and encourage others to get involved and help end this abominable crime.

Although a work of fiction, this story has its roots in the reality of the growing epidemic that is human trafficking. Though the headlines play primarily on the sexual side of this industry, there are many facets to this international crime. The International Labor Organization estimates nearly twenty-one million men, women and children worldwide, have been forcibly held in labor and sexual servitude. Of these, 68% are trapped in forced labor, 26% are children and 55% are women and girls. The most common labor industries are agriculture, construction, domestic work and restaurant help.

The sexual side includes entertainment of many sorts, massage parlors and prostitution. The ILO estimates human trafficking generates more than one hundred and fifty billion dollars a year in illegal profits.

Trafficked persons most often have low self-esteem and come from depressed socio-economic backgrounds. They may be homeless, runaways, immigrants, have a history of sexual and/or physical abuse and may have spent time in foster care. Recruiters search for the weak and vulnerable, offering friendship and comfort in times of need. It is estimated that one in five children reported missing are likely victims of human traffickers. The most common age of victims is thirteen.

Ohio, and in particular, Toledo has a high incidence of human trafficking. A state task force estimates more than eighteen hundred people may be moved in and out the area at any one time. Toledo ranks third in the nation for the youth sex trade and is considered one of four gateway cities. Because of its position in the country, Ohio is one of the states where victims are sold and moved around from city to city. It's proximity to the Canadian border and access to major water and highway arteries, make Toledo a haven for human trafficking.

Deana Lauck, an investigator with the Lima, Ohio Police Department and member of the Lima-Allen County Interdiction Task Force, says, that the days of girls being run by a pimp have evolved into groups who traffic women and girls of all ages and are moved with regularity from state to state. The 23 year law enforcement veteran first received training around 2003 and came away from the initial presentation shocked. Where once girls were arrested for prostitution a new desire to understand the reason behind what they do, began to show a disturbing pattern. "For many of the young girls it is the only life they know. They are taken care of by their handlers, although not well, but are fed, clothed and sheltered, which over time, creates a feeling of loyalty and family for the girls. In essence, they are brainwashed into believing they are contributing to the organization or family and that they are important."

Girls who have grown into women under this type of life style, are often now used to recruit new girls, continuing a pattern of control, abuse, and addiction. According to Investigator Lauck, "the drug and trafficking trade go hand in hand. Most groups who traffic one usually do the other. Getting the girls addicted to drugs is one way for their handlers to have power over them."

Though in recent years, the amazing members of the Toledo and Lima area law enforcement agencies have made headway combating human trafficking, the high profits make it an ever-growing industry. It's important that we, as concerned Americans and human beings, help put an end to this human rights violation, by reporting any suspected trafficking sightings. "However," Lauck says, "the victims have been brainwashed into believing the police only want to arrest them, not help them. They don't trust anyone and often are too afraid to speak up for themselves, fearing reprisals from their handlers."

If you see something or someone that just looks wrong—older men with young girls in suspicious places, anxious nervous behavior by the girls, avoidance of eye contact, afraid to speak for themselves—go with your gut. Make a call."

Contact the Lucas County Human Trafficking Coalition or the National Human Trafficking Resource Center, operated by Polaris, at 1-888-373-7888 for more information, or to call in a tip or report a sighting, twenty-four hours a day, or text to Be Free 233733. You can also join the Blue

Campaign on the Homeland Security Website for weekly updates. Their slogan is: One Voice. One mission. End Human Trafficking.

We can be slaves to our job, to our studies, to our passions and obsessions and to our families, loves, and relationships. That's our choice and we can change when we want, or the circumstances dictate. But at no time should anyone ever *be* enslaved. End of story.

About the Author

Having spent 35 years as a teacher and 25 years as the owner/operator of an Italian Restaurant, Ray now spends his time, reading, writing, hiking, cooking, and playing the harmonica.

You can reach him on the Rebel ePublishers website, or at raywenck.com.

Also by this author ...

The *Danny Roth* series: *Teammates, Teamwork, Home Team*

The *Random Survival* series: *Random Survival, The Long Search for Home, The Endless Struggle*

Warriors of the Court

And for more from this author ...

Please turn the page for a preview of the next exciting book in the *Danny Roth* series, *Group Therapy*

GROUP THERAPY

RAY WENCK

At that time of night and in that part of town, the alley was as dark and eerie as alleys could be. Especially when used some of the things that happened there on a nightly basis; such as what was happening now.

Long and narrow, multi-storied brick commercial buildings bordered both sides by, very few of which were still operating, having long ago fallen victim to the economy and the environment failures of the neighborhood. Typical landscaping adorned the alley: large dumpsters, long forgotten, dotted the walls at various places on either side of the cracked cement driveway. Garbage and broken bottles littered the entire distance. Light seeped in from both ends but wasn't strong enough to fight its way through the bulk of the darkness in the middle of the long path. Though, in truth, it would have looked dark and ominous in the daylight.

Through the years the alley had been witness to illicit deals of all sorts. Drug dealers peddled their slow but sure death; dopers shooting it into their bloodstreams. Hookers doing quickies on their knees, while their pimps watched from the darkness to see if the "john" was worth robbing. Muggings, beatings, stabbings and the occasional gun sale were known to have taken place there. This particular alley had become quite famous for the variety and quantity of crime. Tonight would be no different.

The man walking out of the dim cone of light from the western end of the alley was well aware of its history. In fact, when the message had reached him that the meet would take place there, he mused, "I wonder if they had to get a reservation." His tall slender form moved with such stealth it seemed to glide soundlessly over the debris-filled ground, one benefit of Special Forces training with the Rangers.

His name was Ricardo and those skills had served him well after his enlistment had ended. They had helped him to survive in the underbelly of the city he called home. It wasn't such a large city, like New York or Chicago, and certainly didn't have the underground population that its larger cousins had, but every city had one. The contacts he had culled over the years were loyal to him, first and foremost because he always paid them well for their information. But also because he protected them, never trying to threaten or bully them. They respected and trusted him. They knew he was like them, of the streets. Because of that bond, he had the information he needed, which led him to the alley now.

Knowing what he had to do and who he was meeting should have made him afraid. Anyone else would never have contemplated coming within a hundred yards of the place, especially without backup and at this time of night. Yet Ricardo strode confidently, at least in appearance, down the center of the alley.

His catlike green eyes stabbed at the surrounding darkness as his head swept back and forth. He expected trouble and was prepared to meet it. He knew he would be outnumbered and that those he was meeting would be armed, but being armed did not make you deadly. The drug-addled minds of the street punks he was there to deal with could make them dangerous because of their unpredictability. However, being deadly was more about being trained and clear headed enough to use that training and know your enemy. They knew nothing about him, but he knew everything about them.

Ricardo had pushed all of his usual contacts to give him a name. The word spread and soon he had what he needed. Contact was initiated; first through a third party, then by him as a representative of the kidnapped girl's family.

He had come because of the desperate pleas of an old friend and his wife. Their fourteen-year-old daughter had been the victim. The threat wasn't that she would be killed but that the kidnappers would do horrible, unimaginable things to her. They demanded ten thousand dollars for her safe return.

The kidnappers were small time. That was a lot of money to them. Ricardo agreed to help, as much for his hatred of people sick enough to kidnap and rape a child, as to help his friend. He tried not to think about what he was sure the poor child had already endured at the hands of her captives, because for what he had to do, he couldn't allow emotions to cloud his judgment, or skew his focus.

His goal was to bring her home alive. Whatever had happened to her was too late to prevent anyway.

374 | Ray Wenck

He would keep his anger in check until he was sure she was all right and he could get her to safety. Then he would let his fury loose upon those responsible.

Entering the alley, he scattered a large handful of Wheat Chex cereal behind him as he went. It would serve as his early warning for when they closed in from behind, as he knew they would. They would want to control him. It would be a fatal mistake. They would be overconfident because of their numbers, weapons and having him surrounded. Walking further into the darkness, Ricardo heard the crunch of the cereal echo off the brick walls. He smiled to himself. He guessed there were two of them.

He came well-armed. A Smith and Wesson .40 in the small of his back and a short barreled .38 strapped to his ankle. Another .38 weighed his pocket. But as good as he was with a gun, Ricardo was better with a knife and with his bare hands. He had seven knives secreted around his body in various strategic positions. Some were for throwing, some for slashing and one, his favorite, for stabbing.

They thought he was the girl's father bringing the money. They had no idea who he was or what he was capable of, but in their youthful inexperience and foolish belief that they were immortal, they never bothered to find out. After all, he was just one man. And from their position, they would know if the cops came and would have plenty of time to kill the girl and make good their escape.

He slowed his pace. His hands were in the pockets of his brown leather jacket. His hair was pulled back into his trademark short ponytail; at least when he was working.

Up ahead, on the edge of the darkness, three forms waiting for him. The one in the middle, the large black man known as The Hurt, stood smiling. Thinking he was the one in command of the situation. The other two, a shorter, rounder black man wearing brightly colored, extremely baggy clothes, and a tall muscle-bound white man wearing the red bandana of his gang on his head, stood to the left and right, respectively, of their leader.

Ricardo kept advancing, closing the distance between them. He had hoped that The Hurt would come himself. Now if he was just as stupid and as arrogant as he sounded on the phone, he would have made the one mistake that would seal his fate.

As he drew within thirty feet, he said loudly, "Where's the girl?"

"Ha!" the black man breathed out. He turned his head slightly to his left and said to the white guy, "Get this fool! He believe he in charge here." The white guy laughed. "Maybe she here, maybe she not. Maybe you never live long enough to find out."

"Then fat head," Ricardo closed the distance further, "you'll never see a penny of the money." Twenty feet. "Now show me the girl!"

"Who you think you is? Come up here to my house and make demands. You sure ain't her daddy so you must be someone looking for trouble. You show me the money, I show you the little bitch."

"The girl first, then the money. What are you afraid of, I'm just one guy. Show me the girl and you get your payoff." Fifteen feet. He saw the looks pass between them and it told him the girl was somewhere close by. He slowed his pace. It was about timing now.

The smile left The Hurt's face. The hard stare conveyed his thoughts. He would kill Ricardo and take the money. Well, he would try. The Hurt turned his head to the right and said something to the round black guy. He nodded and disappeared behind the corner of the building on the right. Ricardo slowed again, not wanting to close on The Hurt too soon, but didn't want to stop either. He heard the men behind him approaching, trying to be stealthy, but failing. Their attempts to sneak up would give him time.

The black man came back dragging a young girl who stood almost as tall as he did. She wore nothing but an oversize t-shirt that fell to just above her knees. Her hair mussed, she moved with the staggering gait of someone who was under the influence of some substance. They most likely shot her up with something so they could use her without a fight. Ricardo took one look at her and knew he had been right. The payment was only a bonus to them. They had already abused her. If she was lucky she was stoned when it happened. With any luck, she wouldn't remember her ordeal and wake at night screaming at the nightmare they had put her through.

They had just made a fatal mistake. He breathed a silent sigh of relief and quickened his pace again. Not running just a brisker stride, even though his blood boiled and his desire for their blood a red haze in front of his eyes. At five feet, he withdrew his hands from his pockets and showed them to The Hurt, palms out. He lowered his arms to his sides.

"Now you show me the money, asshole. Or we gut the bitch, and then slice you up." His look turned wary as Ricardo moved to within three feet. "Hey! Stop! Show me the damn money now." He backed up a step and reached behind him for what Ricardo assumed was a gun. For the first time, a look of doubt widened The Hurt's eyes and panic wiped the arrogance from his face. With the speed of Wolverine's claws, a blade appeared in each of Ricardo's hands.

He ran the last step to The Hurt and placed his own hurt upon him. As the gun appeared from behind the big man, Ricardo sliced into the defensive arm with one knife and drove the other into The

Hurt's throat. The gun bounced off the cement as the big man clutched his throat and fell on his ass.

Ricardo was a blur of choreographed movement. He continued toward the white man who had raised a gun. It was hard to hit a moving target for an untrained shooter, and this punk was not trained at all. He snapped a round in Ricardo's direction as if cracking a whip. The bullet flew wide. If a trained man with a knife was within twenty feet of an untrained man with a gun, he would for sure get his cuts in before a shot was accurately directed his way. Ricardo was on the frightened man in seconds. The knife bit deep into a spot at the base of the man's neck as he pulled the trigger one last time on his useless automatic. The shot went back down the alley.

Ricardo pivoted toward the black man holding the girl. He didn't bother to try to remove the knife from the collapsing white man. It would have cost him precious seconds and possibly the girl's life. Without hesitation he continued on toward him.

The third man fumbled a knife from his pocket, opened it and placed the blade to the girl's throat. She didn't seem to notice, staring straight ahead, watching a movie on some invisible screen.

The panicked man backed up. "I'm gonna ... I'm gonna cut her. Don't you come near me." But it was more plea than actual threat.

Ricardo glanced down the Alley. The two men had taken the time to pull weapons and still were not closing in on him. Ricardo kept moving, hand reaching for another weapon to fill his empty hand. "Save yourself. Run! I'll give you till three."

The scared wanna-be thug, glanced down the alley looking for help. It was coming. Running footsteps now echoed off the enclosed alley.

The man's eyes reflected the battle waging in his head. Ricardo saw the fear and knew he was close to breaking and fleeing. It wouldn't matter. He was dead either way. Ricardo started counting and ran toward his enemy, his gun in his hand. "One! Two! ..."

"NO!" the black man screamed, stumbled backward and fell away from the girl.

"Three!" The report was loud and seemed to echo endlessly down the narrow alley. He had no guilt or felt no remorse for the dead man. He shouldn't have raped a fourteen-year-old girl. The running footsteps stopped. Shots chipped at the cement and brick walls around him. He sprinted, staying low, the girl in his arms, to the safety of the corner where he set her down. She seemed to notice him for the first time. Her eyes tracked him and a smile touched her child's face. Leaving her sitting against a wall, Ricardo spun back around the corner and caught the two men in the open, evidently thinking he had run away.

They stopped suddenly, shock transforming their faces. Ricardo put two shots into each one before they had a chance to come to a complete stop. He picked up the girl almost before their bodies hit the ground.

He carried her five blocks to where he'd parked his black Escalade. Sliding her into the back seat he lay her down and hopped behind the wheel. Pausing, he checked for any signs of pursuit or witnesses before driving off, keeping to the speed limit.

In the back seat, the young girl stared blankly at the ceiling and softly hummed to herself.